***Don't miss the next Irish Eyes romance
coming soon from Jove***

Titles by Donna Fletcher

IRISH HOPE
THE IRISH DEVIL
MAGICAL MOMENTS
WEDDING SPELL
WHISPERS ON THE WIND
THE BUCCANEER

Visit the author's Web site at
www.donnafletcher.com.

Irish Hope

Donna Fletcher

JOVE BOOKS, NEW YORK

IRISH HOPE

A Jove Book / published by arrangement with
the author

PRINTING HISTORY
Jove edition / April 2001

All rights reserved.
Copyright © 2001 by Donna Fletcher.
This book, or parts thereof, may not be reproduced in
any form without permission.
For information address: The Berkley Publishing Group,
a division of Penguin Putnam Inc.,
375 Hudson Street, New York, New York 10014.

The Penguin Putnam Inc. World Wide Web site address is
http://www.penguinputnam.com

ISBN: 0-515-13043-5

A JOVE BOOK®
Jove Books are published by The Berkley Publishing Group,
a division of Penguin Putnam Inc.,
375 Hudson Street, New York, New York 10014.
JOVE and the "J" design
are trademarks belonging to Penguin Putnam Inc.

PRINTED IN THE UNITED STATES OF AMERICA

10 9 8 7 6 5 4 3 2 1

Prologue

"Hold still, Lady Gwenth," Hope ordered the large, impatient dog. "You must have a disguise if you are to accompany me on this adventure. Everyone will be looking for a young woman with a large dog of regal bearing. This white mark on your forehead and your lazy manner will dissuade them."

Hope finished her task and planted a generous kiss on the dog's snout. "And, my dear, you shall answer simply to 'Lady' from this moment on. Understand, Lady?"

The big dog eyed her critically and turned her nose up in the air to retreat to her cushioned bedding near the window.

Hope followed her, squatting unladylike down beside her. "Please, Lady Gwenth, I cannot leave you behind, and I know you are accustomed to being pampered, but this is only for a few weeks. I cannot enter into an arranged marriage without experiencing life."

Lady Gwenth sighed and closed her eyes as if not at all interested in her mistress's dilemma.

"You must understand," Hope went on. "Uncle Shamus has arranged a marriage for me befitting my ancestry to the high king of Ireland, but I wish to know the true Ireland. The people who make this land flourish, whose blood has been spilled to keep it free and whose hands toil daily. I want to walk the green fields and meadows, climb the hills, drink from the rivers and talk with the people. And—"

She paused, a generous smile spreading across her pretty round face, and her arms wrapping around herself in a loving hug. "—maybe meet my true love."

Lady Gwenth voiced her objections with a heavy sigh.

Hope lifted a large floppy ear to whisper. "Do you not wish to find a special mate?"

The dog grumbled her response.

Hope hugged her own slim waist. "I dream of finding a man. An ordinary man who wishes to love as deeply and strongly as I do. Foolish dreams, I suppose."

Lady Gwenth agreed with a loud yawn.

Hope stood. "I must do this, Lady Gwenth, or else I will forever regret not taking the chance."

Hope hurried over to the large bed, slipped out of her night shift and continued speaking to the large dog who kept one eye focused on her. "I snatched these garments from the stable lad. I did, of course, leave him sufficient coins to cover his loss, but I required a good disguise for our trip. And since I barely stand three inches over five feet—" She paused and glanced with disappointment down at her small breasts. "And possess a body that barely resembles a female, it was a simple decision to choose a young lad's disguise. And besides, who would think me audacious enough to attempt such an outrageous feat? All who know me describe me as the perfect young lady, which makes me perfectly boring and perfectly predictable."

Lady Gwenth opened her eyes to watch as Hope pulled on dark stockings over petite, slender legs. "If the remainder of my life is to be boring then I must fill it with a bit of adventure and store the lasting memories so that I may recall and savor them in my old age."

Lady Gwenth yawned and dropped her head to rest on her cushion, though her big, brown, concerned eyes remained fixed on Hope.

A worn brown linen tunic covered the stockings to her knees. "Perhaps I am being foolish, and yet . . ." Hope sighed and shook her head. "Yet I feel this need to explore, search and find . . ." Another shake of her head and another sigh. "Life is out there, Lady, I feel it as sure as I feel the cool night air rush across my warm skin. It reaches out to me, urges me, and I must go."

Hope lowered herself to kneel beside Lady. She cupped the dog's large face in her small hands, the heavy jowls hanging off her palms. "I must have my adventure no matter how foolish my dream."

Hope stood and secured the loose tunic with a braided cloth belt. "Now all that is left for me to do is to cut my hair."

Lady Gwenth raised her head.

Hope sighed and ran her fingers through the silky strands of her dark hair. It was her pride and joy, hanging straight to her tiny waist. She combed it herself every night, keeping the rich brown color shiny, and it pained her to reach for the sharp bladed knife on the bed. "I am afraid it is necessary for my disguise."

Lady Gwenth whimpered.

"My hair will grow back," Hope said, though tears stained her eyes, and before she could give her foolish actions serious thought, she grabbed hold of her long, straight hair and sliced a section off at her shoulder.

Lady Gwenth whimpered loudly and dropped her head to her cushion.

"It is done," Hope said with a quiver to her soft voice. She finished the difficult task with quick, steady strokes and when finally done she ran her slim fingers through the short strands. It felt strange with her long tresses gone, but then she had made a choice, and she intended to do what was necessary.

She tucked her hair behind her ears and chewed at her nails while she cast tearful eyes around her room. She had spent many happy years here. Uncle Shamus and Aunt Elizabeth had been good to her, caring for her as their own after her parents' untimely death when she was barely eight. And the marriage they had arranged for her was a worthy one, but a loveless one, and though she could not explain it even to herself, she wanted to know love. Foolish dreams yet again, but what was there to life if one never knew true love? She did not wish always to wonder whether it truly existed. She wished to experience its passion and tenderness. Its pain and sorrow. Its joy. But most of all its simplicity, for only true love could be that chaotic and yet so simple.

Her ancestry had afforded her a claim to a mighty heritage, and while she would not forsake her duties, she wished, if only for a few weeks, to taste the wonders of life and perhaps the simplicity of love. Then she would do as was expected of her. She would marry a stranger and bear him children.

But first she would have her adventure.

One

Colin eased away from the eager mouth but not before squeezing the woman's bare, ample backside. Another squeeze, a gentle kiss, and he was on his feet and slipping into his clothes.

"It is a rogue and charmer you are," the woman said with a teasing smile that made her pretty, full face appear beautiful, and Colin did not waste the precious moment.

He leaned over and grabbed her chin with a possessive firmness that sent a shiver of desire racing through her. "Nellie, only a beauty like you could thoroughly please a rogue and a charmer like me." He kissed her then, roughly, before gentling his lips and stealing her breath along with her heart.

A disappointed sigh preceded her words. "Do you have to go?"

"As much as I would love to remain here with you, I have my duty to my lord."

She nodded knowingly and appeased her disappointment by watching him dress. Her dark eyes lingered over every lean, hard line of him. He stood a good six feet tall, perhaps an inch or two over, and though not broad and thick in size, he possessed a defined hardness to his muscles that large men lacked. Taut muscles ran over his midriff and down his stomach, making one wonder whether, if he took a blow to his middle, it would not be the fist that received the damage.

His long legs possessed that same defined muscular structure, and then there was his . . . She giggled, caressing his manhood with her eyes. It was large and thick, and oh so pleasing, and he knew *exactly* how to please a woman. He was a master of the craft. A charming rogue with good looks to match and a golden tongue that could talk, tease or tempt any woman into sin. But then she was a sinner herself—and there was always confession.

Nellie reluctantly left her warm, tousled bed, taking the memories with her. She dressed in haste, dropping a loose-fitting gown made of soft green wool over her head and gathering it at the waist with a thin leather belt. She donned a pair of worn sandals and walked over to Colin, who had finished dressing in a dark red tunic, dark stockings and leather boots. He ran his fingers through his shoulder-length hair, smiled at her approach, then spread his arms wide.

Nellie ached with the want of him as his arms enfolded her and hugged her fiercely to him.

"It is good memories of you I will be taking with me, lass, and be ever grateful for them."

Nellie kissed him soundly and hurried out of his arms and toward the door. "It will be fresh bread and cheese, enough for you and your men, that you will be taking with you, Colin."

Colin's expression turned serious. "I seek no compensation from you for our enjoyable time together."

Nellie appreciated his words more than he would ever know, for she instinctively knew he spoke the truth. "Aye, and I thank you for that, but I offer this to you as a friend."

Colin smiled and her heart skipped a beat. "Then I accept it as a friend, and thank you for your generosity."

"If only . . ." Nellie said with a sad smile.

"I have often thought the same myself," Colin said with his own bittersweet smile.

Nellie left with a shake of her head, and Colin saw to

collecting the last of his belongings. He smiled at the rumpled bed and the delightful memories. When he and his small band of men had stopped at this single farmhouse early last evening, it was with the intention of requesting permission to camp on the land for the night.

The widow Nellie had other ideas as to where Colin himself would bed down, and he naturally made no objections. It had been over two weeks that he and his men had been away from home on a mission for Eric of Shanekill.

Eric was more friend than lord and while many feared the Irish devil, a name earned by Eric, Colin found him to be a man possessed of an enduring courage and a man true to his word. He was also a man deeply in love with his wife, Faith, who was presently growing heavy with his child. Which was why Colin was on this mission instead of Eric. He simply refused to leave Faith's side.

Colin could not blame him. Faith had a way of doing exactly as she pleased no matter how many times Eric ordered her otherwise. And Eric intended to see that his wife did not do her own digging or planting in her herb garden, and that she did not tire herself by tending to too many ailing villagers, though that was a difficult task in itself. Faith was a healer and all at Shanekill Keep sought her skill. And it was with a tender touch and caring heart that she dealt with everyone.

If truth be told, Colin would have to admit that he envied Eric and the true love he and his wife shared. He had thought to find such a deep, binding love one day, but fate had other plans and while he sincerely cared for the many women he bedded, he loved none. And his worst fear was that he was not capable of truly loving any woman.

He discarded the troublesome thought with a shrug and headed out the door. He had a mission and so far it had not been very successful. His men greeted him with grumbles and complaints when he stepped out of the cottage into the bright early sun.

Spring was near on top of them; the clear blue sky, rich green hills and the riotous bloom of wildflowers announced its arrival. The delightful weather was precisely why the men were grumbling. The nine men were part of Eric's elite warriors and they had fought enough battles and slept on enough hard grounds to last them a lifetime. When Eric was granted land and a wife by the kings of Ireland he gave his warriors a choice of joining him in settling down and creating new life. They all jumped at the opportunity. Some of the men had new wives, barely wed a month, and two or three had wives who were carrying babes.

Colin knew that his night with the widow Nellie had them all thinking of their own wives and comfortable beds.

"We are near to Limerick," he announced with a broad smile, though it was not returned. "Word has it that a young woman with a large dog is traveling that way. If she is not the woman we search for we will return home to Shanekill Keep and seek further instructions."

A resounding cheer split the morning air.

"I say we deliver the troublesome baggage to Lord Eric tied up tightly so she cannot run from her duties again," Patrick said, swinging up onto his horse.

He was one who was recently wed, an understandable reason for his urgent desire to return home, and one Colin could not fault.

"Seems like the lass might fear her marital duties," Daniel said with a smirk.

"Bah," John said, sitting straight on his horse, his large beefy hands light on the reins. "She is a spoiled young lass who needs a firm hand."

"Like the firm hand you take with Maggie?" Daniel asked with a laugh.

John grinned, "It is a firm hand my Maggie likes."

The men continued their teasing with more suggestions of how the missing lass should be treated as they turned their horses away from the small cottage.

After a lingering kiss to Nellie, Colin mounted his horse and joined his men. He listened with half an ear, his own thoughts on the young woman who had run away. Her name was Hope, and she was a descendent of the high king of Ireland. It seemed that her Uncle Shamus had arranged a suitable marriage for her, but she must have disagreed for she disappeared along with her large dog. It was claimed the pair were inseparable.

Eric had been contacted by the King of Connaught with an urgent request that he assist in locating Hope. Eric agreed and instructed Colin to take a small band of men and find her. Eric did not expect Colin to fail in his mission since he himself would not have, but Colin felt a stirring of pity for this young woman he had never met. She was being forced to wed a stranger, to spend the rest of her life with a man she did not know and perhaps would never come to know. Colin knew of too many arranged marriages that were just that and no more. Love was never found, desires never satisfied, all in the name of duty.

Had Hope rebelled? Had she taken flight in an attempt to find true love? He shook his head at his ridiculous musings. True love? Was it real? Did it ever exist or was it merely a figment of a poet or minstrel's imagination?

A more reasonable explanation would be that this Hope was probably a spoiled and stubborn young woman who thought of no one but herself. And because of her willful ways he and his men were stuck on this ridiculous mission.

He was suddenly quite annoyed with Hope. Eric had given him a brief description of the young woman: comely, petite, thin, with dark waist-length hair. How could one pint-sized woman create such havoc?

But then women have a way about them in getting

what they wanted, he thought, though it was usually he who got what he wanted from them. Women were delightful creatures and when handled with care and finesse they would purr like contented kittens in a man's hands.

Colin wondered how easy it would be to make this Hope purr to his touch. A thought he would make sure never saw reality. Eric made it quite clear that he was not to use his charming tongue on the runaway woman. She was to be returned unspoiled to her uncle. A pity. If this Hope had enough courage to take off on her own, he wondered what courage she would display in bed.

As the day wore on the grumbling grew more distinct, especially after they passed through a small village and were told that no young woman with a large dog had been seen. If they did not locate Hope, Colin knew all too well that Eric would order them to continue the search.

Colin grumbled and mumbled to himself as they continued on. The battles he had fought had been easy compared to finding this woman. How could one small woman with a large dog hide herself so well? Or perhaps she had not and was in trouble. That thought disturbed him, for it meant that Eric would then take a formidable troop of men and see to the matter himself.

He hoped his concern was for naught, but the countryside held dangers such as roving bands of thieves, warring factions and just plain difficulty of survival. How in the Lord's name was this pint-sized woman surviving?

It would take a few more days for them to reach Shanekill Keep, and Colin intended to have at least a fraction of information on the woman to take home with him and for his own use when he set out once again in search of Hope.

The grumbling settled along with the setting sun. The small band of men finally sat relaxed around a campfire that slowly cooked two pheasants on a spit over tempered flames. Stories were being exchanged with robust laughter punctuating the embellished tales as the group waited impatiently for the evening fare to finish roasting.

A jug of mead was passed around the camp, each man taking a generous taste along with the cheese and bread supplied by the widow Nellie.

"It is glad I am to be going home," Stuart said. He was the largest man of the group, tall and broad like an ox, and there was not many a man who would raise a fist against him. His wife Mary equaled his size and was soon to deliver their firstborn. She was also the keep's cook and favored by the men for her exceptional skill.

"You think Mary will bake us some of her special meat pies to celebrate our return?" Daniel asked with a lick of his lips as if he could already taste their delicious flavor.

Patrick shook his head. "We are not returning home victorious. What is there to celebrate?"

John did not agree. "We have time yet before we reach the keep. Who knows what will happen? We could find this woman and return in glorious victory. She is after all only one lone woman."

"Do not forget the dog," Stuart reminded. "I heard she is a big monstrous thing."

"Like Rook," Patrick said with a grin.

The men laughed, as did Colin, who sat a distance away from them, leaning back against a cropping of large stones. Rook was Faith's trusty companion; he was big and ugly, though dedicated to Faith and loved by all at the keep.

Colin was glad to be returning home. Eric and Faith were like family to him, as was Borg, Eric's half brother, and his wife Bridget. It had been too long since he had felt close to anyone, and the feeling of belonging was a satisfying one he did not wish to relinquish, even for a short time.

The jug made another circle around the campfire along with tall tales that entertained. The laughter grew

ong was raised and the band of men impatiently
or their supper to finish cooking.

It was then without notice or forewarning that chaos
erupted. A large animal with a spot of white on her head
raced into camp snarling and growling as she made a
mad dash for the pheasant on the spit. She jumped over
John who lay stretched out, her big paw catching him
in the stomach and knocking the breath from him. The
jug of mead was knocked out of Stuart's hand by the
battering tail that swept in front of him. Patrick was
momentarily blinded by a spray of flying dirt as the animal came to a sudden halt in front of him, and Daniel
rushed to catch the second pheasant that fell to the
ground after the animal successfully captured the first
pheasant in her large jaws.

It took a moment for the men to make sense of the
sudden attack, and then they rose swiftly to their feet
and rushed in eager pursuit after the thieving animal.
Daniel righted the remaining pheasant on the spit and
followed his comrades, aware that one pheasant was not
a sufficient meal for all the men, no matter how plump
the bird.

Colin quietly waited in the shadows of the night. He
had a feeling the large dog was not alone, and when he
saw a small shadow advance on the camp, he smiled.

A skinny young lad crept into camp, his head jerking
quickly from side to side, his eyes wide and alert, and
his slow approach awkward yet determined. His steps
were unsteady, faltering too often, which meant he
lacked experience, though he wasted no time in collecting his loot—the sign of a good, if inexperienced, thief.

Colin stood, his movements silent, his instincts alert,
and he remained in the shadows watching the lad's every
movement. He was barely ten and two, if that, and so
frail that a rush of strong wind would blow him over,
and yet. . . .

He was determined, foraging in the sacks, stuffing an
empty one with the bread and cheese and taking time

for a fast gulp of mead. His hunger was obvious, and the fact that he lived on what he scavenged was pathetic. There was no muscle on his skinny frame that would aid him in defending himself. His quick-witted mind obviously made up for his lack of physical strength, and Colin admired his courage.

He was a skinny lad who possessed enough mettle, or stupidity, to rob a sizable band of men and expect to succeed. Colin could not help but grin, though it faded quickly when the lad made ready to steal the remaining pheasant.

His nose had enjoyed the smell of the roasting bird for hours, and his stomach had rumbled in anticipation of the succulent taste. While he had no intentions of seeing the ragged lad go hungry, he was not about to allow him to steal the evening meal.

Colin waited in the shadows for the right moment.

Two

Hope scavenged as much food as she could with the little time afforded her. She was aware that Lady Gwenth could not forestall the band of angry men for long. She did not have the courage nor propensity to do so. She was, however, hungry, and was probably at this moment, while being chased, chomping with delight on the pheasant. When she finished her rushed meal she would undoubtedly sneak off to hide.

In the meantime Hope was given the chore of stealing food for both of them. They had not eaten in almost a full day's time and her own stomach was protesting loudly and incessantly, and she feared the grumbling would be heard over the chaos—a foolish thought, but one brought on by fear of being caught. She had never stolen anything in all of her twenty and two years. It was a sin, and yet . . .

She shoved a sizable piece of cheese in her mouth and continued to scavenge the camp for food. She had never known such hunger. Food had always been plentiful at the castle, and she thought of the many meals she had never finished and the sweets she had taken mere bites of then discarded. If only she had that food at this moment, she would finish every delicious morsel.

With trembling hands she gathered hunks of bread and chunks of cheese, shoving them into a small sack she had hurriedly emptied of its contents. Time was running out and she had to make her escape before any of the outraged men returned. They would surely have no mercy for a young lad stealing their evening meal, but then none of the men looked as if they lacked for food and one night without a meal would do them no harm.

However, she and Lady required nourishment, and she intended to see that they got it no matter how fearful the task.

With her sack full and the roasting pheasant tempting her famished stomach, she reached out to slip it carefully, though hastily, off the wooden spit.

Her fingers were on the bird when she was grabbed by the back of her tunic and hoisted up away from the campfire as though she weighed no more than a feather. She wasted no time in attacking her assailant. She kicked and threw punches, though her frantic actions did little good. Her useless blows struck the night air while her assailant's hand remained firm at her neck.

Still, her pride would not allow her to surrender without a fight. Her rational mind warned her that the man whose hand held her without difficulty had to be a formidable assailant and that her struggles would prove ultimately useless, but she remained adamant in her attempt to free herself.

It was his laughter that finally caused her swinging limbs to cease their senseless struggle. It was a laughter born of ridicule and the sound rankled her pride.

"Finally you grow sensible," the mocking voice said.

Hope was fast to respond. "Hunger makes one senseless."

She was deposited on the ground with a jolt. Her mighty heritage would allow her to bow before no man, and it was with a sense of dignity that she stood and raised a defiant chin to her unknown assailant.

She had been taught that to show emotions would indicate weakness, so she cleverly hid her reactions behind a mask of her own making and for once was pleased that she had acquired such an ability. The man who stood before her was a handsome devil—too handsome for description, though she would admit that he could steal a woman's heart in a minute. And undoubtedly he did on many occasions. Yet his eyes told her a different story. He possessed dark eyes, lonely and aching for love; he probably searched for the elusive emotion in every woman he met, hoping he would finally find himself.

A quick glance at his body told her that many men underestimated his strength. He was lean, hard and determined, a combination that could prove fatal if not judged wisely. He stood a good six feet or more, towering over her meager height and making her feel inadequate to deal with him. But then there was her heritage, and it was with the strength of mighty kings that ran through her blood that she tossed her defiant chin up a notch more, demonstrating her bravery.

He laughed again. "You possess an ounce of courage, lad." He paused and shook his head. "And a ton of foolishness."

"Hunger does that to you," she said, her manner remaining brazen.

"You could have asked for food."

The thought had briefly crossed her mind when she first spied the band of men setting up camp for the night, and with a sense of regret she had dismissed the unwise notion. She feared someone discovering her gender and then possibly her identity; either one would prove disastrous.

She was about to offer a poor excuse for feeling it necessary to steal when shouts of laughter approached the camp and a distinct whine penetrated the revelry. The large men soon appeared out of the darkness towing a frightened and protesting Lady behind them on a rope.

A fierce sense of loyalty and love rose up in Hope as she watched her precious dog try with all her might and sizable weight to fight against the rope that tugged viciously around her neck. Her huge paws pushed at the earth in an attempt to gain leverage, and she snarled and snapped, hoping to appear a formidable opponent. But it was her inability to hide her fearful whines that gave her true character away. She was simply a coward.

"Shut up your crying, you mangy thief," one of the men ordered and gave a hard smack to her snout.

That was it. Hope lunged for the assailant, kicking him fast and hard in the shin before yanking the rope away from the giant of a man who held it and hurrying to free Lady of the menacing noose.

"Cowards the lot of you," she yelled at the men while throwing her slim arms around Lady's wide, furry neck and hugging her tightly. The dog whimpered and hid her face against Hope's chest.

The men stared speechless at the puny lad who fiercely protected the large cowering animal.

"The beast stole and ate our supper," the large man said, offering a sensible explanation.

"Lady is not a beast," Hope yelled back. "She is my best friend and would harm no one. She stole because of hunger." She cast a quick assessing glance over each one. "Something I am certain you men never experienced."

The band of men stared at the bold lad with wide grins, though none made a move or a sound. They simply waited, and Hope realized why. The man who had grabbed her by the neck stepped forward. He was their leader and he would handle the situation.

Colin stood with arms crossed over his chest, sizing up the ragged pair. Besides being hungry, they looked worn out. And they looked to be inseparable, the young lad being the stronger of the two—a fact that amused Colin.

"What's your name, lad?" he asked sternly in an attempt to intimidate.

His tactics did not work; the lad once again raised a defiant chin, to everyone's surprise and amusement.

"Harold," Hope said, having grown accustomed to the name she had chosen.

Colin took another step forward. "On your own, Harold?"

"Me and Lady," Hope said, her arms clasped firmly around the large dog's neck. The animal's head remained buried in Hope's chest and her sizable body shook with fear.

Colin grew curious about the dog. The woman Hope whom they sought was in possession of a large female dog, and he wondered as he rubbed his chin. "How did you come by Lady?"

Hope had planned well, determining questions that would be asked of her and having reasonable answers for each and every one of them. "I found her alongside the road near to starving, and healed her back to health. We have been sound friends ever since."

"Where did you find her?" Colin asked, thinking that perhaps this dog had belonged to Hope and they had become separated. If he could learn of her last whereabouts he would have a good starting point or at least information to take to Eric.

"Connaught," Hope said, deciding that where she had started was a good place to leave Hope behind.

Her answer did not seem to please the man. He frowned and his handsome features turned dark and foreboding. There was another side to this man, a darker side, and the thought sent shivers racing through her.

Colin walked over to the animal and without hesitation or fear he rubbed at the white mark on her head.

Lady whimpered loudly and Hope held her tightly.

Colin looked down at the white smudge on the palm of his hand. "What were you doing in Connaught?"

"I travel the roads," she said with an indifferent shrug.

"The dog was alone?"

Hope kept up the pretense, but wondered over his questioning. "I saw no one about."

Colin offered no more. "You are welcome to join us for the evening and share our food."

His announcement caused the men to disperse, their

laughter and boisterous voices an indication that they did not seem opposed to their leader's decision. This offered her some comfort.

"Thank you," Hope said and stood, the dog moving to hide behind her.

Colin could not help but smile at the odd pair. The lad barely reached three inches past five feet and looked as though a good gust of wind would blow him over. Smudges of dirt marred a pale complexion and dark, curious eyes peeked out from beneath long lashes. The dog looked to actually weigh more than the lad, and with the size of him you would think her a formidable opponent. But large frightened eyes and a continuous low whine told him otherwise.

No, the lad was definitely the stronger of the two and Colin admired his courage and devotion to the animal.

Hope realized he found them amusing; she could tell by the grin on his face. His good looks probably afforded him his choice of women and, being honest with herself, she had to admit his looks did appeal to her, though it was his character she was presently interested in.

Her uncle told her that the truth of a man was defined in his character, so if she was to deal with this man she wished to discover his true character.

At that moment her near empty stomach decided to protest loudly and embarrass her.

Colin stepped aside and pointed toward the campfire. "Join the men and satisfy that noisy belly."

Hope's stomach answered for her, responding with a loud rumble. She walked past Colin with Lady close by her side, stopping a few feet beyond to turn and ask, "Who do I have to thank for this generosity?"

"Colin of Shanekill."

"The Irish devil is your lord?" she asked with wide eyes.

"More my friend," he answered with pride.

Hope simply nodded, turned and walked to the campfire on shaky legs. The Irish devil and his men were known for their fearlessness and tenacity. They celebrated many a victory and tasted few defeats. And they served the kings of Ireland well, which meant that they would be summoned to help in finding her.

Was this band of men searching for her? If so, perhaps it would be the perfect place for her to hide.

With Lady sitting down quietly beside her, Hope joined the men around the campfire. Food was shared and generously, most of the men making comments of how she needed more meat on her skinny bones.

Colin joined them only moments after she had and she noticed he kept a watchful eye on her. She continued eating the tasty chunks of pheasant, sharing them with Lady.

"That animal ate a whole pheasant; she needs no more food," the large man they called Stuart said with a firm nod to Hope.

Hope gave Lady another piece of her portion of meat. "My dog, my decision."

The other men smiled and Stuart even cracked a wide grin. "You have courage, lad, for one so small. How old are you? Ten and one? Ten and two?"

Hope had decided that with her meager size and weight she would be better admitting to a younger age. "Ten and two."

"You have family?" another man asked.

She shook her head, having taken a generous bite of the tasty meat.

"On your own, then?" Stuart continued the questions.

She understood their curiosity. A lone, young and frail-looking boy on the roads alone—what was one to think? She attempted to appease their concern. "With no family ties, I found the road a good home."

"How long have you been on your own?" Colin asked, tearing a piece of pheasant from the cooked bird.

Hope shrugged as if the length of time made no difference. "About six months."

The men looked startled by her answer.

"You have survived that long on your own?" Stuart asked, obviously surprised.

Had she erred? The short time she had traveled the roads had proved difficult, near to impossible. But would a young lad accustomed to a hard existence find the roads more of a challenge than a difficulty?

She shrugged again and answered more truthfully than she realized. "I have no choice."

"Too true for too many," Stuart said with a sadness.

Hope understood his comment. In her travels she had seen too many poor souls in dire need of help and many with too little food to feed their large broods. With a land so bountiful and possessed of such beauty, how could any go hungry?

One of the other men offered her another generous chunk of pheasant and she gladly accepted it, sharing her portion once again with Lady, though no one commented.

No more questions were asked of her and she offered no information. Conversation turned to family and friends and their strong desires to return home. She ate quietly and listened with interest. She learned that these fierce warriors were tired of battle, and while none would shun it or run from it, they preferred life at Shanekill to the battlefield. But then, if she remembered the tales well enough, the Irish devil's contingent had fought an endless series of bloody battles.

Hope finished her food and could not stifle a persistent yawn. Lady agreed with her own loud yawn before settling her large body next to Hope and resting her head in her lap. Hope instinctively laid a comforting hand over her faithful companion.

Colin watched the odd pair with admiration. Puny as the lad was, he stood his ground with courage and he protected the one he loved. But to whom did the large animal actually belong? Was the skinny lad telling him the truth about how he came by the dog? And where the hell was Hope?

He felt like giving the young woman a sound thrashing for all the senseless problems she was creating, and if he found her he just might give her what she so richly deserved.

Another wide yawn from the strange pair attracted his attention and he shook his head. The young boy battled to keep his eyes open while the large dog slept contentedly.

"Harold," Colin said and the lad's head snapped up, his eyes wide. "There is bedding over by that grouping of rocks." He pointed to a spot a short distance from the campfire. "Go settle yourself for the night."

"I will not deprive another of his bed?" Hope asked with concern.

Without knowing it Hope was beginning to win the respect of the small band of men.

"Take what is offered you," Colin said firmly.

Hope thought to protest. She had, after all, grown accustomed to the hard ground and on many a cool night she and Lady had shared their warmth. However, Colin sounded as if he intended to have his way and she thought it better not to protest.

She stood, Lady coming alert and standing up alongside her. "Thank you."

Colin nodded. "Sleep well."

She walked to the bedding spread out on the ground and gratefully crawled between the warm blankets. Lady snuggled beside her, her head resting on Hope's stomach. Hope placed a protective arm over the animal and the pair was soon sound asleep.

The men drifted off to their blankets and without comment one of the men dropped a blanket beside Colin before walking off to his own bedding. Colin accepted the offer, the night air having taken on a decisive chill. He draped the wool blanket over him after stretching out on the ground near the fire.

His glance remained on the young lad though his thoughts drifted to his own childhood days. Unlike Harold he had a family, if it could be called that. His father had been a tyrant ruling with an iron hand, demanding he and his brothers do as he commanded or suffer his wrath. His mother was a frail woman who was weak in character. She followed her husband's every command without question.

However, there was one person who had made a difference in his bleak life and strangely enough she was his father's mistress, Lilith. Beauty was not her forte but charm was. She possessed a smile that could disarm any man and a charm that captivated the coldest heart. She had taught him well those skills and when he grew older she had gladly, though without his father's knowledge, taught him how to turn sex into the art of making love.

He had shed no tears when his mother passed on, but he had wept in private when Lilith passed away unexpectedly from fever. She had made a decisive difference in his life and he missed her to this day. Her passing had caused him finally to make a difficult decision. A week after her burial Colin had packed a few meager belongings and left his home.

He was the first son and was to inherit his father's vast holdings. There were even plans of a marriage, though of course his father had not consulted him on the bride. He wanted none of his father's plans for he was certain they were meant to benefit him and his wealth. He had simply ridden off and never once looked back or regretted his decision.

He met up with Eric a short time later and joined his fighting troops. It was fighting alongside Eric that he came to understand the true meaning of friendship and the value of a caring and loving family.

One day perhaps he would marry, though he often wondered if he could love, truly love anyone. Lilith had insisted love was possible, though rare. She had told him that most times people made do with each other. She had advised him that love was different for everyone and that he should think on what it meant to him and then not dwell on it. Let it go and wait; wait for that love to find him.

He had asked her if she was still waiting herself.

She had smiled and told him that she had been blessed with such a love. When her love had passed on she was wise enough to realize she would never find another so she made do. Her loving memories made her life bearable for she felt she was one of the rare few who had known true love.

He had admired her strength, courage and unselfishness. She had taken a lonely, unloved young boy and turned him into a man full of his own strength, courage and convictions—a man who could not turn a hungry young lad away.

Colin gave the sleeping boy one last glance and closed his eyes. They would rise early tomorrow and he would make certain that he saw Harold delivered safely to the next village.

Three

"*Harold!*"

Hope jumped at the lad's name being called out and both she and Lady turned to see who issued the demanding summons. She had thought it was Colin. His voice was distinct even in a shout, a melodious thunder that caught attention and made the legs tremble.

She, however, approached him on sturdy legs with her attention alert.

"Good morning to you, sir," Hope said, purposely respectful.

"Colin," he corrected, "and it is a good morning. A fine morning for you to be traveling along with us to the next village." Since the lad voiced no objections Colin assumed he favored the idea and continued. "We should arrive there by early afternoon."

Hope was relieved to hear his generous invitation. She had hoped to remain with the band of men for as long as possible. If it were only to the next village then that was fine, though she would have preferred to tag along until she thought otherwise. To remain on her own was not a wise choice.

She had learned relatively early on in her travels that the road was a dangerous place to be and she had been lucky to survive as long as she had. And of course there was Lady to consider; she simply did not travel well. Everything seemed to frighten her, unless she was hungry: when hunger struck she turned courageous.

The journey to the next village would give Hope time to think and plan. Perhaps there was a way to remain with Colin and his men. If she kept her identity a secret there would be no need for worry, and besides, she doubted that any of the men thought she was female. She was much too thin and shapeless.

Hope walked without complaint alongside the men on horses. She and Lady had no difficulty keeping up with the slow, meandering horses and their riders. They seemed in no particular hurry, and with all the walking she and Lady had done lately it wasn't difficult to keep up with their unhurried pace.

The day was beautiful, the sun bright and the land a carpet of brilliant green. Spring was early in the air and the thick buds would soon burst and drench the land in a profusion of color and greenery.

She walked, enjoying the eye-catching sight, and was grateful for the safety of the men who surrounded her. If she was wise she would admit her identity and ask to be returned home. While she did not think of herself as lacking intelligence, she was not ready to return and accept her fate without question. She had not nearly experienced all there was to life. And possibly, just possibly, with this band of men and with Colin in particular she would learn what she wanted.

A quick peek at Colin as he rode past her on his sleek mare made her heart flutter. He was a handsome one and a charmer, though at the moment his charm was replaced by his warrior skills. He sat his mare confidently and his brown eyes remained alert to his surroundings.

Hope sighed and looked to Lady, who walked beside her, issuing a protesting whine every now and then. "I would like to know him better."

Lady released a moanful whine, not at all in agreement with her master.

"He interests me," Hope said on a whisper. "There is more to the man than he shows. I wish to know that man."

Lady whined again, drawing the attention of the riders close by.

"Behave," Hope scolded in a low, threatening voice, making Lady grumble quietly. "If you do not wish to forage for food then it would be wise for us to remain with these men, who could provide us with a daily sustenance."

Lady's eyes widened and she looked with curiosity at the men who rode past her as if she understood Hope's every word.

"How we will accomplish that feat I am not certain, but I intend to see that we do."

Lady issued a low grumbling sound of agreement.

"I am glad you agree and I know I can count on you to help."

Lady whined this time and dropped her head, her large sorrowful eyes fixed on the ground.

"You can be courageous when you must," Hope informed her.

"Does she ever answer you?" a laughing voice asked from behind.

Hope turned wide eyes on the large man with bright red hair. If she remembered correctly, he was called Stuart. "When she wishes."

The man laughed all the harder. "Too bad you do not follow us to Shanekill Keep. I know of a good mate for her."

Hope grew curious. "One she would fancy?"

"Aye, that she would," Stuart said with a firm nod. "A big ugly but lovable dog that belongs to the lady of the manor. And brave. He saved Lady Faith's life."

Lady's ears perked up with interest.

"As brave as the Irish devil himself," Stuart continued. "They would turn out fine, strong pups. And I would be proud to have one as my own."

Someone cried out that they approached the village, and Stuart immediately took himself off to join the impressive line of men.

Colin rode the lead and Hope was certain that with his charming smile he and his men would be greeted with enthusiasm. She actually looked forward to entering with his troop. At least there would be no need for worry of her safety. The men, she was certain, would offer their protection to the young lad.

It was with confidence that she entered the village.

Yet her confidence was fast put to a hard test.

After enjoying an ample fare at the local gathering place, Hope had taken herself off to explore the village. Lady joined her and they slowly strolled the small village together. Colin had warned her to stay near at hand and said that he wished to speak with her before they departed. She had wished the same, hoping to convince him to take her along. But he had been busy with a well-endowed woman who had planted herself on his lap and looked as if she had no intention of going anywhere without him. As he appeared to agree, Hope thought it best to leave him to his dalliance while she saw to exploring.

The few cottages and barns that comprised the village were well maintained. Fields ripe and recently planted spread out from behind the cottages, and fences helped keep the few livestock contentedly secluded. Villagers kept themselves busy with daily chores and the women shared the local gossip as they strolled by with baskets in hand.

It seemed a safe enough place to be on her own. Of course, she had not counted on running up against the village ruffians who were out to prove themselves formidable foes when actually they were nothing more than troublemakers.

Hope always did have a problem with tyranny over the weak, and three boys—for their childish antics certainly forbid them from calling themselves men—who taunted a meek, young lad drew her attention.

The tallest boy, though only an inch or two more in height than Hope, and with a thatch of bright red hair and a preponderance of freckles, appeared to be the leader. He pushed and shoved and verbally belittled the lad who began to cry.

This was a mistake on his part, for it only served to strengthen the trio's bravado. The two other boys, shorter than Hope but sizable in weight, joined in the taunting. No one who passed by appeared to take notice. Lads constantly got themselves into fights and were expected to defend themselves. It was a way of life and one that was better learned at a young age. Obviously the young lad had not learned that particular lesson, but he was about to.

It was a lesson well worth learning if one was to survive and yet Hope felt a tug of sympathy for the distraught lad. He would surely take a beating with three against one and what would it teach him? Fear? Self-doubt? Humiliation?

She shook her head. She could not ignore his plight. She had to help, she just had to. Lady did not seem to agree and took a step back away from her master.

The words rushed from her mouth before her mind gave them consideration. "Only cowards pick on the weak."

The tall boy gave the young lad a hard shove, sending him sprawling to the dirt, then he turned angry brown eyes on Hope. "You calling me a coward?"

The crying lad scurried to his feet and looked about to run when he cast a worried glance at Hope. Though his knees looked as though they trembled, he remained where he stood, gaining an ounce of strength and a wealth of courage.

"I would say the name fits you." Hope supposed that she should give thought to the consequences of her actions and words and the fact that she was a woman of noble birth at that. But at the moment she felt like a lad fit and ready to defend his honor.

The tall lad shoved his two cohorts out of his way and approached Hope with his hands fisted at his sides.

Hope had been in a few scuffles since her departure from her uncle's home, but a fight with fists? Never. She had a feeling that was about to change.

She expected words flung at her but his fist came fast and hard to her face and she felt the blood pour from her lip and her anger boil. She put every ounce of strength she had into her fist and landed a good punch to his jaw, sending him tumbling.

Chaos broke free after that—fists flew, blood ran and Hope learned fast how to fight. She also learned that her dog, for all her impressive size, was a coward at heart—she took flight after the scuffling had started.

Lady ran straight to Colin, inserting her cold, wet nose beneath the snug arm he had wrapped around the waist of the friendly woman who sat on his lap.

"Go away, Lady," Colin ordered firmly.

The dog persisted, this time with a whine.

"Not now." His words were stern and meant to reprimand.

Lady remained persistent. Her nose dug beneath his arm with enough force to disengage it from the woman's waist. That brought Colin to his feet after lifting the disappointed woman off his lap.

Lady took a few cautious steps back but continued to whimper and whine and turn her head in Hope's direction.

Colin suddenly realized something was wrong. "Harold in trouble?"

Lady barked and jumped, ready to take flight.

"Show me," Colin ordered and Lady took off.

Hope and the young boy fought bravely. Unfortunately they possessed limited fighting skills and physical strength. Remaining alert to her opponent's moves and being quick and agile on her feet saved her from several direct punches, but when the tall boy called for reinforcements she knew she was in trouble.

She kicked, swung and battered anything in her line of vision until one staggering blow sent her to her knees and was followed by several kicks to her ribs, landing her flat on her back. This was not a good position to be in, since her grinning opponent was about to pounce down on top of her with fists swinging.

She prepared for the worst and was utterly shocked when the descending boy suddenly stopped in thin air. With a look of disbelief crossing his face, he was tossed aside to land with a hard bounce in the dirt.

In the next instant she was grabbed by the arm and yanked to her feet. The look on Colin's handsome face when he laid eyes on her bloody mouth and bruised eye was chilling.

"I told you to stay close by." He sounded annoyed and angry.

Hope instantly grew defensive. "I take orders from no one."

Colin brought his face to within inches of the lad's. "You will take orders from me."

She was about to open her mouth when he warned, "Do not dare defy me."

His usual charming voice chilled and his dark eyes cautioned.

She wisely held her tongue.

The other lads hurried off, not waiting or wanting to be confronted by the formidable and angry man.

Colin made no attempt to stop them. He cared not a wit for them, though he did care that Harold had taken a noticeable beating. And he wondered over its cause. "Tell me what happened."

Hope wiped the trickling blood at her mouth with the sleeve of her brown tunic and winced.

Colin shook his head. "I would say that you have not a lick of sense in your head."

She shrugged, not really willing to offer an explanation.

Her indifference annoyed him all the more and he grabbed her arm. "Come with me. We need to talk."

A rough yank to her arm had her crying out and Colin abruptly stopped.

Her hand insistently went to her right side over her ribs. "A kick," she explained when he looked at her with concern.

He shook his head again. "Come, I will see to your care."

His words rang with a clear warning in her head and she grew defensive. "I can look after myself."

"Obviously you cannot." This fact irritated Colin for some unknown reason. Perhaps it was the lad's puny size that made him feel protective toward him. And there was his face, much too pretty for a lad even with the blood running from his split lip and the bruise darkening around his eye. His gentle features would surely attract the wrong attention. He needed someone to look after him. Someone to teach him how to defend himself properly. Someone to make sure he got enough to eat and a safe place to rest his head. He needed a home.

The strange, contemplative look in Colin's dark eyes made Hope wonder over his thoughts. She decided not to respond to what was obviously the truth—she could not adequately defend herself. She chose silence and waited for him to clear his mind and speak his thoughts.

It did not take him long. "Since you have no home and obviously require looking after, I think it would be not only in your best interest but wise of you to come live at Shanekill Keep."

Lady, who had been cautiously hiding behind a bush during and immediately following the melee, hurried over to Hope's side and whimpered as if insisting she accept the generous offer.

It was what Hope had intended and yet she felt reluctant looking into Colin's intriguing dark eyes. She realized she found him attractive. What woman would not? He was handsome and charming and a skilled warrior who could protect. And protect he did. He protected a young lad too skinny and helpless to defend himself.

And why should that thought disturb her? She wanted everyone to believe her a young lad. She was, after all, on an adventure.

But she was also a woman and the woman found the man appealing, a dangerous prospect in her current position.

"I will have your answer now," Colin said with annoyance. Here he offered the lad a safe home and the lad paused to give it consideration. What was there to consider?

Lady whined and Hope nodded as if confirming her answer with the animal.

Colin suddenly stopped her from responding. "I must tell you that you will be expected to do your fair share of the work along the way and once at the keep you will be given chores that must be maintained, though it will be a fair exchange for the lodgings and care you will receive."

"I am not lazy. I can do my share and more if necessary," she said, her chin rising with her pride.

"Then it is settled," Colin said as though deciding for her. "You will return to Shanekill Keep with us and make it your home."

For now.

It would be a good place to be for now. She could continue her adventure more safely, and when the time came to reveal her identity, she would simply leave.

"I will go with you," she agreed.

Colin looked at her strangely and she felt as though he understood her thoughts. His words confirmed her suspicions.

"And once there you will stay put."

She simply nodded.

He did not look as though he believed her but made no mention of it. "Come, we will see to your wounds."

She did not care for the "we" for she intended there to be no "we." She would tend to herself. It would do no good having his hands on her and discovering her secret, but then the thought of his hands on her did give her pause to think as she followed him, Lady trailing behind her.

She was not ignorant to the intimate ways of men and women. She had always been an inquisitive child, asking questions, oftentimes embarrassing ones, as her uncle reminded her. But she was lucky that her uncle Shamus was patient and also indulgent with her to a fault. He allowed her to have her way much too often as her Aunt Elizabeth repeated time and again to him, but then Aunt Elizabeth had a way of indulging Hope herself. Her aunt and uncle were never blessed with children of their own and when Hope had come to live with them they had given her everything her heart desired and then some. Add to that an abundance of love and a little girl who was forever grateful.

Her aunt and uncle were the reason she had actually considered this adventure. They were the only married couple she believed truly loved each other. Hope could see the love in their eyes and in their actions toward each other. And she had dreamed over the years of finding such a unique love herself.

She understood that if she found such a man to love that her uncle would not deny her choice of a husband. But if she did not find that man and that love, she would be forced to wed the man of her uncle's choice. Although, she didn't think her uncle would force her to wed a man she disliked; that was part of the problem. He would probably pick a man acceptable to her—but would she love him?

It was doubtful, but she would do her duty and not disappoint her uncle. Which gave her all the more impetus to go on an adventure before she committed herself to a loveless marriage. And of course, once in that marriage she would be confined to her husband's dictates, which was not a particularly pleasant thought. And then there was intimacy.

How was one intimate with a stranger? A man who

was chosen as a husband but knew little of his wife and she of him?

Sex was rarely discussed amongst ladies, though Hope learned early on that the household servants chattered endlessly about it. She had hid many times and listened with delight and interest to the servants' tales of love and sex. She often held her hand to her mouth to prevent herself from giggling at some of the odd stories. But as she grew older and wiser she began to understand all they discussed.

When she was around twelve she finally decided she wanted to view the sex act for herself so she could better understand all she heard. Her plan was to hide in the barn at the time her uncle mated the horses. Her plan worked better than she had hoped. One of the household servants and the stable boy had decided to use the barn for a quick coupling and she had watched from beneath the pile of hay she had buried herself under as they kissed, caressed and coupled with sheer pleasure.

She realized much about intimacy, sex and love after that and if her strange studies taught her anything they taught her that love, true love, made a difference in a relationship.

And that casual love was easy to find, but a lasting love was rare.

Hope's glance settled on Colin's back and her ear picked up the charm in his voice as he answered the women who called out pleasant greetings to him, some daringly approaching him and whispering near his ear.

He would smile, touch and charm all with casual ease.

Did he care only for a moment of casual love? Did he not wish for more?

Or did love not interest him at all?

Hope shook her head and Lady moved up alongside her, her nose poking at Hope's hand. She patted the dog's head as they both continued to follow behind Colin.

Why should she care what Colin thought of love? And

why of late was she giving the passionate emotion so much thought? And why when she thought of love did she think of Colin?

She collided with his back, having not paid attention to her steps to notice that he had stopped. She winced and grabbed her side, and Colin, in turn, grabbed her arm.

"Come with me and let me have a look at those ribs."

Before she could protest, he all but dragged her to where the horses grazed contentedly around a large old tree. And with quick hands he reached for her tunic to pull it off.

Four

Hope shoved his hands away. "I will see to myself."

Colin noted the defensive tone, a tone the lad was in the habit of using all too often. "I will have a look."

His insistent tone cautioned Hope, and she took a step back. There was no way she could match his strength. His lean build might cause some to think him weak but she had witnessed his exceptional strength with the way he had easily plucked the young lad off her as if he were no more than a pesky fly.

"A bruise, nothing more, I assure you," Hope said with a smile that was meant to dissuade and dismiss.

Colin thought otherwise and took a step toward her. "I want to make certain you did not sustain a more serious injury."

Hope retreated another step or two as she answered. "Not serious. A bruise is all."

The lad's reluctance to let Colin see to his wound concerned him. Had someone hurt him? Or did he not trust? He wanted Harold to trust him. He wanted the lad to know that he could rely on him for most anything. But then trust took time, and there was pride. No man nor lad cared for wounded pride.

Colin stepped back. "We will be leaving shortly. See to yourself and then see to helping the men pack the horses with the provisions we have purchased."

"Yes, sir," she answered quickly and with obvious relief.

"Colin," he corrected before walking off with a shake of his head.

Hope hurried to clean herself up though her steps were not as agile and light-footed as she had hoped. She was beginning to ache all over. She washed the dried blood from her split lip and could feel the increased swelling. Her jaw was tender to the touch and she could barely run her hand over her ribs on the right side. The tender area was visibly bruised and would probably worsen in color and soreness as the day advanced, as would the whole of her body.

Her movements took on a decisive strain and slowness. Her attempts to pack the horses quickly took a toll on her. Even lifting the slightest weight disturbed her injured ribs and made her grimace in pain. But she refused to give in or give up. Colin had told her that she must shoulder her share of the work and she intended to do just that—no matter the discomfort.

Stuart was the first of the men to come to her aid. He began lifting the heavier parcels and securing them to the horses while asking "Harold" about the fight.

At first Hope dismissed the altercation as unimportant but she could tell by the time the second man joined them that the men were actually curious and eager to hear a good tale. Hope loved a good tale herself so she found herself embellishing on the incident.

By the time Colin joined them Hope was sitting on a small barrel listening to the men share their first fighting experiences. She jumped up at his approach—a definite mistake. Her ribs protested the unexpected jolt and she would have sunk to her knees from the pain if it were not for Stuart, whose thickly muscled arm lent quick support.

"May be the first, but it will not be the last pain you feel, lad."

Stuart's remark was meant to encourage and Hope had to be cautious in her reaction and remember that her response should be that of a lad of ten and two. And then, of course, there was her own pride. She raised her chin. "It hurts but little."

Stuart smiled and eased his arm away. "And will hurt less tomorrow."

"No lifting until I order so."

The stern command was meant to draw attention, and it did. Stuart and Hope's eyes were immediately drawn to Colin.

"You will see to light chores only." Another order issued just as sternly.

Hope was amazed at how one minute his tongue charmed and the next it commanded. He fascinated her with his rogue charm and warrior strength, which contradicted and yet somehow confirmed his true character. She wished to explore his many complex sides.

Hope acquiesced with a curt nod.

Colin turned to Stuart. "I wish to be on our way shortly and ride until near dusk. We will make stops at a few more villages and cottages along the way and ask if a young woman has been seen in the vicinity."

"Not wishing any harm to the young lady," Stuart said in an apologetic manner, "but it is not likely that she could survive on her own, her being a lady and accustomed to being tended to."

"I would agree, and if that be the truth then I would like evidence to take to Lord Eric. Until that can be a proven fact I must assume the lady is alive and therefore we must continue to search."

Stuart seemed reluctant to speak. "You do realize she may never be found."

"Aye, I have given that thought." Colin smiled. "Though Eric informed me that the lady's uncle mentioned that she was a willful and fearless lass."

It seemed obvious they searched for her, Hope thought. Her uncle had often commented on her willful nature, though he had never made mention of her being fearless. She took his words as a compliment of her strong character.

"Spoiled and ignorant is more like it," Stuart said, a curt nod affirming his opinion.

Hope could not hold her tongue, and besides, she wanted to learn all they knew about her. "Who might that be?"

"Lady Hope," Stuart answered.

Lady whined at the sound of the familiar name and Hope nudged her gently with her foot. "Someone important?"

"Someone who should know her place and do her duty without causing others trouble," Stuart said, annoyed.

Hope shrugged as if it made no difference to her.

"Perhaps she is not content with the decisions being made for her."

Colin's words surprised her. Could he possibly understand how she felt? She did not think anyone did, least of all a man. And yet he spoke her thought.

Stuart disagreed with a snort and a grunt. "She is a descendent of the high king of Ireland and she has her duty to do, content or not."

"Perhaps her willful nature thought otherwise," Colin said with a hint of admiration for her rash actions.

"Her willful nature might just be the death of her," Stuart said, slowly shaking his head.

"Or help her survive," Colin said.

Colin was her champion yet did not know it. He defended her actions and perhaps in his own way understood them. He was a kindred spirit of sorts, an idea that she liked. Somehow it made her feel less lonely on her quest.

"Let us hasten our departure," Colin urged. "I am anxious to be off."

Stuart nodded and returned to his task.

Hope turned prepared to do the same.

"Harold." Colin's tone was authoritative. "Rest, the walk will be difficult enough for you."

She was ready to protest when he crossed his arms

over his chest, shook his head and smiled.

How could he warn with charm? She did not understand though she saw the wisdom of his warning and paid heed to it. She sat back down on the barrel.

They were off before long and Colin's words had proven true. After a few miles her steps slowed and her ribs ached unbearably. She wanted to drop to the ground and remain there for however long it took for the pain to ease. And while she made no sound or mention of it, Lady whined as if she bore her master's entire suffering.

Stuart was the first to offer his horse to her, and she attempted to decline but he insisted and with large yet gentle hands he lifted her onto his horse. He walked alongside her in silence, understanding her need for quiet and rest.

After several miles Hope, with her ache having subsided to a bearable pain, suggested that she once again walk. Stuart insisted that he enjoyed his walk but she did not want to appear a burden nor give them pause to think about her physical weakness, leaving room for doubt about her character.

With reluctance Stuart helped her off his horse.

It took fewer miles than before for the ache to return full force and she soon found herself offered another horse to ride. John was adamant about walking, making mention of a specific part of his body that would never be spoken of in front of a lady and bluntly describing the discomfort.

And so it went as they continued on until the final one to offer his horse was Colin.

"My turn," he said with a warm smile and slipped his hands around her slim waist to lift her up onto his horse.

His smile faltered for a moment and Hope all but held her breath until she was safely seated on the horse. What had he felt or assumed? Was her waist too narrow for that of a lad? Her breasts were so small it was not necessary to bind them and the two layers of clothing she wore sufficiently protected her from being discovered. Why had his smile faltered?

He walked beside her, his smile having returned. "Tell me about yourself, Harold."

Tales were her forte; she spun many for her own entertainment and that of her aunt and uncle. She had fashioned a believable tale and was now given the chance to test its strength, though she thought it best to begin reluctantly.

"Not much to tell."

"Tell me what you will."

Hope liked the fact that Colin did not always insist but instead showed sincere interest, causing one to succumb to his charm. And she did just that.

"My family was a loving lot and while we barely had enough to eat we had more love than most."

She had decided her tale could not do without strong love. When there were strong family ties there was strength; she had learned that firsthand. It was a lesson that kept her going through the most difficult of times.

"We worked hard as most do and then my father took ill." She turned silent for a moment, thinking of her own father's quick demise. Her voice faltered and she cleared it. "My mother took ill shortly after him and it was all I could do to look after them both."

"Was there no sister or brother to lend a hand?" Colin asked.

For a moment Hope's breath caught. The sunlight struck his face in such a manner that it highlighted his features and his face simply stunned her. His good looks could not be denied. But then, he also possessed a good heart.

"There was only me," she said, her voice trembling.

"That must have been difficult for you." His words held a genuine concern and his obvious caring nature touched her heart.

"I did what I had to do." A true enough statement, since it explained her decision for her journey.

"I admire your courage."

She shrugged, feeling uneasy in accepting his compliment. "I survived."

"It takes courage to survive." Seeming to understand that Harold did not take well to praise, Colin persuaded him to continue. "Tell me more."

"Not much to tell. My mother went faster than my father." As was true in her life. "My father fought for his life, telling me that he needed to look after me." She paused, tears clouding her eyes. Her father had held her hand and even in his weakened state she could feel his strength. He did not wish to leave her alone and yet in the end it was he who told her to remain strong for in strength she would find the ability to survive. "When I finally made him understand I would be all right, he quietly passed on."

Colin waited in silence, as if paying homage to her deceased parents.

"After their passing I realized I could not tend the land on my own and I always craved adventure. So I took a few belongings and began my journey."

"What happened to your belongings?"

"Stolen." She had learned that a brief answer was the best when having fashioned an intricate tale.

"And where did you wish your journey to take you?"

She gave a truthful answer. "I did not truly know. I only knew that the journey was necessary."

"Life has provided you with wisdom beyond your young years."

"Nay," she said firmly and with a defiant shake of her head. "There is much for me to learn."

Colin grinned. He liked the young lad's stubbornness. "And learn you will."

Hope suddenly felt guilty about riding Colin's horse. He had warned her about doing her fair share and here on the first day when she could prove her worth, she proved herself defenseless. What ever must he think of her? And did he doubt she was capable of learning? She needed to amend his opinion of her. She needed him to believe her a young lad willing and able to do what must be done.

And she would begin by walking instead of riding as she had been doing since leaving the village hours ago. "I should walk."

That brought a loud whine from Lady and a laugh from Colin.

"Your dog has more sense than you."

Hope attempted to object.

Colin gave him no time. "You will ride until I instruct otherwise."

She did learn quickly, and she had learned that Colin led his men wisely and when he issued an order it was to be obeyed, not questioned or argued. She remained on the horse, her aching limbs grateful.

After a few disappointing stops at villages that had heard or seen nothing of the young woman described to them, and the sun near setting, Colin ordered them to stop for the night.

The men saw to setting up camp. Harold was ordered to gather twigs to help start the fire. This would have been a simple enough task if Hope had not been suffering from the aches and pains of a recent beating.

Her movements were slow yet steady. She intended to accomplish the given task and prove her capabilities.

Stuart suddenly appeared at her side and took the small bundle she had already collected from her. "I have an eye for twigs that start good fires. I will finish this. Go rest."

She thought to protest but a yawn interfered and Stuart grinned.

With reluctance she returned to camp, Lady lagging behind her. The day's journey had proved tiring for them both and at the moment Hope was more in need of sleep than food. But how could she just plop herself down to rest when every man there was busy setting up camp?

She was the only one doing nothing; that she could not tolerate. It was only fair she help.

Hope was tireless in her efforts to share the work with the men and the men were tireless in their efforts to see that the lad rested. It was Colin who finally took her by the arm and forced her to sit by the fire.

"Lady," he addressed the dog with authority. Her ears perked up and her eyes widened. "See that he stays where he sits."

Lady seemed to understand. She placed her large body across Hope, settling her head on her legs.

"Good, Lady." He praised the dog and patted her head before walking off.

Hope had to admit that Colin was certainly a caring soul—as were his men—and she was lucky to have met up with them. There had been a few times she had met men of less reputable character and had barely escaped without serious injury. By the time she had come upon Colin's camp she had been starving and completely disenchanted with her journey. Now, though, she had to admit she found it rather exciting; but then it was the prospect of learning more about Colin himself that excited her.

Yawns continued to attack her as she watched Colin do his share of the work without complaint. He moved with an easy confidence, his hands familiar with even the most menial task. And his smile remained constant, demonstrating that a mundane chore did not at all disturb him. She heard no complaints from him and he issued orders with a quiet authority that was immediately obeyed.

She thought him a man of contrast, charming and personable and yet complex and mysterious. How did he lead with charm? And where had he learned the skill?

Three rabbits were soon roasting on the wooden spit over the fire and one by one the men drifted over to sit as they finished with their chores. By the time Colin joined them Hope had passed out, she and Lady curled around each other.

"He is a tough lad," Stuart said as Colin stood over Hope, his arms crossed.

"A stubborn one, too," John said, "though not a bad trait."

The other men agreed with a chorus of "ayes."

Colin thought to move Hope and Lady but the pair looked comfortable enough so he joined the men for the evening meal. His eyes, however, continued to stray to the sleeping lad. He looked frail for a lad of ten and two and yet he had a depth of strength to him that surprised Colin.

When he learned of Harold coming to a weaker lad's defense even against difficult odds he found himself admiring his courage. Harold must have known he would take a beating and yet he did not walk away from injustice; he stood his ground and defended his own beliefs. For that alone Colin respected him.

Colin wanted to help. Why, he could not say. The need to protect was strong. While Harold was a determined one he did not possess the physical strength to defend himself, so Colin felt compelled to do so.

Then there was the thought, a persistent thought, that Colin could not ignore. He felt that Harold had no intentions of remaining at Shanekill Keep, that given time he would leave and tell no one of his departure. He would simply be gone, once again on his own. The thought disturbed Colin.

Why this young lad's well-being seemed so vital to him he could not understand. He really was not Colin's responsibility. And yet he felt responsible; he intended to see that the lad had a permanent home.

He would see that Harold remained at Shanekill Keep whether he wanted to or not. Colin watched a shiver race through the sleeping lad, causing him to wrap himself more tightly around the large dog for warmth.

Colin was about to stand and get a blanket for the lad when Stuart leaned over from where he sat nearby and gently placed a wool blanket over Harold.

"A good lad," Stuart remarked, "though he needs weight on him."

"Ayes" could be heard making their rounds around the campfire.

Colin smiled and shook his head. Harold had worked his way into the men's hearts and strangely enough the lad had touched his heart as well.

Five

Hope made certain she remained with the men when they entered another village the next day. It was a small one and within minutes they learned that no one fitting Hope's description had been seen in the area.

The men's grumbles grew as they journeyed on, though they continued to offer Harold their horses along the way. She accepted a few times and walked other times. While her injuries continued to cause her discomfort, the pain was not as unbearable as the previous day and she did not wish to appear weak in front of the men. She was, after all, a young lad with pride.

She found that she enjoyed listening to the men and their tales. They spoke far differently than they did when in the company of ladies and the contrast amazed her. She had to turn her head a few times to hide the blush that their raucous words caused her but that did not prevent her from listening or even grinning from time to time.

She had to admit that her adventure was finally becoming adventurous and she was having a grand time.

Colin rode up to speak with Stuart who walked beside his horse, which Hope rode.

"There is a small lake up ahead and being the day is warm and sunny I thought the men might enjoy a dunk."

Stuart nodded. "A good idea." He looked up at Harold. "Do you swim, lad?"

Hope was an excellent swimmer, but Harold? She

shook her head, knowing that it was not possible for him to take a dunk with the men. "Nay, I do not."

"Then perhaps it is time you learned," Colin said, his smile not making his remark sound any less adamant.

Protesting was useless; her wits would be her best weapon. "If you think," she said with an indifferent shrug of her slim shoulders. "Last time I made an effort to learn was on a day like today. Warm and sunny with a faint chill that caught the air every now and then. I guess that was what caused my fever, the chill."

She said no more, planting a seed in Colin's mind and letting it take root.

It rooted fast in Stuart's mind. "Maybe a warmer day would be best for the lad."

Colin rested a steady eye on Harold. The lad was no fool. He chose intelligence over brawn and used it to his advantage, outwitting his opponents.

"It is Harold's choice," Colin said with a sharp eye on him.

Hope forced herself not to squirm and appear restless, but while Colin's smile charmed, his eyes accused with a relentlessness that unnerved.

She forced herself to respond though the lump in her throat made her voice squeak. "Another day, I think."

"Then you will tend the men's horses while they enjoy themselves," Colin ordered firmly.

Stuart was about to voice his objection when Colin shot him a look that warned him not to protest. Stuart wisely remained silent.

Harold nodded, relieved. If there was time she would sneak away and wash herself quickly. It had been several days since she had been able to do more than see to washing her face and hands. Her body required much more attention, and she hoped there would be time and the solitude necessary to see to it.

The horses were tethered near where the men bathed in the chilled lake. They did not strip completely naked especially after testing the water, though they all stripped to their chests and Hope could not help but peek around the horses at them.

They were all impressive, but then she supposed that was because they were trained warriors and elite ones at that, belonging to the Irish devil. They varied in size though each possessed a muscled chest and arms, Stuart being the largest of the group. He could not be called fat by any means. The man was simply a mass of muscles and she wondered why any man would choose to go up against such a powerful opponent.

Why, he looked as though he could squash a man's head with one hand!

She kept herself looking busy and kept peeking past the horses to watch the men. Her adventure was proving so much more educational than she had thought it would be. Here she was learning about men so that when she married she would better understand her husband.

Or perhaps if she was lucky enough she would discover love.

At that moment Colin approached his men bare chested and she was unable to look away. His body was beautifully defined as though each muscle was sculpted by a master artist, and in those defined lines Hope could almost see the strength he possessed. He was a work of art magnificently crafted, and each fluid movement proved it as he reached out to cup water in his hands and splash it over his hard chest.

His muscles grew taut and flexed in a natural rhythm that captivated attention. The beads of water even paid reverence to his beauty, slowly sliding down his chest as if not in a hurry to detach from him.

Hope felt her body rush with a sudden tingle that settled between her legs and caused her to grow uncomfortably moist.

It was time to take herself elsewhere. This would not do at all and she was finished seeing to the horses' care, not a difficult task since she had often spent time in her youth helping with her uncle's horses.

She had always been an inquisitive child, insisting on answers to her endless questions. If no one could satisfy her curiosity then she searched for the answer herself. But her present question haunted her and the answer would not come easily.

She wished to know what it would feel like to touch Colin, to feel his strength beneath her hand and . . .

Hope shook her head, willing away her tormenting thoughts. The more she allowed herself to think of Colin in such intimate terms the more aroused she became and that was not right.

Hope marched off, putting a safe distance between herself and the men—Colin in particular. She wasted no time in splashing a generous handful of water in her face and taking a deep breath.

Lady sat a few feet away, watching her with woeful eyes as though she understood her master's dilemma and sympathized.

Why must she find him attractive? He obviously was a charmer with the ladies, having had several women approach him in each of the villages they had stopped at and he not turning them away. One could only assume that he did not take love seriously. If it was a good romp in the sack she was looking for then he would certainly fill her needs, but she wanted more. She wanted love, but what did Colin want?

She shook her head. She did not think even he knew what he searched for.

She sighed and turned to Lady. "A dilemma for certain."

Lady snorted her agreement.

Hope hurried and saw to her own care before someone discovered her missing and came in search of her. Soreness made her movements awkward and she was certain her recent chores had not helped her healing, but then she was expected to do a lad's share.

She returned as the men were slipping back into their clothes and took a seat on a large stone to wait.

Colin made his way over to her and she fought to keep from inspecting his bare chest as only a woman could.

"Where did you go?"

Useless.

That word seemed to be constantly in her head lately. And of course it was useless to lie to him; he was much too alert and aware of his surroundings, a warrior's trait for sure.

But she was quick enough to reply. "Lady and I went to tend to our duties."

This was a reasonable enough explanation; so why did he look as though he did not believe her?

Uncomfortable with the way his deep brown eyes scrutinized her, she shifted her position on the rock. She lost her balance and slipped off, the sudden jolt causing a stab of pain to her injured side.

Colin's arm went out, grabbing her around the waist, and her hand grasped his solid muscle for support.

His flesh was cool, his muscles hard, and the strength of him tingled beneath her touch. She quickly righted herself and just as quickly stepped away from him.

"Your side still pains you?"

She was reluctant to speak, knowing her voice would tremble. She kept her response brief. "A bit."

"You will ride until we make camp," he ordered and turned to walk away only to stop and turn around. "And if you wish to wander off on your own you will ask permission before doing so."

His remark annoyed her independent spirit and sparked a fire in her eyes that caused Colin to smile.

"Choose your battles wisely, lad."

She understood that he warned her she would not see victory in this situation. Why charge headfirst into a battle when defeat was imminent? But then he was not aware of her tenacious nature, and she knew that with patience she would see victory.

"I always do," she said with a confident grin and

marched past Colin with Lady close at her heels.

Colin watched Harold walk away with an overly confident swagger. He would prove to be a handful—of that he had no doubt—but he liked the lad. He was independent and inquisitive and prepared to face whatever life dealt him. His frail appearance belied his true character and perhaps it was that appearance that always made Colin feel protective of him. When they returned to Shanekill Keep he would make certain he began lessons in self-defense, and hopefully with an abundance of food and proper care he would begin to gain weight and muscle.

He watched as Harold wasted no time in lending a helping hand to the men. He was not afraid to do his share and then some, though it was obvious pain still haunted him. And the fact that the lad suffered disturbed Colin. He did not wish to see him suffer needlessly.

"Harold," he shouted sternly, causing everyone to stop suddenly and look his way. He realized his voice was more firm than he had intended, though he chose not to alter it. "Rest until we are ready to leave and you will ride for the remainder of the day's journey."

Hope almost protested his edict but then thought of his recent remark. . . . *Choose your battles wisely* caused her to hold her tongue.

She simply nodded and found a sunny spot to sit with Lady and wait.

That evening Hope sat by the fire nibbling at the roasted rabbit and listening intently to the men's conversation. Talk had turned to women and Hope was amazed at the comments the men made.

"Women do not make sense," John said adamantly after downing a generous portion of ale.

Stuart laughed. "True enough."

"Your problem is that you try to make sense of them," Colin said, sounding as though he had no difficulty understanding women.

"It helps to understand when you have a wife," Stuart attempted to explain.

John grinned. "He is right. Bedding a woman takes no understanding; marrying one does."

Hope's glance shifted from one man to another as they spoke. She found their comments interesting and was anxious to hear more.

"A foolish thought," Colin said, taking a bite of rabbit.

Daniel, the quiet one of the group, spoke with a teasing lilt. "We are mere mortals, not legendary lovers like you."

The men laughed, humor wrinkling their faces though envy could be seen as well.

"I simply know how to charm," Colin said confidently.

"It is your tongue that charms and in more ways than one," John said with a snicker.

Stuart smiled as he joined in. "My wife tells me that you are the talk of the keep, the lasses sharing tales of your infamous charm."

Colin gave a slight bow of his head. "I only wish to please."

Daniel spoke again. "I have trouble pleasing one woman. How do you manage to please so many?"

"I give them what they want," Colin said as if he possessed a secret.

"What do they want?" John asked curiously.

Hope found herself eager to hear his answer. Lady's ears also perked up.

"Me," Colin said with a proud thump to his chest.

The men laughed and raised their cups in a salute.

Hope was not as satisfied as the men and asked a question only a woman would. "What if it is not you a woman wants?"

The laughter died and the men turned wide eyes on the lad.

Stuart spoke, though they all looked ready and eager to defend Colin. "All women lust after him."

John agreed with a firm nod. "That they do. They cannot keep their eyes off him."

Daniel's voice was adamant. "I have seen women fight over him."

Hope grew annoyed. "Why do they fight? He seems to make himself available to all."

The men laughed again.

"He is but one man, lad," Stuart said.

"With the stamina of ten," John added with a snicker.

Daniel grinned. "I do not think the lad has the experience to understand of what we speak."

All eyes fell on Hope and it was with a false bravado that she spoke. "I know of what you speak."

John sat forward with a teasing grin. "So tell us of your exploits with women."

Hope's bravado grew and she leaned closer to him. "Why? Do you need advice?"

The men roared and John found himself speechless.

Colin laughed along with the men, though he realized that the lad's sharp wit could cause him endless trouble. And yet he dared to speak his piece no matter the consequences. Colin wisely changed the subject when the laughter subsided. "Tomorrow we stop at Croom Abbey."

"You think the lass may have taken shelter there?" Stuart asked.

"If she has, she is a determined one to make it this far on her own," Colin answered. "And I will certainly be curious to discover exactly how she accomplished such an unusual feat for a woman."

"I hope she gets the thrashing she deserves for causing so much trouble," John said without a shred of compassion.

"Her intended will certainly have his hands full with the likes of her," Daniel said, his sympathy for the man obvious.

"She does appear to possess an adventurous spirit," Colin said with a hint of admiration.

"Which needs taming," Stuart said firmly.

"A pity," Colin said, his charming smile surfacing. "An adventurous woman can prove interesting."

"Trouble she is," Stuart warned. "Nothing but trouble."

Trouble.

She was causing her uncle needless trouble and worry by being adventurous and yet she felt the need to continue her adventure. Upon her return she would marry and never again have a chance to explore and learn about life. And then there was Colin.

In a strange way she felt he understood her reason for running away and did not judge her for it. But how understanding would he be when he discovered Harold's true identity? Would he find Hope adventurous then? Or would he consider her a troublesome woman who deserved taming?

And why did his opinion of her matter? Was she like all the other women who fell under the spell of his charming tongue and good looks?

She shifted her glance around the camp, watching the men settle down for the night and allowing her eyes to stray to Colin when she saw that no one took notice.

His good looks could not be denied and yet it was his character that intrigued her. Under that polished charm lay a different man, and she wondered who he was and whether he wished to love instead of always charm.

Did he ever wish to find one woman to please and love forever? Did he ever think of love, a binding love that could not be denied? Or did he think his charm would suffice for love?

Lady whimpered softly, alerting Hope to her need to see to her nightly duty. Also, Lady did not care to be on her own in the dark woods. Hope had to accompany her.

Hope stood, an eager Lady standing along with her. She was making her way to the outskirts of camp when her eyes met with Colin's.

No charm glistened in his dark eyes; instead, they warned with an icy chill that sent a shiver racing down her spine.

She instinctively obeyed his silent caution and approached him. With a tremble to her voice she fought to hide she said, "Lady needs to see to her duty."

How he could manage to intimidate stretched out on his blanket, his braced elbow supporting his weight, she did not know. But the length and strength of him made her knees quiver. He appealed all too often to her senses and at this moment her sense of sight was much too heightened as her eyes reveled in every defined curve, bump and bulge of him.

She wisely averted her eyes to Lady, giving her head a thoughtful pat.

"She cannot see to it on her own?" Colin asked.

Lady answered with a woeful whimper.

Colin laughed softly and with a stretch and a gentle ease of his body, he stood. "I will go with you."

Hope knew better than to protest. She simply shrugged as if his decision made no difference to her and walked toward the night shadows.

Lady took her time, as she always did. She typically sniffed and pawed the ground until she found the perfect spot, and just when Hope thought her ready she would stop and start the process all over again.

Hope thought to take advantage of her dog's intentional lingering to learn more about Colin.

She decided to be blunt; it often caught people off guard and made for an honest response.

"Do you not wish to love?"

Colin was too much of a seasoned warrior to respond without regard, though he did stop in his tracks, the unexpected reaction annoying him.

"And why is one so young thinking about love?"

Her answer came easily, for it was the truth. "I learned about love from my mother and father and realized how important it is. I could not imagine a relationship without such a binding love. So I but wonder if you ever think of loving, truly loving someone."

Colin envied the lad his loving parents. His childhood had been emotionally and physically barren and he had found himself all too often aching for loving arms. And did he still not wish for those loving arms?

His answer was yet a question more to himself than to the lad. "Does not everyone wish to love?"

Hope intended to have her answer. She stood with her slim legs slightly parted, her feet braced firmly and her arms crossed over her chest. "I asked if *you* wish to love."

Colin did not know why he chose to answer the lad. He guarded his emotions well and spoke of his hopes and dreams to no one, yet his answer slipped from his lips on a mere whisper. "Aye, I do wish to love."

Hope heard his ache and understood his reluctance in admitting his feelings. She so often buried her own hope and desire to find love that she recognized another who did the same. And before he could once again shield his emotions, she asked, "A binding love?"

There was no hesitation when he said, "A forever love. I wish to find forever love with a woman and make her *forever mine*."

A tingle rippled in her stomach. "That is a long time."

"When you truly love, forever would not seem long enough."

The dark night prevented her from seeing his face clearly but at that moment she could see without actually seeing. And she knew he wore no charming smile and his dark eyes did not sparkle with sensual mischief. His handsome face portrayed emotions he rarely allowed anyone to see. His eyes betrayed his loneliness and his lips ached to kiss a woman he forever loved.

At that moment Hope felt they shared a common bond and she understood him almost as well as she did herself.

Lady joined them, poking Hope's hand with her nose.

"She appears to finally be finished," Colin said.

This was one time when Hope wished that Lady had lingered longer.

Colin took the lead and walked toward camp. Hope followed with Lady by her side, wishing that she could slip her small hand in his firm one and hold on to him tightly. But he thought she was a lad and at that precise moment she felt more like a woman than she ever had.

Six

Hope walked all morning, although she was offered rides. The day was much too beautiful not to walk. The sky was a clear blue and the ground a carpet of vibrant greens with dashes of colorful wildflowers, which decided it was time to rear their heads to welcome spring. Besides, the pain in her ribs had subsided to a dull ache she could handle, so walking was no great chore.

She was never much for giving in to any degree of pain, though she had learned that emotional pain could cause greater suffering than physical pain. She had learned that lesson when her parents had taken ill and died, so the dull ache she now experienced was easy to contend with.

The men were helping her with most all of the chores Colin gave her, allowing her plenty of time to heal. It seemed that every time she lifted even the smallest weight one of the men would appear by her side and tend to the chore.

She worried that Colin would grow annoyed with their protectiveness and order the lad to tend to his own fair share of the work. She would gladly do the work if the men would allow her to. And yet Colin, while well aware of what was going on, made no mention of it. His silence signified his approval, in a strange way.

The thought of the Irish devil's elite warriors tending to a young lad's care warmed her heart and made the small group all the more endearing to her.

And as for Colin?

"He is handsome, is he not, Lady?" Hope asked, her eye on Colin who sat his horse with discernible confidence.

Lady issued a grumbling growl which Hope took as a positive response, allowing her to continue to speak her mind.

"It is not just his looks."

That remark caused a rolling grumble from Lady.

Hope looked down at the dog. "It is not," she insisted. "He is an unselfish and caring man. Look at the way he treats Harold. He could be much harsher on the lad and he is not. And—" She paused and gave Lady's snout a gentle tap. "He is tolerant of you and your cowardly ways."

Lady whimpered softly.

Hope raised her eyes once again, settling them on Colin. "I think him a fine man with good character."

Her eyes widened as his glance settled on her. Her voice had been low so no one could hear and he was a safe enough distance away that he could not have heard her words, yet he looked at her strangely—almost as if he sensed her thoughts had been on him.

He rode slowly toward her, his mare confident in her strides and in the man who held her reins.

Hope possessed a strong confidence of her own, which Harold demonstrated by keeping a steady glance on Colin as he approached.

Lady, on the other hand, was easily intimidated and one look at Colin caused her to hurry behind Hope as they continued walking.

"Are you feeling well?" he asked as he brought his horse alongside the lad.

"Aye, I am," she answered with a firm nod.

He smiled, a teasing one that Hope favored. "Do you often talk to your dog?"

The truth always came easily. "All the time."

He understood, as she knew he would. "Lady is a good friend."

"My best friend. I can confide in her." She laughed. "And be certain she keeps my confidence."

"And do you harbor dark secrets, lad?" Colin asked in a low, conspiratorial tone that was meant to tease.

Hope played along, looking to the left and right of her, Lady doing the same, and then lowering her voice to a mere whisper so that Colin had to lean down to hear. "Aye, I do. A deep dark secret that no one must ever know." She pressed a finger to her pursed lips.

"Share it with me," Colin said. "You can trust me to keep it."

His teasing manner faded, for his words sounded sincere. He wanted the lad to know that he could trust him to keep his confidence, that he was his friend. The lad surely needed one.

Hope had no doubt he was a man of his word and that the lad could trust him with almost anything—anything, that is, except this secret.

Colin watched as doubt welled up in Harold's eyes and he wanted to climb down off his horse and offer the boy comfort, a comfort he himself had never been offered as a child. But the lad had pride and a strength Colin admired and he did not wish to offend him, so he stayed as he was and instead offered him friendship.

"When you are ready to share your secret I am ready to listen and whatever way is in my power to help you, I will. Remember that and never fear to trust me."

How Hope wished at that moment she could tell him all and that he would help her. But his loyalty was pledged to the Irish devil and if he learned her identity he would do as he must and return her to her uncle. And then she would never get to truly know him or to finish her adventure. She wished for both, though someday the truth would be spoken and then—she did not want to think of the consequences.

"I will remember," she said, her words heavy with the weight of her secret.

"We will arrive at Croom Abbey shortly and end our day's journey at the village, hopefully with good news to take home with us."

"Do you think this woman you seek might be there?" Her necessary deceit disturbed her since she had always spoken the truth. Yet presently the truth was causing him and his men anguish.

"You have barely survived your travels; think then if a woman could do as well. And a woman who is accustomed to being attended to, her every whim met, her every need fulfilled."

"Spoiled, is she?" Hope said with a laugh, recalling how her aunt and uncle often accused each other of doing just that in their own ways. And it was because of their unselfish and loving natures that she now possessed her own spirited nature. She was forever grateful to them for all they had given her.

Colin's charm surfaced easily. "All women are spoiled, Harold. Learn that now and you will better deal with them."

"How so?" she asked, curious to hear a man's view on women.

"All women expect something from a man."

"What do they expect?"

He laughed and shook his head. "They do not know themselves."

Hope wore a confused look. "Then how do you know that they expect?"

He turned a confident grin on her. "Because I know women and each woman I have known has expected something from me. Whether it was attention, a kiss, a touch or more, they expected and I made certain they were not disappointed, which endeared me to them even more."

Hope found their discussion interesting. "And did you do this to please them or you?"

"My pleasure is gained by pleasing them."

She thought a moment, then asked, "So you please but do not love?"

He did not pause in his answer. "I love in my own way."

"And yet you wish a forever love."

"Which is why I search so hard to please so many women." He chuckled at his own response.

Hope, however, found his flippant remark sad and all too telling. "You hope to find the one you wish to love forever. Do you not grow weary and disappointed in your search?"

The lad was much too astute. He ached for the love of one woman. A woman who would care, truly care for him. Not for his good looks or his charming tongue but simply for who he was, a man in need of love.

He kept his thoughts to himself and answered with his usual charm. "The fun is in the search."

Hope stopped walking, which caused Colin to bring his horse to a halt. She looked up at him. "When you are ready to tell me your secret, the one you refuse to share with anyone, then I will trust you and tell you mine."

Hope walked off, Lady prancing beside her, leaving a stunned Colin to himself.

Croom Abbey was smaller than most abbeys that Hope had visited, though it was well maintained and the nuns friendly and welcoming. A generous amount of food was offered to the men while Colin spent time with the abbess.

In return, as the men finished their meal they offered their services to the nuns. Repair work that required a man's strength was soon seen to and Hope found herself on her own since Lady decided a nap was to her liking.

She wandered the ground, aching to bend down and sniff a blossoming spring flower, but a lad would not stop to sniff flowers. So she used her wits and leaned over to pick up a small rock that lay near a bright yellow flower and then gave the rock a forceful toss.

She sneaked more sniffs and tossed more rocks until the sound of Colin's voice brought her to a halt not far from a narrow window at the back of the abbey. The other voice caused all color to drain from her face.

The gentle tone, the clear soft lilt, was all too familiar. It belonged to Sister Bernadette. She was a distant cousin of her aunt Elizabeth and she could have kicked herself for not remembering that she had recently been appointed an abbess.

"She is that stubborn?" Colin asked with a hint of laughter in his voice.

"Determined," the abbess corrected gently. "Hope was always determined. Shamus could never say no to the child. He indulged her most every whim."

"Spoiled her, did he?"

"Nay," the abbess said. "While indulgence can spoil, in Hope it created a remarkable strength of character that gave her determination in all she chose to do. She is intelligent and adventurous and oftentimes fearless."

"Has she ever run away before this?"

"Nay, she has been an obedient child." The abbess laughed softly. "I contradict myself, but you see, Hope always managed to barely remain in the boundaries of her world. She did what was expected of her and found ways to do the unexpected and not embarrass her aunt and uncle."

"Then why run away now?" Colin asked curiously.

"I could but venture a guess, though I must tell you that Hope will do what is expected of her. She will return and marry the man her uncle has chosen, unless . . ."

"Unless?" Colin prompted, all the more curious.

"Unless she finds love, true love. She has searched for it in her own way and I think this is why she ran away. She took a chance that her adventure would bring her the love she ached to find."

"Foolish, romantic notions," Colin said while thinking himself wrong. It did not fit her character.

The abbess sighed. "Hope is far from foolish and romantic." She shook her head. "Hope has much love to give a man and in return needs to be loved just as strongly and deeply. While some young women think to be protected and cherished by the men they love, Hope intends to protect and cherish the man she loves."

The more Colin learned of Hope the more he admired her and the more he wanted to meet her. "I have been told that she is a mere wisp of a woman. However could she protect?"

The abbess laughed heartily. "You must know Hope to know she is capable of most anything."

"Capable of surviving on her own?"

"As strange as it may seem to you, I do not fear for Hope's safety. She is much too intelligent to act unwisely, and I am confident that she is well and will return when she is ready."

"I do not wish to be rude, so forgive me when I ask whether you would tell me if you saw her?"

"You need only to ask me."

"I appreciate your help," he said with a respectful bow of his head.

"Now let me see that the sisters have treated you well."

"And let me see that my men have assisted the sisters where necessary."

"Your help is greatly appreciated and we will reward you with our prayers," the abbess said and walked toward the door.

For a moment Hope stood frozen in place. She could not let the abbess see her; all would be over then.

She heard the door close and silence descended around her. What was she to do? How could she keep from the abbess's sight until they left?

The sound of Lady's anxious barking drew her attention. Lady knew the abbess and liked her. Hope hurried around the corner of the abbey and came to an abrupt halt.

Lady was wagging her tail furiously and running toward the abbess.

There was no time to think—only to react—and Hope reacted. She ran straight for Lady.

Lady, however, was much rested from her nap and was delighted to see an old friend, especially one who had always indulged her with a treat. She ran with an enthusiasm Hope had long thought she had lost.

Colin stood staring in disbelief at the scene in front of him. He had never seen Lady so agile or move so quickly, and Hope ran with a remarkable speed for one recovering from bruised ribs. If they were not careful they would collide and Colin did not wish to see that happen. He stepped forward, about to intercede.

Hope caught Colin's movement and she chanced a glance past him to the abbess. The stunned expression on the short, plump woman's face warned Hope that she had immediately recognized her.

"Lady!" Colin called out in a commanding tone that demanded obedience.

The dog instantly halted in her tracks, though her large paws scrambled to stop herself and she ended up on her bottom only a few feet in front of Colin, wearing a confused expression.

Hope was almost breathless by the time she reached the animal, and she placed a firm hand to her sore side, hoping the pressure would help dull the stinging pain.

The abbess stepped forward. "She is a playful dog."

Lady barked and thumped her tail on the ground.

Hope stared in silence at the abbess, her eyes begging the aged woman to keep her secret.

The abbess reached down and patted Lady's head. "I think she wishes to have a treat."

Lady barked loudly in agreement.

The abbess turned to Hope. "Would you like one as well?"

Hope nodded, understanding that the abbess wished to speak with her privately.

Colin watched the trio walk away and shook his head. He wondered over Lady's strange actions and a thought struck him like lightning.

He called out. "Excuse me, Mother Abbess."

The woman turned around slowly. "Yes, my son?"

Colin approached her. "I was told that Hope traveled with a large dog and the lad here, Harold, found this dog along the road. Would you know if this dog belongs to Hope?"

The abbess looked down at the large dog. "She does seem familiar." She looked back at Colin. "To be truthful, the dog was not full grown when last I visited with my cousin."

"Do you recall the dog's name?"

The abbess answered without delay. "Lady Gwenth."

Lady barked at the woman.

"Where exactly did you find her, Harold, and when?" Colin asked.

"I do not recall," Hope said, knowing if she was not quick with her wit he would begin to piece it all together. "I had been traveling for days. I was hungry and not certain of my surroundings. She was just there on the side of the road looking half starved and lifeless. I felt the same way so I joined her. We have been together ever since and she now belongs to me."

Colin rubbed his chin. "She answers to Lady—"

Lady barked, confirming his remark.

"So she would answer to Lady Gwenth—"

Lady barked again and Hope wanted to hug her.

"As well," Colin finished and looked to the abbess. "Do you think it possible that this dog could belong to Hope?"

"Aye, I think it is possible."

Colin did not wish to voice his suspicions. If this dog actually did belong to Hope then there was a distinct possibility that she encountered trouble along the road, and could at this moment be injured or dead. Neither thought sat well with him. He had grown to admire this spirited woman and he wanted the chance to meet her.

"Think on where you found Lady, Harold," Colin said. "And if you recall anything that may help, please tell me."

"Aye, I will," Hope answered with a firm nod and felt that she was once again in control of the situation, though there was the abbess to deal with.

Colin walked off after a respectful nod to the abbess and the trio continued on their way. They stopped in the small cottage that housed the cook area and gathered a basket of treats. No conversation was exchanged until they reached a wooden rail fence that led to a grove of trees. There under the budding trees they began to talk while Lady enjoyed a fat bone.

"It is good to see you are safe and healthy," the abbess said. "Many worry about you."

Hope lowered her head, feeling contrite for the worry she was causing everyone. "I am truly sorry."

"Then why continue to make those you love suffer needlessly . . . when you know you will do what is expected of you."

"Perhaps that is why I do it. I know I will marry whom my uncle Shamus tells me I must, yet before I dedicate my life to being a good wife, I wish to live, truly live."

The abbess placed a comforting hand on her arm. "You take a dangerous chance. Could you not have confided in your uncle your wishes?"

Hope sighed heavily. "I did and he suggested I travel to visit friends and relatives, but I have done that. I wished to meet new people, go new places, and learn about this land that is my home."

"You are too curious."

"How will I ever learn or know life if I am not curious?"

The abbess shook her head. "You know all you need to know. You will wed and be a good wife and mother to your children. What more do you want?"

Tears threatened her eyes. "I want to find a love like my mother and father shared. A binding love that even death could not separate."

The abbess fought to keep her eyes dry. "They were a unique couple, my child. A love like that is rare."

Hope brushed away the single tear that ran from her eye. "I know, but I can dream and I can at least attempt, if only for a short time, to discover such a love before I must commit myself to a loveless marriage."

"And what if you were to find such a love?"

"I would speak with my uncle and I have no doubt he would allow me to marry the man of my choice."

The abbess smiled. "I have no doubt he would. He could never deny you anything. Which is why you are in your present situation."

"Will you keep my secret?" Hope asked anxiously.

"I cannot lie."

Hope understood the abbess had to be true to her vows, but her disappointment was obvious in the slump of her shoulders.

"But then"—the abbess paused and smiled gently—"the truth need only to be told when asked of me."

Hope's eyes widened and a smile flashed across her pretty face. "Thank you."

The abbess raised a shaking finger to her. "Do not be so fast to thank me."

Her smile faded slowly.

The abbess continued. "I will say nothing because I know you are safe with these men and that they continue on to Shanekill Keep where your safety will be further guaranteed. But once there your time will be limited, for I heard that your uncle may journey to Limerick to speak with the Irish devil himself. If they stop here at the abbey to see me then I will tell them of your whereabouts. So enjoy your adventure, child, for it will end soon enough."

Hope could not complain. She was grateful for the time she had and the time remaining.

"Now take yourself off, child," the abbess ordered gently. "I will take myself to the chapel for prayer."

Hope understood that she intended to keep herself out of Colin's sight so that he would not question her again in regards to Hope. And of course no one would dare to disturb her while in prayer.

The abbess placed a soft hand to her face. "Be well, my child, and may you find what you search for."

Hope watched her walk away and instantly thought of Colin. Was he what she searched for? Could she find love with him? She knew little of him and yet he appealed to her in many different ways. Was that not a good place to start?

She shrugged as she walked off with Lady. What was she thinking? Colin knew her only as a young lad in need of friendship. And he knew Hope as a spoiled young woman in need of finding. Whatever made her think that when the truth was discovered he would feel anything but anger toward her?

She was foolish in her thoughts of him, and yet . . .

She shrugged again and smiled down at Lady. "He appeals to my eye."

Lady released a grumbling growl.

She went on. "And he is kind."

Lady grumbled yet again, as if she tired of hearing her master repeat herself.

Hope's smile grew. "I will get to know him well and then I will know if my thoughts of him prove foolish."

Seven

The men were having a grand time.

Hope was not.

They had met up with a traveling troupe of entertainers late in the afternoon and decided to set up camp for the night together. Ale was flowing freely and so were the three women who were part of the troupe. There was song, dance and merriment and antics the likes of which Hope had never seen but had heard tales.

She understood that some women were free in their ways, though she had never witnessed such promiscuity. Seeing it now before her eyes made her realize she knew little of men, but she was learning quickly.

The men urged her to join in the fun, shoving a jug of ale in her face repeatedly. She pretended to drink her fill, though the ale that ran down the sides of her closed mouth was the only ale she tasted. She laughed along with the boisterous group and watched their actions with interest, especially those of Colin.

A woman with bright yellow hair and a body that was plentiful in all the right places attached herself to him. She made certain the other two women kept their distance from him and she made certain he received more than his fair share of ale.

Hope did not trust her. Her eyes were much too narrow, her look too intent and her salacious movements too intentional. She was up to something.

Lady remained close by Hope's side, growling every

now and then if someone came too near to her. It was obvious Lady did not care for the raucous antics herself.

The night wore on and the men became worn out, most of them sound asleep on the ground snoring loudly. The two women had found willing men for the night and had taken themselves off to more private places, which was what the woman with Colin was attempting to do with him.

"Come on, love, we need to find a spot for ourselves," she said with a teasing laugh and lips that tempted his.

"Why is that, lass?" he asked, his hands reaching out to caress her full breasts.

Being a lady Hope should have looked away, but given the fact that she posed as a young lad who was in need of learning all he could about life, she kept steady eyes on the pair.

"I have something you want," she urged in a hushed breath and ran her hand down over the bulge beneath his tunic.

Colin did not stop her; his hands grew more aggressive with her breasts.

"Come on, love," the woman urged again. "I ache for the taste of you."

Hope watched as they both stood on swaying legs and, with arms wrapped around each other they walked out of camp into the dark night.

Should she follow?

She certainly did not wish to watch them mate. It was none of her concern whom Colin made love with, though he certainly was not about to make love; he was simply copulating, assuaging his sexual desires. And from the way she heard the men speak, their sexual desires needed assuaging frequently.

Women, she had been told, thought and felt differently about the sex act. To many it was a duty performed with their husbands to create a child. Her aunt, however, had told her that if there was love between the couple then making love was a wonderful experience shared often. And she impressed on Hope that some husbands who were experienced and considerate made the act a pleasant experience even though there was no love involved.

Hope wanted nothing less than to love the man she would be intimate with and she had thought most women had similar feelings; yet here was a woman who seemed to care nothing of love. She simply wished to satisfy her lust.

So, then, could women be as lusty as men? And not care with whom they mated?

Her thoughts intrigued her, but then so did her suspicions about the yellow-haired woman. Was the woman really lusty for Colin or was she up to something else? Or was Hope feeling envious that the woman would enjoy intimacy with Colin while she could only wonder what it would be like to make love with him?

And she *had* wondered.

Watching him work his charm on the women in the villages they stopped at and hearing the men speak of him with such awe and envy, how could she not wonder?

And besides, she liked Colin. He was a more decent man than anyone paid heed to and they shared a common wish. He wished for a love as strong and lasting as she did.

She shook her head and sighed softly. How could she ever hope for any emotions between them when he thought her a young lad? And when he discovered her identity, she was certain he would be angry that she had made a fool of him. Her situation seemed helpless, and yet . . .

She grew more fond of him day by day.

The anguished cry that ripped through the dark night did not disrupt the snoring men, but it caused her to jump in fright and Lady to growl.

In moments Colin emerged from the dark, his hand

gripped firmly around the woman's arm while she struggled to free herself.

Jeremy, the leader of the troupe, stepped out of the enclosed wagon half dressed, looking as if he had been roused from a peaceful slumber and was none too happy about it. He took one look at the woman and swore.

"Hell and damnation, Birdie, what have you done now?"

"Will you admit your crime or shall I tell him?" Colin asked, shoving her away from him and sounding much clearer of mind than a man who had consumed a generous amount of ale for the evening.

Birdie attended to her disheveled clothing, ignoring Colin and walking toward the wagon.

"Answer the gentleman," Jeremy snapped, making Birdie jump.

Jeremy was an impressive man in weight and size and though he appeared congenial he also looked to have a temper when it suited him.

"I was being friendly with him," Birdie insisted with a defiant toss of her head.

"It was my coins she was being friendly with," Colin corrected, his smile charming but his tone stern.

"Aye," Birdie said with a lusty smile. "And it is a large set of coins he has."

Jeremy shook his head. "The gentleman offers us safety for the night and shares his food with us and you mean to steal from him?"

Birdie stamped her foot like an irate child. "I wanted to be paid before I serviced him."

Jeremy shook his head slowly this time. "Look at the gentleman, Birdie. Do you think he needs to pay a woman to bed him?"

She tapped her full chest. "No man touches me without sharing his coins."

"And did you tell him this?" Jeremy asked.

"He looks to possess a good wit, he should have known," Birdie insisted.

Hope found the scene quite entertaining, occasionally laughing softly so that no one would hear her. She moved her hand to her side without thought, a dull ache reminding her that though her ribs were healing nicely they required her to be vigilant in her rest.

Colin addressed Birdie while he walked toward Hope, to her surprise. "If you would have been honest with me, I would have been honest with you." He stopped right next to Hope and looked at her with questioning eyes.

"What do you mean?" Birdie demanded.

Jeremy shook his head again.

Colin turned his glance from Hope to answer the irate woman. "It means I would have told you what Jeremy already knows. I do not pay a woman to bed me."

"I am not good enough for you, then?" Birdie all but screeched at him.

Colin's dark eyes filled with that icy chill that always caused Hope to shiver and his men to step back in respect or fear, Hope was not certain which.

"Nay, it is because I do not wish to degrade you or disrespect what you offer me."

Birdie looked ready to kill Colin, her eyes rounded wide and her face turned bright red.

Jeremy stopped her before she could say a word. "Get in the wagon, Birdie."

"He insulted me," she yelled.

The words spilled from Hope's mouth before she could stop them. "You insult yourself."

"Why, you little . . ." Birdie flew at Hope in a rage.

Colin immediately stepped in front of Hope and Jeremy grabbed for Birdie.

"In the wagon," Jeremy ordered again, his large hand firm on her upper arm.

Birdie attempted to protest. A forceful shove from Jeremy stopped her, and with angry steps and continued assistance from Jeremy she entered the wagon.

Colin turned back around and placed his own hand

over Hope's where it rested on her ribs. His touch was warm and gentle and her body responded as only a woman's could. She felt the tingling sensation down to her toes.

"Your side still pains you?"

His voice was filled with concern and his dark eyes had lost their icy chill. He stared at her with a sincerity that warmed her heart. He cared, honestly cared about the lad's well-being.

She wanted to rest her head on his shoulder and gently cover his hand with hers, not an appropriate reaction for a young lad.

So instead she took a step back so his hand would fall off hers and said, "I get a painful twinge now and again, but nothing I cannot tolerate."

"Still, it concerns me," he said. "When we arrive at Shanekill Keep you will have Lady Faith see to it and make certain all is well with you."

That was not a possibility, though Hope chose not to argue with him. She would handle the problem when the time came. She simply nodded as if in agreement and decided it would be best to find out what she could about Lady Faith before their encounter.

She lowered herself back down to her sleeping pallet which consisted of a warm dark red wool blanket and a curled-up Lady. "Lady Faith is a good healer?"

Colin appeared in no hurry to sleep. He sat down beside the lad. "She is exceptional and well loved by all at the keep."

"*All?*" she questioned.

"None speak poorly of her. She is a loving and generous person." Colin chuckled. "And determined to do as she pleases no matter what the Irish devil orders."

"She defies her husband?"

"Often."

"He does not grow angry with her?"

Colin nodded and laughed. "Often."

"You make light of it."

"No," he said with a smile. "I am but pleased to see two strong, courageous people in love."

Suddenly Hope was eager to meet Lady Faith. "They married for love?"

"Nay, but love found them anyway."

"It is good to know that love can find you no matter the circumstances." She could not help but think of her own strange circumstances and wondered if love could defy such odds and find her.

"Love does whatever it pleases," Colin said with a laugh. "It defies sensibility and attacks impulsively."

"And love did that to Lady Faith and the Irish devil?"

"Love defied all rhythm and reason when it found them and it was a delight to watch."

"You are happy for them."

"They are meant for each other, as are Borg and Bridget."

She looked confused. "Another couple found love?"

"Love attacked often at Shanekill Keep."

"You avoided it."

He stared at her a moment before he softly said, "Perhaps it avoided me."

The eventful day and longer night caught up with Hope and she yawned wide and long.

"Lay yourself down, lad, and get some rest," Colin said firmly and reached out to make certain the boy was tucked warmly beneath his blanket. "We rise early. It is but two days' ride to Shanekill and I ache to return home."

"Your home sounds like a good place to be."

"It is," he said with pride. "You will like it there and will make many friends. It will soon feel like home to you. Now sleep."

He left her then, though she wished he had not. She soon fell into a slumber fraught with dreams that warned her that her adventurous journey might soon turn perilous.

The traveling troupe left at dawn the following day

and Hope was glad to see them go—especially Birdie.

The day dawned cloudy and grew worse with the passing hours. Gray skies darkened further by midafternoon and promised heavy rain within hours. The men had been generous and offered the lad heavy covering for the inclement weather to come.

Moods grew somber and grumbling could be heard. Hope knew the men looked forward to their return home and she could not blame them.

Thunder rumbled but the dark clouds did not open up and Colin ordered the men to prepare to make camp early.

Colin rode up to Hope who walked with a trembling Lady beside her.

He laughed and shook his head. "She is afraid of thunder."

Hope nodded. "And lightning."

He looked to the trembling dog with concerned eyes. "We will stop soon, Lady. Then you may find shelter and comfort in your master's arms."

Lady whined as if she understood his every word and thanked him.

"It will be a difficult night, Harold, so keep yourself warm and I will see that you have sufficient shelter from the storm."

He rode off without expecting an answer or allowing Hope to thank him for his generosity. Every time he saw to the lad's care he won another small part of Hope's heart.

The group rode on with the thunder growing louder, as if they rode into the very heart of the storm instead of away from it. Everyone huddled beneath extra coverings, waiting for the fat drops of rain to soak them.

But the rain turned out not to be their foe.

The attack came suddenly, though the men responded with the speed and agility of seasoned warriors, and the band of thieves was surprised by the group's instant and fierce response.

Hope froze for a moment and then took action. She knew she was no match for the burly men who fought ferociously. She attempted to maneuver her way around the battling men.

Lady, God bless her, growled and showed enough impressive, sharp teeth to deter any men from approaching her.

The men fought like trained warriors, never once worrying about their own lives, concerned more with the battle and victory—and the protection of the skinny lad.

"Get yourself cover, lad," Stuart shouted, deflecting a charging sword with his own.

The clash of metal against metal reverberated in her ears as she attempted to make her way through the melee to the cover and safety of a large rock. Lady trembled yet kept a constant growl that continued to keep men at bay, though Hope was not certain how long the dog could maintain her false courage.

Anguished cries filled the air and Hope prayed none of Colin's men knew harm. She prayed even harder that Colin survived the battle. Her quick glimpses of him confirmed his skills. He wielded a sword with the ability of one born to the task.

She ducked and swayed and made her way to the rock, pushing Lady behind it, intending to follow. Just as she was about to take cover she saw a man descending on Stuart, his sword raised high and aimed for Stuart's back.

She did not waste time on thought or on the consequences of her actions. She simply knew that Stuart's life was in danger and she could not stand by and do nothing.

Without weight or physical strength to aid her she did what she thought was sensible. She leaned low and threw her body at the charging man.

She connected with his knees, hearing a brittle crack of bone and an anguished cry of pain from the unsuspecting assailant. She rolled away quickly, rising to her feet and running for the safety of the large rock.

The clash of swords and the crack of thunder brought her hands to her ears in an attempt to deflect the terror surrounding her. She charged forward, her path clear, the rock a short distance away.

Tears were stinging her eyes; her throat felt tight and dry and she was unable to utter a single sound. The thought terrified her. She raced for the safety of the rock.

She was yanked backward by her hair and before she could think or had time to react, her assailant swiftly raised a knife to her throat. She could not scream, she could not move.

She was going to die.

Eight

Hope offered a silent prayer for her soul, when suddenly she was yanked out of the man's hands and shoved behind Colin. It took mere seconds for her assailant to realize he was no match for the skillful warrior and that his pitiful attempts only shamed him. He made a wise choice and fled as fast as his stumbling feet would carry him. The other thieves began to do the same when they finally realized that they would not see victory that day.

Hope was so relieved that she gave no thought to her actions. She threw herself against Colin with such a force that he had no choice but to wrap his arms around her.

She came to her senses when she realized that if it was not for the extra clothing the men had given her for protection against the rain, Colin at this moment would realize she was a woman.

Her foolish actions propelled her to pull away from him though she continued to tremble.

Colin seemed concerned and offered the comfort of a supporting arm around the lad's shoulders. "First battles have a way of putting the fear into you."

Hope nodded; she could do no more.

Colin continued to offer counsel. "Once at Shanekill I will personally see to teaching you how to defend yourself."

More problems she did not presently need. Her only need at the moment was to wrap herself around Colin and linger in the comfort of his strength and courage.

Instead she received a pat on the back and more encouraging words from a man to a young boy.

"You will grow strong, I will see to it, and one day you will have no trouble taking on an opponent."

She responded with another nod.

"You did well for your first encounter," Colin said in an attempt to praise. "You should be proud."

"That he should be," Stuart said as he approached them. "He saved my life."

Colin looked to Harold. "Is this so, lad?"

Hope shrugged and made an attempt to speak, but her throat was too dry. Instead she once again resorted to a single nod.

"Then you not only do yourself, but all of us proud," Colin said, offering another pat on the back.

Hope barely broke a smile and was glad that Colin was summoned by one of his men. She in turn went to find Lady, who she was certain remained hiding behind the rock.

Stuart gave her a manly hug before she could walk past him and thanked her, insisting he would be there for "Harold" whenever needed.

Hope found Lady shivering behind the rock and instantly fell to her knees to hug her. The large dog whined in her ear and licked her face clean, so relieved was she to see her. Hope felt the same overwhelming sense of relief and held onto the animal until both of their trembling subsided.

The rain began as they resumed their journey.

Hope did not think she possessed the strength to walk but she found it was wiser to keep moving than to stop and think about how close she had come to death. She told herself that she would be fine, that all was well. Her stomach, however, told her differently, and she wondered if her next battle would be to keep from making a fool of herself by losing what little food she had eaten that day.

Colin watched the lad with concerned eyes. He was pale and his steps uncertain, yet still he did not utter one word of complaint. He continued walking. He could not help but worry about the boy. After having the lad plastered against him he realized he had much physical maturing to do. He was much too slim, his body too frail. He needed nourishment and someone to care for him.

What it was that drew him to the lad he could not say. He only knew that the more he came to know the lad the more he admired his strength and courage and the more he wished to help him.

Once at Shanekill there would be time to spend with him. Time to make him realize that they could be good friends, always good friends.

He shook his head at himself. Why did he feel a need to keep the lad around and see to his safety? Why did he feel so protective of him? The redundant thought annoyed and perplexed him and yet he could not shake it. He felt *compelled* to take care of the lad.

He watched as Harold struggled along on trembling legs, the heavy rain soaking him to the bone. Colin shook his head and rode toward him.

Hope fought against her rumbling stomach, knowing it was a useless fight she was bound to lose. But she fought anyway. She was glad she tried to walk. She had to concentrate on taking her steps, thereby keeping her mind occupied by anything other than her protesting stomach.

It rumbled again and she moaned softly.

"Are you all right, Harold?"

Hope jumped, not having heard Colin's approach over the heavy rain and her own deep thoughts.

"Aye, I am fine," she said, though her lips chattered and her face was pale.

"I think it is best that you ride."

Hope shook her head. "Nay, nay, I am fine."

"It is an order," Colin said, meaning to be obeyed.

Hope had been gallant in her efforts to maintain her

courage and her dignity, and surrender was not to her liking. Unfortunately, her stomach thought otherwise and at that moment she decided that surrender was precisely what was necessary.

Hope made a dash for the grove of trees and bushes off to the left of the road, Lady fast on her heels.

On her knees with her arms wrapped tightly around her protesting stomach, Hope lost what little food had nourished her. She wished Colin would not follow her or that no one would come upon her when she was so weak and vulnerable. Then as suddenly as the thought came she felt a strong arm wrap around her own arms and she knew she had not gotten her wish.

Colin was there.

"Easy, lad," he said. "It is a common enough reaction. There is no need to be embarrassed."

The thought that he understood her upset her all the more and she continued to heave even though her stomach had long since lost its contents.

When she finally regained control of herself, she sighed heavily and leaned back against Colin. His arm remained firm around her.

"I did the same myself when first I tasted the threat of death."

She understood he tried to console the lad, but presently all she wanted was to melt in his strong arms and forget that the world existed. She wanted to be swept away from the reality of her situation and into the comfort of his protective arms.

That, unfortunately, was not possible and as much as she yearned for the fantasy, she knew it was not to be.

She took command of her senses and addressed Colin as a lad in need, not as a woman in need—a woman in need of a man to love her.

"I can take care of myself," she said with the bravado of a young boy.

"I have no doubt you can," Colin said, impressed by the boy's determination. "But I want you to know that

I am a friend you can rely on when needed."

Need.

Her need for him seemed to be growing day by day. And the more he showed a concern for the lad the more he stole her heart. She saw a man who cared, truly cared for those less fortunate, for those in need, for those who truly needed a friend.

She managed to show her appreciation with a simple "Thanks." Then she pulled away from him to lean on Lady, who sat nearby. The dog welcomed her with a swipe of her wet tongue.

"You will ride until we camp," he ordered in his no-nonsense tone.

She chose to argue. "I prefer to walk."

"You do not feel well. You will ride." He was adamant in his directive.

"I will do better walking."

"You will ride." His stern tone promised he would have his way.

Hope wisely chose reason. "My stomach continues to protest. I feel riding will only make it worse."

Colin gave it thought, then nodded. "You may walk for a while but as your stomach eases you will tell me and then you will ride for the remainder of the way."

She agreed with a nod and stood, Lady rising to stand beside her.

"It is only two days' journey to Shanekill."

She understood his words were meant to ease her worries, but they only added to her trepidation. Once at Shanekill her time would be sorely limited. Her journey was fast coming to an end, and what had she accomplished?

"Something troubles you?"

Much troubled her, especially her attraction to Colin. Her adventure was turning more complicated than she had planned. Or was her adventure turning too adventurous for her?

"What if I do not like Shanekill?"

Colin had expected the lad to have doubts and he hoped to ease his worries. "I think you will be surprised at how much you favor Shanekill."

They walked back to the road, the men having waited for them and the rain having settled into a steady drizzle. Once they were spied coming through the grove of trees the men continued on, leaving Colin to walk alongside the lad. His obedient mare followed close behind him.

Hope was persistent, needing to confirm her suspicions. "So say you, but what if I do not favor it?"

Colin would not lie to the lad. "When I feel you are well and capable of defending yourself, you may go where you choose."

So he did feel responsible for the lad. While Hope thought it amiable of him, it hindered her plans and posed the threat of discovery for her. She refused to consider her growing feelings for him—that would only complicate matters more. Her adventure had certainly turned perilous and she wondered how she would handle it all and how she would cope with the consequences.

For now she intended to hold fast to her independence as best as possible. "You have no right to force me to remain at the keep."

"I have every right," he insisted, though his tone was far from stern. He seemed to want the lad to understand and offered reason instead of demands. "You accepted the Irish devil's protection."

"I thought it was given freely," she said, annoyed with herself for not being wiser in her choice of words when he had offered for her to join them. Now she feared she had made a commitment she had never intended to keep.

"And you freely accepted it. Now Eric of Shanekill is responsible for your protection and you in turn are answerable to the Irish devil."

That thought did not sit well with her and her mighty heritage reared its regal head. "I answer to no one."

"Nay, lad," Colin said with a warning in his voice that sent a chill through her, and the words that followed caused goose flesh to rise on her damp skin. "You answer to the devil."

An involuntary shiver trembled her body and she wrapped her own arms around herself. She had heard tales about the infamous Irish devil and had believed them to be just that—tales. But now she wondered.

"He is a fair and just man," Colin said, attempting to ease the lad's apparent concern. "He expects what he himself gives to others—respect, honor and truth. Show him these and you will have no problem with him."

One question haunted her and she had to ask it though she thought she already knew the answer. "How will the Irish devil feel about you returning without the woman you search for?"

Surprisingly, Colin laughed. "He will grow angry, though he will display no temper. He probably has already formulated another plan and has a another troop ready to leave if we should return unsuccessful in our quest. If they should return unsuccessful, then he himself will search and he *will* find her. And God help her when he does."

Hope kept her voice from quivering. "What will he do to her?"

"Make her regret the day she met him, though"—he laughed once again—"from what I have learned about Hope she might make the Irish devil rue the day he found her."

His remark caused her to smile and say, "You seem to admire this Hope."

"She has courage. Foolish courage, but—" He shook his head. "She must possess a strong character even to think that her foolish adventure could succeed."

Hope grew annoyed; after all, she had succeeded so far. "But has she not been successful? She has avoided the Irish devil's troop and remains free to enjoy her adventure."

Her remark annoyed him; she could hear it in his voice. "She may not be free. She may be in harm's way, and she has lost her dog." Colin glanced down at Lady who walked close beside the lad.

"You do not know for certain if Lady belonged to Hope."

"Lady Gwenth!" Colin called out, intending to prove his point, but the dog kept her head down and continued walking as if she heard nothing.

Hope kept her lips pursed, forcing back a persistent grin. She had nudged Lady with her leg when she realized Colin's intention. It was the one and only command that Lady ever obeyed. It was meant for her to remain as she was and respond to no one.

Hope wanted to kiss her for being so obedient. Instead she said to Colin, "Looks like you might have the wrong dog."

"Lady!" he shouted and the dog raised her head and barked.

It was Hope's turn to laugh.

"The two names are too similar to be certain which she answers to," he insisted.

"True enough, though you would think a lady of such importance would have a dog that protected."

"I have given that fact consideration, but since this woman is not of the common mind, I am led to believe she would not have a common dog."

"But a coward?" she grimaced and shook her head. "That does not make sense."

Lady whined at the insult and Hope nudged her silent.

"Time will tell and time is running out for Hope," Colin said with confidence.

She made no comment. She could not deny the truth of his words.

Colin mounted his horse and looked down at Harold. "You may walk until I send one of the men with his horse, then you will ride."

She did not argue. He would have his way and besides she had suddenly grown weary. Riding sounded appealing at the moment.

He seemed to sense her tiredness, his glance running over her with concern. "I will send Stuart. He feels obligated to reward your courage."

"I did what any decent man would do."

"You did what any courageous man would do and not all men are courageous." He smiled. "And besides, you are but a mere lad yet to grow into his manhood."

She wondered what he would think if he only knew the truth. She spoke without weighing her words. "I will never be the man you are."

"No," he said gently. "You will be your own man and a fine one at that."

He rode off, leaving Hope to stare after him. He forever encouraged the lad and saw to it that he was looked after. He never once ridiculed or abused him. She felt a pang of regret for being deceitful and yet she felt as if her adventure truly began when she met up with Colin and his men. She had grown to be part of them and she sensed the men had grown to like the lad.

It was a strange situation, to be sure, but one she did not wish to change. She looked forward to her continued adventures and learning more about Colin. He was so much more than just his charming smile.

Stuart interrupted her musings. "Time to ride, lad."

He hoisted her up onto his horse as though she weighed no more than a feather, but then Stuart was a large man. She recalled the ease with which he handled his sword and the way he ploughed through his opponents in battle. He was a man of might and yet at times he appeared a gentle soul. And he, like Colin, felt protective of the lad.

"I think the sky is fighting off the rain," Stuart said with a nod toward the heavens.

He was right. The gray storm clouds appeared to be drifting off, and though the sky lacked its usual intense blue color, it was clear.

Hope cast a look at her surroundings. The land lay drenched from the rain. Raindrops glistened on blades of grass, dripped from tree branches and kissed the blossoming buds of spring. The horses plodded along the mud-soaked road and the men began to discard their wet garments.

She had always thought the land beautiful after a rainstorm, but none so beautiful as today. Today she had the chance to view the countryside as a lad free of responsibility or burdens. A lad who had all the promises of all the tomorrows in front of him. A lad who could make his own choices and a lad who could find his own love.

Harold was fortunate, Hope was not. She could almost feel the weight of her responsibilities descend on her and too soon it would be necessary for her to shoulder them. She had no other choice. She could not disappoint her aunt and uncle. They had been too good to her.

"Something troubling you, lad?" Stuart asked, interrupting her thoughts.

She spoke the truth. "I was thinking of my family."

"It is not easy being on your own, but take heart, lad, you have us now. And you will find many more at Shanekill Keep who you will call family."

Hope smiled her appreciation. Stuart was a good man and Shanekill Keep sounded like a good place to call home. Unfortunately Hope realized she could not linger there for long. She could not take the chance of anyone discovering her identity, and she could not risk hurting or disappointing those she now called friends.

If the men discovered that Harold, the lad they had grown to admire and respect, was actually Hope, the spoiled woman for whom they searched, they would feel she had made a fool of them. They would no longer call her friend.

The thought upset her and made her decision all the more necessary. She would remain at the keep for a week or two but no more.

One day Harold would simply slip away from the keep and return to Croom Abbey. Once there, she would send a message to her uncle that she was ready to return home.

Harold would be no more and her adventure would live forever in her memories.

Her glance drifted to Colin who rode slowly toward her and he smiled with the charm of the rogue that he was. Tears stung her eyes and she felt a tug at her heart.

She would miss him. Much too much.

The thought disturbed her and made her wonder about her feelings for Colin.

And made her think twice about remaining for any length of time at Shanekill Keep.

Nine

Hope rose as dawn was breaking. The men lay sleeping except for John who stood watch, his eyes closing and his head nodding every now and again. She made a point of walking past him, Lady by her side.

He did not stop her, assuming the lad was going to relieve himself. In reality, Hope needed some time to herself. She had slept little the previous night, her active thoughts keeping her from a restful slumber.

In the predawn light, she made her way to the nearby stream. While Lady drank the cold refreshing water, Hope splashed a handful in her face. The cold water sent a chill through her and she shivered.

A heavy sigh followed, along with a shake of her head.

She did not know what to do. Part of her wanted so badly to remain at Shanekill Keep and continue her adventure, but another part warned her to return home. Perhaps she should remain and learn more about Colin; though if she was truthful with herself she would admit that the reason she wanted to remain was to learn of her own feelings for Colin.

She sighed again, knowing what the wisest decision would be, and knowing it was the hardest decision of all to make.

"Thinking of running away?"

Hope fell back on her bottom, so startled was she by Colin's voice.

He did not wait for an answer. He walked to the stream, went down on bended knees and scooped up a handful of water to splash in his face and then another handful to drink. He wiped the excess water off his face with his hand and then stood and walked over to sit beside her.

"What troubles you, lad?"

At that very moment she wished she could confide in him and tell him all. She wanted him to know who she was, why she had run away and all about her dreams and hopes for the future. She felt he would understand; if anyone could, it would be him.

But she maintained her facade as she knew she must and spoke to him as a young lost lad. "I do not know if I should go to Shanekill Keep."

"I thought you were reluctant. Can you tell me why?"

He spoke so gently with the lad and made no demands on him. Would he be the same with the woman he loved?

How to speak the truth and not give her secret away? She chose her words wisely. "I fear I will disappoint many."

"Nay, lad, these are foolish thoughts."

She remained silent, knowing her thoughts were far from foolish.

"Give yourself and the keep a chance."

She reminded him of his own words. "You tell me I must remain at the keep, that I no longer have my freedom."

"In all honesty, lad, I cannot allow you to go off on your own when I know you cannot adequately protect yourself."

"But is that not my decision to make?"

"You are young and headstrong and think yourself capable of defending yourself."

She shook her head. "I am no fool. I know my skills and physical strength are limited."

"Then why would you wish to be on your own?" He

sounded agitated that he should have to ask.

Hope lowered her head along with her voice. "I know not where I belong."

Colin placed a firm hand on the lad's knee. "Then allow yourself time to find out."

His hand was so warm and the strength of him palpable. At that moment she thought of him as a virile man and her body reacted, sending a sensual shiver racing through her. She disguised it with a strong hug of her arms around her shoulders.

"Chilled?" he asked, and without waiting for a response he placed his potent hands on her arms and rubbed vigorously.

She closed her eyes, not wanting to look into his dark eyes that promised endless pleasure or see his handsome face that could charm with a smile or warn with a chilling stare. And in doing so she allowed her other senses to take command and she felt more than she was prepared to feel.

The strength of him never failed to surprise her. His lean build suggested he lacked the power of a large muscled man and yet his hands betrayed his potency. His skill with a sword was phenomenal. He swung it with the ease and grace of a man born to it and a man strong in courage and strength. He was so much more than he appeared to be and she wondered how many men had judged him unwisely and paid for their foolish decision.

And she wondered how those potent hands would react if he knew he touched a woman. She mentally shook some sense into her head and eased back away from him. "I need to know that I am free to leave if I so choose."

Colin hesitated and his brief pause did not bode well. "I cannot promise you that, lad. If the Irish devil feels you should remain at the keep then so you shall. You will need to address that matter with him."

Colin did not bother to tell the stubborn lad that he would advise Eric that the lad was to remain at the keep until he was grown enough to defend himself properly. He had no intention of allowing the lad to continue on his own. And once Eric met him he would no doubt agree. In time Harold would understand and come to think of the keep as his home. Until then the decision would be made for him, whether he agreed or not.

Annoyed that her life never seemed to be her own, Hope grew sharp with him. "And if I should choose not to continue on with you?"

"That is not an option, lad." His stern voice warned her that he expected her obedience, and the thought rankled her.

She stood, her hands firm on her slim hips. Lady stood to move behind her. "Are you telling me that I must go with you?"

Colin rose slowly, towering over her. His impressive height and confident stance would cause most to back away or surrender.

Not Hope. It only made her more stubborn and she stuck her chin up to prove she was not at all intimidated by him.

He made the mistake of smiling, which only fueled her annoyance.

"I can go where I please," she said, not realizing she was shaking a tightly gripped fist in his face.

This time he laughed. "You'd best learn how to throw a good fist before you challenge someone."

His laughter did not help and she unwisely maintained her clenched fist while she spoke. "I will do as I please."

Colin nodded, his smile remaining. "I'll tell you what, lad—since that fist of yours is ready for battle, if you can land a solid punch on me, I will allow you to do as you please."

How could a pint-sized woman land a potent blow to a man of his solid muscular structure? Her small fist certainly did not possess the power to inflict the slightest damage, thus he was simply toying with her. The idea further fueled her temper.

"It is not a fair offer."

Colin looked at the lad with surprise and a bit of admiration. "Life is not fair. You learn to deal with what is dealt to you."

He was teaching the lad a lesson, a lesson Hope had already learned and one of which she did not need to be reminded. But arguing with him would be futile.

She decided her wit would be a better weapon and relaxed her fisted hand. "What if instead of a solid punch, I manage to get past you?"

"Use wit instead of brawn, an intelligent choice, especially in a situation where your opponent outweighs you." He nodded as if approving her sound reasoning. "I agree, lad. Get past me and you shall win your freedom."

Hope counted on his approval and the stance he took. He extended his arms out, spread his legs, braced his feet firmly on the ground and waited for her to advance.

"Any time, lad."

"Follow me, Lady," she whispered to the dog and swiftly bent down to scoop up a fat rock, toss it at Colin and make a mad dash between his legs.

Colin was prepared; he swatted the flying rock aside and reached down to grab for Harold. He did not count on the swiftness of the lad or the trailing dog and when he reached down it was Lady's rump he grabbed.

Lady's screech echoed loudly in the bright light of a new dawn and caused Colin to jump out of her way. He swung around in time to see that Harold was not far in front of him and without hesitation, he threw himself at the lad.

They hit the ground with a solid thud, Colin coming down on top of her.

Hope threw her hands out in front of her to prevent her face from hitting the hard ground. The impact knocked the breath from her and caused a jolt to her ribs, sending a sharp, stabbing pain resonating through her body.

Regaining her expended breath, she let out a yell that rivaled Lady's screech.

Colin was off the lad in a flash and just as quickly he turned him over and reached down to run a gentle hand over his sore ribs.

When Hope realized his intentions she quickly rolled away from him, wincing and crying from the pain, and with much effort got to her feet, her own hand firmly holding her side. She looked at him with accusing eyes. "I was past you. You had no right to jump me from behind. You cheated."

His face betrayed his concern for Harold's condition, but his tone warned he would accept no argument. "You involved Lady in your escape. The agreement was for you and you alone. Since you saw fit to cheat, I followed suit."

"I won my freedom," she insisted loudly, instantly regretting her action since it sent a piercing pain through her side. She pressed her hand firmly to her aching ribs, hoping to ease her self-inflicted suffering.

Colin stepped toward her. "You have injured your ribs again."

Hope took a cautious step back, wanting to keep the pain at least bearable. "I am fine."

"You are stubborn," he said firmly.

"It is my freedom that is in question, not my stubbornness," she insisted, though this time she kept her voice at a normal tone.

"You forfeited your freedom when you chose to cheat," Colin said, his tone as normal as hers. "Now let me have a look at your side."

Hope backed away from him as he stepped toward her. "I will see to my own care and it is not my care that concerns me. It is my freedom."

"That issue is settled. You remain with me."

She spoke as one highborn. "You cannot dictate to me."

His soft laughter soon turned hardy and then quieted

to a ripple. "You have much to learn, lad. You will follow my edict whether you like it or not."

Hope thought to protest, then suddenly realized the futility of such action and chose to remain silent. She had no intention of following his edict. She would have her way whether he liked it or not. When the time was right she would take her leave and he would have little to say about it.

He seemed to read her thoughts and responded accordingly. "You will remain at the keep, Harold. If you intend to leave without my permission then know that I will come after you, and I promise you that you will not like the consequences of disobeying my order."

Her chin went up defiantly. "We all do what we must."

"Aye, that is true and I will do what must be done if you choose to disobey me."

She shrugged, as if his warning mattered not to her. "Do what you must, as will I."

Colin softened his tone. "I do what is best."

Bewilderment filled her eyes. "Best for whom?"

"For a young lad who requires guidance and help."

"And what if this lad does not want guidance and help?"

Colin spoke patiently. "The lad is too young and inexperienced to know otherwise."

Hope attempted to voice her objection but he quickly continued. "Therefore, one who is wiser must take charge, teach him and become his *friend*."

Her anger faded when she realized that he truly wished to call the lad his friend.

"Give Shanekill Keep a chance, Harold. It will not disappoint you."

Nay, it probably would not disappoint her, but she certainly would disappoint many there and perhaps that was why she felt the need to take her leave. Colin and his men had been good to her. She could not help but concern herself with their reaction to her true identity.

She would certainly disappoint people and lose many friendships, and that thought disturbed her.

"Now let me have a look at you."

Before he could step forward she took a few quick steps to the side. "It pains me little and besides, you say we will reach Shanekill Keep before nightfall. The healer can then have a look at it. I trust her skills more than yours."

"That is a wise decision and one I will respect," Colin said. "Now let us be on our way; I am anxious to get home."

He turned to walk away and Hope called out to him, her voice strong as that of a young lad filled with conviction. "Colin."

He stopped and settled an attentive glance on the lad, letting him know he was willing to listen even though he had addressed him with a demanding tone.

"I ask for nothing and make no promise, but I do wish to thank you now for your generosity, your protection and most of all for the friendship you offer me."

Colin admired the way the lad spoke the truth and his courage for admitting that although he had been warned there still remained the possibility that he would not remain at the keep. He smiled and shook his head. "Brave or foolish, lad, I am still not certain which you are. But I am pleased to call you my friend."

"And I you," Hope said, and with a wide grin walked past him along with a trailing Lady. "And I still won the wager."

Colin laughed at his audacity and in a few effortless strides caught up with the lad, placing a firm hand on his shoulder. "Let me teach you about cheating."

The men were in a festive mood, all of them happy that they would soon be home. Laughter and merriment filled the campsite as they prepared to take their leave. Some of the men, mostly the married ones, had washed up and changed to cleaner garments.

Colin did the same and took much teasing for it as

they began the final part of their journey home.

"Which fair lass will be the lucky one tonight?" Stuart asked with a grin.

John added to the teasing. "How dare you insult him, Stuart. It will be two lasses he entertains this night."

Hope listened with interest and a twinge of disappointment as she rode Colin's horse. He walked alongside her, his smile as potently charming as ever and his own tongue adding to the good-natured ribbing.

"Only two?" Colin shook his head. "What little faith my men have in me."

The men laughed.

Hope did not. She had not expected the thought of Colin being with other women to disturb her so, and yet surprisingly it did. Why should it matter to her who he dallied with?

"Harold," John said, startling the lad. "You look annoyed. Could you be jealous? And in need of a woman yourself?"

Hope was fast to reply. "Why? Are you needing some lessons?"

The men shared a good laugh, though John scowled at her.

The day continued on much in the same manner. The men's moods grew more lighthearted as they neared home.

Hope spent most of the time lost in her own thoughts. She did watch the surrounding countryside, since it was important that she be familiar with the lay of the land when it came time for her to take her leave.

She made a mental note of the location of the stream and the direction in which it ran. She added to her memory the rock formations that sprang up amongst the green fields, knowing they would help guide her on her return journey. And she made certain to notice the best places to take refuge along the way in case she felt the need to conceal herself.

One factor she had not given enough consideration to

when she had begun her journey was a sufficient supply of food. This time she would not make that mistake. She would become friendly with the cook at the keep and make certain to hide enough food away in preparation for when she needed it.

She had learned much in her travels. She understood it was necessary to avoid certain people and places and that it was not always wise to trust a trustworthy-looking person. She was now secure that her gained knowledge would guarantee a safe return journey to Croom Abbey.

"Are you all right, lad?" Colin asked.

Hope looked down at him and his concerned glance rested steady on her.

"You wear a worried look," he said when the lad did not reply.

She shook her head to bring herself fully alert. "I but wonder about Shanekill Keep."

Stuart heard and replied. "It is like no other keep. It is a bit of heaven."

"Spoken like a man in love," John teased.

"And married to a wonderful woman," another called out.

"Who works miracles with food," another added.

"He is lucky to have such a fine woman," Daniel said.

Colin offered an explanation for such avid praise. "Stuart's wife Mary is the keep's cook and she does create miracles with food."

"No one misses any of her meals," Stuart said with pride.

"Only a fool would miss her meals," John said with a laugh.

Hope licked her lips. "It has been some time since I have tasted fine food."

Colin patted the lad's leg. "You shall taste it tonight."

"What is your favorite food, Harold?" Stuart asked. "I shall have Mary prepare it for you."

"I thank you," Hope said with a smile and her heart filled with emotion at the thought that this giant of a man could be so caring. "But I do not wish to cause your wife extra work."

"Mary loves to cook. It would be no extra burden for her and I know when she glances upon your skinny body she will see to it that you receive extra portions at mealtime. Now tell me your favorite treat."

"Aye, tell him, Harold," John insisted. "It could be mine as well and then there will be extra to share."

"The treat is for the lad," Stuart said, his manner teasing.

"Aye, for him and him alone," Colin agreed, his manner also light.

John accepted defeat graciously. "For you, lad, then."

Hope thought differently. "I will share my fruit tarts with you, John."

"I love fruit tarts," John said with a grin and looked to Stuart and Colin. "The lad offered freely."

"Aye, that I did," Hope said in agreement.

Stuart laughed. "Then I will tell Mary that it is fruit tarts for you and John."

John cheered, his shout filling the late afternoon air, and when the men joined in their joyous voices it caught Hope by surprise.

She realized soon enough when all the horses were drawn to a stop and all eyes settled in the distance that it was not the fruit tarts that caused the cheer. Her own eyes followed theirs and her breath caught and her stomach tightened. In the distance sat a castle of impressive sight and she knew that within a short time they would arrive at Shanekill Keep.

Ten

Their entrance caused a celebration. Cheers greeted them. Drink was offered to them and wives eagerly greeted their absent husbands. It did not surprise Hope to see that the men remained in formation, their wives walking alongside them with anxious smiles.

Hope understood that Colin needed to enter the castle on his horse and she chose to walk behind him, Lady close to her side. The stop afforded her the luxury of viewing her new surroundings without much thought being paid to the lad. Her eyes hastily took in the well-maintained cottages, a chapel and a marketplace, and then her eyes caught hold of the keep itself. It was a magnificent structure built mainly of stone and the craftsmanship was remarkable. It looked impenetrable and she wondered in some way if it did not represent the devil himself.

She remained behind Colin as he came to a stop before the keep and continued to stay behind him when he dismounted and climbed the steps to the keep's door.

Her legs trembled and her heart raced when she peered around him and caught sight of the two men standing on the top steps of the keep.

One was a giant—there was no other way to describe him. He was tall and broad, though Hope sensed from the softness in his eyes that he was a gentle giant, which eased her concern. It was the man who stood in front of him that caused her the most worry. He was large, his muscles thick, his features handsome, his look stern. His hair was dark and the length reached his chest. Two tight braids ran down each side and he wore a black tunic with barely a trace of red running through the fine wool. Black stockings hugged his powerful legs and his confident stance made him appear as impenetrable as the keep itself. He was a warrior of impressive status. He could be none other than the Irish devil.

"Welcome home, Colin." The voice was deep and sincere, as was the bear hug the Irish devil gave him.

Colin returned the hug, his wide smile confirming his joy at being home. "It is good to set eyes on you again, my lord."

The giant was next to hug Colin and give him a slap on the back. "It is good to have you home."

"Aye, that it is," Colin agreed.

"Where is he, let me at him," an insistent female voice said from behind the large men.

"She has been waiting for your return," the Irish devil said with a grin and stepped aside.

Hope felt her breath catch. A beautiful woman stepped forward, her brilliant red hair a mass of ringlets that fell past her shoulders and down over her ample chest. She was round with child and the smile on her face complimented her true beauty.

"Colin," she said with outstretched arms that he insistently went into. "I have missed you."

"And I you, Lady Faith. It is good to be home." He stepped an arm's length away from her, holding her hands. "You are well?"

"I am healthy and happy," she said with a smile that caused every face to light around her, including Hope's.

Colin hugged her once again.

"You must be starving for a decent meal, and I know that Mary is starving to see her husband." Faith looked around Colin to Stuart who had dismounted and awaited further instructions. "Go to her."

Stuart first looked to Colin and then to the Irish devil for permission to take his leave.

The devil himself ordered, "Go!"

Stuart gave a grateful bob of his head and whispered to the lad. "I will have Mary see to those fruit tarts." And with that he disappeared inside the keep.

Colin stood tall and in charge as he addressed the Irish devil. "May I dismiss the men? They are anxious to be with their families."

"Aye, and I am anxious to speak with you."

Colin gave a respectful nod, turned and discharged the men, who eagerly ran to their waiting wives and families. He then looked at the lad and directed him forward to present him to the Irish devil.

Hope took cautious steps forward, coming to stand beside Colin. A sense of vulnerability ran through her, and she eased her worries by convincing herself that it was the sheer size of the men who surrounded her that caused her insecurity.

Lady chose to remain hidden behind her—not that a 150-pound dog could hide behind a skinny woman, though she did try.

Colin placed a firm hand on the lad's shoulder. "Lord Eric, I would like to present Harold, a young lad who joined us on our return journey."

The Irish devil stepped forward and Hope had to force her feet to remain planted firmly to the ground since her first thought was to turn and run. She worried that his blue eyes probed too deeply and that he would in some magical way determine her true identity.

To her surprise and relief he held out his large hand. "Welcome, lad, I am pleased to have you here."

Hope accepted his offer, her small hand disappearing into his large one. She almost winced from the pain of his forceful handshake, though she realized he had tempered it when he felt the lad's meager strength.

"I have offered Harold a home here at Shanekill," Colin said and the look the two men exchanged warned

Hope that the lad's fate had been quickly decided.

The thought did not sit well with her and she voiced her own opinion. "I appreciate the offer and will give it consideration."

Colin's hand went tight on her shoulder and with a whisper he said, "This matter has been settled."

Eric crossed his arms over his impressive chest and Hope thought she caught the giant smirking, though a hand to his mouth covered the evidence. Lady Faith watched with a pleasant smile.

She was not one to be dictated to, so with a shake of her shoulder to disengage Colin's hand she stepped forward to have her say.

Colin thought otherwise. He stepped forward along with her. "Harold accepted my protection on our journey."

It seemed that was all the devil needed to hear. "Then you are part of our family, Harold. Welcome."

How did she disagree with the devil? She thought a moment and realized that it was not a possibility—compliance was expected. With a smile she gave the two men what they wanted. "Thank you for your generosity."

Lady Faith, however, sent her a smile that made her realize the lady understood much more than the men. And *that* she would have to remember.

A loud bark followed by pounding footsteps caused everyone but Hope to smile. It took only seconds for her to realize from where it came. A huge, ugly yet adorable dog came bounding around the corner of the keep and headed straight for Colin. That is, until he caught sight of Lady.

The two dogs spied each other and Lady instantly turned female. Her head went up, as did her tail, and her chest went out. She stood regally as the large dog tentatively approached her. Then with a sniff here and a sniff there, the two began prancing around each other.

"Be a gentleman and offer the lady a treat, Rook,"

Lady Faith said and Rook answered with a loud bark.

Lady's ears perked up at the mention of a treat. Rook barked at her and ran a distance ahead, then turned to bark at her again as if telling her to follow him. Lady turned to look at Hope.

"Go and behave," Hope instructed, happy that Lady looked so joyous over her newfound friend and of course the offered treat.

The two ran off, their combined weight making the ground around them quake.

"Come, there is much for us to discuss," Eric said to Colin and his hand went out to his wife. She took it and slipped comfortably into his arms.

The look the couple exchanged made Hope realize that they were deeply in love. The thought warmed her heart and almost brought a sigh to her lips. She changed it to a rough cough and then winced when she felt a stab of pain in her ribs.

It was a severe pain that caused her knees to give way, and if it were not for Colin's strong arm that wrapped around her she would have collapsed.

Lady Faith was instantly at the lad's side, and Eric followed.

Colin offered an explanation. "He suffered a damaging blow to his ribs, saving Stuart's life."

Eric looked with a stern glare at the lad. "You risked your life for one of my men?"

Hope attempted to dismiss it. "I did what needed to be done."

"You did what a courageous man would do," Eric corrected. "Faith will see to your care and you will remain here at Shanekill and learn a warrior's skills."

"Not until I deem him well," Faith said with a firm voice that expected no opposition.

She received none, to Hope's surprise and relief. It would afford her time to heal and set plans for her departure.

"Colin, take Harold to my healing cottage so that I may have a look at him," Faith directed.

Hope knew that was not possible and she thought quickly, sniffing the air. "Something smells mighty good."

The giant spoke. "The lad's hungry. Let him fill his belly before you go poking at him."

"I agree with the giant," Hope said without thought to her words and instantly regretted her rash remark.

The giant laughed and held out his hand. "I am called Borg."

Hope smiled and took his hand. "I am pleased to meet you, Borg." And she was. He was a gentle man though there was no mistaking the fact that he could be a fierce warrior when necessary. Hope liked him. She sensed he could be a true friend—one whom someone could trust with his or her deepest secrets.

"Come," he said, helping the lad forward. "You will sit beside me for the evening meal and we will feast like kings."

Hope gave a quick glance around her. "My dog Lady?"

Faith answered her. "Rook will return her safely to you. They are probably at this moment enjoying a treat in the kitchen. Mary and"—she paused to poke at Eric— "my husband spoil him terribly."

Hope laughed. "Lady is already spoiled, so they will make a good pair."

Borg walked beside the lad, making certain his steps were slow, and Hope was grateful. Her side did ache and she wanted nothing more than to sit and ease the dull persistent pain.

She could hear Colin mumbling as he trailed behind them along with Eric and Faith. She was certain he spoke about the lad and even more certain that he informed the Irish devil of Harold's intentions to leave when he saw fit. They would be keeping a watchful eye

on the lad, but then they did not know how tenacious
Hope could be.

Hope had never tasted such delicious food. She ate
and ate and ate, and when she thought the meal finished
another dish was brought forth. She sat on the dais beside Borg as he had promised. Borg sat beside Lady
Faith, Eric sat beside his wife and Colin occupied the
chair next to Eric.

Hope listened more than she conversed. By lending a
keen ear, she learned about those around her; she also
possessed a sharp eye to evaluate her surroundings. She
did not miss the way the female servants gave Colin
extra attention or how his hands gave them a familiar
hug or pat to their backside. Nor did she miss the charming smile he bestowed on each one and damned if he
was not sincere about it. He seemed actually pleased to
see the women and his sincerity was reflected in his
smile.

So why did his heartfelt intentions disturb her?

"Where do you call home, Harold?" Faith asked, leaning past Borg who was talking with Eric.

"Up north," Hope said, having learned a general direction usually appeased a person.

Faith nodded as if accepting the answer. "You have
heard of this Hope, then? The woman Colin searched
for. She comes from the north."

Hope answered without hesitation. "Nay, I knew nothing of her until I heard Colin and his men speak of her."

Faith looked at her strangely. "Hope is a descendent
of the high king of Ireland. It is strange you should not
have heard of her."

Hope attempted to add credence to her story. "Our
village was situated in a remote area."

Faith smiled and nodded again. "Where legends flourish."

She was much more astute than Hope had realized.
She would need to be careful around Lady Faith. "Legends abound in all of Ireland. There is not an Irishman

who does not fancy telling a story or two."

Faith laughed. "This is true enough." Her laughter softened to a gentle smile. "So tell me a story, Harold. One whose origin comes from your remote area."

A burst of boisterous laughter caught their attention and drew their glances toward Colin who had his arm wrapped around the waist of a well-endowed servant girl. It was her laughter and provocative voice that interrupted the conversation.

"I have missed you," the young woman said in a whisper that was meant to be heard.

Colin spoke low and softly, so it was with a strained ear that Hope heard him answer, "And I you, Colleen."

Colleen smiled and leaned down to whisper in his ear; as hard as Hope strained to hear her words, it was useless. Her remark was meant for Colin and Colin alone.

Colin appeared quite pleased since he smiled, nodded as if agreeing with her and then kissed her cheek before she moved off him to finish seeing to her chores.

Hope realized that Faith was watching her and she was quick to shake her head and answer her question. "A story escapes me, perhaps another time."

"Aye, there will be time for us to share stories and to come to know one another."

Eric peered over his wife's shoulder to address the lad. "My wife knows all that goes on in the keep. It is rare that a secret can be kept from her." He kissed the side of her neck lightly and Faith smiled and rested back against him.

"I am merely more observant than most."

Hope took her remark seriously. If she was as observant as she said, then it would do Harold well to be on guard.

Colin leaned around Eric to join in the conversation. "Careful, Harold, it is the endless questions that Lady Faith asks and the answers given without serious thought that make her knowledgeable of those at Shanekill."

Hope was not certain if he teased, though he did wear

a purposeful grin, or if it was from experience that he spoke. Regardless of the reason, Hope intended to mind his warning.

Faith yawned and then issued Colin a warning of her own, and not on a favorable subject. "Which reminds me, we must talk soon regarding inquiries I have made concerning a wife for you."

Hope turned an intent ear on Colin's answer.

He laughed briefly and gave an adamant shake of his head. "I have no interest in marriage. I have too many women yet to please."

Faith disagreed. "I think I can find the perfect woman for you."

Eric and Borg laughed along with Colin.

"I think your wife's condition affects her senses," Colin said with a slap to Eric's back and then he looked to Faith. "Besides, perfection would make for a dull marriage."

"He has you there, wife," Eric said with a gentle rub to her rounded belly.

The men's teasing did not disturb Faith in the least. Her determination remained strong. "I think not. I know Colin well, therefore I know the type of wife best suited for him."

"Surrender now, Colin," Borg warned with a grin. "She has you outflanked."

Hope watched with the same enthusiastic amusement as the men, her grin wide and her attention eager.

Colin shook his head, laughter filling his words. "Never. I will go down fighting."

Faith remained firm in her intentions and continued on, ignoring the protests. "The woman you take as wife must equal your own strength. A woman weak in character will never do."

"Finished you are," Borg insisted, his hand reaching out to grab for a tall, attractive woman as she attempted to hurry past him. She smiled as she willingly let him

capture her and he settled her down to rest on his knee.
"Do not say I did not warn you."

Colin directed his remark to the lad. "Take a good
look at these two men, Harold. They are besotted by
their wives and wish for me to be as ridiculously in love
as they are."

Hope responded quickly. "Then they are true friends
if they wish such happiness for you."

"A wise lad," Eric said with a sharp elbow to Colin's
side.

Hope continued. "I am curious, Lady Faith. What
other qualities must this woman best suited for Colin
possess?"

Colin attempted to divert the issue. "Harold, perhaps
Lady Faith should have a look at you now."

"No need," she answered. "The rest and delicious
food has me feeling fine."

Faith agreed. "There is time for me to see to the lad's
health; for now I will settle his curiosity."

Colin moaned and threw himself back in his chair.

"I warned you," Borg teased again.

"He is right," Eric said with a deep chuckle. "You are
finished and I for one will be pleased to see you wed.
It is time you settled down."

"You are both jealous of my freedom," Colin insisted.

The two men burst into laughter.

Hope enjoyed their teasing banter. It demonstrated
how much they cared for each other. Colin truly did
have a wonderful family here at Shanekill. A family who
cared tremendously for him.

Faith interrupted them. "Freedom is one of the qualities the woman must possess."

Borg looked at Faith, confused. "If this woman wishes
freedom, why would she marry?"

"She would bring to the marriage her own sense of
freedom, thus combining both their individual needs, at
times, for independence."

"A woman cannot be independent. She needs a man

to look after her." Eric cringed at hearing his own words.

"Shall I give you a chance to recant your words, my lord?" Faith asked with a soft smile and a gentle pat to her husband's arm.

Hope looked on with envy at the loving and knowing exchange between husband and wife. That they loved was obvious and she silently wished for such a strong, enduring love for herself.

Faith demonstrated the strength of her character when she said, "A woman does have need of a man's protection now and again."

"You, my friend," Colin said with a hand to Eric's shoulder, "have a wise wife."

Eric took full advantage of his remark. "Then, my friend, trust her to find a well-suited wife for you."

"I am doomed," Colin said, and hung his head in mock surrender.

"This is good," Faith said, her victory confirmed. "I will make certain I find a favorable wife for you. One you will be pleased with."

"Find me one with the courageous spirit of this woman Hope that we searched for and marriage might interest me," Colin said with a seriousness that had them all turning an intent glance on him; especially Hope.

She could not believe that he thought her courageous when everyone else thought her foolhardy. Was he a kindred spirit? Did he truly understand her?

Eric spoke as most did about her. "You admire a woman who runs away from her duties?"

Colin answered without hesitation. "I do not think it is her duties that she runs from, nor do I think she runs at all."

"You make no sense," Borg said, shaking his head.

"I think she searches," Colin continued, his remark a surprise to them all.

"What does she search for, Colin?" Faith asked with sincere interest.

Hope held her breath and tried to still the rapid beating of her heart, afraid that someone would hear its wild rhythm.

Colin hesitated only briefly, as though he did not wish to divulge a secret. "I think she searches for herself."

His answer almost caused Hope to gasp out loud, but she caught herself in time, making it sound as if she merely coughed lightly.

Eric and Borg looked at Colin oddly while Faith and Bridget smiled at him.

Hope realized then why Colin attracted so many women. He understood them, in a way more than they understood themselves.

Bridget spoke. "You will make some woman a good husband, Colin."

"Aye," Faith agreed. "And I will find that good woman for you."

Eric and Borg shook their heads, though Borg grinned and directed his glance toward the far end of the long table.

"Looks as though someone wants your attention."

Colin turned and caught sight of Colleen, whose smile invited and promised pleasure.

Hope grew annoyed—so annoyed that she jumped to her feet, ready for battle. This was an unwise move since the sudden jolt sent a fiery pain through her side, the intensity of which caused her head to spin.

She placed a firm hand to her temple in the hope of regaining her balance but it was too late. She hit the floor in a dead faint.

Eleven

Hope heard the frantic voices in the distance. One sounded calmer than the others and it was to that voice that she was drawn. Its soothing softness helped pull her out of the hazy fog she drifted in.

"He is fine, just a bit worn out from the tedious journey and an injury that has yet to heal properly."

"He is a stubborn lad, thinking himself capable of anything."

Hope recognized Colin's voice, though it was fraught with worry. And it was Faith's voice that possessed the calmness that helped clear Hope's head.

"Do not worry so."

"He does too much for a lad so young and frail. He needs someone to look after him."

"That he does," Faith agreed. "But it would seem that he has someone. You care much for the scrawny lad."

Colin answered most eagerly. "That I do. I admire his tenacious character, his courage and his determination. He boldly handles life's trials and tribulations with an audacity that maintains his bravado." He paused and his voice softened. "Even when painful memories haunt him he struggles to survive, any way he can." He paused again and looked to Lady, whom Eric ordered to keep her distance along with Rook, though the large animal whined incessantly, heartsick at not being able to get to her master. "The lad even protects a dog that is more coward than not."

Hope came awake at the mention of Lady and her pitiful whines that filled the air. And it was she to whom Hope called out. "Lady."

The large animal crawled on her belly, whining all the way as if her solemn cries would prevent anyone from stopping her. They did, of course, everyone too concerned with the lad to stop the animal from going to him.

Lady poked her head around Colin since he refused to move out of the animal's way.

"Lady," Hope repeated, wanting to make certain that her dog was all right.

A wet tongue licked at her cheek and a sorrowful whine brought a smile to Hope's face. "I am fine," she assured the worried animal.

"Faith will make certain of that," she heard Colin say, though her eyes remained closed and for some unexplainable reason she wished not to open them.

Faith addressed Colin's obvious distress. "I think the lad requires a good night's sleep before I go poking at him."

Hope sighed with relief.

"What is wrong, Harold?" Colin demanded with concern as he rested a gentle hand over Hope's injured ribs.

The truth. How she wished she could speak it, confide in him her identity and the reasons behind her daring adventure. Instead she addressed the issue at hand, making him believe the lad's sound reasoning. "Lady Faith is right, I but need to rest."

"Your injury?" Colin inquired adamantly. "It must be seen to."

"It is but a bruise that will heal," she said patiently.

Before an argument could ensue, Faith attempted to ease Colin's concern. "I will help settle Harold for the night and take a quick look at his ribs."

"I will assist you," Colin said, sounding more like an order than an offer.

Now what was she to do? She wanted to cry out her

frustration or pound her fist, when all she could do was shake her head.

"Something ails you and you will not admit it," Colin said with a frustrated rake of his hair. "You are a stubborn little fool who needs a good thrashing."

His senseless threat ignited Hope's temper, and to everyone's surprise she sat up with a jolt, her hand instinctively going to her side. "You cannot dictate to me."

Her adamant reply and quick movement startled Colin and fired his own temper. "I do as I please and—"

"As do I," Hope said, her finger poking at his chest.

A collective chuckle could be heard, which only managed to fire the simmering situation.

"*And*," Colin said emphatically, "*you* do as I please."

Hope was not in the habit of obeying orders and she decided neither was the lad. "I take orders from no man."

Another round of chuckles brought a frustrated moan from Colin.

Before the small skirmish erupted into a full-scale battle Eric stepped in. His authoritative voice left no doubt that his words were meant to be obeyed. "Enough! Harold, you will go with Lady Faith so that she may see to your care, and Colin, we shall talk."

Hope stood and tapped her leg, directing Lady to her side. The large animal eagerly obeyed, slinking around Colin as he stood to his imposing height, his dark eyes staring at her with the concern of a loved one.

Hope realized then the foolishness of her actions. Once again Colin demonstrated his sincere concern for the lad and she reacted ungratefully—more like a spoiled child than a grown woman. Had he not willingly offered his friendship to Harold? Did she not realize that he took that friendship seriously? Colin cared, actually cared about the lad's well-being. Was that what disturbed her so? Was she annoyed because she wanted him to know and care for her as a woman? Her unsettled emotions alarmed her, but she could address only one emotion at a time. Her present emotion, guilt at attacking him, needed attention.

She offered an apology. "Colin, I meant no offense. You have been generous with your help and your friendship, which is much appreciated." She paused, attempting to find the right words. "It is just that I am accustomed to being on my own, alone, and not answering to anyone."

Colin placed a comforting hand on the lad's shoulder. "I understand, but it is time you realize that you are no longer alone. You have friends, and friends look out for each other."

"I will remember that."

Colin smiled. "Nay, you will forget soon enough, but I will remind you when necessary." He turned to Faith. "When you finish with him I will take him to the men's quarters and see that he gets a bed."

Hope almost panicked. She could never sleep in a room full of men.

Faith solved her dilemma, and Hope silently blessed her. "I think it would be best for Harold to rest comfortably by himself for the night. He may use the bed in my healing cottage."

Eric effortlessly lifted his wife from where she kneeled on the floor, his thick muscled arm going around her waist. "Do you require any help?"

As Faith was unable to answer, her husband answered his own question. "Bridget, please go with Faith in case she requires your assistance."

Borg grinned. "You worry incessantly now about your wife. What will you do when her time comes?"

Eric cringed and spoke honestly. "I will remain by her side and suffer along with her."

"The devil suffer? This I cannot wait to see," Colin said jokingly.

Eric pretended to whisper to his wife, though his words were meant for all, or at least one person in particular. "I wish to help you decide on whom Colin will wed."

"I wish to help with the choice as well," Borg said, his grin spreading.

Hope smiled and nodded. "I see now, Colin, what good friends can do for you."

Laughter filled the room and Eric left his wife's side after kissing her cheek, then slapped Colin on the back.

"Come, Borg and I have missed drinking with you." Eric paused and cast a glance toward Colleen who waited in the distance. "Unless of course you have other plans."

"Plans that can wait," Colin said and let Colleen know with a smile and a nod that lighted her face that their time would come later in the evening.

Harold frowned, his eyes on Colleen.

"Something wrong?" Faith asked and slipped a soft, deep red wool shawl that she had retrieved from the back of her chair around her shoulders.

Harold shrugged. "Nothing."

Faith took hold of Harold's arm and looked to Bridget. "I really have no need of assistance if there is something else you wish to do."

Bridget smiled, her full face glowing. "I have been anxious to spend more time on a stitching project I have recently started."

Faith hugged Harold's slim arm. "Bridget has a gift with the needle. Her work is quite exquisite."

Hope would have loved to view Bridget's work, being talented with a needle herself, but a young lad would find no favor in such womanly things. So she nodded and followed it with a hefty sigh, as if uninterested.

"Harold, Lady and Rook shall see me safely to the cottage and Rook shall return me home safely," Faith said with a gentle pat to Rook's head.

"The devil will be at your cottage door to see you safely back at the keep as soon as he learns you will return alone," Bridget said with a soft laugh.

"And who will tell him?" Faith asked with a hint of an accusing smile.

"The question would be better asked, 'Who would not tell him?'" Bridget replied and walked off laughing.

Faith directed Harold to the two large doors that led out of the great hall and out of the keep itself. The night air held a chill to it, with spring still held at bay by the persistent winter chill.

Hope breathed deeply of the sharp air, having grown accustomed to spending the majority of her journey outdoors. At first the night darkness had frightened her and Lady. Every strange sound—though at first most sounds were strange to her—had caused her to shake in fear. And then there were the night shadows—those dark looming shapes that drifted over the land at night and gave rise to tales of evil spirits.

It took many fearful nights of shivering beneath a large tree with Lady also cold beside her to come to understand the secrets of the night. The sounds finally began to make sense, and she was able to determine the identity of the nocturnal creatures that created the melodious symphony. She also began to understand the shadows of the night and the drifting clouds over the moonlight that caused many of them.

She now saw the beauty in the dark night and relished the secrets she had learned, and no longer feared the dark.

"You walk with confidence," Faith said, praise evident in her voice.

"As do you." Hope had also learned fast to be aware of her surroundings, not only places but people as well. She had observed how surefooted Faith was and how secure she felt in her safety. It actually added to her own confidence.

Hope failed to catch the yawn that spilled from her mouth, though her hand attempted to do so.

"You are very tired and need more rest than you admit

to." Faith did not speak accusingly; she simply spoke the truth.

Hope did not agree or disagree. She just kept walking, her mind suddenly alert to her dilemma. How was she to keep Faith from discovering her secret when she would probably want to poke and probe her wounded area?

She did not have time to ponder her query since they came to a halt in front of a small cottage not far from the keep's kitchen. A wreath laden with berries, pinecones and sprigs of various herbs hung on the door, giving off a rich scent that delighted the nostrils.

Faith set to lighting candles inside the one-room cottage then said to Hope, "Please set the logs to burning. I do not wish you to catch a chill tonight."

Hope had no trouble getting the logs to light. A basket of kindling sat nearby and she chose the best of the splintered wood. She had made certain to learn, before she began her adventure, how to light a good, dependable fire.

She took a moment to glance about the room and found it much to her liking. There was a feeling of warmth and welcome to it. And with the numerous dried bunches of herbs hanging from the ceiling rafters and drying on a wooden rack not far from the stone fireplace, one would assume a healer occupied the cottage.

A narrow bed braced against one wall looked awfully welcoming to Hope. A soft blue woolen blanket was folded down at the foot of the bed and clean white linens covered the plump straw mattress. Hope wanted nothing more than to drop her tired body on it and sleep.

Hope watched Faith step outside, a small bucket in hand, and return with it partially filled with water. She poured it into the black metal pot that hung from a pole in the fireplace and swung it over the flames. Then she plucked dried leaves off the bunches of herbs on the drying rack, dropped them into a wooden bowl on the table in the center of the room and set to crushing them.

When she finished she dropped them into the pot of water.

"Sit, Harold, you are exhausted."

Hope did not argue. Her exhaustion had caught up with her all at once. She simply wished to sleep as long as she could. A yawn and droopy eyes attested to that fact.

Faith pulled out a chair from the table.

Hope sat resting with her chin in her hand and her elbow on the table.

"I think you are too tired for me to poke at your ribs. I will help you clean up your face and hands and see that you are tucked into bed. Tomorrow is soon enough for me to examine your wound. And besides, the healing of bruised ribs must take place in its own good time."

Hope listened to her chatter. She was too tired to respond, though relieved that her secret remained safe.

Faith poured the warm water mixture into a bowl and soaked a cloth in it. She rinsed the cloth and began gently to cleanse Hope's face.

Hope closed her tired eyes, the warm wet cloth on her dirty face feeling incredibly soothing.

"Your journey was a long one."

A soft sigh was Hope's reply.

"It was more difficult than you had thought."

Another stronger sigh followed.

"Sometimes we think ourselves stronger than we are and discover ourselves stronger than we thought possible."

Hope was lost to the gentle strokes of the warm cloth running over her face and around her neck, and she answered without thought. "Aye, that is true enough. I have discovered strengths I did not know I possessed."

"But strengths needed for such a perilous journey."

"Aye, more perilous than I had thought."

"But one you knew you must take. One that was necessary to you," Faith said softly.

"Aye, necessary," Hope said, her closed eyes having grown too heavy to remain open.

Faith's gentle voice lulled like a soft melody. "And have you found what you searched for?"

Hope instantly thought of Colin, his charming smile, his caring nature, his kindred spirit, and her answer came easily. "Aye, I have found it." She fought back the tears that suddenly threatened to spill from her eyes, though her quivering voice betrayed her heartfelt emotions. "But what good is the discovery when it cannot be mine?"

Faith did not respond; she remained silent, her thoughts her own as she continued to administer to Hope's needs.

Colin continued his endless diatribe and his endless pacing in front of the large stone fireplace in Eric's solar. "He possesses tremendous courage."

Eric and Borg occupied the two chairs before the hearth, a tankard of ale in each of their hands and their heads following Colin's pacing.

"But he is stubborn to a fault and does not always pick his battles wisely, though I feel with proper training he could make a fine warrior one day." He paused briefly, rubbed his chin and continued his pacing. "Of course he will need to add weight to his frail frame, but that should be easy now that he is *remaining* here at Shanekill."

He paused again.

Eric and Borg waited in patient silence, knowing he would continue.

"I will start the lad's training as soon as Lady Faith agrees that he is well enough for strenuous labor. If she feels he needs time, his lessons can always wait since he will be staying *permanently* at Shanekill."

Another short pause.

Eric and Borg grinned at one another.

"He has a way of speaking his mind and his remarks and observations are most intelligent for one his age. I wondered if perhaps he had some bit of tutoring. That was another thought of mine, to have the lad receive some formal education. His wit is too sharp to simply ignore. It should be nourished. And with him *making his home* here at Shanekill there would be time for lessons."

Eric finally interrupted. "So, Colin, do you think the lad should remain here at Shanekill?"

Borg hid his laugh behind the tankard of ale that he purposely raised to his lips.

Colin looked as though the remark startled him. "I thought that decision was already made. Of course the lad will remain here at Shanekill."

Eric's grin faded to a concerned smile. "You have a protective spot in your heart for this lad."

Colin was about to disagree when he stopped to give it thought. The lad had somehow become important to him. He could not quite understand why, though his tenacious spirit had something to do with it. He was determined to live life his way and damned if he did not possess the courage and strength to do it.

Life had not been fair to him, but he did not complain or cry in his cups. He did what needed doing as only a man of true character could, and even though young and frail in body he survived and continued to do so. He was on his own with no one to help him.

Colin understood that feeling of having no one.

He answered Eric. "He needs a friend."

"He seems to have found one, and a good one at that." He leaned forward in his seat, his hand firm on his knee and his smile wide. "And now that we have listened to your endless tirade on the lad, and established that he will be remaining permanently at Shanekill, do you think we could speak of the reason for your mission?"

"Hope," Colin said with a shake of his head. "I cannot for the life of me understand how she eluded us or continues to do so."

"You do not think she may have met with foul play?"

Borg asked. "She is, after all, a mere woman on her own and from what we have been told a small one at that."

"True enough," Colin agreed. "But after speaking with the abbess at Croom Abbey I learned that what she lacks in size she certainly makes up for in determination."

Eric nodded in agreement. "Shamus mentioned her propensity for doing as she pleased."

"Sounds as though she is a spoiled one," Borg said.

Colin looked to Borg. "I thought the same myself at first, but I have wondered of late if there was something else that drove her to leave."

"Why do you say leave, not run away?" Eric asked.

"I do not know why but I feel that her intentions were to take her leave for a time and then return."

"A taste of freedom before wedding a stranger?" Eric asked, rubbing his jaw and giving the idea thought.

"A possibility," Colin agreed. "Her determination gives her an adventurous spirit and perhaps she felt compelled to—"

"Have an adventure?" Borg suggested, incredulous. "Everyone is worried about this pint-sized woman and she is off on an adventure? You cannot be serious."

"I think he is," Eric said. "And I believe he may be correct in his assumption. Considering her spirited nature, it would be a sensible conclusion."

"But do you really think it possible for a woman to survive on her own this long?" Borg asked.

"A bold woman might," Eric suggested.

"And we have determined she is just that—bold," Colin concluded.

"Or very foolish," Borg said.

"Our next step then, Colin?" Eric asked and clarified when Colin looked questioningly at him. "You seem to understand this woman, so tell me what you think her intentions are from this point on."

"I have been giving it thought and while there is always a chance she has been harmed or has possibly met with foul play, I do not believe that either is the case. Somehow she has found a way to keep herself hidden away from those who search for her."

"Any thought on how she has managed that?" Eric asked.

Borg answered. "She could have met up with a family who was in need of coins and she paid them a handsome amount to keep her identity secret while sharing their home."

"Another possibility," Colin said, "though I do not think such a situation would give her the freedom she had intended. Nay, I think she prefers to keep on the move."

"And do what?" Eric asked.

The answer came easily for Colin. "Discover."

Twelve

Colin searched the keep for Harold. It was a senseless search; he had told himself that when he first began. He knew where he could find him. Ever since their return to Shanekill a few days ago Harold could be found in the same location.

He was at the healing cottage helping Faith, and of course sleeping there. How the place had become the lad's home escaped Colin. It seemed his first night at the keep, and every subsequent night, had been spent there and it did not seem that he planned to vacate the place any time soon.

Colin, however, had different ideas. It was time the lad began more manly chores and left the healing to the women. And while his ribs might not be sufficiently healed to participate in the daily practice of combat skills, he could at least watch and learn.

Today he intended to see that Harold began to do as he directed. It was, after all, for the lad's own good.

He marched out of the keep and directly to Faith's healing cottage. His usual charming smile that warmed the ladies' hearts was gone, replaced by a look that warned everyone to clear out of his way. It was a look he seldom wore, but one that was instantly obeyed.

Colin rounded the corner of the cottage to find Harold leaning over the large rain barrel with a bucket in hand. He grabbed the lad by the back of his shirt, startling him and causing him to drop the bucket, splashing the water over them both.

The commotion brought Faith to the cottage door.

"Look what you did," Hope accused, wiping the water off the clean dark red tunic Faith had given her only two days before. It had been a relief to change out of the dirty garments she had worn since the beginning of her journey and a pleasure to have washed herself from head to toe one night when alone in the cottage.

"What I have done?" Colin asked with a shocked expression and a swipe of his hand over his face where the water had splashed him. "You have other duties and responsibilities. I have come to make certain you see to them."

"I do not think Harold's wound is sufficiently healed enough to partake in any strenuous duties," Faith said.

Her remark made Hope suspicious. Her ribs had healed nicely and Faith had even commented on her fine condition just yesterday. So why today did she think otherwise?

"I will see that he takes care, *but* he should at least learn what will be expected of him when he faces an opponent."

Faith looked about to protest when she suddenly asked, "He will but watch?"

"My word, my lady," Colin said and executed a courtly bow followed by a dashing smile.

She laughed. "You are a rogue."

It was that rogue manner that had caused Hope to purposely avoid Colin the last few days. Since the first night of their return she had watched him work his charm on many women, and she had watched many a woman invite him with a smile or a sway of her hips. Some were audacious enough to approach him openly with their intentions.

And while he was cordial to them all, he did not accept every invitation, though he turned down few.

"You know me well, my lady," Colin said with a wink.

"I know all my friends well," Faith replied. "Do I not, Harold?"

Hope wondered if Faith did not know Harold better than anyone. The feeling that she knew the truth about her had haunted Hope's thoughts for the last few days.

Hope nodded slowly as only a lad can do when not sure of his reply.

Faith looked to Colin. "You promise me he will do no more than watch the men practice?"

"I promise." He crossed his heart as he answered.

"Then take Harold with you, but . . ." She warned with a pointing finger. "You will return him to me right afterwards. I have chores I need help with."

Colin grew concerned. "If you require his help, my lady, I will leave him at your disposal."

"Nay," she insisted, "and besides, I think a change of pace will suit the lad. He must grow tired of spending so much time with me."

"Nay," Hope was quick to respond. "I do not mind helping you." And she did not. Faith was a wise woman with much knowledge and Hope took pleasure in what she could learn from her.

Colin slapped Hope on the back, causing her to stumble, and surprisingly received a fast reprimand from Faith. "Be careful, the lad still heals."

Hope spoke up like a lad in defense of himself. "I am fine and can take care of myself."

"We shall see," Colin said with grin.

"Colin, you will keep your promise," Faith said, her tone sharp.

"You upset my wife, Colin?"

The deep, stern voice caused Harold to jump aside, bumping into Colin, who righted him with a firm hand to his thin arm. But then how could one not stumble when the devil himself was bearing down on him.

The imposing man went straight for his wife, slipping

his arm around her waist and drawing her into his powerful arms. She rested her head on his thick chest and smiled at Colin.

Faith answered her husband, her eyes on Colin. "I am being demanding, my lord, and Colin is attempting to appease me."

"Is that the way of it, lad?" Eric asked, startling Hope.

Colin laughed, folding his arms over his chest and fixing his glance on Harold.

The devil might try to intimidate Harold but he rankled Hope's temper and it was she who answered, "You doubt your wife's word, my lord?"

Colin looked stunned, Faith smiled and Eric was speechless for a brief moment.

Eric shook his head. "Foolish or brave, I cannot decide which you are."

"Finally," Colin spoke as if relieved. "I am not alone in my thought."

Harold shrugged indifferently. "You asked a question and I answered honestly. I do not think that makes me either foolish or brave—simply honest."

Faith continued to smile, though she gave a brief nod as if confirming a silent thought. And Hope was more concerned over her musings than the devil himself.

"I respect your honesty," Eric said, "therefore, I expect an honest answer to my query."

Her stubborn tenacity remained. "And the answer to my question, my lord?"

Colin shook his head and Faith laughed.

Eric stared at Hope for a moment, a moment too long for Hope's comfort. She wondered over his thoughts and grew uncomfortable with the way his dark eyes scrutinized her. Had she gone too far? She was, after all, a mere lad without a trace of noble blood, though it was her noble stubbornness that had gotten her into her present predicament.

"You require no answer, but I do," Eric said and waited.

She had behaved poorly for a lad who had been extended such generosity by the lord of the castle and while her nobility afforded her a certain respect, it did not extend to the lad. She had forgotten her place, forgotten who she was supposed to be, a lad, a mere young lad who knew better than to be disrespectful to a lord and especially to the Irish devil.

The lad finally answered. "My lady speaks the truth."

Eric nodded. "I had no doubt she did."

"Then why ask me?" Hope shook her head, realizing the answer. "You inquired not of your wife's honesty, but of mine."

Eric looked with admiration at the lad. "You have a quick mind; use it wisely."

"Come, Harold," Colin ordered. "You have disturbed Lord Eric long enough."

The lad gave a respectful bow of his head to the lord and lady before hurrying after Colin. But Hope paused in her thoughts to wonder if she was now about to face a skirmish of a different kind.

Eric leaned down and nuzzled his wife's neck, his large hand splaying across her protruding stomach. "The lad should have been born of nobility—he possesses the arrogance."

Faith caressed her husband's cheek. "Aye, I agree."

He turned her around in his arms. "Then tell me what nags at me about the lad. What am I missing?"

Faith gave her husband a soft kiss. "Think on it. I am certain you will understand soon enough."

Eric kissed her back, though his kiss promised passion and she responded with a gentle moan. He scooped her up into his arms, entered the cottage and kicked the door shut with a solid thud.

Two women passing by giggled and spread the word that Lady Faith would not be seeing ailing villagers for a couple of hours.

•   •   •

Harold sat on a stump watching the men practice their battle skills. Colin had ordered the lad to pay close attention to their body movements and the way in which they handled their weapons. The lad had no trouble doing so.

Hope, however, had difficulty keeping her eyes off Colin. His tall, lean frame would make one think him less of an opponent than the men with thick muscles. But his defined muscle structure possessed more strength than some of the more heavily muscled men.

And she thrilled in watching him skillfully take down an opponent or brandish his sword with the ease and grace of a man born to it.

Why were her eyes always drawn to him? Why did she always concern herself with him? Why did she care that he smiled at women? Why did her heart flutter when he stepped near her?

She sighed and slowly shook her head. Could she be falling in love with him? Or was she already in love with him? And why? He knew her only as the lad Harold. And yet she knew him as a caring soul. A man who would befriend a young boy and see that he was looked after and see that he would have a family who cared for him.

If he worried so about Harold, a lad he barely knew yet befriended, then how would he treat a wife whom he loved with all his heart? The thought haunted her, as did his words.

Forever mine.

He wished to love a woman and make her forever his. It was important to him that he find an enduring love, not a passing one or one forced on him, but one that lasted forever. One of his own choosing. One equal to his own courage and strength.

A kindred spirit.

The clash of metal snapped her out of her musing and brought her attention back to the practice field. Tempers seemed to have heated amongst the men and arguments ensued.

Colin stepped in the middle of two large men and barked orders at them. At first they hesitated but Colin issued the orders again in a tone that warned he would be obeyed or else. The men parted, though tempers remained high.

The practice continued for a time and the two men who had exchanged heated words kept their distance. It was when the practice session ended that the two men lost control and raged at each other.

Fists flew, shouts filled the air and chaos reigned.

Colin stood aside and allowed the men time to settle their dispute.

Hope sat and watched the skirmish with interest. Even when blood was spilled Colin did not stop the men. And the other men cheered as if they watched a favorite sport.

She would at one time have been appalled at such a display of aggression. She would have thought it senseless, but having come to understand men, at least in a small way, she could watch with an understanding not afforded to most women.

She even found herself standing up on the stump and cheering. Not for any opponent in particular but because there was that feeling of victory in the air. And she did not think it mattered if any man won as long as the battle was fought.

The two large men stumbled over the practice field, blood and sweat flying off them onto the cheering crowd. And the excitement grew as the two men continued on, fists flying.

Colin stepped forward as if prepared to end the fight when chaos took hold and the two men lost their balance and went tumbling to the ground, rolling over and over as their fists kept flying, blood kept spurting and onlookers kept cheering.

Hope told herself to move, get out of the way, clear the path, when all of a sudden the two men crashed into the stump, knocking her off her perch and landing her in the middle of the melee.

Colin was on top of the trio in seconds but not before Hope suffered several blows to her face. He and Stuart tossed the large men off the lad as if they weighed nothing, and when they finally reached Hope their eyes rounded.

There was blood everywhere. Around Hope's eyes, running from her nose, dripping from her split lip. And when the two men took notice of the wounded lad, their tempers settled.

"Is he hurt bad?" one asked.

The other waited for an answer with wide eyes and a concerned look.

Hope moaned and spit out the blood that had pooled in her mouth. She let out an angry shout, the action having caused pain to her split lip. She forced her eyes open, though one eye refused to comply and she knew that was the one that had taken the hefty blow.

Colin peered down at her with worried eyes; at least she thought that what she saw were his eyes, though she was not certain. The blood clouded her vision and she could only see a ghostly image.

"Harold, can you hear me?" Colin asked.

His voice was filled with concern. Hope thought she heard it tremble but that could not be. He was a warrior accustomed to battle injuries to himself and to others.

"Harold!" he said anxiously.

She cringed. "Stop shouting, I can hear you."

"Where does it pain you?" Colin asked, his hands at his sides, afraid to touch the lad.

"Ask me where it does not hurt me," she said caustically and heard Colin laugh.

"I have sent for Lady Faith."

"I am fine. I need only cleaning up," Hope assured him.

"Sorry, lad," she heard a deep voice say.

"We did not mean to involve you," another voice echoed behind him.

Hope thought to respond as the lad but her womanly nature was also curious. "Who won?"

In unison she heard, "You!"

A cheer split the air and she felt herself rejoicing along with the men, her own triumphant shout filling the air.

Colin shook his head, though his shouts joined the others. The lad possessed a tenacity that was uncommon. He did not allow life to trample him. He faced it full force and with the fierce determination of a warrior. And he survived and grew stronger.

"What have you done?" The familiar voice caused silence to reign and a path to be cleared for the lady of the keep.

The Irish devil was at her side and his expression warned all that he was none too happy.

Faith, with the help of her husband, went down on her knees beside Harold. "Dear Lord, what have they done?"

Faith's distress caused Eric to grow more annoyed. "I will have a full explanation, Colin."

"Not his fault."

All eyes turned to Harold.

Hope realized she must keep her senses about her. She had to address this from a lad's perspective. She wiped at her blood-soaked eyes with the back of her sleeve, though the woman in her wanted to cringe that she was staining her new garment.

Better vision afforded her a sense of confidence and she spoke candidly after raising herself to a sitting position. "Colin gave his men what their frustration needed—a good fight. I just happened to get in the way. It was no one's fault, and besides," she said with a wide grin that further split her lip and had blood running down her chin, "I won!"

Cheers once again filled the air.

Eric even joined in, but it was the strange look that Faith sent her that worried her the most.

Faith knew her secret. She had no doubt. What would happen now?

"I think we should get you back to my cottage so I can clean you up and see to your wounds," Faith suggested.

Hope did not argue; her body was beginning to suffer from her altercation and the soft bed seemed a welcoming place.

Colin helped Harold up. "You did well, lad, and I appreciate you defending me."

"I spoke the truth," Hope said, his strong arm braced firmly around her, sending tingles through her aching body.

"I admire your honesty," Colin said and took most of the lad's weight on himself as he assisted him to walk.

His remark brought a moan to her lips; most thought it was her injuries that caused her pain. And she caught many of the men sympathetically cringing for the lad.

"I will go slow," Colin said, easing his steps.

Honesty.

A trait she herself admired and strived to maintain. Unfortunately her present situation did not afford her much honesty. What time she had here was limited. She did not dare allow Colin to learn the truth about Harold. She feared the disappointment she would see on his face.

She would watch and learn and take good memories with her.

The thought caused a pain to her heart and tears to pool in her eyes.

"You are in pain," Colin said when he noticed the lad's unshed tears and how hard he fought to keep them from spilling.

"Aye, I am," Hope admitted, though the reason for her pain was better blamed on her injuries. How could she explain that she loved a man who did not know her at all?

Thirteen

Hope sat under the large tree that partially shaded Faith's herb garden. The soil had been tilled and prepared for planting and new sprouts could be seen making their way through the rich earth.

Lady and Rook were playfully busy nearby, having become inseparable since they first met. And Faith stood at the edge of her garden with her hand braced on her back detailing where she intended to plant the various herbs.

For the past three days Hope had worked closely with Lady Faith, who had insisted upon it after the incident on the practice field. And it was that very incident that made Hope more alert to her suspicions that Faith understood much about her—much too much.

Faith had chased Colin and Eric from the cottage when it came time for her to examine the lad. It was with gentle hands to her arms, legs and ribs and brief questions that she completed her examination. But it was her final words to the lad before leaving him to get a restful sleep that had disturbed Hope.

"You can trust me; we are much alike."

Hope had heard her words resonate over and over in her head for the past few days.

We are much alike.

Could she trust Lady Faith with her secret?

They were alike in many ways. They were both strong in character and determined in their efforts. Lady Faith spoke her mind when necessary yet honored her husband and his name. And she was a true friend to many.

As much as Hope wished she could confide in her she realized it was not possible. She, too, must honor her name and her heritage and do what was necessary.

"I hope I have sufficiently expanded my garden," Faith said, tapping a finger to her lips. "I found myself running low on a few herbs this past winter. I want to have a sufficient crop for drying this year."

Hope jumped to her feet with the enthusiastic bounce of an eager young lad. "Anything I can do to help?"

Her enthusiasm waned when she caught sight of Colin and Lord Eric approaching. Their determined expressions signaled trouble for the lad. But then if she was busy helping Lady Faith perhaps they would leave her be.

She picked up a shovel and asked, "How much bigger do you want your garden?"

Faith rubbed at her back. "Two arms' lengths I think will do nicely. But do not tire yourself. You have healed well and I wish you to remain so."

Hope took several steps back when she watched the way the devil's eyes narrowed and he grew annoyed.

"You should be resting," Eric said, his strong hand going to his wife's back and gently brushing her hand aside to rub where it obviously pained her.

Faith leaned her head back on her husband's chest. "I feel fine. A backache is not uncommon when a woman carries a babe."

He kissed her cheek. "I do not like to see you suffer."

Colin chuckled. "Whatever are you going to do when Faith gives birth?"

"Stop reminding me of that," Eric ordered with a grimace.

Hope found herself consoling the devil. "Lady Faith is a wise healer; she will do well when her time comes."

"The lad speaks wisely," Eric said, Hope's remark having indeed consoled him.

"And in his wisdom he knows that it is time for him to join the men on the practice field," Colin said, crossing his arms over his chest as if waiting for Harold to defy him.

"Lady Faith needs help," Hope said and waited to hear Colin deny assistance to the lady of the keep.

The lady spoke for herself. "Harold has become indispensable to me. Would you mind if he continued to help me, Colin?"

Hope admired Lady Faith. She did not feign feminine weakness or act as though she expected help; she simply spoke the truth.

Eric looked about to answer for Colin, his concern for his wife obvious, but Lady Faith placed a firm hand to his hand that rested on her rounded belly, cautioning his silence.

The action was not lost on Colin and it was with his own concern that he answered. "You may have the lad's help as long as it is necessary."

"I appreciate your consideration," Faith said with a tender smile.

Eric looked to the lad. "You will do whatever Lady Faith orders."

"Requests," Faith corrected sweetly.

The devil looked about to argue when Hope spoke up. "Whatever she asks of me I will do without question."

"You are a good lad and will be rewarded for your diligent service," Eric decreed.

Hope sounded like an arrogant lad who thought to fend for himself. "I need nothing nor want nothing."

Colin decided to step in. "You have what you need— a place to call home and good friends."

Hope stuck her chin up, along with her pride. "I decide what I need."

Colin's usual charm faltered and his determined strides took him to within only inches of the lad. "Sometimes I think a good thrashing would serve you well."

Hope had to admit that Colin certainly could intimidate, especially when his dark eyes turned cold and his lean body grew taut like a bow. And while many a young lad and woman would obey without question, Hope would have her own way.

Her chin rose another notch, to Colin's annoyance. And she spoke with the defiance of a stubborn lad, though her remark brought a smile to the devil. "You would have to catch me first."

Colin was quick to respond. "Is that a challenge?"

"Nope," Hope said with a slow shake of her head and purposely tilted her chin another notch higher. "It is a promise."

Colin looked ready to jolt forward and grab the lad when a large hand clamped down on his shoulder.

"There is work to be done," Eric said, keeping the humor out of his voice though his grin was hard to contain.

"Get busy with your chore," Colin ordered the lad.

"Like I said, whatever Lady Faith needs," Hope said, looking directly at Faith.

To everyone's surprise Faith sighed heavily, an unusual sound for her since she rarely if ever complained or drew attention to herself.

"What is wrong?" Eric demanded immediately, his arm going around her waist and holding her close.

"I feel a bit fatigued."

Hope eyed the lady suspiciously. In the short time she had known the lady she had never known her to complain about her health or feeling tired. She possessed more energy and stamina than the average woman who was not heavy with child.

Eric grew alarmed. "We will return to the keep and you will rest."

"Nay," Faith said with more verve than a fatigued woman would possess. "I think a cup of my own special brew and a brief rest at my healing cottage will do." Eric was about to accommodate her when she shook her head. "You have much to do. Harold will help me."

Hope had a strong feeling that Faith was up to something and she decided to follow along and see what the lady intended. "My pleasure, my lady."

Eric reluctantly turned his wife over to the lad's care, though he added his own directive. "You will find me if necessary."

"Aye, my lord, I will waste not a moment if the lady needs you."

Eric seemed pleased, though he cast a suspicious glance at his wife. "Follow your instincts, lad, and fetch me when it pleases you."

Hope was wise enough to contain her smile. "Aye, my lord, as you say."

Faith placed her palm to her husband's thick, muscled chest. "I am in good hands. Do not worry."

"I worry when it pleases me," Eric insisted, his hand going to the back of his wife's neck to knead the tender muscles. He kissed her then, not sweetly but demandingly, letting her and those around her know how he felt about her.

His unusual actions touched Hope's heart. The devil loved Faith and that was a joyful thought. She looked to Colin then, and saw the envy in his eyes. He wanted to love as strongly as the devil himself.

"Look after my wife, lad," Eric ordered briskly and turned to leave.

"Later," Colin said to Harold with a warning that meant he intended to continue their encounter at a later time. With that said he walked off to catch up with Eric.

Hope watched him go and felt a tug to her heart.

"You care about Colin."

Faith's unexpected though accurate remark caught Hope off guard and she instantly attempted to deny the obvious. "He thinks he can tell me what to do."

"Because he cares for you as well."

That annoyed Hope even more. She threw the shovel down. "I do not need him caring for me."

Faith held a calming hand out to the angry lad. "Why?"

As a woman Hope longed to reach out and accept her comfort but the stubborn lad would deny any need. And so she responded accordingly—she stomped past Faith. "Because I can take care of myself."

Faith, who showed no signs of fatigue, quickly caught up with her. "Can you?"

Hope slowed down, a sense of guilt attacking her for making Faith rush her already labored steps.

Faith's hand came to rest on Harold's arm. "Can you truly take care of yourself?"

Hope was fast to defend herself. "I may not look strong but I am determined."

Faith looked as if she were about to laugh. "Of that I have no doubt." She hooked her arm in Harold's. "And Colin does admire determination, since he possesses an overabundance of it himself."

"I thought it was charm that he had an abundance of."

Faith laughed this time, a light melodious laughter that brought a smile to Hope. "He charms the ladies, but he befriends you. There is a large difference."

Hope shook her head as they walked to the cottage. "But I thought he cared for the women he *charmed.*"

Faith nodded slowly. "Colin has a big heart. He cares in his own unique way for the women he, as you emphasized, charmed. But friendship means much to Colin, and I can tell that he cares for you as a friend and would do anything to protect you."

"I did not ask for his protection."

"It does not matter; he gives it freely. That is what a friend does." Faith then asked a question that startled Hope, though she answered it quickly enough. "Would you not protect Colin?"

"Of course I would."

Faith nodded as if confirming a silent query. "Then you consider him a friend."

Why did the thought upset her? It was the truth. She

did think of Colin as her friend. A good friend who
certainly would protect her with his life. But friendship
was not the only thing she wanted from Colin, and she
realized that was why she had kept her distance from
him since her arrival at Shanekill. What good would it
do to get to know him better when she could not remain
at the keep? And she could never confide her true identity to him for then she was afraid she would lose the
caring friendship they now shared.

"You do, do you not?" Faith asked when she received
no forthcoming answer.

Hope's answer was a sobering one. "Aye, I do consider him a friend."

"Then you have formed a bond between the two of
you."

"A bond?" Had they formed a bond without her realizing it? If they had, it was a strange one. "I suppose
in a way we have."

"You have," Faith insisted. "You both care as only
friends can care for each other. Think about and know
how very lucky you are."

Silence followed them the rest of the way to the cottage and Hope was grateful for the quiet time. She
needed time to make sense of the dilemma she had gotten herself into. While she felt she had experienced a
grand adventure, a better one than she had anticipated,
she had foolishly allowed herself to taste the wonders
of falling in love. And try as she might to convince
herself that her romantic emotions were simply a temporary condition, she knew otherwise.

She could not, if asked, explain how her feelings came
about. She did know she was attracted to him when first
they met, but then his handsome features would catch
any woman's eye. Nay, she realized it was spending
time with him daily and coming to know him, his true
character—the essence of the man he actually was rather
than the charming rogue he played so well—that captured her emotions.

Knowing all this did her little good, however; after all, to him she was a young lad who needed a friend and a home. While he had provided both, she could accept neither.

Her thoughts lingered and nagged at her as she entered the small cottage. She was grateful Bridget had arrived and was busy conversing with Faith. They were close friends and Hope envied their relationship. She yearned for female companionship. It had been much too long since she had talked as a woman about womanly matters. And she missed the comfort of it.

She listened to their conversation while sitting on a small stool near the hearth and removing dried plants from their stems into a large wooden bowl at her feet.

Her ears perked up when she heard Colin's name mentioned.

"So many village women worry that Colin will marry," Faith repeated.

Bridget nodded, her fingers busy stitching a perfect embroidered line along the hem of the tunic she worked on. "Most are hoping you have no luck in finding him a wife or"—she laughed briefly—"you find him a wife who does not please him and he seeks his pleasure elsewhere, after doing his duty, of course."

Hope held her tongue. She wanted to let both women know that when Colin found the woman he loved, he would make her forever his and never once think of wanting another woman again. True love meant too much to Colin ever to betray it.

"Colin would never enter into a forced marriage," Faith said with confidence.

"I tried to tell the chattering women the same myself," Bridget agreed. "Colin has a mind of his own, especially when it comes to females. He will have a wife his way and that is all there is to that. But would the stubborn, foolish women listen?" She shook her head, answering her own question.

Faith smiled. "The women around here favor Colin like no man I have ever seen."

Hope silently agreed.

Bridget giggled. "There is Lord Eric."

"Handsome as my husband is, his size and manner tend to intimidate women and they give him a wide berth when he passes by."

Hope bowed her head to hide her smile; Faith certainly knew her husband.

"Colin, however, can charm most any woman." Faith gave her remark thought and then shook her head. "Nay, not most women; all women. I have never seen Colin not be able to charm a woman. That is why I must find him a wife who sees past his charm and understands him for who he truly is."

"I do not envy you your chore," Bridget said, her brow furrowing with concern. "Not many women will look past his attractive features or that breathtaking charm of his. I even find myself caught up in it from time to time. The man does know how to deal with women."

Hope bit her tongue. She wanted to tell them both that he used his charm as a shield. He shielded himself from falling in love; though he wished for love, he also feared it—feared he would not find the true love he hungered for, and therefore his charm protected him from the hurt and pain of loving.

"Colin deals with women by not dealing with them."

Bridget raised a brow and Hope raised her head at Faith's surprising and astute remark.

Faith continued. "He pleases a woman for a night or an afternoon interlude and while he commits himself for that time he will not allow his heart or mind to take it any further. He keeps himself a safe distance apart. That is why Colin must first befriend a woman before he can love her."

Hope's eyes rounded like two bright moons.

Bridget simply spoke her mind. "Colin, be a woman's friend?"

Faith was adamant. "Precisely; he must be a friend before he is a lover. Only then will he find the love he searches for."

Bridget had trouble accepting the concept. "I cannot see that happening. Colin just does not view women as friends."

"He accepts me as a friend."

"You are Lord Eric's wife. He would not think of you in any other way."

"Well then, if Colin can be a friend to me, why not another woman?" Faith asked and sent Harold a sweet smile.

Hope instantly was on guard and remained silent minding her own business, though she was much interested in their conversation.

Bridget paused to consider her response. "I suppose it is possible, though his charm often precedes him. I cannot see him approaching a woman without his charm intact; therefore, how could he ever first befriend a woman?"

Faith looked to Hope when she spoke. "Perhaps he will be blinded by her charms."

Bridget laughed. "Colin blinded by a woman's charms? That I would love to see, and I am certain Lord Eric and Borg would also be dutifully entertained by such an occurrence."

Hope remained silent, her eyes steady on Faith.

"Anything is possible," Faith said with such confidence that Hope felt her own heart soar with possibilities.

"Aye, that is the truth," Bridget agreed. "I never thought a man like Borg would wish to marry a lowly servant like me."

"But he did not marry a lowly servant," Faith said, reaching out to pat her friend's arm. "He married a beautiful woman whom he dearly loves."

"Anything is possible," Bridget said with a tear in her eye. "I would never have believed it so before, but I do now."

"Good," Faith said cheerfully. "Then you can help me find Colin a wife."

Bridget grew excited enough to halt her stitching. "I would love to help find Colin a wife. A wife he could first befriend."

Faith turned to the lad. "Would you care to help us, Harold?"

Hope regarded her with cautious eyes.

"You have come to know Colin and I am certain you could provide us with insight that we as females fail to recognize," Faith said, that sweet smile of hers a little too sweet.

"I know nothing that will help you." Her tone held a hint of defense.

"I think you know much," Faith said softly. "You need only to trust."

Hope stared at her and realized at that moment that Lady Faith knew her secret.

Fourteen

Colin searched the great hall for Harold and grew annoyed when he could not find him. Of late the lad was never around, and he found himself missing his company. He favored talking with him. He was extremely intelligent for one raised in poverty. His insight into human nature amazed Colin, though his stubborn manner could irritate. But he had no business complaining about such a trait. He had possessed the same manner as a young lad and it had served him well. It had taught him to survive just as Harold was doing. Surviving was not enough, though, and he hoped to give Harold more.

"Lose someone?" Eric asked with a laugh.

Colin reached for his tankard of wine. "Misplaced."

"The lad certainly has a mind of his own."

Colin could not argue. "His wit is too sharp."

"I like him," Eric said. "No matter his size, he holds fast to his convictions."

"He is not strong enough to defend himself."

Eric noted the concern in Colin's voice. "There are many here who would protect him."

"Of that I have no doubt. It is when he is off on his own that I worry."

"You do not expect the lad to remain at Shanekill, do you?"

"I have my doubts," Colin said, casting another glance around the boisterous hall.

Eric spoke his mind. "It puzzles me as to why a young

lad on his own would choose not to remain in a good home when finding one."

"I have thought the same myself and I wonder if he hides."

"From whom?"

Colin shook his head. "I do not know. I only know that since I first met the lad I felt as if he kept something from me. A secret that he would share with few, if any."

"Do you think someone hunts him?"

Colin rubbed the back of his neck. "I am not sure. I only know something is not right. And then there is that large dog of his."

Eric smiled. "The one Rook is smitten with?"

Colin laughed this time. "They do make a fine pair, but I doubt the lad speaks the truth of how he came by the animal. And I cannot help but wonder if he knows something about Hope and her whereabouts."

Eric's tone turned serious. "Do you think he keeps information from us?"

"I think if he gave his word he would keep it and I wonder if he gave Hope his word."

"I can see you have given this much thought."

Colin shook his head. "It is all I have thought about lately. How can a woman of distinctive breeding simply vanish without a trace? If someone wanted her done away with it would have been a simple matter to see to her death. But this Hope appeared to be loved and respected by many. Her own uncle wished her happy and believes her adventurous enough to take off on her own. Then there is the fact that no one has seen her. Not a village I passed through had even caught a glimpse of a woman fitting her description. Why?"

"She hides herself well," Eric suggested.

"That she does, and to do so she would not be able to keep her faithful dog with her."

"This is where Harold comes in?"

"I believe so," Colin said with near certainty.

"Have you discussed this with the lad?"

"He insists he found the dog half starved beside the road, and I must admit when I met them both they were starving, though they worked well together."

"Which leads you to believe that Hope directed the dog to remain with the lad for safekeeping," Eric said, refilling their tankards with more wine.

"It makes sense when nothing else does."

"Talk with the lad."

Colin picked up his tankard. "I have tried and gotten nowhere." He took a generous drink.

"You admire him."

Colin did not bother to deny the truth. "You would think his pint size and small frame would make him lack confidence." He laughed. "Not Harold. He plunges in without thinking, defends the weak when he cannot defend himself and stands beside friends with courage. Aye, I do admire him. For one so young and scrawny he possesses much strength."

"From what you say of him it makes sense to believe he would not betray a friend."

Colin frowned. "You think him a friend of Hope?"

Eric shrugged. "Anything is possible. You met up with the lad along the road and fast became friends. Why not this Hope? A woman in need always attracts men— even the youngest lad."

"True enough; men instinctively wish to protect."

"Children as well as women," Eric said with a knowing smile and a slap to Colin's back.

"Harold is no child," Colin said adamantly and shook his head at his own remark. "But he is no grown man as yet."

"And therefore he needs guidance as a woman needs protecting."

Borg joined them at the table on the dais. "I would not let your wife be hearing you talk like that."

"My wife," Eric boasted, "is intelligent enough to realize that in certain situations a man's strength is needed."

"Or a boy's," Borg said with a laugh and a nod of his head toward the front of the great hall.

Harold had entered behind Bridget and Faith, her attention on Lady who immediately followed Rook in the general direction of the kitchen. She was glad her dog had made a friend though she felt neglected at times. It was a moment after turning her attention away from the dogs that the scuffle had broken out and the two men paying no heed had tumbled directly in Lady Faith's path.

Hope wasted not a moment nor gave her action thought; she simply tossed herself into the two brawling men, sending herself tumbling to the ground along with them.

Colin was over the dais before Eric and they both charged into the melee. Eric grabbed one man, Colin grabbed the other and Harold was left in a crumpled heap on the floor.

Faith grew alarmed and was about to go down on her knees beside Harold when her husband's arm stopped her. "Nay, the lad can stand on his own."

Faith objected most adamantly. "He needs help. He could be seriously injured."

Eric often allowed his wife her way, understanding her need to help the ailing, but he realized of late she had been extremely protective of the lad and it puzzled him. He certainly did not need coddling. "Harold, stand up."

Faith turned wide eyes on her husband, his command holding not a shred of concern.

Eric glared back and repeated his command even more staunchly. "Stand up, lad."

Faith knew better than to defy her husband in front of everyone but her look told him that he would answer to her later this evening.

He simply smiled.

Colin watched with concern, having tossed the man he held aside after ordering him to his quarters along

with the other man involved in the brawl. He would deal
with them later. His worry was now for the lad. He was
not moving and he agreed with Faith; the lad could be
seriously hurt. But he would not go against his lord's
command. So he waited, his worry mounting as Harold
lay motionless on the ground.

The first groan cut into Colin like a sharp knife and
he grimaced, recalling his many altercations when he
was young and the pain that had accompanied them.
While he wished to spare Harold the ordeal, he knew it
was part of the maturing process.

"Up on your feet, lad," Eric ordered more sternly.

Hope heard the devil's command and she wanted
nothing more than to tell him to go to hell but then she
figured he was already there, so what difference would
it make. That crazy thought brought a smile to her face
and another groan to her lips. She realized then that her
lip was split and bleeding, as was her nose, and that one
of her eyes was difficult to open. But the devil had issued a command and she had to obey, did she not?

She grinned to herself, got up on bended knees and
looked up at the devil himself. "I will stand when I damn
well please."

A collective gasp could be heard and from the corner
of her eye she caught the smug grin on Colin's face. He
actually looked pleased with her audacity.

"Good," Eric said, not at all annoyed but well satisfied, "then stand."

"Are you deaf?" Hope all but shouted; at least, to her
ears it was a shout. "I stand when I am ready."

Another collective gasp was heard and Hope thought
she heard Colin chuckle, which quickly turned to a
rough cough—presumably the devil had cast him an accusing eye.

"Good," Eric said again, "then we will all wait for
you."

Hope had not realized she had an audience. The gasps
should have alerted her but her mind remained foggy no

matter how hard she tried clearing it. And it took a moment for her to realize that the devil meant to help her, not harm her. He wanted her to stand on her own, to show all present that the lad was strong and courageous.

The devil truly did have a heart.

"Good," Hope reiterated. "Because now I feel like standing." With that proclamation issued she rose up on weak legs and stood swaying, blood running from her nose and mouth.

Silence followed. Hope chose to break it. "Are you all right, Lady Faith?"

Colin looked on the lad with pride and Eric with admiration; Faith, however, burst into tears.

Eric was taken by surprise and was even more surprised when Faith went to Harold and hugged him, crying on his shoulder, "You are so brave."

Hope was stunned herself, though her womanly instincts kicked in and she slipped her arms around her, offering comfort. "I could not allow anyone to hurt you."

"But you could have been hurt," Faith insisted between tears.

Eric and Colin looked on the scene, a bit confused.

"Better me than you," Hope said, meaning every word.

"And I had thought my situation was difficult." No one understood her remark, though Hope suspected.

Hope lowered her voice, wanting only Faith to hear her words. "I know what I do; do not worry."

Faith collected herself then and drew back away, wiping at her teary eyes. "I apologize for my unmannerly actions. My emotions of late seem to have a mind of their own."

"The babe," Hope said with the shrug of a lad who felt a bit uncomfortable referring to her delicate condition.

"Let me see to your wounds," Faith said with a sniffle.

Hope responded as a lad of twelve would—she stepped back, swiped her sleeve across her nose and mouth and shook her head. "I can see to myself."

Faith seemed upset. "But you need tending."

Eric stepped in, placing an arm around his wife. "The lad is fine; leave him be."

Colin agreed. "A drink or two will clear his head and dull his pain."

"Absolutely not," Faith said with such horror in her voice that the two men glared at her as if she were a complete stranger.

"I could use a drink," Hope said, hoping to divert their attention from Faith who was being too unreasonable about the whole situation.

Faith continued to be unreasonable, however. "You are too young to drink."

Colin laughed. "Quit fussing, my lady; the lad deserves a drink after seeing to your safety." He walked over to Harold and placed an arm around his shoulder.

Hope fought the urge to collapse in his arms. She remained, with much courage, standing on her own.

"Colin is right," Eric said. "The lad deserves praise for a job well done and I myself will raise a glass or two with him."

A chorus of "ayes" circled the hall and tankards began to flow with ale and wine and were passed from hand to hand until one reached Hope.

She took it without hesitation, knowing the drink would dull her senses and the pain.

Eric raised his tankard high. "To Harold, a lad of courage."

"Harold," the crowd echoed his name, raised their glasses and swallowed back their drinks.

Hope joined them, the wine spilling from the corners of her mouth, though she did not care. She was too sore to care about anything. She wondered how anyone could survive being a young lad. She had suffered more bruises, cuts and pains since assuming a lad's identity than she ever had in her entire life.

The drinking and feasting continued with Faith casting a questioning eye to Harold as he downed glass after glass of wine.

The night activities grew more boisterous, or so Hope thought. The singing grew louder, the laughter more robust and voices seemed to resonate throughout the hall—which was a good reason for Hope to continue drinking the offered wine. Wine was known to dull the senses—or was that heighten the senses?

She shook her head at her own confused thoughts.

"What troubles you, lad?" Colin asked, leaning closer to Hope.

Hope smelled the sweet wine on his warm breath and felt the swell of his arm muscle next to her . . . and then there was the scent of his hair—like spring rain.

"Nothing," Hope said with a sense of disappointment for what would never be. Holding hands. A first kiss. A tender touch.

"You need a woman."

Hope choked on the wine she had just swallowed.

Colin hit her on the back.

When she caught her breath, she spoke. "I need nothing."

Colin lowered his voice to a whisper. "The first time is always the most difficult, but you learn after that, and besides—after a fight you need a woman."

Hope lowered her voice, too embarrassed for anyone to hear them, but too curious not to ask, "Why?"

"A rush of excitement. It follows any fight or battle. It rushes the blood and stimulates the senses and makes your passion run hot and heavy until you want nothing more than to drive yourself into a woman."

Strangely enough, she understood him. After her unexpected encounter she felt she was ready to face down the devil himself with a sense of determination that could not be denied.

"Pick a pretty woman for yourself, lad. You deserve a night of fun."

Hope was fast to respond with an adamant, "Nay."

Colin grinned. "There is always a first time, Harold."

She gave a careless shrug like a lad indifferent to his remark.

"I know you are not ignorant of the act itself. You are too intelligent not to know the intimacies of a man and woman. So I assume you are nervous about your first time—a common enough reaction."

Nervous?

If he but knew how she looked forward to sharing the intimate union with a husband of her choice. Someone she cared for and loved and someone who felt the same about her. And love made a difference when two people shared intimacy. She had learned that by listening to the men and from watching the devil and his wife and Borg and Bridget. Aye, love certainly did make a difference.

"Perhaps a good talk man to man would ease your worries," Colin suggested when no answer was forthcoming.

It was an interesting prospect—learning about intimacy from a charming rogue.

She purposely gave pause before answering, allowing Colin to believe that the lad was seriously considering his suggestion but was reluctant to agree.

Colin placed a hand on his shoulder. "I think a talk would do us both good."

Hope was about to agree when Colleen worked her way between them to refill their tankards, an action that was also a blatant effort to capture Colin's attention.

And how could she not succeed, with her full breasts practically shoved in his face.

Colin turned on his charm and with a touch here and a kiss there and a pat where his hand had no business being Colleen bent to whisper in his ear and he agreed with a laugh and a shake of his head.

He looked around Colleen at Harold. "We will talk soon, lad."

Hope could not hide her disappointment or annoyance. "I need no talk from you." She stood and shoved her way past a surprised Colleen. Ignoring all around her on the dais, she stormed off to the kitchen.

Several glances followed the lad's departure, including that of a concerned Colin. He was about to tell Colleen that another time would be better when Faith stood up.

"The lad's wounds need cleaning and tending," she said and with a kiss to her husband's cheek and a whispered promise of her hasty return, she walked off.

Colleen captured Colin's attention once again and with a quick promise to himself to speak with the lad soon, he and Colleen left the hall.

Faith discovered that Harold had left the kitchen as fast as he had entered it, commanding Lady to follow him. Rook of course went along with them both since he followed after Lady wherever she went. It was becoming more and more apparent that they did not wish to be without each other.

Love had struck them both. Faith found Harold at the healing cottage. He was sitting at the table, his face in his hands, softly crying. Lady whined just as softly in sympathy with her head on his lap and Rook looked completely helpless sitting beside her.

The dogs did not announce her entrance nor did Harold realize he had company. He simply continued to cry.

Faith entered the cottage and soundlessly shut the door, closing the world out so that Harold would have his privacy. She approached him slowly. Though the tears were gentle ones Faith recognized the sorrow behind them, and it was with a kind voice she asked, "You care for him as only a woman can, do you not, Hope?"

Fifteen

Hope raised her head slowly and with a gentle swipe of her finger wiped the tears from her eyes. "How long have you known?"

Faith smiled at the feminine lilt in her cultured voice. "Since first we met." She joined Hope at the table, taking the seat opposite her. "I cannot understand how Colin mistakes you for a lad. Your wide eyes alone speak of femininity."

"It has nothing to do with my appearance. A man simply would not think that a woman of good breeding would do something as shocking as disguising herself as a young lad and taking off on her own. The ridiculous thought is not even considered, so therefore Colin would accept how I present myself—a scrawny young lad alone in the world."

Faith nodded in understanding. "And a man would also think a woman too vain to cut her long hair."

"That was difficult." Hope grimaced. "I did it in haste before I could change my mind."

"Was it worth it?"

Hope wiped at the last tear that slipped down her cheek. "I have learned much about life and have learned what it is to truly have a friend." Her tears started again. She could not stop them, nor did she want to.

Faith reached a hand out to her and Hope grasped at the comfort she offered. "I understand how you feel. My husband is my best friend and I would have it no other way. He and I care for each other in ways many would not understand. And I can only assume that Colin touched your heart by befriending the lad."

Hope nodded and took a moment to collect herself. "He was so kind to him, feeding him when he had stolen his food, protecting him and seeing to his care when he was injured. Other men and women I met couldn't care less if the lad lived or died. Colin has taught me much about friendship."

"And by having a chance to come to know him, you have come to care for him."

Hope shook her head at herself. "Foolish. I think myself in love and I barely know the man."

"Do you?"

"Why of course," Hope protested. "The thought is ridiculous. I am probably just enamored by him, as so many women are."

"There is that possibility," Faith agreed, "though you do not speak of his good looks or his charm. You instead speak of his true nature, which you have come to recognize and understand and admire." Faith smiled and patted Hope's hand. "You looked past that charming mask he wears and saw a man worth loving."

"I always thought that when love struck it would be sharp and that my emotions would soar to such dizzying heights I would not be able to deny it. But this?" she shook her head, trying to make sense of her own confusion.

"I sometimes think that love sneaks in when we least expect it."

"Did it with you and Lord Eric?"

Faith grinned like a young girl in love. "Aye, it sneaked up on me and then struck full force until I thought I would go mad for the want of him. But I am glad for the way love found me. I came to know my husband and I discovered he was a good man whom I could easily love."

"There is a kindness to the devil that many do not see."

"Your disguise as a lad has afforded you a rare insight into people; men in particular, I think."

Hope laughed, recalling her journey with the men. "Aye, that it has and I do not regret a moment of my adventure."

"How long do you plan on continuing your charade?"

Hope looked puzzled. "You do not intend on informing Lord Eric of my identity?"

"Heavens no," Faith said with surprise. "I would not betray your confidence, and besides—" She giggled. "I wish to see Colin's face when he learns you are the young woman he searches for."

Hope's own smile faltered. "I did not plan on revealing my identity to him. I thought it best if he never knew."

"Why?"

"He would think I made a fool out of him and then I would lose his friendship, and that would hurt not only him but me."

Faith sounded upset. "But you care for him. How can you simply walk away?"

"What choice do I have? I must wed according to my uncle's arrangements."

"Eric would intercede on your behalf. You must at least give Colin a chance to come to know you as a woman, as Hope."

"Hope is not that different from the lad. She is stubborn and determined like him."

"Then she must also possess the courage and strength the lad demonstrates," Faith insisted.

"Some call it foolishness."

"Fools all of them," Faith said with a laugh.

Hope laughed in spite of her mixed emotions. "Will your husband not grow angry with you if he discovers that you kept my secret?"

"Honesty means much to Eric and I would not lie to

him, but I see no reason for him to question me about the lad's identity. He assumes you are who you say."

"Then he would be angry with me if he discovered my deception," Hope said, growing upset.

"Aye, it would probably disturb him. You have, after all, caused many to worry."

"It was not my intention to cause worry. My uncle and aunt know me well and I had often expressed interest in taking off on an adventure. And many times they attempted to dissuade me."

"But you were determined," Faith said.

Hope attempted to explain her rash actions. "Even as a child I felt the need to explore and learn. I was forever curious and forever asking questions. My parents indulged me and encouraged me. I was lucky that when I went to live with my aunt and uncle they did likewise. But for all my adventurous ways I also knew that I must do what was expected of me. I suppose that was why this particular adventure was so important to me. I realized it most certainly would be my last. And I so wanted to taste life at its fullest."

"And have you?"

Hope thought a moment and shook her head, her eyes gentle in their sadness. "I feel I have barely begun and my heart is heavy with regret, for I know my time is limited." Her expression turned serious. "You will not stop me when I decide it is time to go?"

Faith was honest. "I must know your intentions first."

Hope understood she only wished to protect a friend and so she confided her plans to her. "I will return to Croom Abbey and have the sisters send word to my uncle."

"I must insist that you allow me to have someone accompany you to the abbey so I know that you are safe." Faith sensed her reluctance, and added, "Someone I trust and who will keep your confidence."

Hope nodded. "I thank you for caring and for your help and friendship."

"You would do the same for me; of that I have no doubt."

"Aye, I would, you need only to ask."

Faith smiled. "Then we are true friends, are we not?"

Hope reached out and they grasped hands. "Aye, we are and I am grateful. I have so missed speaking with a woman."

They were sharing an herbal brew when Eric entered the cottage and Hope instantly reverted back to the guarded stance of the young lad.

"You told me you would not be long and I grew worried," he said, his potent size filling the small room.

Faith was honest in her response. "Harold needed a friendly ear to listen."

Eric went to his wife, his hand resting on her shoulder. "Then you are lucky, lad, for my wife listens well." He paused and smiled. "That is, to all but me."

Hope laughed softly. The love the devil had for Faith was so obvious it was palpable and the strong emotion helped ease the ache in Hope's heart.

"I listen," Faith said, feigning indignation.

Eric enjoyed teasing his wife; she proved to be a worthy adversary. "Aye, and then you do as you wish."

Faith leaned her head back to rest against her husband's solid stomach and to look up at him with a smile that stirred his blood. "I wish to do something now."

"Be careful what you wish for, wife," he warned in barely a whisper, as if he fought to control his passion.

Hope, realizing their exchange grew heated, decided her presence was not needed and stood. "I think I need the night air."

"You do not feel well?" Faith asked, concerned.

"Leave the lad be; he knows of what he speaks," Eric said and nodded his silent appreciation.

Hope returned his nod and hastily left the cottage, Lady and Rook on her heels.

The dogs decided her direction, heading straight toward the cooking area for a night treat.

No chill touched the night air, making it clear that spring had come to stay. The dark sky was clear with a partial moon and hundreds of stars winked repeatedly across the sky.

Hope hugged her arms and smiled. She had learned to appreciate the night's beauty, especially the night sky; it never failed to please the eye or warm the heart with its majestic splendor.

Her stomach rumbled, reminding her that she had not eaten much at the evening meal. "A fruit tart would do well right now." She picked up her pace to catch up with the eager animals.

A charming voice in the darkness stopped her as she was about to follow the dogs into the large cooking room.

"I have tarts to share—come join me." Colin stepped out of the darkness to hand the lad a warm wild berry tart.

The sweet scent made Hope's stomach rumble in appreciation and she eagerly reached for it.

"Covet it, lad; Mary's tarts are worth their weight in gold and many a man would risk all to have one. I have taken the last two."

Hope smiled and hugged the tart close to her. "Then we should let no one know of our prizes."

Colin lowered his voice and continued to conspire. "Where should we go with our treasure?"

"The darkness conceals."

"Wise, lad," he said and together they made their way to the large tree that in the daytime partially shielded Faith's herb garden.

Hope sat cross-legged beneath the sheltered branches and Colin sat beside her, his knee resting against her thigh. She wondered over Colleen. Had he hastened his time with her? Had he not spent time with her at all? And why had it seemed that he lay in wait in the darkness? Had he been expecting someone?

She asked him none of the questions that filled her

head. She remained silent and ate the delicious tart.

He unknowingly surprised her with an answer. "I thought you might venture this way. I noticed you barely touched your food this evening."

With a mouthful of tart she was unable to answer, but he supplied it for her.

"Your split lip must have made it difficult to eat."

She nodded, thinking it a perfect excuse. Her lip was tender but it was her emotions that caused her lack of hunger. And now she wondered if perhaps he had dismissed Colleen to tend to Harold. The thought brought a smile to her face.

"Enjoying the tart?"

She was about to nod when she caught Colleen's anxious approach. "Colin, my patience wanes. The lad appears fine and he does not need you worrying over him."

He worried over the lad? And made Colleen wait while he saw that Harold was well? She liked the thought that he cared enough for the lad's well-being to place his passion on hold. And besides, the idea that he would spend an evening pleasuring Colleen and being pleasured by Colleen suddenly did not sit well with her.

"A few minutes, Colleen," Colin coaxed, his hand running along her calf.

"If you must," she said reluctantly, "but only a few. I grow hungry." She ran her tongue slowly over her lips before turning to walk away.

Colin offered Harold his uneaten tart and Hope knew he had taken both tarts for the lad. "I wish to talk with you."

"About what?" she said, her mouth half full and her eye on Colleen, who sat nearby on a stack of chopped wood, seemingly counting the minutes.

"I realized that I never did bother to ask you what you wished of life."

Hope stopped chewing the tart and stared at him.

Her perplexed expression brought a smile to his face, as did the berry stain around her mouth. "When we are young we have dreams and sometimes those dreams are possible if we but try. I would like to know about your dreams."

While she would very much love to discuss her dreams with him—she felt they had much in common— she knew it was the lad who interested Colin, certainly not the spoiled young woman who had selfishly run off.

She answered as she felt the lad would. "Dreaming is a waste of time."

"I am surprised, Harold. I would think you a dreamer of possibilities; all adventurous people are."

Aye, they did think alike. She shrugged. "Life interferes with dreams, so I do not waste my time on what will never be."

"You are too sensible for one so young."

"Life forced maturity on me. I did not ask for it nor want it. But once it was mine I accepted the responsibility that went with it. I will do what I must in life." Truer words she had never spoken, and the truth of them tore at her heart.

Colin placed a comforting hand on the lad's knee. "Shanekill is a good place to find one's dreams."

The warmth of his hand penetrated her stocking and ran a pleasurable tingle up her leg. Why? Why could she not ignore this attraction to him? Had she fallen so blindly in love that she could not make sense of her senses?

"Colin," came a whining plea from Colleen. "The night grows late and I grow more eager."

Hope felt like shoving the last of the fruit tart right in her smiling face. This was her chance to spend time talking with Colin, and the annoying wench had to interfere.

"A moment," Colin said.

A moment was not long enough for Hope. Her time was limited and she suddenly wished to spend much of it with Colin—to come to know him well and to have good memories of him to take with her when she left.

She had to find a way to keep him talking with the lad while ridding them of Colleen. She took another bite of the tart while giving thought to her dilemma when suddenly her stomach cramped. Instinctively her hand went to the pain and she moaned out loud.

"What is wrong?" Colin demanded, his arm slipping around the lad who sat doubled over.

"An ache—that is all," she insisted when she realized her monthly time was near and making itself known. Unfortunately another cramp seized her and she could not stop the suffering sound of another moan.

"You are not well," Colin insisted. "I will take you to Faith."

Hope recalled what the devil and his lady were doing and did not wish to interrupt them. And she told Colin just that. "The lord and his lady are busy at the cottage."

Colin seemed to think nothing of it. "Then I will settle you in my quarters and seek Bridget's aid."

Hope knew she could have no one tend her but Faith. She purposely moaned again and this time more loudly. "Nay, I wish Lady Faith; she will know what ails me."

Colin would agree to anything the lad asked, as long as he suffered no longer. "I will fetch Lady Faith for you once you are settled."

He stood, leaned over and scooped the lad up into his arms.

Hope was stunned not only by his actions but by the feel of his hard chest and the strength of his strong arms and the tenderness of his heart. The last bit of tart fell from her hand to the ground and Hope clasped her hands together to rest on her stomach, so fearful was she that she would throw her arms around his neck and hold on tightly to him.

"Another time, my love," he said to a disappointed Colleen as he neared her. "I promise."

Colleen's smile was bittersweet and her offer generous. "If there is anything I can do to help the lad."

"Aye, there is. Find Bridget and tell her to go fetch

Lady Faith. She is at the healing cottage with Lord Eric."

Colleen nodded. "As you wish." And off she went.

Lady's head came up instantly from where she lay curled by the hearth with Rook. She whined and immediately rushed to Hope, sniffing frantically at her dangling legs and following as Colin carried her into the great hall and up the stairs.

Rook followed Lady, though remaining calm and on guard.

Hope was surprised at the comfort of Colin's room. The bed was large and draped with fine linens in the deepest of blues. Several beautifully crafted tapestries covered the walls. A desk with numerous candles, parchment, ink pots and quills sat against one wall and two large chests with scarves in foreign designs draped across them sat against another. In front of the burning hearth that toasted the room with an even warmth were two wooden chairs with intricately carved arms and legs.

It was obvious Colin had made this room his home, his refuge from the world, his solace. And Hope knew then that he had never brought a woman here. Never, that was, until this night.

He gently laid her on the bed, placing his hand to her head.

"I do not suffer from the fever. An ache in my stomach pains me." She grimaced at the cramp that tormented her.

"Something you ate, perhaps?"

"Lady Faith will know what to do," Hope assured him, wanting to ease his needless worry.

He nodded and walked away from the bed for a moment to return with a cloth that he used to wipe the berry juice from around her mouth. He gave a gentle pat, applying a slight pressure in the corners of her mouth. "You enjoyed the tarts."

"They were delicious." She smiled, and for a brief second his finger slipped into her mouth, faintly brushing her tongue. She shuddered from the taste of him.

He seemed momentarily stunned and then he shook himself as though forcing himself to wake. "You are chilled." He pulled up the wool blanket that lay folded at the foot of the bed and covered the lad to his chin. He then sat beside him on the bed.

Hope wished he would remain there by her side. His presence alone made her feel better. But dreams were not meant to be—she shut her eyes tightly against that disturbing thought.

Colin seemed instinctively to know the lad's need. "Rest, Harold; I will remain by your side."

Until Faith came, she thought, and then he would remain beside her no more and this private time with him would be done.

"Rest; I am with you."

His caring words brought tears to her eyes and she kept them tightly closed, refusing to cry, refusing to admit what her aching heart told her, refusing to love.

Refusing to dream.

Sixteen

Faith chased Colin from the room, insisting she required privacy to tend to the ailing lad. He paced the hall outside his quarters along with Eric who patiently leaned against the stone wall.

"What draws you so to this lad?" Eric asked.

Colin stopped pacing and pondered the question with serious concern. "I cannot say for certain. There is something about him that makes me wish to protect him, though if he were larger in size I have no doubt he could protect himself, given his sheer determination."

Eric agreed with a smile and a nod. "He can be stubborn, but then I suppose his stubbornness aids his courage."

Colin ran a quick hand through his hair, his frustration obvious. "He gets himself involved in countless situations that he does not possess the physical strength to tackle."

"Like this evening, when he used his puny body to protect my wife?"

"Aye, precisely," Colin said and realizing his remark, shook his head. "Eric, I meant no disrespect to you—"

Eric held a hand up to silence him. "I understand your concern, but I think you fail to realize the lad's true nature. He cares deeply enough to think of others before himself. He has a strength of character that is remarkable in one so young and he should be guided wisely so that he may reach his full potential."

Colin attempted to respond but Eric's look warned he was not finished.

"What I want to know, Colin, is why this deep concern for this lad?"

Colin looked about to protest his remark when he suddenly changed his mind and simply shook his head. "I cannot say. Since first we met I felt the need to see to his safety. He is bold and blunt and often too foolish and yet—" Colin shrugged. "As you said, he cares deeply. He thought nothing of risking his own life to save Stuart's."

"The character of a true warrior. He goes into battle with not himself in mind but his courage strong and his mind prepared."

Colin threw his hands up. "But he is scrawny with barely an ounce of muscle on him and those wide eyes of his sometimes remind me of a frightened deer caught in the sights of a marksman."

"A deer that obviously will not surrender."

"True enough and with a large, fearful dog who should protect but instead requires protection. They make a strange pair."

"Rook seems to find her attractive," Eric said with a grin.

"Do you see how Lady sits beside the bed, her head near Harold's hand, and whines as if it is she that suffers and needs consoling rather than her master?" Another rake of his hair and another pace or two saw to his frustration before he once again stopped. "When I met him he barely knew where his next meal would come from but he made certain Lady ate. When the men dragged the thieving, whining dog into camp he ran to her protection, caring not of his own safety or hunger. And he shared every morsel of food with that dog."

"Obviously the lad knows how to love."

"I think he hungers for it."

"As do you," Eric said firmly.

"You are not going to start again about finding me a wife, are you?"

Eric laughed. "I need to do nothing. It is in Faith's hands."

"Lord help me."

"I think he is on her side." Eric laughed harder, to Colin's annoyance.

"I have met no one that I wish to spend the rest of my life with."

"You never take the time to know any woman," Eric accused. "You bed them and forget them."

"It is the best way."

"Why? Do you fear being hurt? Disappointed?"

Colin went to lean against the wall next to Eric. "I have known few marriages where the husband and wife loved each other. They married out of duty and necessity."

"I love Faith."

"Not when you married her."

"Soon after I realized that I did," Eric insisted.

"Then I should take the chance and wed a stranger and hope that I fall in love with her?" He answered his own question with an adamant shake of his head. "Look at this Hope and the trouble she causes. However will her husband deal with her spirited nature?"

"Spirited, not spoiled?" Eric asked.

"Perhaps a little of both."

"If he were wise and cared for her he would give her spirit free rein and love her for who she truly is. That is love, is it not? Allowing the one you love to be who she is."

Colin smiled. "You have grown wiser since becoming a husband."

Eric grinned and laughed. "My wife is a good teacher."

"I wonder if this Hope will teach her husband so well."

"Or will he allow her to?"

"So we return to the question," Eric said, his dark eyes intent on an answer. "Why do you fear love?"

Colin was trapped. His lord expected an answer and that meant he had to face the question. He remained in his own thoughts for a moment, attempting to formulate a good answer. In the end he answered as honestly as he could, surprising himself. "I fear I will never find it. Never find the love that I desire. Never find the woman I can make forever mine."

"Which is why you envy the lad."

Colin looked confused.

"The lad loves unconditionally. He does not care if his dog is a coward and needs protecting; he loves her. He does not care that he is puny in size; he fights anyway. He charges into life with the strength of his convictions and loves with an undaunting courage."

"And you think I do not possess the courage to love?" He sounded indignant.

Eric placed a firm hand on his shoulder. "You have courage, Colin, but you refuse to let it guide you, where love is concerned. How can you ever find a woman to love if you do not take love seriously?"

Colin thought over Eric's words.

"You wish to teach the lad what he needs to survive in this world and yet he can teach you as well. Learn from each other and you both will benefit."

Faith stepped out of the room, softly closing the door behind her. "I have given Harold something that will help his ailing stomach, though I suspect he will have a fretful sleep. I thought I might stay with him throughout the night, so if he wakes I can see that he takes more of the brew I prepared."

"I will sit with the lad and see to his care," Colin offered without hesitation.

Faith worried that such intimate quarters might cause a problem for Hope, and her reluctance showed.

Eric slipped his arm around his wife's expanded

waist. "Colin is capable of seeing to the lad and you need your rest."

Faith's need to protect her friend brought a protest to her lips but she caught it before it slipped out, her instincts informing her that perhaps the two needed time alone to become better acquainted.

"I will give you instructions," she said to Colin with such a sweet smile that her husband furrowed his brow and rested a curious look on her—one she chose to ignore.

Eric waited just inside the room as his wife instructed Colin about his duties. She then joined her husband, taking his hand, her smile remaining much too sweet. She was up to something—he knew it. He could question her, for she was forever honest with him, but she did know how to evade the issue if she so chose. Nay, he would watch her carefully and discover for himself what she was about.

They quietly left the room, leaving Colin to watch over the lad.

Colin moved a chair near the bed to keep a watchful eye on Harold. Faith had borrowed a soft linen tunic of his for the lad to wear as a night rail and had scrubbed his face so clean that his split lip and bruised eye stood out in stark contrast to his pale complexion. He looked small and helpless huddled beneath the wool blanket, and Colin felt a surge of protection rush over him.

What was this compulsion he had to protect the lad?

Why this need to look after him? Especially when the lad asked no favors of him. He was content enough on his own. Yet Colin could not let it go; his need to see to Harold's safety and well-being forever haunted him.

Lady whined softly, her head resting on the bed beside Harold.

"Hush, Lady, your master needs his rest," Colin said in a soft yet firm whisper.

Lady simply whined again, her large eyes resting on

Harold and then turning to Colin as if the animal expected him to do something.

Colin called Lady to him. She was reluctant to leave her perch, but Colin's command turned firm and with one last whine she moved to Colin's side.

He gave her head a pat and her ear a rub and offered consoling words. "Harold is fine. You need not worry. I will take care of him."

Lady seemed to understand and rested her head on Colin's knee, her whining at an end.

"You are lucky, Lady," Colin whispered. "Harold loves you even with all your faults."

A soft whine told him she agreed, and then Lady settled herself at his feet to sleep.

Colin rested his head back against the chair. Was that what he was searching for? Someone to love him unconditionally, faults and all, just as he was willing to love someone. He was not interested in perfection. Perfection harbored selfishness and boredom. He did not wish to be trapped in a loveless marriage where the husband and wife tolerated each other and mated to produce the expected number of heirs.

He wished a wife who sought her bed with enthusiasm and bore his children out of love.

Colin closed his eyes. Eric did not know how very lucky he was to have Faith. Their love was enduring and would last this lifetime and beyond—a forever kind of love.

Harold understood such a love. He gave it to Lady and he would give it to the one he fell in love with. Unconditionally. Forever.

Colin faded off to sleep, love heavy on his mind.

Hope woke near dawn and stretched slowly beneath the covers. She had a restful sleep and her body felt good. No cramps, no pains or aches; she felt refreshed and the feeling brought a smile to her face.

The smile faded when she caught sight of Colin slumped over in sleep in a chair beside the bed. She instantly came awake, though she hovered protectively beneath the covers.

The previous night came rushing back to her and her heart set to beating irrationally. She had spent the night in Colin's bed with him asleep in the nearby chair. This was not good. It was dangerous, much too dangerous.

She should be grateful that she had not woken at all during the night or talked in her sleep or any number of incidents that could have occurred with them in such close proximity. Her disguise at the moment, a linen tunic she assumed belonged to Colin, was too precarious. There was not a sufficient amount of clothing between him and her.

Her most pressing problem, though, was slipping out of the room without waking him. She wanted to place as much distance between them as possible, at least until she could dress and resume the role of the lad Harold. At the moment she felt too much a woman and he was too much of an appealing man to completely ignore.

His body slumped in deliberate invitation. His muscles, while relaxed, possessed definitive structure that caught the eye and his long legs stretched out in welcome. And since Hope was not one to waste time or ponder whether her action was right or wrong, she focused a purposeful glance below his waist.

Her smile grew. He certainly seemed endowed from what she could see, a fact that naturally stirred her interest.

He moved restlessly in the chair before settling once again, and the thought that he would wake while Hope was in his bed set her into action.

She spied her clothes folded neatly near the fireplace and she leaned over the bed, certain she would find Lady sleeping beside it. She was surprised to see her sleeping at Colin's feet—and a sound sleep at that, since she snored lightly.

Hope quietly slipped from beneath the covers, hunching down beside Lady to wake her with a gentle tap and a finger to her mouth. She had learned quickly enough that this command meant silence.

Hope walked past Colin on tiptoes and Lady gave him a wide berth as she made her way past him to follow her master. With a snatch of her clothes from the bench she flew to the door.

"Do not touch that handle or you will be sorry."

She froze, all the blood draining from her face, leaving her pale and shaken. She turned to face him, a definite mistake since he had stood and looked a more formidable adversary than the slumped, sleeping man.

"I am feeling fit." Her trembling voice opposed her remark.

Colin made no move to approach her. "Back in bed."

His order was firm, leaving no room to doubt that he intended to have it obeyed. She thought otherwise. She could not possibly remain in his bed. She attempted to inch herself closer to the door. If her hand could reach the latch, she could make it out of the room in a flash, and she was fast on her feet when necessary.

She decided a few words of appreciation might keep him occupied as she took cautious steps. "I app—"

He moved so fast she barely had time to catch a breath. His hands reached out and she shut her eyes tight and cringed.

His hands landed with a solid thud against the door.

She was trapped between him and the door. She felt the warmth of his body just fresh from sleep and smelled the scent of him, a woodsy odor so crisp and clear that it tantalized the senses.

She warned herself to keep her eyes closed, not to peek or even look up at him, but her own potent desires were fast grabbing hold and sensible reasoning was fast slipping away.

Mistake.

She knew it as soon as her eyes focused on his face. He was near, much too near, and he was much too appealing. He wore no charming smile; actually she liked this look he wore so easily. It was one of concern and caring, though tempered by his stubborn side; but it fit him well. And his dark eyes were soft and warm; no chill or indifference stared back, simply the knowledge that he cared. This touched her heart and caused a flutter to her stomach.

It was his lips, though, that caused her legs to tremble. They seemed so inviting, as though they begged for her to nibble at them, become acquainted with them, to taste to her heart's content.

A sudden change in his expression warned her that she was treading on dangerous ground. Had he noticed something in her eyes? Did they betray her feelings? Was she foolishly behaving like a woman?

She sought to correct her mistake and spoke with the brashness of the lad. "I take care of myself."

Colin shook his head slowly, his hands remaining firm against the door and his voice gentle though unyielding. "We are all family here, Harold, and we look after each other. Whether you like it or not, I care and wish to see you well. And since you are a stubborn lad who does not think before he acts, I will see to it that you do not suffer from your own foolishness. Now into bed with you."

Hope thought to protest and in that brief moment she realized that if she did object that he would only reach down, hoist her over his shoulder and place her in bed. And if that happened then he surely would discover her gender.

She wisely nodded her obedience and Colin stepped back and pointed at the bed, his action reiterating his command.

He snatched the clothes from her arms as she ran past him and on rushed feet she hurried over to the bed and slipped beneath the covers, pulling them up to her chin.

Colin shook his head again and dumped the bundle of clothes back on the bench. "Your legs are much too skinny, as are you. You need to put some weight on that puny body."

Hope understood that he thought her a lad and spoke out of concern. But his words hurt anyway. She had always thought of herself as shapeless, much too thin, her small breasts barely a handful. She worried her narrow hips would cause her birthing difficulties, or so she had been warned by older women.

She often wondered if her husband would be disappointed in her body and find himself not at all attracted to her. But then he had a duty, as did she. Still, it would be so nice to have someone love her for her and her alone, shapeless as she was.

"I meant no offense, Harold," Colin said, sitting in the chair by the bed. Lady sat beside him, her nose slipping beneath his hand in an attempt to let him know she wanted attention. Without hesitation he rubbed behind her ear.

Hope was not at all surprised. Lady was content here and becoming more familiar and friendly with everyone with each passing day, especially Colin. Lady and Rook, who were inseparable, followed him around almost as much as they did her.

Sadly, this place was feeling more and more like home and leaving would be difficult.

Colin continued when the lad failed to respond. "You will need strength to defend yourself."

Hope decided to demonstrate just how capable she was of defending herself, though in a manner unfamiliar to men. She chose wit and words as her weapons. "Size does not matter if one possesses intelligence."

Colin admired the lad's bravado and how he chose to defend himself. Most men did not possess the intellect to verbally spar with an opponent and here this pint-sized lad dared to challenge with wisdom. "A formidable weapon, intelligence, though a cunning mind still at times requires the aid of physical strength."

Hope shook her head. "A weak mind would resort to

physical strength. The cunning mind would discover a way around it or through it."

"You speak with confidence." He braced his one foot on the edge of the bed and steepled his fingers. Then he smiled, charmingly. "How then was it that I caught you so easily the night you attempted to rob my camp?"

A soft laughter mingled with her response. "How then was it that I ate your food and slept well protected after attempting to rob you?"

Colin dropped his foot off the bed and leaned forward, annoyance evident in his tone. "Words failed to prevent you from being beaten in a fight. Physical strength was what you needed."

Hope sat up and spoke firmly. "There comes many a time when a man must stand up for his convictions no matter the consequences. My words fell on ignorant ears, but that did not mean that I should not speak them, for then I would betray my own beliefs. And a few cuts and bruises would do me no permanent harm, but betraying myself would do everlasting damage."

Colin was impressed. The lad possessed a wisdom far beyond his young years. "Who taught you so wisely?"

Hope answered honestly and with pride. "My father."

"He must have been a very wise man."

"He taught me much of which I am grateful."

"And one day I am certain he would have taught you to defend yourself as every man must learn to do." Colin spoke calmly like a father attempting to teach a son.

Hope opened her mouth but it was not her voice they heard.

"This young man is not partaking in any physical activities unless I grant permission," Faith said from the open doorway, the devil standing beside her wearing a large grin.

Seventeen

Hope kept a watchful eye on Colin. Within a day's time she felt fine and required no further bed rest. She was anxious to be up and about, exploring and learning before it was time for her to depart. Faith had seen to it that she was given no cumbersome chores or practice sessions with the men. Her duties consisted of helping Faith, and Faith seemed to understand that she yearned for time to explore and generously gave it to her.

Her explorations gave her the freedom to discover, which she loved doing. One of the discoveries she was not pleased with was that Colin seemed to be in her presence more often than not. He would suddenly appear out of nowhere and engage the lad in a conversation or a challenging debate.

She had the feeling he wished to discover as well, but what was it that he wished to discover? The thought unnerved her and made her more attentive to his actions and whereabouts. She could not chance discovery now, particularly not under her present conditions, here at Shanekill. The knowledge of her identity would upset too many people.

The evening meal was presently being served and Hope sat at a table not far from the dais watching the way one particular servant woman was being overly attentive to Colin. He did not have to lift a finger. She was there beside him whenever his goblet needed filling or if he required another serving of stew.

She would lean her shapely body into him when she poured ale from the earthenware pitcher and her breasts would graze his cheek when she refilled his bread trencher with the tasty rabbit stew.

It was obvious she desired him and what annoyed Hope was that the thought actually disturbed her. And that made her realize just how much her emotions and desires were growing in strength. Then, to make it worse, there was the thought that she could do nothing about it. Unless of course she divulged her identity and then he would probably be angry at her deception and never speak to her again.

The situation was hopeless.

Colin turned on his charm, obviously interested in an audacious and, to Hope's dismay, attractive woman.

Lady appeared to agree with her sentiments, offering a low growl followed by a sympathetic whine which caused Rook, who sat beside his ladylove, to give her a gentle lick on the face.

Hope watched the woman work her female wiles and it did not take long for Colin to stand and, with the slip of his arm around her waist, direct her out of the hall.

Hope frowned and then grew annoyed. She looked down at the two animals who looked up at her as if in wait of a command, and she smiled. "I think Colin wishes to see the two of you."

Lady gave her master a quick lick on the face, barked softly and ran toward her intended mark. Rook eagerly followed.

Hope sat at the table, her hands firmly around her goblet of wine, and watched a bit of chaos begin.

Lady instantly went for Colin's hand, forcing her nose beneath his palm and barking loudly. Rook, as though understanding her actions, followed suit, pushing his way between him and the woman.

"Whatever do you two want?" Colin asked, his smile fading as he attempted to move Rook out of the way.

This was not an easy task since a simple shove would have no affect on the large animal.

Lady barked again and looked to the doors of the hall.

"You wish to go for your nightly walk?" he asked.

Lady barked and started for the door, Rook joining her.

"Lady, go find Harold. He will take you."

Lady barked, jumped and turned in circles, as if demonstrating she could not wait. It was urgent that she go out immediately.

Colin shook his head, grabbed the woman's hand and headed for the door. "You will hurry and be done with your duties."

Lady barked her agreement.

Hope smiled and then downed her wine. Lady would do as she pleased, a thought which pleased Hope. She poured herself more wine and joined in the conversation going on around her.

Colin decided the cool spring night air and the star-studded sky were conducive to romance and he drew Kathleen into his arms, intending to kiss her.

Lady had other ideas and her loud bark snapped the pair instantly apart.

"What is the problem now?" Colin asked, irritated.

Lady jumped up and down, or at least she attempted to—her large size barely allowed her to get off the ground. Rook joined in, realizing she wanted to play.

"Absolutely not," Colin said sternly, understanding the pair. "It is not time to play. It is time to do your duties and be done with it."

Lady had no intention of listening. She would have it her way. She ran off and in a moment's time returned with a fat stick, dropping it at Colin's feet.

Kathleen laughed softly. "I think Lady has a mind of her own."

"Just like her master," Colin grumbled.

Kathleen defended the lad. "Harold is a fine lad, respectful and helpful."

"And obstinate."

Lady barked again and it was Kathleen who reached down, picked up the stick and tossed it for Lady and Rook to fetch.

"He is confident and determined for his young age," Kathleen said.

"Obstinate," Colin repeated and tossed the stick Rook had dropped at his feet.

Kathleen bristled and took a step away from him. "I like the lad and I admire him. He is good to all he meets and he is wise with his words."

Colin crossed his arms over his chest and turned a chilling stare on her. "The lad seems a bit young for you, Kathleen."

"That is not the way of it and you know that, Colin," she said, her own arms crossing her generous chest like a shield. "Though I daresay the lad has had no interest in females since his arrival. I would say his experience and possibly education is lacking considerably when it comes to intimacy."

It was the way she addressed him accusingly, as though it was his own fault that Harold had experienced no interludes since their arrival that annoyed Colin. "Say what you mean, Kathleen."

She did. "You seem to feel responsible for the lad. The whole keep gossips about your fatherly instincts and how you see to his care. Well, it seems to me you have neglected a vital area that all young men need direction in." She had to smile when she finished, and added, "And one that you excel at."

Colin noticed that it had grown quiet and looked to see Lady and Rook sitting side by side as though patiently waiting for the two of them to finish their discussion. "So you are done."

Neither dog made a sound; they simply stared at him. He shook his head.

Kathleen walked over to him with a gentle sway of her hips and slipped her arm through his. "I think you will make an excellent father when you find the right woman to wed. Tonight, though—" She kissed his cheek softly. "I wish to have a lover."

He turned his lips to hers and he was suddenly propelled away from her. He looked down to see that Lady had wedged herself between them.

She barked at him.

"Now what?"

She ran toward the great hall doors.

He shook his head and took Kathleen's hand. "Come, let me make certain that Lady is safely delivered to her master. And then . . ."

His sensual smile told her all that she needed to know. She eagerly followed along.

Hope felt good. She had downed countless goblets of wine and shared congenial conversation and her constant grin affirmed the fact that she was content, though no one guessed it was because her dog was at this moment keeping Colin from bedding a woman.

"Have another, lad," Stuart said, filling Harold's empty goblet.

Hope did not argue. She had never tasted such fine wine and the food was always was delicious. She found herself eating and drinking nonstop this evening and sharing good company. Even the devil, whose keen eye fell often on her this evening, could not disturb her good feelings.

And besides, Faith had a way of diverting her husband's attention often throughout the meal.

Mary, Stuart's wife and the keep's cook, joined them, placing a plate of fresh hot rum cakes on the table. Everyone eagerly reached for one, including Hope.

Merriment reached its peak when Colin entered the great hall. Song filled the air, boisterous conversation circled the room and wine and ale flowed freely.

He thought to remain and join in the revelry, but Kathleen's warm body pressing close to his as they made their way around the tables made him think twice.

Lady hurried to Hope, and Rook went to Faith, dutifully checking on her as he so often did throughout the day if she was not close by.

Colin was about to turn and take his leave when he noticed how Harold swayed when he stood to greet Lady. He watched a moment more and realized that the lad was well into his cups and one of the men at the table was filling his goblet again.

"Let him be," Kathleen whispered in his ear. "He is young and must learn his own lessons."

Colin realized the truth of her words, though he did not wish to see Harold suffer because of too much drink. He also knew the truth of Kathleen's words. It was the lad's lesson to learn.

He slipped his arm around Kathleen's waist and, deciding he had wasted enough time, directed her with hasty steps out of the hall.

Hope caught sight of the pair leaving and her heart felt heavy, as though someone had squeezed the life from her. She sighed loudly and Lady whined in sympathy. Rook had returned to Lady's side and decided he would add his own mournful whine.

"What is it, lad?" Stuart asked, concerned.

The generous amounts of wine she had consumed added to her already courageous nature and she said directly, "Tell me of love, Stuart."

Stuart drew back and shook his head. "Lad, there is not a man alive who can tell you of love. Men simply do not understand it."

"Why?"

His answer was simple. "It does not make sense."

"Why?" Hope asked again, swaying in her seat.

Stuart shrugged. "Love is not reasonable. It is much like a battle. You think you are prepared, you charge in, but chaos reigns."

"Love is chaotic, then?"

"Continually," he answered with a laugh.

Mary added her own thoughts on the subject as she

placed a rum cake in front of her husband and another one in front of the lad. "Love is different for each person. Some fall in love fast, some slowly and some without noticing it at all."

"So what you are saying is that there is no definitive answer to love," Hope said, shaking her head in disappointment.

"Do not worry, lad," Stuart advised. "You will know love when it strikes you."

Hope munched on the cake, licking the crumbs from her fingers. "But will I know if it is the right love? A true love . . . a forever love." She shook her head again and then plopped her chin in her hands, her elbows resting on the table.

Mary smiled. "You will know different loves in your life or think them loves until one appears and then . . ." Her words drifted off and her smile widened as she looked into her husband's eyes. "Then you will have no doubt. You will simply know."

Hope sighed heavily.

"That sounds like a sigh of someone who already fancies himself in love," Mary said with a wink.

Hope shot up straight in her seat. "Nay," she protested quickly, then realized that Mary could not know of her feelings for Colin, for she thought her a lad.

Stuart joined in the good-natured teasing. "What woman has caught your fancy, lad?"

Hope had come to understand the ways of men more than she ever thought possible and she chose her words with her newfound knowledge in mind. " 'Tis your wife who has won my heart, Stuart."

Stuart laughed and leaned across the table. "Every man fancies my Mary, not only for her beauty but for her cooking skills."

"Go on with your tall tales," Mary scolded playfully, though her full cheeks blushed pink.

Stuart gave his wife a sound kiss on her lips and her cheeks turned scarlet. Stuart laughed and nuzzled her neck. She giggled and leaned more closely against him.

Hope envied the loving couple. They had found true love. But then no marriage had been arranged for them. They had made their own choices. Their lives belonged to them.

"Let yourself love, Harold," Stuart said. "It will be the only way you find the love you search for."

Was it that obvious she looked for love that she could not keep it out of the eyes of a young lad? Or had these feelings for Colin surfaced without her realizing it? Did she actually wear her heart where all could see?

She stood grasping the edge of the long table. Her head grew light and the hall spun in front of her eyes.

"Are you all right, lad?" Stuart asked.

"Aye, that I am, Stuart, though I would be better if I could call Mary mine."

Her teasing brought a laugh from them both and on swaying legs Hope took herself off, Lady keeping close by her side.

Hope thought to go to the healing cottage. She had called it her own since their arrival and enjoyed the privacy it afforded her. But her thoughts continued to center on Colin. At this moment he was with that woman being intimate.

Her stomach rumbled and her head spun. She did not feel at all well. She could seek out Faith and ask for a calming brew, but the last time she had looked, the devil and his lady were snuggled tightly to each other and it seemed they did not wish to be disturbed.

She took slow steps to the great hall doors, the distance she had to travel to get to them appearing miles away. It seemed like an endless journey until her hand finally touched the metal latch and she opened the door.

The cool spring air would normally have invigorated her but with all the wine and food she had consumed, the night air only managed to worsen her condition. She wanted nothing more than to make her way to the healing cottage and fall into bed.

She stumbled over her own feet as she attempted to get to her destination. The more steps she took, the more her stomach protested, the more her head spun and the more she doubted she would remain alive.

She braced herself against almost every cottage she passed by and she knew eventually the cottages would end and she would be on her own. There would be nothing for her to lean on. She doubted she had the strength to stand without support.

"Lady, I do not think I will make it," she said, rounding the last cottage and seeing the void of darkness stretch out before her.

Lady whined in worry and watched as her master took cautious steps forward, her hand reluctantly moving off the wall of the nearby cottage.

It took only seconds for Hope to realize her error. She had drunk far too much wine this night and was now reaping the consequences. She took two more steps when suddenly her protesting stomach revolted and she was forced to her knees to empty it.

Lady whined loudly, paced back and forth beside her and, after listening to Hope wretch for a moment or two, took off.

Hope felt too sick to worry that her dog had abandoned her. Besides, she was dying—she had to be, she felt so horribly ill. The sooner death claimed her the better off she would be.

Tears trickled down her cheeks. She would never know love. She would never wed. She would never bear children. She would die a drunken young lad.

Hope wretched again.

Colin stood bare-chested, about to remove the last of his clothing and his boots, ready and eager to join Kathleen who was lying naked in her bed, when he heard the bark, sounding loud and clear.

He shook his head, intending to ignore it.

It sounded again, this time frantically.

Colin looked to Kathleen. "My apologies."

Kathleen gave him a sorrowful smile. "Another time, Colin, promise me."

"You have my promise," he said with a smile that made his departure all the more difficult for her.

Colin slipped on his tunic as he followed a frantic Lady.

He heard the sound of retching before he rounded the corner of the cottage.

Lady stopped beside her master and barked as if she expected Colin to make her well.

Hope breathed a heavy sigh. "Thank God you have returned, Lady. I am dying."

"Nay, you are not."

Hope did not have the strength to turn and look at Colin and she preferred not to gaze upon him one last time. The sorrow would be too much to bear, but then she was dying, so what difference could it possibly make.

She shook her head at her own confused musings.

"You drank too much," Colin said and stepped forward.

"Go away," Hope ordered, her hand waving him away. "I wish to die alone."

Colin laughed and went down on bended knees beside the lad. "You are not dying."

"I must be," she insisted. "One cannot feel this horrible and not be dying."

"Believe me, one can."

"Death would be a relief compared to this suffering."

"I have thought the same myself often enough."

"And still you drink?" she asked incredulously. She herself did not intend to take another sip of wine. Never, ever again.

"As will you." His soft laughter irritated her.

"I am no fool to cause myself to suffer so again."

"Believe me, Harold, all men are fools when it comes to drink and women."

"I know not enough of either, nor do I wish to," she

said adamantly. She hugged her sore stomach and yawned, wishing she was in bed and wondering how she would get there.

Colin realized the lad possessed limited knowledge where women and drink were concerned and required guidance and understanding—but not right now. Now he needed a soothing brew to help settle his aching stomach and a soft bed to sleep his suffering away.

"Can you stand?" he asked.

Hope did not even want to try, but what choice did she have? If he scooped her up in those powerful arms of his she would be absolutely lost and probably do something terribly stupid.

So with as much strength as she could muster she brought herself up to stand on trembling legs.

"The cottage is not far," Colin said as if offering hope.

Unless it was directly in front of her, it would do little good, she thought. Her legs were barely supporting her and she did not know how she would ever find the strength to make them obey her.

She closed her eyes and whispered to herself. "You must have strength."

She had repeated those words often after her parents had died and she had always found the strength needed. But then that was an emotional strength she sought. This was purely physical. Still, she would not surrender to any weakness. She would fight and keep fighting.

She took a step forward.

Colin admired the lad's effort but knew it was useless. He stepped forward and caught him just as he fell face forward toward the ground.

Eighteen

"Out!" Colin shouted. "Out and stay out!"

"Do not yell at the lad," Kathleen scolded, holding the soft wool blanket up over her bare breasts.

Colin looked ready to kill. Ever since two nights ago when he had tucked Harold safely and soundly into bed, the lad had plagued him. He seemed dauntless in his intentions of disrupting his social life. Whenever he was with a woman Harold suddenly appeared. And if it was not Harold it was Lady. She would whine and grumble and make a complete nuisance of herself until Colin finally paid attention to her.

He felt as if his intimate life was being sabotaged and he had no intention of allowing it to happen. It stopped here and now.

"Go away, Harold," he ordered, sitting up in bed and glaring at the lad who peeked around the edge of the door.

"But the devil wants you," Hope insisted, though the devil had only mentioned Colin's name, never actually demanded his presence. Hope merely wanted to make certain that Colin's interlude was interrupted. She had of late felt the need to rescue him from senseless liaisons. She told herself it was for his own good, that if he thought of it he would realize that he should concentrate on a permanent relationship, not on meaningless encounters.

At least, she attempted to convince herself of that.

"I think you need to talk with the lad," Kathleen said, disturbed by the interruption since the last three times Colin and she attempted to get together, Harold had interrupted. "He needs some fatherly advice."

"I am not his father," Colin said in a harsh whisper.

"You are a fatherly figure to him and have looked after him since first finding him. He is your responsibility."

Colin mumbled incoherently beneath his breath as he threw the bed covers off himself and stood.

Hope quickly diverted her eyes from his naked body, then, realizing she had no reason not to look upon him, took full advantage of the fact that she was thought of as a boy. She watched Colin with indifference as he shoved his garments on in annoyance.

He possessed a magnificent body—lean and muscled and flowing in a fluid strength that pleased the eyes and senses. Kathleen seemed to agree, watching him with an appreciative eye herself.

"I will be back momentarily," Colin said with certainty.

Kathleen laughed. "Somehow I doubt that."

He sent her a scathing look for doubting his word.

She thought better of her remark. "But I will wait with high hopes of your immediate return."

"I suggest that you do," he said with none of his usual charm.

Hope decided now would be a good time to take her leave. She had accomplished what she had set out to do, keeping him from Kathleen's bed. She slowly moved away from the door.

"Do not dare move," Colin shouted, approaching the partially closed door with determined strides.

Hope almost ran, but thought better of it. Colin would only search her out, and then? She leaned against the stone wall, waiting for him.

Colin ran his fingers through his tousled dark hair. "The devil had better want me, lad."

Hope shrugged indifferently. "I heard that he did."

Colin crossed his arms over his chest and glared at the lad.

Hope glared back.

Then in a flash Hope was grabbed by the back of the neck.

Lady barked, whined and then let out a howl that would surely bring the walls of the cottage crashing down around them.

"Quiet!" Colin ordered and the dog instantly obeyed. "And you"—he said with chilling eyes focused on Hope—"have explaining to do."

With a firm hand Colin directed Harold through the village and into the keep. Many villagers glanced their way but none made a comment. It was early evening and many were busy finishing their chores for the day. Colin stopped but a moment in the great hall when he caught sight of Eric talking with Stuart and two other men.

"Did you wish to see me, my lord?" Colin asked with a formality that raised Eric's brow.

"Nay, I but wondered if you were about, though I had no cause to seek you out."

"As I thought," Colin said, annoyed, and tightened his hand around the back of Hope's neck. "We need to talk."

Hope thought otherwise. "Lady Faith waits for me."

"Then she waits."

"She needs my help."

"Eric," Colin called out as he would to a friend, his casual address bringing a smile to Eric's face. "Please tell your wife that Harold is with me and I will send him to her when I *finish* with him."

"I have need of him now," Faith said, entering the hall in a hurry, her rounded stomach not at all hampering her progress around the tables.

Hope breathed a sigh of relief—a short sigh, since the devil spoke.

"Colin has need of the lad. I will send a man to assist you until Harold's return."

Faith did not agree. "I require Harold's assistance."

"Why?" her husband demanded to know.

Faith did not fear the devil and it showed in her eyes. "Harold knows my ways."

Eric paused in silence, his eyes regarding his wife and then focusing on Harold.

His dark eyes looked as if they pierced a person's soul and Hope worried for a brief moment that he recognized her identity, but his remark indicated otherwise.

"Colin requires time with the lad."

Faith looked to Hope with regret. She could not or would not argue her husband's edict.

Colin gave the devil a respectful nod and looked to Faith. "I will send him to you as soon as I am finished with him."

"Remember he is but a lad," Faith reminded him and hoped her words weighed on his mind.

Colin nodded knowingly. "Do not worry. I do not intend to thrash him."

"I should hope not," Faith said firmly.

"Women," Colin muttered and caught Eric and Borg grinning at him. He shook his head. "Harold will be returned to you safely, Lady Faith." He wanted to hear no more or be delayed no further so he directed Harold with a firm hand on his neck out of the hall and to his chambers.

Lady attempted to follow but he ordered her to remain behind and she reluctantly did, though a whine and soft howling echo followed him.

Harold tore free of Colin as soon as they entered his bedchambers, but then there was no place for Harold to run so there was no need for Colin to detain him physically.

Colin sat in the tapestry-draped chair by the fireplace, a small fire keeping a chill from the room. "Sit down, lad, we need to talk."

Hope did not want to be alone with Colin nor did she
wish to talk with him. Actually, she did not know what
she wanted of Colin—she felt so confused by the whole
matter. Reflecting on her recent actions and attempts to
keep Colin from Kathleen, she felt foolish. But then,
were not all her actions foolhardy of late?

Hope dropped into the chair opposite Colin and kept
steady eyes on the flickering flames.

"Talk to me, lad."

Hope did not expect understanding; she thought he
would rant and yell and order Harold to keep his distance. His reaction only confirmed what a good man
Colin was, which upset her all the more.

She knew not how to respond. She could do nothing
but sit there and shake her head and produce a solemn
frown.

"Come, lad, your worries cannot be that great."

If he but knew the truth, he would realize the mag-
nitude of her worries. That thought deepened her frown.

He leaned over and placed a firm hand on Hope's
shoulder. It always concerned him that the lad was of
such slim build, but it was no wonder since his appetite
was pitiful for a growing boy. Those concerns, however,
were better left for another time. At the moment he
wished Harold to confide in him, for something obviously troubled the lad. "Talk to me, Harold, I am your
friend. And true friends can confide secrets and feel safe
that such knowledge will go no further."

A friend.

Harold's friend—not Hope's—she had to remember
that. She shrugged, as if not sure she could trust him,
and yet knowing she could. Still, there was nothing she
could really confide in him.

Colin recalled Kathleen's words and remembered Stuart telling him of how the lad had inquired about love;
perhaps he did need to offer him fatherly advice. And
he did it in the best way he thought possible. "I will be

blunt with you, Harold, for I know no other way to approach the matter."

Hope suddenly grew nervous. Whatever was he talking about?

"Have you ever been intimate with a woman?"

Hope stared at him wide-eyed. Did he intend to discuss sex with her? She was about to attempt to divert the subject elsewhere when she realized this was an opportunity she could not deny.

She squirmed in her seat, rubbed at the back of her neck and cast her glance about the room, playing the part of a nervous young lad who attempted to forestall answering.

Colin patted his shoulder then leaned back in his chair with a satisfied smile. He had assumed correctly and would handle the matter accordingly. After all, this was one area in which he possessed a definite expertise.

He spoke with confidence. "Intimacy between a man and woman is nothing to worry about. It comes naturally—"

"Easy for you to say," Hope interrupted, relaxing back in her seat and deciding to be blunt herself, to her own surprise. "Did it come naturally to you the first time?"

Colin smiled, recalling the fond memory and feeling comfortable in discussing it with Harold. "I was lucky. My first time was with an older woman who had experience and unselfishly guided my fumbling hands."

Hope should have been embarrassed by such a personal discussion but instead she was curious. "So you fumbled?"

Colin laughed. "My hands trembled and I was so aroused that I ached with the want of her. I was not certain what to do first."

"Then it did not come naturally."

Colin laughed again and shook his head. "Not exactly. I understood what needed doing, but I was not certain how to go about doing it. I remembered hearing a man, a friend of my father's, boast about his talent with the ladies. He spoke of how he took his time and made certain that the women never forgot him and how he had often received requests for repeat performances. Then there were the younger lads like myself who were un-skilled, and when they boasted it was of quick sessions they themselves enjoyed."

Hope tucked her legs beneath her in the chair and listened intently.

"I wanted my first time to be memorable not only for myself but for the woman I was with. Fortunately, I met a woman with the patience to guide a young, inexperi-enced lad and make his first time unforgettable. I learned something very important that first time. And you will do well to remember my words."

Hope nodded and waited silently, anxious to learn what he had learned.

"I learned that when you care you give and that makes a difference when you make love."

"This woman gave to you that night?"

"She gave freely and taught me more than she ever realized."

"You speak fondly of her," Hope said and understood that while he did not love the woman, he cared deeply for her.

"She was beautiful, wise and loving and I shall never forget her and what she did for a lonely young lad." Colin cleared his throat and his thoughts and once again spoke bluntly. "Have you ever seen a naked woman?"

Hope almost laughed then caught herself and biting down on her lip shook her head. Then thinking better of her remark, she amended it to, "Bare breasts I have seen."

Colin nodded. "Have you ever touched a woman's breasts?"

"Nay," she said quickly, thinking it best to act igno-rant.

"Did you ever want to?" he asked casually, as if he asked if she ever wanted to taste wine.

She thought a moment, thinking of his bare hard chest and the way his golden skin glistened when wet and her answer came easily. "Aye."

"That is the natural part, Harold, the desire to want to touch, to feel, to join together. A young age brings haste to the act, most young men wanting nothing more than to please themselves and most not able to control themselves to make it last long enough to reach true pleasure."

His words were igniting her senses and her eyes were steady on his fingers and the way he would steeple them in front of his face then bring them close to his lips. Hope wondered what magic he worked with those long skilled fingers.

She squirmed in her chair, a gentle throb between her legs warning her that his words touched places she would much prefer his fingers to touch. The improper thought should have shocked her, but then if she had been proper she would have never attempted this adventure.

Colin continued, relaxed and at ease with their conversation. "You will learn control as you mature and become more experienced, but I would advise you not to completely rush your first time." He went on as if advising an apt pupil. "Most women's nipples are very sensitive."

Hope could attest to the truth of his words since her own nipples were presently hard and aching.

Colin rubbed his thumb and forefinger together and smiled. "A light touch does wonders to start and a gentle tongue works magic."

Hope remained completely still and silent, her nipples aching with the want of his fingers upon her.

"Do not think of what you do; simply allow yourself to enjoy the feel and taste of her and you will both benefit." Colin saw that the lad seemed adrift in his own thoughts. "Are you listening, Harold, or dreaming?"

Hope refused to blush like a foolish woman being

caught in improper thoughts. And Harold was too bold to demonstrate self-doubt. Nay, he would hold his own. "I was giving your advice thought, and wondering things."

"Good—then you were listening."

"When one listens, one learns much."

Colin gave a tilt of his head and his eyes narrowed as though he examined the lad more closely.

Hope wanted him to see nothing more than a young lad aching to mature. She silently admonished herself for speaking out of character and sought quickly to correct her mistake. "My father taught me that."

Colin seemed to accept her remark. "What were you wondering?"

Hope plunged ahead. "Do women touch and taste men's nipples?"

"Women with experience do and they often do it well."

His smug grin told her that he definitely spoke from experience.

She decided to ask a more pertinent question since he was so willing and so ignorant of her true identity. After all, she would never have this opportunity to speak so candidly, so man-to-man again. She would be foolish not to learn all that she could.

"What about virgins? I hear tell it is painful for them and I do not wish to hurt a woman."

"A considerate and skillful lover can lessen a woman's pain, and a woman who desires as strongly as the man will find the pain but a brief annoyance."

Hope bit at her bottom lip, thinking of what to ask next, so many questions filled her head.

Colin understood. "You will have endless questions and all my answers will do little good, for you must experience the magic of intimacy to know what it is about. It is not the same for everyone. You have listened to the men's tales"—he laughed—"and some of them are just tall tales, but you have heard each one speak from his own experience and desire. The act itself is basic. It is what each man and woman make of it for themselves that make it special and magical."

"It can be disappointing?" she asked, foolishly sensing that she would be disappointed if she made love with anyone but Colin.

He nodded slowly. "It can be disappointing for some."

She had to ask, "Have you been disappointed?"

He smiled, that devilishly charming smile. "I have never disappointed, therefore, I have never been disappointed."

His confident remark annoyed her. "You have never been with a woman who was not talented?"

"I guided those who lacked experience." He held up his hand, preventing an anxious Harold from asking another question. "And I enjoyed guiding as well as reaping the results."

Hope decided to ask the one question that often came to her mind. "Many women are attracted to you and some are bold in their pursuit. You seem to please as many as you can. What, then, when you marry? Will you be a faithful husband? Or will you mind not your marriage vows?"

Colin voiced his surprise at the question. "Why do you ask me this, lad?"

She shrugged her slim shoulders as if she did not know, but she felt it was necessary for her to hear the answer.

"We spoke of love once and you mentioned the forever kind. I but wondered whether forever meant you loved enough to be faithful."

Colin looked to the flame that flickered in a chaotic dance in the fireplace and pondered his answer.

Hope waited. Her breathing was normal but her heart beat wildly.

Colin felt comfortable confiding in the lad. "I sometimes wonder if I will ever find my forever love, the woman I can make forever mine. If I am lucky enough

to find her I would want no other, need no other, care
for no other. She would belong to me and I to her and
I would love her forever more."

Hope understood at that moment how very much she
wished she could be the woman whom he thought of as
forever his.

Nineteen

Hope had dallied long enough at Shanekill. She had to make immediate plans to leave no matter how difficult the decision. It was time to return home and accept her fate. Her adventure had been grand and she had made many friends she would long remember. Also, she had learned about love—the hard way.

An afternoon spring shower was dusting the land and Hope ran toward the keep, Lady close at her heels and Rook beside her. The three shook the sprinkle of rain off themselves when they entered the great hall.

Hope noticed how busy the hall was—an unusual occurrence for this time of day—and she wondered what it was about.

Bridget hurried past her, linens in hand and needle and thread on top. "Faith could use a hand, Harold. Unexpected company arrives tomorrow."

Hope nodded and made her way around the row of trestle tables that filled the great hall. Colin, Lord Eric and Borg stood by the dais in deep discussion and she ventured close enough to hear but not distract.

"Having no significant news for him is not to my liking. I thought by now we would have located her," Eric said, annoyance evident in the deep timbre of his voice.

"Do you think she has eluded our efforts in locating her or do you think she has met an untimely end?" Borg asked as if it were a riddle that needed solving.

Colin answered. "I think she knows exactly what she

does and does exactly what she pleases. She has a mind of her own and an intelligent one at that."

"Admire her all you want," Eric said. "But understand she has made a fool out of us, and that I will stand for no longer. After speaking with her uncle tomorrow be prepared to find her, for she is about to taste the devil's wrath."

Hope stood frozen. They spoke of her. Lord help her if she was correct in her assumption that it was her uncle who was the unexpected company tomorrow.

"Harold," Colin said, though the lad made no move to respond. "Harold," he attempted once again, his voice raised. "Harold!" he finally shouted when Hope failed to respond.

Hope jumped and stared at Colin with fearful eyes.

"Are you all right?" he asked, concerned.

She nodded vigorously. "Faith needs me."

"Then go to her, lad," Eric said, his firm tone making it a command.

"Aye, my lord," she said and hurried out of the hall.

Colin watched him scurry off.

"Something troubles you?" Eric asked.

"Something, but I do not know what it is," Colin admitted. "I feel it is important that I know and the importance of the matter seems to strike me when I look upon the lad and yet . . ." He shook his head. "I cannot understand what it is. Of late, though, the troubling feeling plagues me more and more."

"Then let it plague you about Hope," Eric said. "The idea that she has eluded all our efforts astounds me. She is, from what her uncle says, a pint-sized bundle of sheer determination. If she were a man she would make a formidable opponent. But she is not, she is a mere woman. A woman I want found."

Colin shook his head and rubbed at his chin. "We are missing something. Something obvious and yet . . ." He threw his hands up in the air as if in surrender.

"She thinks differently than us," Borg said.

"What do you mean?" Eric asked with interest.

"She is a woman and thinks as a woman, but not just an ordinary woman. She has many years of sturdy and courageous blood running through her veins. She possesses the strength to do what other women cannot. You look to her weaknesses as a woman when you should look to her strengths. They will tell you something you do not know."

"Wise words, and ones I will think on," Eric said. "In the meantime preparations are necessary for Shamus's arrival."

Hope heard it all and turned pure white. She did not dare move from her hiding spot behind the steps. Her heart beat madly and her legs trembled so much that she was afraid they would not hold up her slim weight. She took several deep breaths before attempting to sneak off to join Faith in her bedchambers.

Whatever was she to do? She certainly had dallied here too long and now there was no chance of escape. She was not foolish enough to venture out without thought to her actions. She knew that would be a dreadful mistake and she would not suffer from her own ignorance again.

Her only recourse at the moment was to confide in Faith and see what choices she might have, though she did not think there were many.

Feeling her legs return almost to normal, she made her way around and up the stairs, taking them slowly and quietly. Only when she rounded the second flight and caught sight of Faith's closed chamber door did her feet take flight. She was in the room after a sharp knock, swinging the door open and closing it with a hefty shove.

"My uncle arrives tomorrow," she said, braced against the door and attempting to catch her breath.

"That was why I wished to see you," Faith said.

Hope noticed that she sat in the chair near the fireplace, a wool blanket thrown across her legs and a shawl tucked around her shoulders. "Are you feeling well?" She hurried to her side, suddenly concerned for Faith's welfare, forgetting that her own was in peril.

Faith placed a protective hand on her rounded stomach. "The babe tires me out today and makes me realize that I would do well to rest every now and again."

"You have much to concern yourself with," Hope said, sitting on the floor, her legs crossed in front of her. "You do not need my problems."

Faith smiled. "I love adventures and it pleases me to be enjoying yours when I cannot enjoy one myself."

"My adventure is fast coming to an end. I must leave tonight."

Faith grew alarmed. "You cannot leave. We have made no plans for your departure or safety. I cannot permit you to endanger yourself. You must stay."

"But my uncle arrives tomorrow. My secret will be known." She lowered her chin and felt tears sting her eyes. "Then all is lost."

"You love Colin, do you not?"

Hope looked up in haste, her wide eyes pooled with unshed tears. "Is it that obvious?"

"I know your identity and see the truth where others only see what they wish to see."

"It is a love that will never be," Hope said on a sigh.

"And you have decided this?"

"What else is there for me to do? My uncle has made arrangements for a marriage and I must honor his wishes."

"Unless, of course, there was a discretion born out of love that could not be denied," Faith said.

"What do you mean?" Hope could not keep the eagerness from her voice—or perhaps it was hope itself that sounded there.

"If you and Colin were caught in an indiscretion your uncle would have no choice but to see you marry him."

For a moment the idea that she could possibly wed Colin brought a shred of joy to her heart but it quickly faded. "I could not deceive him. It would not be right."

"Colin needs someone like you to love and in his own way he already loves you. Look at how he cares for the lad's well-being and how he protects him from harm."

"That is Harold, not me."

"But you are Harold. Harold is you and that is who he feels for—you. When he discovers your true identity he will begin to realize the feelings that are there. He only needs a chance. A chance to love."

Hope wondered over the wisdom of such a notion. "I do not think Colin would like being deceived. I have already deceived him enough."

"It is not deception; it is an arranged marriage."

"By whose authority?"

"The Irish devil's wife," Faith said proudly. "I told him I would find him a wife and he made no adamant protest. Therefore, he accepted my edict and will marry the woman I deem proper."

Hope shook her head. "Uncle Shamus will have something to say in the matter."

"If it is handled wisely he will see the wisdom of it and make no protests."

"I do not wish to deceive Colin," Hope said, though she did wish to wed him. She thought she could love him as no other had, but was it her own desires and wishes that made her feel so confident—or was it the love she felt for him that gave her the confidence?

"You have doubts?"

Hope nodded slowly and then followed it with a shake of her head. "I cannot deceive him. It would not be right to do. He does not love Hope; he cares for Harold."

"But in Harold he sees the strength and courage of Hope."

She shook her head adamantly. "He knows nothing of Hope. He thinks her a spoiled young woman."

"Nay, he sees the strength of an adventurous woman who fascinates him. And he cannot understand his interest in someone he has never met."

"How do you know this?"

"I know Colin. He tries to keep himself a mystery, a man whose smile charms but whose heart aches. I know him, for at one time I felt as lost as he did, and then I met Eric."

"Eric and you were meant for each other," Hope argued.

"As are you and Colin."

Hope continued to shake her head. "How can you be sure?"

"How can anyone be sure that two people are meant for each other? One but feels and knows when it is right. Tell me you do not feel this."

Hope at first thought to argue the matter but it would do no good. She felt exactly as Faith implied. "I cannot deny my feelings, but the situation is hopeless. Colin would never love me. And I do not wish to have a marriage based on deceit."

Faith thought of her own circumstances and the consequences and she spoke from the heart. "Sometimes we must take a chance and allow fate to decide. Colin needs a wife and you require a husband. Fate saw fit to bring you both together. Will you deny what the heavens decree?"

Hope pondered her dilemma and could find no satisfying answer. "I know not what to do. Colin knows not who I am. And yet I know him and I have come to love him."

"For who he truly is," Faith said with certainty. "I think that is what Colin searched for in a wife. Someone to love him for himself, for his roguish ways, his charming nature, his caring soul."

Hope smiled. "I see all that in him and more. He will make a good father, you know."

Faith nodded. "Aye, I think he longs for children of his own."

"I thought the same," Hope confided, happy that someone held the same opinion.

"Then why deny him your love?"

"How do I deny him something he does not know he possesses? He thinks me a common lad who is but sharp with his tongue and weak in physical strength. I mean nothing to him. He knows nothing of Hope—only the lad." Frustration was evident in the rise of her voice.

Faith shook her head. "Hope is the lad, and all of her qualities, her strengths and her weaknesses are part of Harold. Once he learns your identity he will realize this."

"And do what with the knowledge? Grow angry at me? Accuse me of deceit? Condemn me for being a spoiled woman?" Her words hung heavy on her and she lowered her head.

Faith reached out to her, her fingers lifting her drooping chin. "He will see Hope, a young woman of courage and determination and a woman whom he can admire, respect and love if given the chance."

Hope produced a sad smile. "I think his anger would shadow all thought or reason."

"If you choose to walk away you will never know. Can you live with the thought of never knowing?"

Could she?

Could she walk away and forever wonder what if? What if she had taken the chance? What if she had dared to love no matter the consequences?

"The choice is yours, Hope, and now you must decide," Faith said and waited.

Hope sighed, lowering her chin and closing her eyes. If she shut out the world would she have to answer? Could she make her problems go away by not facing them? She was too intelligent to believe she could hide from her precarious situation. She understood that by lingering at Shanekill she had created her dilemma and now she had to address it.

But what to do?

Did she run or did she take a chance?

She raised her chin and squared her shoulders. "What do you suggest?"

"First," Faith said with such confidence that Hope felt her own courage soar, "you must not lose hope no matter what happens. You must remain confident and determined as Harold always does."

"I sometimes think that Harold possesses more courage than Hope. The lad has a way of getting away with things that Hope could never dream of doing."

"But she has, has she not?" Faith said with a certain laugh.

"I have so enjoyed myself," Hope said enthusiastically. "I wanted to see and do so very much and I have done more than I could ever have imagined. I have fond memories to recall of this time."

"And fonder memories to create."

"Then I suppose I should begin."

"Aye, that you should."

The two huddled together, making preparations, determining the wisest course of action and the possible outcomes. When all was set, all plans confirmed, Faith looked to Hope and placed a gentle hand on her arm. "If at any time you wish to reconsider your decision you need only to step away and carry it through no further."

"And if I do, then what?"

Faith understood her concern. One way or another Colin would learn of her identity, but which way was it to be? "I will make certain that you are escorted to Croom Abbey immediately."

"Thank you for being a good friend when I need one the most."

"I will always be your friend," Faith said and stood spreading her arms out in a gesture of welcoming friendship.

Hope wasted not a moment, hurrying into Faith's comforting embrace with tear-filled eyes and silently praying that she was making the right choice.

Hope left Faith's bechambers just as the devil entered. He gave a curt nod to the hastily retreating lad.

Hope returned the brief nod and fled in fear of the devil.

"You could have smiled," his wife scolded with a pleasant smile of her own.

He walked straight to her, taking her into his powerful arms. "The lad can hold his own. He is a bold one for his age and size." He kissed her cheek. "You feel well?"

She laid her head on his hard chest. "The babe tires me today."

He scooped her up gently in his arms and carried her to their bed. "Then you will rest."

"I have rested," she said anxiously. "There is much for me to do."

He went down on the bed beside her, keeping her in his embrace. "What is there for you to do?"

She had spoken without thought, so anxious was she to set all plans into motion.

"Is there so much for you to do that you cannot remember it all?" He ran a lazy finger down the side of her face. "Or is my wife keeping something from me?"

She could not and would not lie to him, but she could avoid the subject. "The evening meal requires attention."

"Mary will see to it."

"But she is also with child," Faith protested earnestly.

"And has much help thanks to you," he reminded her. "And I will ask Bridget to help her as well."

She had not counted on that. She had hoped to have Bridget aid her in this scheme. She was a trustworthy friend.

Faith ran her loving hand along her husband's chest. "I think Bridget has other plans."

The devil slipped his hand down along his wife's rounded belly and stroked gently. "Do those plans include you?"

He knew she was up to something and there was only one way to distract him, and she did so enjoy distracting him. Slowly her hand roamed down his stomach, over muscled thighs to finally cup him solidly in her hand. He hardened instantly.

"I thought you were tired."

His concern always touched her heart and she felt a tinge of guilt for misleading him, though not for wanting him. She looked up at him. "I am never too tired to love you."

He kissed her softly first and then it turned quick and hungry. She responded with her own hungry need and when his hand slipped between her legs she moaned with a heated passion she ached for him to satisfy.

Clothes were hastily discarded and with an equal urgency the devil and his wife came together in a loving that left them both breathless.

"You are so beautiful." He stroked her damp skin with the tender touch of a man who loved deeply.

She sighed and smiled in contented pleasure. "You make me believe it is so."

"It is," he said as if declaring it a proclamation. "And you will not deny it nor can you hide it."

"Anything can be hidden, my lord; one must only desire it to be so."

They both knew she spoke of the scar she carried from a vicious attack and how she had managed to keep it hidden from him. But her words gave him a different reason to pause.

"And where is the perfect place to hide that which we want hidden?"

Faith still lingered in the aftermath of their lovemaking and answered without thinking. "Where it can be seen."

"And no one would see it, for it is not really hidden— merely disguised."

Clarity hit Faith like a splash of cold water and she wisely held her tongue.

"I must say I admire her audacity and courage not only to attempt such a feat but to succeed at it."

Faith remained silent, allowing him to continue.

"It was all so obvious. She could not risk discovery nor could she travel about freely without some type of protection. And what better protection than a disguise, and what better place to hide than in the home of the one who searched for her."

Eric jumped out of bed and paced the floor naked with a joy that was hard for Faith not to smile at. Then, of course, there was that magnificent body of his to focus on, a better focus than the fact that Hope was about to be discovered by the devil himself.

"I cannot believe that I did not realize this sooner or that Colin was so easily deceived. He knows women so well. Why did he not see through Harold's disguise? Why did not anyone know that—"

He stopped abruptly and stared at Faith with a potent glare that chilled and forced her to take refuge beneath the bed covers.

Eric approached the bed and slowly leaned down over his wife, his hands braced on either side of her face.

She pulled the covers up to below her chin and smiled.

"You knew that Harold was Hope and said nothing?"

"She asked me to keep her confidence. If you had asked I would have told you. I would not lie to you."

Eric knew without her saying that the truth was always spoken between them. "And you carefully avoided the subject."

Faith touched her husband's face gently. It was a familiar touch that told him how very much she trusted and loved him. "Hope needed time to think and to understand her feelings."

"Feelings?"

Secrets could no longer be kept. Two lives were in danger of losing a special relationship and Faith took the chance and confided all.

Eric stretched out next to her and took her in his arms, her head resting on his chest. "You think this Hope is good for Colin."

"Aye, I think her strength matches his in many ways and she searches for a forever love, as does Colin."

"How do you know so much of what Colin searches for?"

"I listen when he speaks and hear what he does not say."

"I do not want Colin forced into a marriage. I want him happy," Eric said, planting a firm kiss on his wife's forehead.

"Can we really force Colin to do anything he does not wish to do?"

Eric gave that thought. "Nay, he is much like me. If I had not wished to wed you when your father ordered that I do, I would not have done so."

Faith snuggled against him. "You wed me because you wished to wed me."

"Aye, that I did. I lost my heart to you and dared not admit it to myself."

"As I did to you, and if given an opportunity I think Colin would lose his heart to Hope."

"But he thinks her a lad and he will think her deceitful."

"Will he?" Faith challenged. "Or will he want to come to know the woman he once thought of as a lad and felt the need to protect?"

"I will not force him to wed her," Eric said firmly.

"And I told Hope that if she chose otherwise she need only walk away."

Something in her voice made Eric ask, "You do not think she will see this plan through?"

"She fears Colin will think her deceitful."

"A good possibility."

"But one she needs to face."

"As you did with me?" He hugged her to him.

"If I had not we would never be." Her own words upset her.

"But you did and I am forever grateful for your courage." He kissed her gently. "You made me understand love and gave me a gift I will cherish forever—your unconditional love."

Tears stung her eyes. "I want Colin to have a chance to love as we do. He deserves it."

"What are you asking of me, Faith?"

"I worry that Hope will change her mind and walk away without ever knowing if Colin could love her."

"And what will she do then?"

"I told her that I would provide protection back to Croom Abbey where she could contact her uncle. Then she would wed the man of her uncle's choosing and forever think of Colin and what might have been."

Eric agreed. "Aye, her stubbornness matches Colin's."

"Another reason they would make a fine pair."

Eric laughed. "You are determined."

"I wish them both to discover the love that I know is there."

"Her uncle Shamus wishes her happy and would not object to a marriage of her choosing; he has told me this."

"Then there would be no problem."

"Unless Hope runs off before giving it a chance," Eric said, shaking his head.

"I have been giving that thought," Faith said with the grin of a child at play.

Eric laughed and hugged her to him. "Tell me of these thoughts and we will see what we can do."

Twenty

Hope doubted herself. She wanted to take the chance—Lord how she wanted to take the chance—and see if Colin could love her. But in her heart she was not comfortable with deceiving him. And she wanted no marriage based on deceit.

When the great hall filled for the evening meal and she saw that Colin's tankard was forever being refilled she knew then that she could not see this plan through.

She left the table where she sat with Stuart and approached the dais. Lord Eric was deep in discussion with Colin. Borg was busy speaking quietly with his wife Bridget and Faith sat contentedly beside her husband. It was a good time to tell Faith that she could not go through with their plans and that she would be prepared to leave tonight for Croom Abbey. If for some reason Faith did not help her then she planned on traveling alone. Well, not entirely alone, since Lady would be with her, though separating her from Rook was going to be a problem—a problem Hope completely understood and empathized with.

"Harold, you are enjoying yourself?" Faith asked with a knowing smile.

"Much, though I grow tired," she said, leaning on the table. "I think it is best I retire early. . . ." And on a softer note added, "Get away."

Faith's disappointment was evident in the slow nod of her head. "As you wish, but are you certain?"

"I feel there is no other way."

Faith nodded once again and Hope did not see her slip her hand beneath the table to rest it on her husband's leg.

Eric casually turned his head, a smile adding to his handsome features. "Harold, join us for some wine."

Hope had had a glass or two already. She wanted a clear head when she departed the keep this evening. "I am tired, my lord—another time."

"Nonsense," Eric's voice was firm. "Share one drink with Colin and me."

Colin filled a goblet and motioned Hope to come around the table and take the empty seat beside him.

Hope had no choice in the matter. Eric made it a command and she had to obey dutifully. She promised herself as she walked to the end of the dais and around the long table that she would take but a few sips and be on her way.

"Sit," Colin said with a slap on the seat of the chair. "We will share adventures."

Hope could see that Colin had been enjoying his wine and she thought of her plan to get him drunk and drop him in bed, then climb in beside him. He'd wake in the morning and discover that Harold was not a lad but a woman—the very woman he searched for.

Hope sat in the chair and took the goblet Colin pushed in front of her. After careful consideration she came to the conclusion that her plan was flawed and much too full of deceit. She could not bring herself to see it through.

Would she always wonder over his reaction if he had found her such? Aye, the thought would forever haunt her. But haunt her it would, for she could not place him in such a difficult position. Instead she would leave and never know what might have been.

Hope sipped at the wine to ease her anguished musings. She would get through this night. She would spend these last moments with Colin and forever remember his face, his smile, his laugh and remember how much he had cared for Harold.

"Drink and smile," Colin ordered, raising his own glass. "Tonight we make merry, for tomorrow we begin our search once again for the elusive Hope. Will you join me, Harold?"

Hope raised her glass.

"Nay," Colin said shaking his head, though he more tilted than shook it. "Join me in the search."

She stared at him oddly.

Colin placed a heavy hand on the lad's shoulder. "Your wit is sharp, your wisdom sharper and your company pleasant. I would enjoy having you join me and the men."

"I think it is a good idea," Eric said. "You will learn much at Colin's side."

Hope smiled pleasantly and nodded at the crazy idea of going in search of herself. But had not that been her intention in the first place?

"Good," Colin said, his hand falling off Hope's shoulder to reach for his goblet. "Tomorrow when I speak with Hope's uncle you will be at my side."

The devil's smile sent a chill through Hope.

"Another good idea," Eric said, slapping Colin on the back. "I think Shamus will like the lad."

"And this time," Colin said, sounding determined, "Hope will not be able to hide from us."

Eric leaned closer to Colin. "Hide, that is the clue to finding her. She hides well and we must learn to think as she does. Where would a pint-sized woman hide and not be noticed? What say you, lad?"

Eric spoke low but in his deep voice was a strength of command that could not be denied.

Hope took a generous swallow of wine before answering. "I know not how a woman such as her would think."

"Aye," Eric said as if the lad had given him the answer for which he searched. "That is what we must remember. She does not think as you and I and, therefore, we must think as she does."

Colin agreed after downing more wine. "True, Eric, I failed to consider her own reasoning or perhaps I failed to realize this Hope is much more intelligent than anyone suspects. She would do what one least expects instead of the obvious."

Hope found herself asking, "Why think you that?"

Colin answered easily. "She is not the ordinary woman."

Eric seemed in agreement. "Aye, she possesses a skilled mind."

"You both speak as though you admire her," Hope said, another sip of wine following her words.

Colin responded. "She evades skilled warriors who search for her and survives the hardships of the road on her own. For a privileged woman this is a rare accomplishment. And while I wish to find her, I also admire her fortitude and endurance. She is not an ordinary woman by any means and her husband will do well to keep his eye on her."

"Tame her, you mean," Hope said curtly.

Colin paid no heed to her testy remark. "Nay, to tame such a free spirit would be wrong. To encourage, guide and share her enthusiasm, though possibly difficult at times, would be the wise choice."

"One not many men would make," Hope said adamantly.

"You speak with admiration for her as well," Eric said.

"Respect," Hope corrected.

"You do not think of her as spoiled? Wanting her own way and behaving improperly?" Eric asked as though he suspected she had the exact answers for which he searched.

Hope answered with caution, another sip of wine preceding her words. "I cannot say with certainty for I know nothing of this woman but what I have heard. I can only wonder why one would think so of her when she took off on her own not worried about her safety or well-being but adventurous in thought and action. If she were spoiled would she not have made certain that she had run away with the amenities she was accustomed to?"

"I have thought the same myself," Colin said. "Why, when she had everything, did she choose to go off with nothing?" He shook his head. "Strong of character or very foolish."

"With both of you beginning to understand her I would not be surprised if you find her faster than you think."

Eric's remark disturbed Hope, as did his broad smile. She downed the last of her wine and had no sooner placed it on the table than Eric refilled her goblet. She was too late to protest, for he went on to add more to Colin's goblet and his own.

He raised his goblet and Colin followed suit, leaving her to do the same. "To finding Hope and a happy ending for her."

"Aye," Colin agreed wholeheartedly. "A happy ending for her."

How could Hope not drink to that? It was what she wanted and the devil had even added his own well wishes. She feared a happy ending was not in her future, however, but joined in the toast anyway. What harm would it do?

Toast followed toast, goblets were refilled time and again and before Hope realized it the night grew late and she grew drunk. The devil swayed on his feet—or was it Hope who swayed when she stood staring at him?

Her swaying grew worse when Borg joined the devil and Hope attempted to look up at his full height. He was a giant of a man and the more her eyes traveled up the length of him the more dizzy she grew.

Colin reached out for Hope just as she was about to topple over. "Easy, lad."

Hope rested gratefully against Colin, thinking that his solid weight would still her endless motion. She was mistaken. They swayed together.

"The lad needs a bed to steady him," Eric ordered. "See to it, Colin."

Hope attempted to gain a bit of clarity but her foggy mind would have none of it. She knew there was something of extreme importance she was to do this night but she could not make sense of her thoughts and a bed sounded like a good place to be at the moment.

"Need help?" Borg offered and stepped forward.

Eric placed a firm hand on the large man's shoulder, stopping him. "Colin can see to the lad himself."

Hope thought she caught a strange and silent exchange between the two men before Borg stepped back. But then her mind was foggy—why not her sight as well?

"Aye, the devil is right," Colin said, his charming smile surfacing. "I can handle a mere lad. It is an elusive, pint-sized woman who gives me the most trouble."

Borg laughed. "I cannot believe my ears. He admits there is a woman he cannot charm."

Hope came swiftly to his defense. "He can charm any woman. I know," she insisted with a thump to her chest. "I have seen him work his charm."

"As have I," Borg agreed. "But this woman he has yet to find, and somehow I think she would not submit so easily."

"Aye, she would," Hope continued to insist, especially since she was the woman and had already succumbed to his charm—or was it his good soul that she favored?

"Borg has a point," Eric said. "Colin very well may have met his match."

"He has not," Hope said indignantly and took a step forward. She swayed, the room spun and the floor rushed up to greet her.

Colin grabbed for the falling lad and with little effort

swung him over his shoulder. "He definitely needs a bed."

"It is late," Eric said. "Find him a sleeping palette in the keep."

Faith listened from where she sat in her chair and waited.

"He can share my quarters for the night."

"Good," Eric said, as if pleased by his choice. "Then you can make certain Harold is with you to greet Shamus in the morning."

"We will be together."

Faith smiled and stroked her rounded belly, pleased with the news.

Eric came to her side, his hand resting on her shoulder as they both watched a swaying Colin carry Hope out of the great hall.

Lady moved lazily to follow her master but a sound command from Eric kept her beside Rook.

Colin made his way to his quarters with little difficulty. Harold was barely a bundle, his weight was so light. He feared the lad would never gain the muscle he needed to defend himself, and that often worried Colin.

He carefully placed Harold on the tapestry-draped chair while he went to the bed to roll the bed covers back and strip out of his own clothes before seeing to the lad.

He discarded his own garments quickly, the wine fast catching up with him and knowing that shortly he would be able to help no one. He turned to see that Harold had wrapped himself up in the tapestry and slept contentedly, rolled up as he was.

Colin thought it best to leave him and dropped naked into the bed, pulling the bed covers over himself and falling fast into a deep sleep.

Hope stirred in the middle of the night, her head pounding and her neck sore from it, resting on the arm of the wooden chair in which she found herself. She stretched her cramped body, slowly attempting to focus her bleary sight.

The fireplace was directly in front of her and she could make out a bed to her right. The room seemed familiar and she assumed with relief that it was the healing cottage. All she needed to do was make her way over to the bed and climb in. There was getting herself undressed first, though she could remain in her clothes.

She shook her head at her own suggestion. She was much too warm from sleeping in front of the fireplace. She much preferred to slip her clothes off and crawl naked beneath the covers.

Her spinning head and weak legs told her the task might prove difficult. Still she was determined, and with fumbling hands she attempted to undress herself. It took several attempts with much effort and deep breaths to boost her strength. Her leggings proved the most vexing for the hose refused to disconnect from her toes. The garment simply refused to let go of her toes. It tangled around them and hung on tight.

It was with a heavy breath that she finally managed to free her imprisoned toes and cast the stubborn garment aside.

Now she had to make it to the bed.

She ran her hands through her hair and for some odd reason began to cry softly. Her hair, her beautiful long hair, was gone, the length now barely at her shoulders. Why had she been so foolish? Why had she cut her hair?

She stopped crying as suddenly as she had started.

She wiped at her wet cheeks and then at her bare chest where the teardrops had fallen. She remembered why. She had decided to go on an adventure. Not just any adventure, but a grand adventure.

Her fumbling hand drifted once again to her hair but this time it was to rub her head. There was something about this adventure she should remember. Something important.

She shook her head briefly, the action causing both

her head and the room to spin. She would remember in the morning, she promised herself. After all, it was important.

"Very important," she whispered as she made her way slowly to the bed.

She climbed beneath the covers and as her head hit the pillow and she drifted off to sleep, she remembered. She was to leave Shanekill tonight. It was important. Very important.

Twenty-one

Loud, shouting voices penetrated Colin's sleep and his aching head. He did not know who was arguing outside his bedchamber door but when he found out there would be hell to pay.

He told himself to open his eyes but somehow the thought of bright morning sunlight kept his eyes firmly shut. He had entertained himself with much too much drink the previous night and from the feel of the warm feminine body next to his, drink was not the only entertainment in which he had indulged.

Usually he never forgot taking a woman to his bed—actually he had never forgotten a night of lovemaking no matter how much drink he had consumed. But at the moment he could not recall who he had invited to his bed, and stranger still was the fact that he never brought a woman to his bedchambers. He always went to their quarters, enabling himself to take his leave when he chose.

From the feel of her cuddled against him she was a small one in height and weight. Not that size mattered to him. He had had his share of women of all sizes and discovered fast enough that it was the woman's character that attracted him the most and made her a good lover. So it troubled him that he could not recall anything about the sleeping woman beside him.

The voices grew louder and if his head had not hurt so badly he would have yelled back at them for disturbing him.

He was about to peek beneath the covers where she was curled with her back against him when a sudden pounding shook his door. He was about to jump out of bed and pound on the person who dared disturb him when his door flew open and slammed against the wall.

A short man, rotund and balding and with thick fists, entered followed by Eric and Faith.

"Where is she?" the man demanded, shaking his fist at no one in particular. "Where is my Hope?"

Colin realized then that the man was Hope's uncle Shamus—but why did he think his niece was here?

He ran his fingers through his hair and pushed himself up to sit with the bed covers slipping down to below his waist. He decided to address Eric since the short man obviously was not making sense, and Colin himself felt a faint tickle of apprehension rush down his spine. "What is this about, my lord?"

"Where is Harold?" Eric asked.

Last evening came flooding back and he realized then that the slender figure asleep beside him must be Harold, though he could have sworn it was feminine curves that rested at his side. "Right here beside me."

"He admits it, he admits it," Shamus shouted, his full face turning a bright red.

Colin held his tongue and waited. Something was amiss, seriously amiss.

Eric approached the side of the bed where Harold slept and lifted the covers just enough for Colin to see who slept beside him.

He jumped out of bed when his eyes caught sight of a small woman just rousing from a deep sleep. When he realized he stood naked before Faith he hurried back beneath the bed covers but kept a safe distance from the mysterious woman.

"He will do right by her," Shamus demanded with a mighty shake of his fist toward Eric.

Eric glared at the small man and his fist fell slowly to his side. "I will see to this matter."

"I have no doubt you will," Shamus said more calmly. "I am told you are an honorable man."

Hope peeked from beneath the covers, her sleepy state leaving her confused. "Uncle Shamus?"

Colin turned chilling eyes on the woman he had thought a lad. "You are Hope?"

Hope stared at him speechless. She could not find the words to offer a reasonable explanation, one that would make any kind of sense. She remained silent.

His look turned furious, his tone was icy. "Answer me."

"Do as he says, Hope," Shamus ordered firmly. "You owe the man that much."

Hope owed him much more but she realized he would never listen to her now or understand. She decided to rely on her own strength and brave the consequences of her foolishness.

She sat up, pressing the covers against her chest to conceal her nakedness. She held her head high and spoke with a confidence that surprised everyone. "Hope and Harold are one."

Colin stared at her in complete silence. He had no words to express his shock. How had he ever missed the fact that Harold was a woman? Hope had played the role well. He had never once doubted the validity of the lad's tales.

Now, looking at her sitting there bold and confident, he saw signs he had never noticed before. Her eyes were wide and curious and fringed with long lashes, her lips were a pale pink and plump though slim and her neck was slender and looked soft to the touch. He could only imagine how she would look when her hair grew in, for now it fell to her shoulders, though slight waves here and there gave it a gentle softness that spoke of femininity.

He shook his head at his own stupidity, running a hand over his face in frustration. How could he have been so blind?

"We need to talk, Colin," Eric said and though it did

not sound like a command there was no doubt it was.

Shamus spoke with impatience. "I will hear him say now that he will do right and wed my niece."

Hope saw the fury rise in Colin's eyes, sending a shiver through her. Her fear had been realized. Her deception weighed heavy on him and he felt the fool. There would be no love between them and she would not wed him without it.

"I will not wed him," Hope declared adamantly with a defiant toss of her head.

"You have no choice," her uncle said just as adamantly and he looked to Colin. "Give me an answer, son."

"I gave you my answer," Hope said with a sharp insistence that drew all eyes to her. "His answer is not necessary."

"Your own foolishness has brought this down upon you," her uncle said with a shake of his fist at her. "You will do what is right, as will he."

"I will not marry him," Hope repeated with a calmness that chilled and she looked with imploring eyes to Faith.

Faith understood her silent request and walked over to her, holding out the warm white wool shawl she wore. Hope took it and slipped it beneath the covers to drape around her. She then moved the covers and stood up wearing the shawl, safely concealing her nakedness.

She walked to Faith's side, needing the support of a friend. Faith slipped her arm around her and together they approached the door.

"You *will* marry him," her uncle said as if he had not a doubt.

She stopped and with tear-filled eyes said, "Nay, I will wed no one."

Colin's curt, firm voice stopped her. "You will wed me."

"It is settled," Shamus said with a sigh. "We celebrate."

Hope shook her head at them all and left the room.

Faith held her closely as she cried. Between sobs she attempted to express herself. "I did not"—she choked on her words—"want this."

Faith had wrapped her in a warm robe and they sat huddled together before the fireplace in the devil's bedchamber. "You have not given it a chance."

"Chance?" Hope looked at her with incredulous eyes. "There is no chance for us. I deceived him. How will he ever trust me?"

"You did not purposely deceive Colin. Your deception was for your own protection."

"I kept my identity from him." She hiccuped.

"You felt the need for autonomy. He will come to understand this."

Hope shook her head and allowed pooled tears to flow freely. "He will never understand. He will always think I tricked him and he will hate me."

Faith hugged her. "When he calms down he will begin to question and begin to realize and he will attempt to make sense of it all. That is when he will begin to talk with you and understand you."

"Uncle Shamus says that I make sense to no one and that it is because of my heritage that I will not bow or submit to any man no matter the reason or fault."

"Then hold fast to such courage and give Colin a chance."

Hope rested her weary head on Faith's shoulder. "You did not let me leave last night, did you?"

Faith shut her eyes as she answered. "A chance, Hope. If you had not taken it you would always have wondered and possibly always regretted."

"What if I regret now?"

"Then you know it and can go on, but if you did not learn that, then every day of your life you would think what might have been and never *ever* fully live your life. I am sorry if I hurt you and perhaps I had no right, but it is for the best. You will see that."

Hope sighed and hiccuped again. "I forgive you. You did what you thought best. And you are right—I would have forever wondered. But," she said with the obstinacy of Harold, "I will not enter into a forced marriage. Colin must have time to consider whether he wishes to wed me or not."

"I do not think your uncle will agree to such conditions."

"I will have it no other way," Hope insisted.

"You are as stubborn as your uncle," Faith said with a smile.

"Aye, that I am, but it is I who will have my way, not my uncle."

Somehow Faith had no doubt she would.

"A week's time?" Shamus shouted, though it was unnecessary to raise his voice. Eric and Colin were the only ones present in Eric's solar and could clearly hear him. "Not acceptable."

Colin chose silence so he could listen.

"This is not an ordinary situation," Eric attempted to explain calmly.

"It matters not how it came about that my niece was in his bed naked. It only matters that he wed her and as fast as possible."

"A week's time is hasty enough," Eric insisted.

"Not for me." Shamus was just as insistent. "Two days' time."

"A week," Eric countered, refusing to rush Colin into anything without giving him sufficient time to think it over.

Shamus was stubborn. "Two and he is lucky I give him that."

Colin decided to speak up. "Four days and I will marry her."

Shamus wasted not a moment. "Agreed." He extended his hand to Colin to seal the agreement.

Colin did not hesitate; he shook the man's hand, sealing his fate.

"Now we only need to see that Hope obeys my orders to wed you," Shamus said, a weary smile warning that it would not be an easy task. "She is determined to do as she pleases and has the intelligence to accomplish it."

"She fooled all of us," Eric said with admiration.

Shamus's smile turned to one of pride. "She shares the blood of courageous kings; I should expect no less of her. And you should know, Colin, that marriage to her will forever be eventful."

Colin had to smile at the challenging prospect. "We will come to understand each other in time."

"Good," Shamus said, pleased, and rubbed at his rotund tummy. "Now I hear that your cook is greatly skilled."

"She works magic," Eric said with pride.

"Good, then I am ready to taste magic."

Eric summoned a servant to escort Shamus to the great hall, requesting a few moments alone with Colin. He did not object and took his leave when the servant arrived.

The two men sat in the broad wooden seats in front of the fireplace. While the warm spring weather filled the meadows and hills, the castle itself held a chill, so fires burned in the many hearths.

"Do you wish this marriage?" Eric asked directly.

"Are you telling me I have a choice in the matter?"

"We have been friends far too long for you even to ask that of me."

Colin nodded, knowing Eric's words were all too true. "I remember when your wife thought you were forced to wed her. Until she truly came to know her husband, she did not realize you married her because you wished to."

"That is why I ask this question of you. Do you wish this marriage?"

"An honest answer would be that I am not certain.

Part of me is angry at the deception she played on me and part of me admires her audacity." Colin sighed, frustrated. "At least I realize why I felt so protective of the skinny lad; perhaps something inside me knew but was unwilling to accept. And even now I find myself wanting to protect her from her own obstinacy." He shook his head. "Am I making any sense?"

"About as much as I did when I met Faith."

"You sound confident that Hope is a good match for me."

"I cannot take all the credit. Faith had a strong hand in this."

Colin sat forward with a look of disbelief spreading across his handsome face. "You mean to tell me that Faith knew Harold was Hope and never told you?"

"I never asked," Eric said, as if the few words explained all—yet they did make sense to Colin. Faith would not lie to the devil, but then she would offer no information that was not asked of her.

"Then Faith thinks that Hope is suited for me?"

"I think what she feels is that you both should at least give it a chance and see what happens. If four days is not sufficient time, we can extend the marriage date."

"I gave my word," Colin said.

Eric understood. A man's word was his honor and one did not give it lightly. "Then I suggest you become acquainted with your soon-to-be wife."

"I feel as if I know her and yet I do not."

"You know her as a bold, stubborn lad full of pride and tenacity. Those qualities and flaws do not change. Now, though, you must come to know the woman within."

"You know me well, Eric, and know that I enjoy women and the challenges they present. What troubles me is her deception. Which brings up a trust issue."

"You need to ask yourself why she went to such lengths to deceive and why you were so tenacious about protecting the lad. Also, you must know that Hope did not wish to deceive you last night. At first she had considered it but in the end she told Faith that she could not deceive you and requested help in leaving Shanekill immediately."

"She intended to leave here without telling me?" The thought angered him more than the deception.

Eric answered with a nod. "It is my understanding that she did not wish you to feel foolish over her own foolish actions."

"If she had thought more carefully over her foolish actions she would never have found it necessary to worry about making fools of anyone."

"She never purposely made fools of anyone. She actually attempted to avoid such errors, keeping her distance from the men as much as possible while she was here."

"Though not from me," Colin said. "She seemed to be around whenever I was—"

He stopped suddenly and frowned, which caused Eric to smile.

"Whenever you were what?" Eric asked.

Colin rubbed at his chin. "Of late whenever Kathleen and I attempted to find time alone either Harold—I mean Hope—or Lady would haunt us."

"Why do you think she did that?"

He shook his head and then dropped it back against the chair with a groan. "Damn, I spoke to Harold about women and sex."

Eric laughed. "That must have been an enlightening conversation. Were you as detailed in your explanation as you are in your liaisons?"

Colin grinned. "Very detailed."

"How did Harold react?"

His grin quickly faded. "He asked questions and seemed intent on answers."

Eric's laughter echoed off the stone walls. "For a skinny lad Harold possesses a large pair of—"

"Enough," Colin said with a grimace. "Harold is

Hope, a woman and a bold one at that, and I will do well to remember it, as should you."

"I admire her," Eric said more seriously. "She has much courage and the strength to stand for her convictions. She refused marriage to you though it would mean her reputation. She will not be forced and it makes me wonder what plans she has to make certain her word is taken seriously."

Colin jolted forward. "Do you think she would run away again?"

"I suppose since she did it once and survived she would have no trouble doing it again, and probably with more confidence this time."

Colin stood in a rush. "I will thrash her if she attempts to run away from me."

Eric enjoyed another laugh. "You would never raise your hand to a woman in anger."

Colin settled his turbulent emotions and leaned one hand against the stone hearth. "Aye, you are right, though the hand I raised would certainly have her surrendering to me fast enough."

"Then perhaps that is the hand you should use with her and see what it brings."

"First I must accept the fact that Harold is a woman. Now when I look at her I can see distinct signs of femininity. She is quite lovely."

"Is it her features that delight you or is it really what lies beneath that fascinates you the most?"

"She is far different from any woman I have known and she is—" He paused in silent thought.

"A challenge," Eric finished for him.

"Life would not be boring with her. She will keep a husband alert and always interested, though he may get gray hair faster than other husbands."

"But he will have a story for every gray hair he suffers," Eric said with a chuckle.

Colin stood away from the hearth to stand tall, his shoulders back and his smile disarming. "I think it is time for me to speak with Hope."

Twenty-two

Hope felt odd in women's garments. The many weeks she had lived as a boy had given her a strong sense of herself and her strengths. Now in feminine attire, she felt vulnerable. As Harold she could say and do as much as she pleased, but now a certain behavior was expected of her. The short taste of freedom she had experienced made her realize she was no longer the same person— nor did she want to be.

She paced the small confines of the healing cottage knowing that she would soon be expected to make an appearance in the great hall and dreading it. She would not be able to hold her tongue if ordered to wed Colin, and then what choice would she have?

A convent?

The door creaked open and she did not bother to turn around. She had been waiting for this moment—waiting for Colin to appear and demand answers—answers she often wondered over herself.

"We need to talk, Har—Hope."

Hope turned and her heart jumped. He wore a charming smile and stood with such ease and confidence she thought to surrender there and then, whether he loved her or not. Would her love not be enough for them both?

She knew the answer and it made her task all the more difficult.

"There is naught for us to discuss," she said firmly and with a defiant toss of her chin. "I will not wed you."

"If you so choose," he said much too calmly and approached her slowly. "Though I wished to speak of Harold."

"I am Harold." She could not keep the obstinacy from her voice though it did not seem to bother him. He kept his approach steady and slow.

"True enough, though I would like to know what made you choose such a disguise?"

"A man's world is freer than a woman's. I could not hope to see the things I wished to see and experience life by remaining a lady. But a lad?" She smiled and her face lit with delight. "A lad would afford me entrance to places a woman could never hope, dare or wish to go."

"And these places interested you?" He stopped a few feet in front of her.

"Places, people, life itself. I had the urge to explore. My world seemed so narrow and confined. How could I ever make a good wife or mother if I did not know life?" She did not add that she had hoped to learn about love along the way. He did not need to hear that.

"So Harold was born."

"Aye." Her smile turned tender. "Harold made my adventure possible, and I will be forever grateful to him."

"So will I."

She looked at him oddly. "Whatever for?"

"He possessed an undaunting courage that I admired and a sharp wit that challenged. He stood strong for his convictions and that is to be respected in a man."

"And a woman?"

"Harold taught me that those same qualities are possible in a woman. Rare, but possible."

She shook her head. "You admire and respect Harold but are angry with Hope?"

"Strange as it may seem, aye," he answered. "I suppose I feel that if Harold trusted me as a friend then so could Hope, and that trust could have allowed her to confide in me."

"You were a good friend to Harold."

"And to Hope?"

She looked away. How could she admit the truth? How could she tell him that Hope loved him and wished to learn more about him? She could not, so she had held her tongue and remained disguised as the lad. She turned wide eyes on him and asked a question of him that she could not answer herself. "What would you have done if you had known me to be Hope?"

Colin spoke honestly. "I would have seen you returned safely to your uncle."

"And my adventure would have fast come to an end."

"You were starving when we first met," he reminded and took another step toward her.

"I found food." She stood, confident and strong.

"You could have gotten yourself killed."

"I survived."

"Pure luck." Another step and he was only inches away from her.

"Pure determination," she recounted and folded her arms across her chest.

It was a puny protective shield at best and one Colin knew he would have no trouble penetrating. He reached out and she stood firm, showing not an ounce of fear. He tugged gently at her hair. "I never thought a woman would shear her hair so."

"The reaction I expected from a man."

"And one that kept you safe in your disguise."

"Of course, who would expect a spoiled woman to cut her hair and don male garments? Nay, they searched for a female and completely ignored a skinny lad with a large cowardly dog who fit Lady Gwenth's character perfectly."

"And where and when did you plan for your charade to end?"

"The time and place would be of my own choosing."

"Was your choice made last night?"

She defended herself. "I did not choose this ending, but I will see that I have my way."

"Nay, no longer will you have your way," he said adamantly. He ran a tender finger along her jaw and faintly across her lips. "You will be my wife in four days' time and—"

"I will not wed you!" She raised her voice and refused to pay heed to the way his gentle touch stimulated her senses.

"We will wed and I will make you a good husband."

She stared speechless at him. At that moment she realized that he planned to do his duty, wed her and play intimate with her as he did with the many women who sought his bed. There was no love in his eyes though she did feel he admired and respected her, but that was not enough. She wanted him to love her.

She was calm when she announced once again, "I will not wed you."

Hope moved to walk past him and his hand reached out, grasped her slim waist and swiftly drew her up against him. She attempted to protest—an unwise move, since it left her mouth open and vulnerable.

His mouth descended on hers quickly.

She had never been kissed and often wondered how it would feel. She had never imagined the taste to be so potent and had never thought to lose her senses so quickly. She could barely keep a coherent thought. His lips, his tongue worked magic, casting a spell that enveloped her entire body and made her want to melt against him.

But then he was an expert lover.

The thought was like a rush of water dousing a fire. She returned instantly to her senses and pulled away from him.

His smile irritated instead of charmed. She wanted deep, genuine emotions and he was giving her surface feelings. She would have none of it.

"I will not wed you."

"We shall see," he said confidently.

She refused to be manipulated, dictated to or seduced. She had done well on her own and would continue to remain independent, no matter the demands made upon her. And when she married? She answered her own question out loud.

"When I wed it will be because I love my husband. Because I want his hands upon me, because his touch thrills me and because our love will be long-lasting. I will not doubt his love nor will he doubt mine. If you cannot offer me this, Colin, then do not insult me and take my hand in marriage."

She turned and walked out of the cottage, her head high and unshed tears rushing to sting her eyes.

Colin was stunned by her words and even more stunned by their implication. Was she implying that she loved him? And that she wished that love returned?

He grew agitated. What did she know about love? She was a mere naive child when it came to such strong emotions. She knew nothing of the depth or breadth of love and its consequences.

He stormed toward the door, his footsteps heavy. She would do her duty as her uncle directed and she would obey her new husband. He would see to that.

He slammed the cottage door shut behind him and stomped toward the keep.

Hope entered the great hall and took her usual seat beside Stuart at the long table in front of the dais. All eyes settled upon her and conversation hushed.

Her uncle glared at her, his mouth hanging open in bewilderment.

Faith was not surprised by Hope's rash action and she was pleased by the way her husband handled it.

"Lady Hope, please join us," he said, standing and extending his hand in invitation for her to take the empty chair beside the one she knew to be Colin's.

Hope answered sweetly. "Thank you, Lord Eric, but I prefer to sit here."

Her uncle shook his head in dismay but remained silent, allowing the lord of the keep to handle the potentially volatile situation.

Eric spoke more firmly and directly. "I am certain that Stuart enjoys your company, but your place is beside your soon-to-be husband."

Colin entered the great hall at that moment and remained standing near the door listening.

To everyone's surprise Hope went to battle with the devil.

"You must be mistaken, my lord; I intend to wed no one."

Shamus shook his head harder and Faith smiled.

"Then join me so we may discuss your objections," Eric offered, his hand remaining extended though his tone took on a note of authority.

Hope remained steadfast. "I see no need for discussion, my lord. I have made my decision."

Faith held firm to the chuckle that tickled her throat and offered her husband a comforting pat to the hand he had extended in invitation that now lay fisted at his side. It was obvious that he was irritated.

"There is always room for discussion," Eric said with a firmness that raised brows and caused a rush of whispers to circle the room.

Hope thought differently. "I think not. I am content with my decision."

Uncertain how to proceed without creating a scene, Eric looked to Colin and smiled, seeing that he was bearing down on his future wife with intentional strides.

Eric extended his offer for the last time. "Are you certain you will not join us, Lady Hope?"

"Nay, I—"

Her arm was seized in a tight grip and she was propelled off the bench in a flash.

"My Lord Eric, Lady Hope will be only too happy to

join you," Colin said pleasantly but firmly.

Hope attempted to free herself. It was a useless endeavor, his grip being much too tight and she, of course, lacked the physical strength to combat him. The only weapon to defend herself, therefore, was her mouth. "I possess the intelligence to speak for myself."

Colin's whispered response was for her ears alone. "Then speak wisely or not at all."

She returned the whisper. "Is that a threat?"

"To be more precise, a promise."

Words were ready to spill forth from her anxious lips when Colin rested his cheek next to hers.

"I always keep my promises."

His warm breath tickled her cheek and drifted down her neck, sending a shiver racing through her. She could continue to battle or withdraw and save her strength for a more important encounter. She chose the wiser course of action and acquiesced.

"I would be pleased to join my lord and lady."

A collective sigh could be heard circling the room as she walked with Colin to the dais.

Hope took the seat beside her uncle who sat beside Lord Eric, and Colin took the empty seat on her opposite side, effectively trapping her between them. If they thought to keep her well in hand they were wrong. They could not keep a constant eye on her. She had learned too well the artful art of dodging.

Conversation soon developed around her and while she answered questions that people asked, she did not voluntarily join in the conversation. She preferred to listen.

Colin leaned in close when he spoke, making it seem that he was an attentive and caring husband-to-be. "I have watched the lad react like this before. Harold would often grow quiet and contemplative and I realized he was taking in much. Is that how you learned to fool those searching for you?"

Hope was in the mood to battle. "It was not hard to fool the foolish."

Colin's jaw tensed and Hope instantly regretted her rash remark. He and his men had been far from foolish. They had cared for the lad and she did not wish to belittle their treatment of him.

Colin made ready to enter the skirmish when Hope spoke in a hushed voice. "I never counted you and your men among the foolish. You saw to Harold's care and protection and for that I am grateful."

"Not grateful enough to confide in me."

His annoyance was obvious and Hope attempted to alleviate it. "It would have made for a difficult situation if I had done so. I chose to continue my charade so as not to disappoint or make it more difficult for those around me."

Colin decided to be direct. "In simple terms, you did not trust me."

"I was not certain whom I could trust." She hesitated and then spoke as directly as he did. "I still do not know whom I can trust."

"Since I am to be your husband I would hope you would trust me."

While he sounded sincere and she wished that he was, there was always that charm of his that he used so easily. She wanted none of it. She simply wanted the real Colin—the one who cared for the lad's safety and well-being. The one searching for a forever love.

She spoke candidly. "Forcing someone to wed does not invoke trust."

"We shall wed." He sounded as though he delivered an edict and no amount of debate would persuade him otherwise.

"Since you command that we wed will you also command us to be happy?"

He turned on his charm. "You will find happiness in my arms—that I promise."

Hope wanted happiness born of love—otherwise his

arms would feel empty. She had four days to decide her own fate, and decide she would. If she felt this marriage was wrong then her decision would be a simple one. She would leave and take up residence at Croom Abbey.

With a plan in mind she felt more confident and since time was sorely limited she needed to do as much discovering as possible. "Could we find a more private place to talk?"

Colin obliged her without hesitation. "The healing cottage would afford us privacy." He stood and offered his hand to her, confident she would not object.

She placed her hand in his and rose to stand beside him. "A most welcoming and quiet place."

Colin excused them from their present company, explaining they intended to enjoy the cool night air.

Hope directed Lady to remain beside Rook where she rested comfortably. Besides, she did not look the least bit interested in following.

They walked in silence to the cottage, keeping a proper distance from each other though Hope's thoughts were anything but proper. She wanted time alone with Colin. She wanted him to kiss her. She wanted to know if there was a possibility that he could love her.

Hope entered the cottage first and walked over to stand in front of the fireplace, extending her nervous hands out to warm them. She heard the door shut and the slide of the latch effectively shutting all away from them and she shivered, realizing that she had thought of this moment many times. Now that it was here she was fearful—not of being kissed, but of what that kiss might bring.

Colin moved up behind her and slowly slipped his arms around her waist. "We are strangers yet we are not."

She relaxed back against him. "Aye, that we are. I have come to know much about you through the eyes of the lad."

Laughter spilled gently from his lips. "The lad taught

us both well, but it is the woman I wish to come to know now. Tell me about Hope."

A slight shudder raced over her, his warm breath tickling her sensitive neck. He tightened his arms around her waist and placed a tender kiss on her temple.

She decided to be direct. "Hope often thought of how it would feel to kiss you."

Colin turned her around in his arms and one look in his smoldering dark eyes told her she was about to find out.

He cupped her face in his hands and placed faint kisses to her forehead, her eyes, her nose and her chin.

Each kiss sent a tingle racing through her and made her eager with anticipation to taste his lips on hers.

He did not hurry the moment but continued at his own leisurely pace. "I cannot believe I never realized you were a woman. You have the softest skin, stunning eyes and lips." He shook his head slowly. "Lips that beg to be kissed."

He was certainly right about begging—if he did not kiss her soon she was going to beg him to kiss her.

With a faint brush of his lips across hers he began their first kiss and she moaned from the pleasure of the subtle taste and the promise of what was to come.

Another brush of his lips over hers and she found herself reaching up to try and capture his elusive kiss, her moan growing with her desire.

"Such passion," he whispered, his mouth a mere breath away from hers. "We will do well together."

She looked in his eyes before his mouth claimed hers and she saw a heated passion there that surprised her. His lips took control, tempting, teasing and tormenting her until his tongue swiftly entered her mouth and soared her passion near out of control.

She brought her arms up and around his neck and pressed her body against his without thought to her actions. And he welcomed her intimate gesture, holding her firmly to him and pressing his own body more intimately to hers.

Hope never knew such a powerful emotion existed. It stormed her senses, leaving her to feel senseless. Nothing seemed important at that moment except being there in his arms with his mouth on hers.

Nothing.

Nothing, that is, but love.

Twenty-three

Hope rose early the following morning, donned the lad's garments and, with Lady and Rook as companions, left the keep and made her way to the herb garden. She had been forced in the nicest of possible ways to sleep in the keep. She had wanted to remain in the healing cottage, but it was not proper for a lady to remain unattended, so she had no choice.

All her choices of late had been taken from her, though with good reason, as she was told. That did little good when she so missed the freedom she had enjoyed as the lad.

Her time now was expected to be spent on her wedding preparations and her husband. It appeared that everyone expected her to pay Colin extra attention and focus on pleasing him. That she loved him she had no doubt.

She wished to spend time with him, but the kind of time they had once spent on the road together, talking of interesting subjects and sharing similar interests. Now he treated her as a lady, courteous and attentive. And since their first kiss he had kissed her often, touched her gently and treated her as the charmer he was.

But she did not want Colin the charmer. She wanted Colin the deeply caring man, who had befriended Harold. Somehow she had a feeling that that man would kiss her differently than would Colin the charmer.

Prickly with agitation, she decided digging in the garden would be good for her, and she set herself to work thinning the young seedlings that had sprouted and needed dividing for optimum growth potential.

Lady could not be bothered helping her or getting her paws dirty in the rich dark soil, but Rook would fetch her a tool when asked while remaining attentive to his ladylove.

She had but three days to make a decision and she realized it would not be an easy one. At the present moment she wanted nothing more than to think about her digging in the earth, feeling its rich life and knowing it would create abundant blossoms in the near future.

She intended to dwell on this good thought.

The morning meal was being served in the great hall and all were present but Hope.

Eric and Borg enjoyed watching their friend have to deal with a woman who obviously could not be easily charmed. Over the years they had seen him successfully work his charm on every woman that he met.

Not so his future wife.

Their smiles grew broader.

"Not one word," Colin said to them both and looked at Shamus. "Hope obviously lacks proper behavior."

Shamus nodded with a wide grin that brought a laugh from Eric and Borg. "That my niece does. I am afraid her aunt and I spoiled her, but she was such an intelligent young girl and had such a passion to learn about life, we simply could not deny her. Her pleasant and caring personality made it all the more easy to indulge her."

"Now I, as her soon-to-be husband, am stuck with the consequences of your actions," Colin said, though his thoughts did not reflect his remark. He actually admired Hope's audacity. He had dared to hope that Hope the woman would retain some of the lad's qualities and he was learning that she most certainly did. The idea fascinated him.

A boring wife who performed womanly tasks all day did not at all interest him. A woman, however, who possessed a zest for life and wished to live it differently was more to his appeal.

He had even been surprised when he had kissed her and she responded so willingly. He had worried that perhaps she would be uptight and rigid when it came to intimacy but he was beginning to realize that Hope faced all of life's challenges with gusto. And he was suddenly interested in finding out how much gusto she possessed in bed.

Presently he wondered where she was and what she was up to. He did not for once think that she sat sulking in her room; that was not her way. Nay, she was off somewhere, not caring for the time or her obligations.

Lord, but this woman appealed to him.

With a broad smile on his face, he stood. "I am going to find Hope."

Eric kept his grin from spreading. "I think you are going to need some hope to find Hope."

Borg chuckled. "Aye, he is hopeless right now."

Shamus was the one to give a hardy laugh. Even Faith giggled quietly.

Colin spoke with confidence. "I will use my charm and have her here in time to share the morning fare with us."

"I wager you cannot do that," Borg said with just as much confidence.

"A foolish wager since I know the outcome, but I will take your coin as usual, Borg." And with that he left the hall, his strides as confident as his words.

Hope finished a row of seedlings and wiped at her perspiring brow, leaving a streak of dirt across her forehead. It felt good to dig in the earth and see the rewards of her chore. The tiny seedlings stood straight and proud, their small green leaves stretched out as if in thanks for a job well done.

She scratched at an itch on her cheek, leaving another bit of dirt to mar her soft complexion, and sat back on her haunches to inspect her endeavors and bask in her partially completed task.

That was when Colin saw her and stopped where he was. He remained near the corner of the cottage so that he could watch her without her being aware of his presence. She looked like a forest nymph; her skin and garments sprinkled with the earth's essence, her cheeks flushed from her busy chore and the pure delight on her face filled him with an intense passion that he had never experienced before in his life.

It was as if his heart and soul ached and for a brief second the strange thought frightened the hell out of him.

Damn, but he wanted her at that moment. He wanted to rush over to her, lay her down in the earth and make love to her with a rushing need that bordered on pure undeniable lust. He could not remember ever wanting a woman with such an overpowering intensity and he fought the odd urge with great difficulty.

She moved forward, her hands busy in the dirt, and he watched.

He had always thought of the lad as scrawny but viewing her now as a woman he thought of her as petite. Dressed as she was, it was hard to see curves and such, but thinking back to yesterday when her body was pressed firmly to his he realized just how shapely she was.

Her breasts were small, but then he never cared about size; he much preferred the nub that capped the soft mounds. Some hardened more than others and he liked the feel of a hard nipple in his mouth. It seemed that Hope hardened quite nicely from what he remembered of yesterday.

Her waist was slim and her hips rounded just right. There was also that petite, firm backside of hers that he enjoyed seeing in the lad's garments. And there was the thought of removing the garments from her body and seeing for himself what lay hidden beneath.

Hope groaned and stretched her arms out, her muscles obviously beginning to pain her. The tunic stretched across her chest and gave him reason to smile. Her nipples were hard and ready for a man's tongue.

It was his turn to groan and he kept it low as he moved from his hiding spot, realizing his spying had done him little good. Actually it had made him most uncomfortable.

"Hope," he called out more abruptly than he intended. She looked up at him, startled by his appearance.

Rook ran up to him and received a generous pat on the head. "The morning meal is being served." He kept his tone more neutral and his smile pleasant.

With a shake of her head she said, "I am not hungry."

While extra weight would not hurt her it was not a matter of her hunger he was concerned with. He wished her presence beside him for the meal. He liked talking with her. They never shared boring conversation. She always managed to stimulate his mind and now she stimulated him in other ways as well.

"A light fare, then," he said with a bit of firmness.

She shook her head again. "Nay, nothing. I am busy."

"Digging," he said as if her task was unimportant.

She did not seem to take offense. She smiled at him. "Helping life to flourish."

He came to stand beside her, looking down to watch her hands carefully separate the abundant seedlings and gently replant them.

"Now they will grow hardy and flourish," she said with a sense of excitement that he could almost feel himself.

His skin prickled with the intensity of her passion and it heightened his own senses and desires. He silently cursed his own flourishing and went down on bended knees beside her. She was much too happy for him to force her to leave her chore, though it most certainly was not a chore to her. He did not wish to partake of the morning meal without her so he decided to join her right where she was.

"Can I help?"

She gave him a glowing smile and his heart melted. The way he reacted to her was not at all good. He did not understand it, know how to deal with it, or know how to control it. And as a seasoned warrior, that was frightening.

"Your hands are gentle; this I know from watching you and how you administer to those more vulnerable. It is a caring side you have, Colin, but seldom allow others to see."

She was certainly astute in her observations. And damned if those streaks of dirt did not make her more attractive. Then there was the smell of the rich earth, so natural to the senses that it only made him more aware of her.

"Show me what to do," he said, though he really wanted to kiss her, touch her and . . . "Show me."

"It is dirty work," she said with a smile, squeezing a handful of dark earth.

"Dirt has never bothered me and I have had my share of being dirty."

"How so?" she asked and demonstrated what he was to do.

He followed her lead. "During battle it was not so easy to keep one's self clean. There were many times when I was covered in dirt and blood for days on end, wanting nothing more than to cleanse myself in a river or lake."

She placed a tender hand to his arm. "That is dirt, this is soil, and it gives life not takes it."

"You are much too intelligent for a woman," he said with a smile that complimented not charmed.

Her hand returned to digging and she gave him a wide grin. "I am unique."

He had to laugh, she said it with such conviction. "You are that."

Her smile faded and she looked at him with serious concern. "I am not like other women, nor do I wish to be."

Colin stopped digging. "I know this, Hope."

"But can you accept this in me?" Her voice seemed to plead for understanding as though his response would make a difference.

"Aye," he said without hesitation.

She beamed, feeling there was hope for them. Now all she needed to discover was that he could love her as much as she did him. "It is a good start."

"A good start," he repeated and gave her lips a quick kiss.

The kiss ignited a passion in them both; it sprang to life in their eyes and their hearts, and even Rook and Lady felt the surge of feelings for they both raised their heads where they lay beneath the tree and stared at the two humans with compassion.

Hope felt her breath catch and her heart race wildly and she watched his eyes heat with a passion that could not be denied.

Colin looked to the healing cottage that was a few feet away, then back at Hope. She understood his silent question, but how did she answer it?

She wanted him—that was obvious—and he her, but there was still love to consider and if she lay with him there would be the possibility of a child. She had yet to decide if she wished this marriage to take place.

"Hope?" He placed a firm soil-covered hand on her arm.

What did she do? She wanted him—lord how she wanted him.

Stuart rounded the corner of the cottage and smiled. "I have been sent to find you, sir, and Lady Hope. They hold the morning meal for you and everyone grows impatient."

"We will be there shortly," Colin told him and Stuart, understanding, nodded and retreated in haste.

"We have our duties, but later this evening the time is ours," Colin said, making his intentions clear. "Come." He stood and extended his hand to her. "Eat what you wish or not at all, but make your presence known."

Hope took his soil-covered hand. "I will clean up in the cottage, change my clothes and join you."

He nodded, though he wished her to remain as she was, in the lad's garments. "As you wish, but do not be long."

"I will hurry," she said and slipped her hand out of his to rush toward the cottage, not looking back at him.

Colin walked to the great hall, wishing her hand was in his. Eric and Borg smiled at him as he approached the dais and before words could be exchanged Faith intervened.

"Have you seen Rook, Colin?"

"He is with Lady. He was helping Hope in the garden while Lady rested."

Faith laughed softly and eased herself from her chair.

Her husband stood to help and she gratefully accepted his assistance, her stomach having rounded considerably in the last couple of weeks.

"I think I will go join Hope."

Eric looked about to object when Colin spoke. "She will be here soon."

Eric looked relieved, though it was short-lived.

"Then I will walk back with her. I feel the need for fresh air and I am not that hungry."

"What is wrong?" Eric demanded, his worry obvious. "You are not feeling well?"

"I feel fine," Faith insisted, hoping to ease her husband's worries. "I but wish to join Hope and get a breath of fresh air. And I wish to see Rook. He has been absent of late and I miss his company. There is no reason to hold the meal. Eat. I shall return with Hope shortly."

Eric was not satisfied. "I will go with you."

Faith sighed softly. "It is not necessary. I am fine."

"I will go with you and make certain you arrive safely, then I will leave you and Hope alone."

Faith smiled and shook her head before resting it on her husband's wide chest. Her words were meant for him alone. "You understand me well, husband, and for that I love you even more."

Eric smiled and kissed her lips gently before announcing, "Serve the meal; I will return soon."

A grateful sigh circled the room as the lord and lady left the great hall.

Hope was pleased to see Faith enter the cottage and glad that the devil but kissed his wife and bid her a quick greeting. Before he took his leave, he stopped abruptly at the door.

"Look after her," he said firmly.

"We are friends. I will always see to her welfare."

Her response brought a smile to his face. "Colin will be lucky to have you for a wife."

Hope was shocked by his words.

Faith simply smiled and sat in the chair at the table. "Eric understands Colin well."

"I wish I did," Hope said on a sigh. She had washed up and was getting ready to change garments when they arrived.

"Perhaps it is not Colin whom you need to understand."

Hope cast Faith an odd look.

Faith explained. "Perhaps you need to understand yourself."

Hope took no offense; she knew Faith only meant to help. "I thought I understood me."

"Sometimes we think we do, but when we take a closer look we find that is not so and we need to look with clearer eyes."

Hope found her remark interesting and joined her at the table, not bothering to change out of the soiled garments she wore. "You think my vision blurred?"

"I think you see what you wish, but ignore the obvious. Colin is a good man and with time—"

Hope interrupted. "There is no time."

"There is no need to rush."

"I have but three days to decide whether or not to wed."

"Why not wed Colin?" Faith asked.

"What if he does not love me?"

"What if you do not give him the chance to love you?"

"He has only three days."

Faith laughed. "And you expect him to discover his love for you in three days' time?"

It did seem absurd that she should allow him only three days to fall in love with her. But what was she to do? Wed him and hope?

She voiced her concern. "What if I wed him and he does not fall in love with me?"

Faith placed a tender hand on hers. "What think you of love? Do you understand its complexities? Do you understand the emotions involved? How can you think love can be decided on so easily?"

"Did you not love the devil easily?"

"The devil is not easy to love," she answered with a teasing smile. "I had to come to know him first, understand his ways and understand my own feelings for him."

"You questioned your love for him?"

"I wed him knowing little of him, but I learned quickly enough."

"That you loved him?" Hope asked, attempting to understand.

"That he was a man I could love if given a chance."

"You are saying that I should give Colin the chance to love me."

"I am saying," Faith said softly and with heartfelt compassion, "that you should give him more than three days."

Twenty-four

Colin stormed through the keep in search of Hope. In two days' time she would be his wife and she had yet to obey even the simplest of commands. He had planned for them to take a leisurely ride outside the castle grounds, giving them time alone. She had only to meet him in front of the keep at the designated time. That time had come and gone and she was nowhere to be found.

He was angry and had every right to be. She had turned his whole life upside down and was continuing to do so. He was caring, cordial and attentive to her and what did she give him in return? Obstinacy, stubbornness and selfishness. She did whatever she wanted.

That was about to end.

He walked through the kitchen and for the first time the female servants drew back from him. "Has anyone seen Lady Hope?" he asked in such a chilling tone that two servants shivered and the remaining servants vigorously shook their heads.

He almost bumped into Mary on his way out the door, moving aside to allow her to enter. His face softened to a concerned smile. "Feeling well?"

"Fit as can be," she beamed, her full cheeks rosy.

"I am glad to hear that." His smile faded and his glance drifted past Mary out the door to the surrounding area.

"Looking for someone?" she asked.

"Lady Hope," he answered anxiously. "Have you seen her?"

"She left the castle with Lady and Rook some time ago. I think I heard someone mention she was going to collect a few plants for Lady Faith."

"Thank you, Mary," he said and marched off with a look he often wore into battle—a harsh look that had brought many an opponent to his knees.

Colin wasted no time in going to the stables, getting his horse, mounting and riding out of the keep. He paid no heed to those who waved or called a greeting and tongues soon began to wag.

The charmer had met his match.

Hope was running through a meadow with Lady and Rook nipping at her heels in excitement. She was having a wonderful time and wished life could remain as it was at this moment—carefree and simple.

She had gathered several plants that Faith had requested. Her basket was near full and she was about to return to the keep when the open meadow with its high lush green grass and patches of wildflowers called out to her. It had been too many years since she had run through a meadow and felt the grass beneath her bare feet and the warm air rush across her face.

She felt as if she were a child at play and it felt delightful, the blades of grass tickling her bare feet and the lad's garments giving her the freedom to move and run as she could never do in female attire.

The dogs barked their pleasure and she turned in circles, throwing her arms out, dropping her head back and closing her eyes to let the bright sun toast her face.

Hope felt the earth rumble beneath her feet and knew instinctively that a horse was bearing down on her. She stopped and spun around to see who was headed her way. Horse and rider were upon her before she could yell—

"Colin!"

He scooped her up with one arm and deposited her fast and hard in front of him.

She stared with startled eyes at him and her arms went quickly to his waist, though she grabbed hold of his tunic, attempting to avoid any intimate contact—a foolish thought, since her lower body was planted firmly against his.

"Where are your senses?" she demanded as he brought the horse to a slower pace and the two dogs caught up with them and followed in peaceful strides.

"I lost them the day you entered my life."

Her temper flared but his was already well ignited.

"Did you forget we had plans?"

"*You* had plans. *You* made them, therefore, *you* should enjoy them."

Her anger brought her to full glorious life. It raged over her with a vitality that stimulated the senses and heated the blood. Lord, he had not felt this alive with a woman in a long time. And she was just a bit of a thing. He barely had to use his muscles to scoop her off the ground and yet the body pressed so intimately against him was every inch female.

He felt her heat mix with his own and damned if he did not want her as he had for the last two days. His passion for her was ridiculously out of control. He had desired women—many women—over the years. But damned if he did not want, ache and feel an overwhelming need for this woman.

What was different about her? Was it that she did not appear eager for him? He could see in her eyes that she wanted him with almost the same intensity as he did her. He knew if he reached down and touched her she would be moist with desire for him. But she never voiced her passion or demonstrated it. She held back, almost fearful of admitting her true feelings for him.

The horse slowed to a gentle trot and he stared down into her heated eyes. She waited, ready and prepared to battle him. He decided it was time to change tactics.

He moved his hand from her waist to grab hold of the back of her head while his mouth swooped down on hers.

She was too late to defend against the unexpected assault and the results were devastating to her senses. He tasted simply much too good and she could not deny him or herself. She kissed him back with all the raging desire that raced through her.

The horse stopped though the couple locked in each other's arms did not notice. They kissed like long denied lovers and their hands touched with a frantic urgency. They became lost in their own world, one of pleasure and promise.

Colin ran his hand down to where their bodies joined to intimately stroke her. She moaned into his mouth and moved against him.

He pulled his mouth from hers and rushed his words. "We need to find a secluded place."

"Aye, we do, we must," she pleaded.

He wrapped a strong arm around her and directed the horse off to a clump of trees in the near distance. The dogs followed, though they stopped to sniff and forage along the way.

He eased her off the horse first, then followed in haste, taking her back in his arms.

Hope felt the difference immediately. Colin the charmer had returned and intended to work his skills on her. She wanted the Colin who had kissed her only moments ago. The one who had lost all reason and knew nothing, wanted nothing but to love her. She wanted the man who hid behind the charming mask. The one born of deep emotions, caring naught for learned skills but surrendering to the love he kept hidden and locked away.

She reluctantly took a step away from him. "Why do you hide from yourself?"

His arms felt empty when she left them and it was

not a feeling he liked. He looked at her strangely, not having expected a question or her retreat.

"You think to charm me into intimacy?"

He had to laugh, though he did not think it funny. "My charm pleases women."

"I look for more than just meaningless charm." She took an adamant stance, crossing her arms over her chest in defiance, though it was disappointment she felt. She ached to be in his arms and feel that rush of uncontrolled passion rage through him and into her. She wanted all his defenses down so that he could finally love.

"I will not allow you to anger me, Hope," he said with a smile that could charm the devil himself. "And I will not force my charm upon you. When you are ready."

"And if I am never ready?"

He laughed gently. "You already are."

"I will not wed you," she spat at him in anger.

"Aye, you will wed me," he said calmly. "You have no choice in the matter." His smile teased. "And I will *charm* you every night of our married life."

"Never," she all but snarled at him and rushed past him.

He grabbed her arm. "Never say never, Hope, for then it will surely come to pass." He grabbed her around the waist then and hoisted her with ease onto the horse.

She looked ready to jump off but he was quick and swung up behind her before she could make a move.

"Now we can talk while we leisurely ride back to the castle," he said, reaching out to take hold of the reins and to keep a firm arm around her small waist.

She decided that resisting would be futile. Talk was what was necessary—perhaps then they could find a way to settle this situation.

Briefly she wondered how he would react if she admitted her love for him. Would he respond kindly so as not to hurt her feelings? Would he suggest that perhaps one day he could love her as she did him? Or would he admit that while he cared for her there was no love for her in his heart?

He seemed to read her thoughts. "Why do you oppose this union?"

She asked the question that rested on the tip of her tongue. "Why do you wish this union?"

His answer was simple. "Honor."

"Yours or mine?"

"You wound me," he said with soft laughter and a gentle hug to her waist. "Allow me my chivalry and allow us time."

"There is no time," she said sadly.

He pressed his cheek to her temple. "We have the rest of our lives."

She shut her eyes tightly, hoping to stop the tears. He was being kind and nice—it was his nature to do so—yet it was not enough. Her heart ached with love for him. His heart weighed heavy with duty and honor. She did not want love born of necessity.

She decided to be truthful. What else was there for her to do? "I wish a marriage born of love."

He paused a moment before answering and that brief pause gave Hope her answer. "In time I am certain a degree of love could flourish in our marriage." He seemed to want to comfort her and alleviate her doubts. "I will make you happy, Hope. I will not force rigid rules upon you but will allow your free spirit to soar and I will always, always protect you."

He pressed her back firmly against him and she rested willing in his embrace. His strength felt good and she had no doubt that he could well protect her.

"And you will find pleasure in our bed, that I promise," he said in a whisper with a kiss to her temple.

A single tear slipped free and she casually wiped it off her cheek then opened her eyes. Her decision was made. She would set her plans in motion immediately. Until then she would keep up a pretense of following through with the wedding plans.

"I suppose you are right. I have no choice in the matter. Our marriage must be."

"I am glad to hear you say this. Everyone will be pleased with your wise decision. And in time you will come to realize that it was for the best."

"Aye," she said softly. *But best for whom?*

"We will do well together, Hope, and you need not worry about intimacy. I will treat you well and teach you to enjoy the marriage bed."

"I have no doubt you will," she said, "after all—you do charm."

He nuzzled at her neck. "Aye, that I do."

She allowed herself to relax and enjoy the play of his lips on her sensitive neck. After all, this would be the last time she ever felt them. Tonight she would leave Shanekill and travel to Croom Abbey where she would seek permanent shelter. She would have no problem convincing her uncle that it was for the best.

"I look forward to the many nights we will share together as husband and wife."

Again he attempted to console her and alleviate her doubts, and he was so sincere, so charming. Where was the other Colin? The one who displayed his true emotions when they surfaced. The one who searched for forever love.

Hope excused herself when they returned to the keep, wishing to bathe and change her garments. Colin seemed reluctant to let her go, suggesting they spend time together. She knew better than to be alone with him, however. She understood that with the way she felt she would easily surrender to him and then, once intimate, she would not be able to retire to the convent for there would be the risk of being with child.

Nay, she needed to keep her distance from him and make her escape this evening. There was no other way.

"A short walk," Colin suggested, realizing his need for her was reaching an aching throb, which alarmed him. He had never felt this needy for a woman.

Hope shook her head. "Later, perhaps." Though a convenient headache would put an end to that. She just could not risk being alone with him.

"Later," he said, as if his word confirmed his intentions.

She hurried away and he drifted off to sit with a tankard of ale in front of the large stone fireplace in the great hall. It was quiet with only a few servants scurrying about. A gentle fire kept the room roasted to a pleasant warmth, though with summer not far off the hearths would soon lie cold and barren. For now, Colin enjoyed the gentle warmth of the flames and the warmth of the ale as it made its way down to his stomach.

He sat on a bench, his elbows braced on his knees as he leaned toward the hearth staring at the leaping flames. He did not know what disturbed him but he felt unsettled as though a secret that he could not grasp gnawed at him and demanded his attention.

The last couple of days had been a sudden jolt to his senses. Discovering that Harold was Hope—a woman and not the lad he had found himself caring about—weighed heavily upon him. The fact that he found himself attracted to Hope made the situation all the more confusing.

He was attempting to remove the lad from the woman and yet they were really one and the same. Harold was merely a shield that Hope had used to protect herself. A shield she continued to keep strong and steady around her. A shield he intended to penetrate.

There was something about Hope that fascinated him. She was uncommon in her demeanor and forward in her convictions. She possessed a tenaciousness he admired and a strength that was gentle yet oddly powerful. She seemed to know and understand what she wanted. And she intended that no one stand in her way.

He smiled and shook his head. Her determined nature warned him that she would be a handful in bed and he looked forward to the challenge. He was certain she would not respond like most women but would demand and delight in the pleasures of intimacy. The thought excited him and made him eager for their wedding day.

Tonight when they had time alone he would tempt and tease her, but he would wait until they were properly wed to join with her physically. His smile grew, thinking of the way she so easily responded to him, though there was something, something he did not quite grasp about her that made him pause and ponder.

That secret that gnawed.

Love.

The word roared in his mind. She had been honest when she told him she wanted a marriage of love, but then he had wanted the same. He wanted to love the woman he wed, or he would not wed at all. If that was so, then why did he seem not to object to this marriage? Why did it not seem like a forced arrangement but actually one he looked forward to? Could he have deep feelings for Hope?

Nonsense.

He shook his head again.

He didn't really know Hope—or did he?

At first when he was sent in search of her he was annoyed that a spoiled woman of such sterling heritage should be causing so much difficulty for so many, but as he discovered more about her character he realized she was living the strength and courage of her heritage. And she continued to do so, no matter the consequences of her actions.

Hope was not an ordinary woman and that fact appealed to him. She would not be a boring wife, and her demands would be ones he could certainly handle, deal with and perhaps enjoy. An adventure or two would suit him well, especially sharing them with a wife.

He was content with his decision in regards to this union. He actually felt that Hope belonged to him. He was not certain when he had made that discovery or whether it involved the fact that he felt so heavily responsible for the lad, but Hope and the lad being the same person made his responsibility even more weighty.

He ran a hand through his hair before downing a generous gulp of ale.

"Heavy thoughts?" Eric asked, joining him on the bench with his own full tankard.

"Are not thoughts of a woman always heavy thoughts?" he asked with a grin.

"They are a trying lot," Eric agreed.

"But a lot we cannot do without."

"Aye, I will drink to that," Eric said and raised his glass in a toast.

Colin clinked his tankard to Eric's.

"Are you certain you want this marriage?"

Colin grinned. "I was waiting for you to ask that of me."

"I will not have you in a forced union. You have fought hard by my side and protected my back many a time. While I think this union is a good one for you, I will have it only if you wish it."

"You are a true friend," Colin said with a hardy pat to Eric's back. "But I find that I do wish this union. Why?" He shrugged. "I do not know and I do not think it is important. I only know that I wish Hope to be my wife."

"I am glad to hear that you wish to wed Hope."

"So do I," Borg said, joining the two with his own tankard of ale in hand and raising it in another toast. "To a joyful, prosperous and loving union."

Eric raised his tankard.

Colin raised his, clinking it with the other two, love heavy on his mind.

Hope huddled beneath the wool blanket, feigning a horrible headache. She squinted her eyes and moaned softly, feeling guilty about lying, while Faith hurried quietly around the room preparing an herbal brew to help alleviate the pain.

Colin entered the room quietly, and Hope caught his entrance from the corner of her eye, hoping he would speak with Faith and take his leave. But she was not that lucky.

He approached the bed.

He leaned down beside the edge of the bed that she clung to and spoke in a whisper. "I am sorry you are not well, but I feel confident that Faith will help ease your pain and bring you comfort."

He reached out and gently brushed her hair out of her eyes. She moaned, feeling guilty with her deceit.

"Rest," he urged. She heard his distress and wondered if he actually felt love for her. "Tomorrow we will spend time together and the following day we will exchange vows and seal our fate forever. Then, Hope, you will be *forever mine*."

She shut her eyes tightly and though he assumed it was from the ache in her head it was the ache in her heart that caused her pain. She recalled how he had wanted a woman to love and one he could call forever his. She had wanted so very badly to be that woman. But he would marry her out of honor and duty. Love had nothing to do with their forthcoming union, and she would have a marriage no other way.

He kissed her gently on the forehead and she moaned softly, knowing this was their final farewell. "Rest, I will see you on the morrow."

She whispered a gentle good-bye and forced her eyes shut against the tears that threatened to spill. When she heard the door close behind him she could not stop the flood that rushed forward.

Faith was instantly at her side. "Drink this and the pain will ease."

"Will it make me sleep?"

"Aye, you need to rest."

She could not sleep. She needed her wits about her for her journey. She pretended to shiver. "I am so cold."

"Take this and drink. I will get another blanket to warm you."

As soon as Faith's back was to her, she spilled the contents of the cup beneath the bed, bringing the empty cup to her lips as Faith turned and approached her.

Faith spread another blanket over her, then took the empty cup from her. "You have been through much in the last few days. Rest now, for in a day's time it will be over and life will finally begin for you."

Hope fluttered her eyes as if they were too heavy to keep open and wished to drift shut. She waited while she felt Faith tuck the blankets around her, clean up around the room then check on her one more time before extinguishing the candle and quietly leaving the room and closing the door softly behind her.

Hope did not waste a moment. She hurried from the bed, changed into Harold clothes yet again, gathered the stash of food she had squirreled away over the past couple of days and alerted a sleeping Lady that it was time for them to leave.

The only problem she did not count on was that Rook intended to join them. He refused to leave Lady's side and no amount of prompting or coaxing would change the fact. The dogs were obviously inseparable and in love. She had no choice but to take Rook along.

She made her way safely out of the keep, off the castle grounds and into the dark night, praying that her journey would be a safe one.

And praying that her broken heart would someday heal.

Twenty-five

"She is gone?" Colin asked as if he did not hear or understand Eric.

"She probably left sometime last night," Eric confirmed, his annoyance obvious.

Faith hurried into the solar, her hands gripped tightly together. "I cannot find Rook anywhere, Eric."

Eric was instantly at her side, his arm going around her shoulder and hugging her solidly to him. "He more than likely went with Lady and Hope."

Tears spilled from Faith's eyes and tore at her husband's heart. "I never thought he would leave me."

"Love causes foolishness," Colin said, his heart heavy for Faith.

"But I raised him since he was a pup. He has never been away from me."

Eric looked ready to kill when he cast a furious eye on Colin. "We go to find her and that coward of a dog of hers that Rook insists on protecting."

Faith pulled out of her husband's grasp. "I will join you."

"Absolutely not." Eric knew his remark was unwise as soon as he spoke the words.

"I will go find my dog with or without your approval," Faith said with a childish stamp of her foot.

"You will not jeopardize the safety of our unborn child," Eric insisted, knowing full well she would never do such a thing but not knowing what else to say to dissuade her.

"You know me better than that, my lord."

Eric and Colin winced. Whenever Faith referred to Eric as "my lord" it was on purpose and with intention.

Eric attempted to reason with her. "I will see to returning Rook safely to you. It is not necessary that you accompany us."

"Not necessary, but I wish to," Faith said with a firmness that meant she was not to be dissuaded.

Eric decided it was time to put his foot down. He reached out and grasped her chin. "You are not going."

Two hours later Eric, Colin, a band of six men and Faith were ready to travel.

Eric was not in a good mood; Faith, however, was in a fine mood. Colin was simply furious.

He could not still his growing anger. He had assumed all was settled between him and Hope and that there would be no further problems. He had not expected her once again to disappear. And when he found her, he intended to—

"Calm your anger," Eric ordered as he rode up beside him. Colin looked ready to rebel. "You will do yourself and us little good if you do not possess a clear head."

Colin understood the truth of his words and attempted to calm his warring emotions. "I do not understand why she ran away. Does she so oppose this union that she takes flight?"

Faith joined them, guiding her horse between the two men, and answered his disturbing question. "She fights for what she wants."

"What does she want?" Eric asked.

"Love," Faith and Colin said in unison.

Faith smiled. "You begin to understand her."

"Only begin," Colin said. "I realize from dealing with Harold that he was tenacious when he thought himself right or was firm in his beliefs. He would place himself in jeopardy to prove himself or to defend his actions. I admired his courage."

"And do you admire that same courage in Hope?"

"Watch how you answer that," Eric warned him with a smile.

"I do not need to," Colin said confidently. "I admire Hope's courage, yet it worries me, for she takes risks she should not take and places herself in dangerous situations."

"And this worries you, you say?" Faith asked with a rub to her back.

"You are uncomfortable?" her husband asked, slowing his horse and forcing all those around him to do the same.

Faith hated to admit that she already grew weary. She did not wish to slow them down, and she herself was worried about Rook and wished to find him. "I am fine."

Eric focused narrowed eyes on her and she attempted to avoid that knowing glare of his by insisting Colin answer her question. "About your worry."

Eric answered. "Any man involved with a stubborn woman who does not know any better than to do what she is told is doomed to worry endlessly."

"Thank you for that bit of wisdom, my lord. Now may Colin answer the question?"

"His answer sounds good to me," Colin said with a grin.

"Men," she said, feigning annoyance and trying to move and alleviate the dull pain in her lower back without notice from her husband.

It was useless. He took immediate note of her discomfort.

"That is it—we stop now for the night," he ordered firmly.

"We are barely away from the castle," Faith said, feeling guilty she had disrupted their search mission.

Colin put her at ease. "Hope could not have gotten far on foot, especially if she left in the dark of night.

We would do well to search the surrounding area while you rest."

She did not argue, wanting desperately to get off the horse and ease her back pain. "If Rook is close by he may sense our presence and find us."

"If I were not familiar with that big ugly dog—"

"He is not ugly," Faith insisted, and seemed hurt by his remark.

Her obvious reaction upset Eric and he halted his horse along with hers, dismounted in haste and gently scooped her off the horse into his powerful arms. "Nay, Rook is not ugly, but you are weary and need rest."

She snuggled her face into the crook of his neck. "Aye, that I do and I am sorry for being stubborn and not listening to you. Now I will slow your progress down in finding Hope."

Colin intervened. "My lord, though your presence and skills are appreciated, I do not require your help. I have sufficient help in finding her. We are still close to the keep; I would suggest you return there tomorrow morning with Lady Faith."

"A wise suggestion and one I will follow," Eric said. "For now I will see to her comfort while you search the area."

Two men remained behind to help set up camp and for added protection. Eric never took chances, especially where his wife was concerned.

By nightfall a fire burned, a rabbit roasted over the spit and Colin seemed more irritated than ever.

"I cannot understand how the woman just disappears in clear sight. She could not have gotten far, and yet there is no sign of her or her cowardly dog." He looked regrettably to Faith. "And no sign of Rook."

"He can take care of himself, I am sure; I just miss him so." She rested her head on her husband's shoulder.

"Find them all," Eric ordered, not caring to see his wife so upset and certainly not accustomed to it, since she possessed a spirited nature of her own. But he knew the babe was beginning to take its toll on her and he wanted her where she could have rest and care, and that was the keep.

Colin nodded in understanding, his own concern for Faith obvious. "I will return them all safely to Shane-kill."

His confident remark brought a smile to Faith and they were soon eating and enjoying a lively conversation about the perils and pleasures of wedded bliss.

Faith suddenly sat straight up and cocked her head as if to listen.

Eric was about to ask her what she heard when Rook burst out of the surrounding darkness and headed directly for Faith. He licked her face, wagged his tail and bounced around her in excitement.

"Calm down, calm down," she said mildly.

Colin and Eric immediately stood and the men went to walk the perimeter of the small camp at close attention.

"The others cannot be far off," Colin said.

"Aye, but why is Rook separated from them?" Eric asked the question more to himself than to the others.

"I think something disturbs him, Eric," Faith said, alerted to the dog's eagerness for her to follow him.

"We cannot race off into the dark," Eric said, noticing how agitated the dog appeared.

Colin grew alarmed. "Hope could be hurt."

"Eric," Faith said in alarm and fumbled to stand, her rounded stomach not making movement easy. He immediately reached down and assisted her up with one powerful arm. "We cannot leave her out there all night."

"We cannot search the darkness," Eric insisted.

As much as Colin hated the thought of not immediately searching for Hope he had to agree with Eric. "He is right, Faith. It would be foolish to attempt a search now."

"But Rook can direct us," she insisted.

"And if we lost him in the dark?" Eric asked.

Faith watched how Rook anxiously looked to her to follow him and she grew worried. "Something is wrong, Eric, dreadfully wrong."

Eric suddenly felt the hair on the back of his neck go up and he looked to Colin, but before he could issue a command their camp was rushed by a band of zealous thieves who surrounded them in an instant.

Eric and Colin took a guarded stance in front of Faith, their hands braced on the hilt of their swords. Rook stood at her back, a warning growl for all to keep their distance.

A tall man with confident strides stepped from the darkness. He was a sinfully handsome one and astute, his eyes taking in his surroundings in a quick yet studious glance. He spoke with an eloquence that belied his trade and bordered on arrogance, and he carried himself with the pride of one accustomed to privilege.

"Please forgive our intrusion. We will take only a moment of your precious time."

"Speak your piece then and be gone," Eric ordered in a commanding voice that the band of thieves immediately respected.

The man acknowledged his worthy opponent with a gracious nod. "I seek a donation for the needy. Whatever you have on you I am sure you will be willing to share with those less fortunate."

Colin realized that if it were just the men there, Eric would waste not a moment putting the thieves in their place, but because of Faith the devil would relent and give the thief what he asked, though he doubted it would be the last the thieves saw of the devil.

"Be generous, men," Eric ordered and stared straight at the thief in charge. "My wife has nothing to donate. She will be left undisturbed."

The man wisely nodded in agreement. "I will take your word, my lord, for I know you yourself will be generous. And I"—the man said with a wide smile— "have a helper who will collect your donations."

Rook whined and Colin felt dread grip the pit of his stomach.

"Lad," the man called out. "Make haste."

Colin and Eric both shook their heads when Hope, dressed in the lad's garments, stepped out of the darkness. Lady followed close by her side, whining pitifully with fear, which caused Rook to growl all the more.

"Be done with it, lad," the man instructed. "We do not wish to keep these fine people waiting when they are so willing to share with the needy."

Hope walked the perimeter of the camp first, collecting from the men who stared at her with wide eyes and grins. They seemed entertained by her plight—or was it the consequences that entertained them?

Hope finished up and with steps that were far from hasty approached the trio in the center of the camp. Did she step up to the devil first or did she face Colin? She somehow thought that in this situation it would be easier to face the devil.

The choice was not left to her. As soon as she was in close distance of them both, Colin reached out, grabbed her arm and yanked her to his side. Lady hastily hurried to Rook's side where she leaned against him and whimpered.

"One word," he warned her, "and I will throttle you."

The tall man took quick steps toward Colin.

Colin halted him with a raised hand and a firm voice. "The lad belongs to me."

Though startled by his words and the strength with which they were issued, Hope remained silent, displaying no emotions and hoping no one could hear how wildly her heart beat.

"How so?" the man asked, his hand cautiously resting on the hilt of the knife tucked in his leather belt.

Colin stood with a warrior's pride and arrogance and a tight hold on Hope. "First tell me whom I address."

"A reasonable request, as long as it is reciprocated," the man said.

Colin nodded, intending that he receive his answer first.

"I am called Rath. And you?"

"I am Colin and this is—"

Rath finished when Colin looked to Eric. "The Irish devil himself."

Eric demonstrated not an ounce of surprise, though he asked, "You know me and yet you attack my camp. Not a wise move."

Rath smiled as if he knew better. "It is common knowledge how much you favor your wife. I knew you would do nothing to jeopardize her safety."

Faith attempted to step forward and protest, feeling she had made this trip difficult for her husband. His large body blocked her attempts and no amount of shoving would budge him from his protective stance.

Rath looked back at Colin. "And the lad—who is he to you?"

"*The lad*," Colin said with the annoyance of a frustrated man, "is a *lass*, and she is *my wife*."

Hope glared at him and was about to protest his lie when he turned a chilling stare on her that warned of his mounting wrath and the dire consequences if she should choose to disagree with him.

Colin continued. "She is a temperamental woman who has yet to learn her place and duties, though I intend to teach her well to obey me."

That brought a laugh from Rath. "I have known the lad but a few hours and I would say that you have taken on more of a chore than you realize."

Laughter circled the camp not only from the band of thieves but from Eric's men as well. Though strangers, they all seemed to be in agreement.

When the laughter subsided Rath asked, "Tell me, Colin, how much is your wife worth to you?"

Colin laughed when he answered, "Not much."

Hope grew furious but felt disappointed. Naturally, she wished to hear that she meant the world to him and that no monetary value could be placed on his feelings for her. Her anger made her react and she pulled to free herself.

Colin only tightened his grip on her and whispered harshly, "Stay as you are."

Reluctantly she obeyed, seeing that she had no other choice.

Rath grinned and shook his head. "Come now, Colin, she must be worth something—even a small purse. She does, after all, possess a courage and strength not found in many women."

Colin realized that the thief wished to barter and that the man fully understood the value of the possession he bartered over. "And what do you think her worth?"

"A heavy purse, for sure," Rath said with confidence.

Colin had to keep up a pretense that he thought her worthless when her worth, to him, was priceless. "A weighty purse?" He shook his head. "I think not."

The two men seemed to take joy in their bartering, as did the others in camp. In the end when all was settled it was a heavy purse that Colin agreed to.

"Now for delivery of my reward for seeing to your wife's safe return," Rath said, finishing negotiations. "The two women will remain behind in my protection while the rest of you see to collecting my coins and returning them to me."

The devil's voice boomed in the darkness. "Absolutely not."

A few men shivered; Rath merely stood his ground. "I am afraid I must insist, my lord, but fear not—your wife will be safe in my protection."

"My wife will remain protected for she will remain by my side, and I am sure Colin feels the same about *his wife*," Eric said emphatically.

Colin agreed with the devil. "Aye, that I do. Hope will not leave my side." It was then he finally released her and gently pushed her to stand behind him.

"I can understand your misgivings," Rath said, "but

it is the payment of coins that I am concerned with. Your wives will remain with me until the payment is received. If you wish to join them so be it, but then make arrangements for the payment so that your stay with me is a short one."

Eric spoke up. "I will arrange for my men to return for the coins and instruct them as to where payment will be made."

Rath seemed satisfied. "An acceptable arrangement. We will finalize the plans this evening. Until then we all might as well make ourselves comfortable for the night." He looked to the devil. "I think your wife has been on her feet long enough. She must be tired."

Eric was impressed that the man actually showed sympathy for his wife and was curious that a common thief cared. But then the man looked anything but common.

Colin seemed to agree, for he exchanged knowing glances with the devil, understanding full well that they both intended to keep a watchful eye on the man.

Faith gratefully settled on a bed of blankets her husband had arranged and used his wide chest as a comforting pillow for her aching back. Rook and Lady sat by her side, both dogs snuggling together to drift off into a much-needed sleep.

Hope was made to join Colin on the spread of blankets on the ground not far from the fire's warmth. She sat straight and stiff beside a prone Colin, his arms cushioning his head.

He said but one word to her. "Why?"

She feigned confusion.

"Do not play ignorant with me. You know full well what I ask."

Hope spoke low, her reasoning for his ears alone. "I did not feel our union a valid one."

Again he asked, "Why?" His eyes settled on her lips and he wondered why they suddenly seemed so inviting;

but then he remembered how they tasted and ironically he missed their robust flavor.

She sensed his attention was elsewhere, especially when his glance rested on her lips. She attempted to keep the question focused. "You do not wish to wed me."

He turned to his side, his head braced in his hand. "I agreed to wed you."

"Agree and wish are vastly different."

"So for this difference you ran away?"

Hope stared at him. "Of course, and given that you do not understand my reasoning, it was a wise decision for me to run away."

"A foolish decision," he corrected firmly. "You will be my wife soon, that I promise you, but for now everyone will *think* you my wife." He avoided her protest by continuing on. "You will behave accordingly, follow my dictate and perform your wifely duties without question."

Hope eyed him critically. "You think this to be so?"

He sat up and brought his face to within inches of hers. "I know it to be so. Defy me and suffer the consequences."

"A threat?"

His charming smile irritated her. "A promise."

"You think you have won—"

He did not allow her to finish. "I know I have won."

"Borg tells me that you always wager foolishly."

"And I always win," he said, planting a quick kiss on her lips.

She pulled back and wiped at her lips with the back of her hand. "There is always a first time."

Colin could not help but grin and lean in close to her. "Aye, Hope, that there is and it is me who you will be sharing your first time with."

Twenty-six

The next day found them on a tedious journey to a remote area that sat well secluded from prying eyes. The small village was tucked between hills and buried in a thicket of heavy trees and bushes. Only those who called the village their home knew of its existence and it seemed the inhabitants intended to keep it that way.

Eric's men had been sent back to Shanekill with a message to Borg who was to secure the agreed upon coins and bring them to a designated area within a week's time. Until then Eric, Faith, Colin and Hope were guests of the thief Rath.

Colin and Hope were secluded in a small cottage not far from a similar cottage that Eric and Faith were placed in. They were provided with drink and food and a continuous guard outside their doors.

Colin had little time to speak with Eric before they were directed to their temporary residence, but one look in the devil's eyes told Colin he was not at all happy and that concern for his wife was uppermost in his mind.

Colin understood that Eric would not risk his wife's safety and, therefore, they were to be patient and wait. Colin, on the other hand, found his patience seriously waning. The reason for that was a pint-sized woman named Hope.

It was dark by the time they were secured in the cottages. A generous serving of food was provided for them, a warm fire chased the slight chill from the air and a narrow bed sat prepared for husband and wife to share.

Unfortunately Hope and Colin were not in a loving mood. They were ready to argue. Over what they could not say, though any topic would do.

Colin chose it, and Hope was ready to defend herself. She stood in front of the small hearth, warming her chilled hands.

Colin tore a chunk of bread off the freshly baked loaf on the small table in the center of the confined room. "Upon our return to Shanekill I intend to see those garments you wear burned."

Hope shrugged, though her chin rose. "No matter; if I wish to wear a lad's garments, I will."

"No more you will," he said firmly, ignoring the warm bread in his hand.

"You are not my husband and have naught to say over me." Her words were issued with the bearing of one accustomed to giving commands.

Colin tossed the bread on the table. "I will be your husband; it would be foolish of you to think otherwise. And it would be foolish of you not to heed my words."

Hope gave a defiant and emphatic toss of her head. "I will not marry you and I most certainly will not bed you."

Colin smiled with the charm of the devil himself and caused Hope's knees to tremble. "Guard your words wisely, sweet Hope, for you respond most ardently in my arms."

Hope intentionally fussed with warming her hands in front of the flames; the pause gave her time to consider a response. "You do charm." Her curt reply was meant as an explanation for the way she responded to his intimate touch.

Colin would have none of it. "You refuse to admit the truth."

"And what truth is this that you speak of with such confidence?"

"That you enjoy my touch."

Hope shrugged indifferently. "As I said, you do charm."

Colin understood women by their actions and their words, though it was often what they did not say that betrayed their true feelings. He realized that Hope fought against what she felt; the nervous warming of her hands alerted him to her unease.

Did she actually war with the possibility that she loved him? And if she did, why fight a union with him? Their confined time together would give him a chance to discover answers to his questions. Patience, however, was not one of his virtues—especially, it seemed, when it came to Hope.

So he decided to be forthright. "Do you love me, Hope?"

She abruptly stopped warming her hands and turned around to face him with stunned eyes that glistened with pooled tears.

He waited what seemed like forever for an answer and realized that her response was more important to him then he had thought. She seemed small and fragile, standing there dressed as a lad, her eyes on the verge of tears, her soft lips fighting a tremble and her hands clenched tightly in front of her. But then there was her courage, which always seemed to take charge and defend. He expected it to spring forth any moment and retaliate with a wise response.

Her answer, therefore, stunned him speechless.

"Aye, Colin, I do love you." She had thought briefly about avoiding the truth, but what good would that do? He knew women well enough and would soon come to realize it on his own, especially now, while sharing such confined living quarters. It was better she admit it herself so that he would understand why she could not marry him.

Colin took time to clear his head. He had not expected such a definitive answer. He had thought perhaps she would throw the question back at him, demand he speak of his feelings, and yet she simply spoke the truth. He decided to do the same.

"I did not expect such honesty." He took a step toward her and her hands went up, warning that he step no closer. He obliged her silent request and stood a short distance from her.

"What good would it do me to deny it?"

Her sorrowful eyes caused his heart to ache. He wished to reach out and offer her the comfort of his protective arms but he understood that her pride and courage would force her to refuse his offer. He stood with his hands at his sides hoping to comfort with words.

"I think you are wise not to deny your feelings."

She seemed relieved, her hands lowering to her sides and a soft sigh whispering from her lips.

He continued to comfort. "I am honored by your love."

Honored.

She cared naught about honor. She only wished that he loved her in return, though she understood his words were meant to soothe and comfort her. He was always the charmer, always fulfilling a woman's needs. Perhaps this was good, for then he would understand her reason for not wedding him and would no longer object to voiding the arranged marriage.

His next remark warned her otherwise. "I am pleased that I will have a wife who loves me."

"I cannot wed you," she said in disbelief.

"Why not?" he asked, his own confusion obvious. "You love me."

"That is precisely why I cannot wed you."

He ran his fingers through his dark hair in frustration. "This makes no sense."

"You are right, it does not," she insisted and paced in front of the hearth several times.

Firm hands on her shoulders forced her to stop her nervous pacing. "You love me yet refuse to wed me?"

A warm, safe feeling wrapped around her and she suddenly wanted to surrender to the comfort of his arms. That was an impossibility, however, for if she succumbed she would surely be lost forever.

She could ask him if he loved her; perhaps then he would understand why their marriage could not be. But she feared his answer, for her heart ached enough without hearing him admit only that he cared.

She chose a simple response. "It is best this way."

"It makes no sense." He lifted her chin for their eyes to meet. "I will be good to you, Hope. I will give you all that you need and treat you decently. I will make a good husband and father."

She so wanted children, lots of children, so that her home would be filled with much laughter and love.

Love.

It always came back to love. And if she gave it thought, would it not be better that she wed someone whom she at least loved compared to someone she did not love at all? Any sensible woman would agree on such a wise decision. So why, then, did Hope feel she could not wed Colin?

Love.

She wanted his love, not his charm, and she feared that the years to come would only serve to destroy the love she felt for him. She would know every day of their lives that he cared and provided for her out of duty— and that she simply could not endure.

She preferred to love him and walk away with cherished memories than to watch those memories fade or turn bitter.

The tears she had fought so valiantly not to shed began to fall and Colin wiped them away one at a time.

"I care for you, Hope."

His words tore at her heart and she knew without a doubt that she could not, would not marry Colin. She must prevent their marriage; she must. And she must not surrender to his charm and chance getting with child, a difficult prospect since their confined quarters would afford ample opportunity for surrender.

Colin kissed her damp cheeks, her tears having subsided. "We will do well together—I promise you."

She ached with the love she felt for him and surrender would be all too easy, but when had she ever chosen an easy path?

He kissed her gently, lovingly, his hands cupping her face, his body moving closer to hers.

She needed to distance herself from him or she would soon be lost in his charm. Her hand moved to rest on one of his. "Please, Colin, I need time. So much has happened so soon and I feel confused."

He placed his forehead to hers. "I will not rush you, but do know that I want you and these confined quarters will prove difficult for me to keep a distance."

"I understand." All too well. She knew the strain it would cause them both.

Colin stepped away from her, going to the table, taking a seat and reaching for a piece of bread and cheese. "Tell me how you met up with Rath."

Hope smiled and felt the tension drain from her body. She also suddenly realized how hungry she was and joined Colin at the table, reaching for a large chunk of cheese.

She was only too glad for the change of subject and the tasty food that filled her stomach. "My intentions were to seek refuge at Croom Abbey."

He raised a brow. "You thought to make that journey on your own?"

"Lady and Rook were with me."

Colin laughed as he filled their goblets with wine. "Lady is presently returning with Rook, whose side she refuses to leave, to Shanekill. We both know that she is a coward at heart."

Hope ignored his disparaging though accurate remark. "My previous experiences on the road gave me the confidence to attempt this easy journey. I saw no reason to believe I would have difficulty in reaching my destination."

"Please do not tell me that you attempted to thieve from a thief," he said teasingly.

She shook her head. "Nay, I brought sufficient food with me and kept off well-traveled roads. He appeared out of nowhere and at first I thought nothing of it. He was but one lone man and Rook was there to help. It was Rook who alerted me to the others' presence. His senses are keen and his reactions quick."

"He took off, did he not?"

She nodded, a yawn following. "I realized he went for help, knowing it was the only choice possible and I hoped he would find it. The men thought him a coward and besides, Lady remained by my side shaking with fear, confirming that they were a pair of cowards."

"What did Rath want of you?"

"He offered me safety, shelter and food if I but helped them in their thieving."

"You wisely agreed?"

Another yawn prevented an immediate answer. "What choice did I have? While Rath did not seem ready to harm me, he also did not seem eager to let me go."

"What do you think of this place?" he asked, valuing her opinion.

"Secure and maintained from what I could see. The people seem content and grateful for Rath. Did you see the way they welcomed him upon our arrival?"

"Aye, they were attentive and respectful and relieved to see him safely home, as if his safety truly mattered to them."

Hope agreed with a nod. "He does not appear a common thief. The short time I spent with him made me think that his background is anything but common. He is highly intelligent and his manners impeccable."

"He is not who he seems to be."

"True enough, but then who is he?"

"A question that needs answering," Colin said and

watched another yawn attack Hope. "You are tired."

"The day has been long," she said, and looked reluctant to follow with what was on her mind.

"Something troubles you?"

"I worry over Faith," she admitted after a brief hesitation. "Why ever did Lord Eric allow her to join the search?"

Colin laughed. "You know Lady Faith well enough to answer that yourself. She simply refused to be left behind."

"Do you think the devil is mad at me? He has said not one word to me."

Colin leaned his arms on the table. "Be grateful he has chosen silence. His wrath is something you do not wish to taste."

"He pays the coins demanded without question."

"For now," Colin said. "His wife's safety and yours are what is important at the moment. When that is seen to he will deal with the thief."

"Rath does not seem at all intimidated by the devil."

Colin smiled. "A fool he is, but he will learn that soon enough."

Hope yawned again, stretched her arms above her head and arched her back, attempting to ease her sore muscles.

Colin watched the way the worn tunic formed to her body and he could just about make out a small pair of breasts. She was petite and slim with a strength of character that belied her physical form. She had responded to his touch eagerly and with a confidence not usually found in one so inexperienced. He looked forward to making love to her. He wanted her first time to be memorable and satisfying and he would do his best to see that she was pleasured.

Hope lowered her arms and looked to the single bed.

"We will share it," he said emphatically.

It would do no good to argue and she was much too tired to debate the issue. Tomorrow she could disagree.

Tonight she would sleep in the bed with him, fully clothed of course.

She walked over to the bed, sat down and slipped her boots off her feet. She made her way beneath the warm wool blanket and rolled to the far side of the bed, the edge of which was braced against the wall, and immediately fell into a much needed slumber.

"A stubborn lass you are," Colin said, speaking to himself, then blew out the candles on the table before joining Hope in bed. He refrained from slipping completely naked beneath the covers and instead left only his chest bare. He kept to his side of the bed, his thoughts busy and sleep elusive. But the long tiring day quickly caught up with him and he slipped into a deep slumber.

Soft whimpers pulled him from his heavy sleep and it took him a moment to remember his whereabouts. It was not long before he realized that the soft cries came from the huddled pint-sized body next to him. She had rolled toward him and had pressed herself firmly against his back as if the closer she could get to him the more protected she would feel.

Colin turned without hesitation and wrapped her into the comfort of his strong arms. She went willingly, her cries subsiding as his arms closed solidly around her.

He wondered over her troublesome dreams. What did she fear? What caused her cries and need for safety and solace? And why did she instinctively seek it from him?

Love.

She loved him and turned to him in need.

Need of what? he wondered. The love she sought? The safety she felt she needed?

And why did he feel compelled to provide her with anything she asked of him? Why had he always felt such an overwhelming need to protect the lad? What was it about Hope that made him lose all reason and agree to things he would never have thought possible?

Marriage.

Why had he agreed to their marriage so easily? Did he *wish* to marry her? Did he think she would make a good wife?

She stirred anxiously in his arms and he soothed her with whispered words and gentle rocking.

Was he being honest with himself? he wondered as she quieted in his embrace and once again settled against him. Was he not admitting that perhaps she was special, different from the other women he had bedded and loved in his own way?

He grew weary of his jumbled musings, wondering if he could ever solve this raging dilemma that plagued him. The simple matter of it all was that she would be his wife. She had no choice—it had been made for her and would be seen to accordingly.

Whether she favored it or not was not of consequence. She had a duty to perform and she would do as she was told. Why, then, did he feel it was not as easy as it sounded?

His present situation had provided a golden opportunity for him to become better acquainted with Hope the woman. The one who had decided on the adventure and who had created Harold in an image of herself, garnishing him with attributes she herself possessed but seldom had the chance to express.

If he could understand the two who were now one perhaps then he could understand the situation and know best how to proceed.

Love.

The word haunted him and simply refused to let go. He would accept her love for him, cherish it and guard it safely, for it was a precious gift she gave to him.

And in return he would take care of her, be a good husband and father and provide well for her.

Love.

He shut his eyes and gently shook his head. That was all that she asked of him, but could he give it? Could he love her?

Twenty-seven

Hope thought she would go crazy confined to the small room with Colin. He seemed not at all perturbed with their forced circumstances and never lacked in finding a subject to discuss with her.

She, however, wished for the outdoors and the freedom to which she had grown accustomed. Rath had not made himself known since their arrival at his village two days ago. Food and such were generously supplied to them but contact with anyone was kept to the lone person who brought their meals. And that person changed daily.

It was near nightfall and it was raining out. The downpour pelted the cottage incessantly and wore on Hope's already frayed nerves.

Colin appeared not at all distraught with the weather or their confinement. He sat at the table lazily enjoying the fine meal provided for them.

"You can do nothing about the situation," he said, as if attempting reason.

She was not feeling reasonable. "And you accept this?"

He turned a charming smile on her, which irritated her all the more. "What else is there to do?"

She had no answer for him, which frustrated her all the more.

"See, your silence answers for you."

He was right, of course. There was nothing they could do. Presently their only course of action was patience and he possessed more of that virtue than she did.

"Sit. Eat and talk with me."

"We have talked," she said, plopping down in the chair.

"I have talked, you have listened."

She glared at him, prepared to disagree, when she suddenly realized the truth of his words and admitted her feelings. "There is naught for me to say. All this is my fault and my guilt overwhelms me. I pray that Lady Faith fares well and that the devil does not turn his wrath on me, and I pray that the ordeal I have caused you can be rectified with haste and satisfaction."

His smile lingered. "You remain adamant in your decision not to marry me."

"I feel it unwise." She tore a thin piece of meat from the cooked rabbit on the platter. "I will not make a dutiful wife."

"What makes you think I wish a dutiful wife?"

"What *do* you wish of your wife?"

He paused, his answer near to spilling from his lips. That answer had rushed forth without forethought and it had startled him. He wished to love his wife.

"You do not know," Hope said after he had remained silent for several minutes. "Therefore it would be unwise to wed without considering the qualities you wish in a wife."

He leaned his elbows on the table and glared at her. "She would most certainly be patient with her tongue."

"A quality I lack," she said firmly as if striking a mark against herself.

"One that can be learned."

"If one wished to learn it."

He shook his head. "Were you always this stubborn?"

"Aye, and it is a fault that is not good in a wife," she said, tallying another mark against herself and reaching for a piece of bread. She felt confident that their conversation was finally making sense and that perhaps, just perhaps, he would see reason.

He changed tactics, a skilled warrior's trick that left

an opponent unprepared. "I wish for a beautiful wife."

It seemed to work—she looked at him with startled eyes—before her emotions took hold and her eyes misted with regret. "Another quality I sadly lack."

He regarded her strangely and then realized she believed her words. She did not think of herself as beautiful. His heart suddenly ached for her. He, however, chose to remain combatant, for if he attempted to convince her with sweet, flowery words she most certainly would not believe him.

"Do not play foolish with me."

There was a bite to her own tone. "I cannot say I have never been foolish, but I play no foolishness now."

He leaned forward and said it simply. "You are beautiful."

"Now who is being foolish?" she snapped at him, though truthfully she wished badly to believe him. No one had ever told her she was beautiful and his words had touched her heart.

He defended himself. "Not I. I speak the truth."

She shook her head. He was a charmer and she had to remember he charmed the ladies, each and every one of them. She would not be as foolish as they. "You attempt to charm, as is your way. I need no foolish charm worked on me."

"You fear your beauty?" he asked, leaning back in his chair and deciding it was time to discover the deeper side of his soon-to-be wife.

A small voice nagged at her to accept the compliment instead of denying it, but her stubborn nature prevailed and she chose reason as her defense. "Everyone views beauty differently."

His response surprised her. "Do you think me handsome?"

Her answer came easily. "Aye, everyone comments on your good looks."

"Do you think me handsome because everyone else does?"

"I have eyes of my own to see with," she said with a grin that told she thought his question foolish.

His attack had been a strategic one, his weapon the truth, and he moved in on his opponent. "As do I, and when I look at you I see a beautiful woman for I see her with my own eyes."

Her grin faded and she tugged at her shoulder-length hair. "How could you ever think me beautiful?"

"It is what my eyes see. There is a beauty about you that I cannot deny. Your face simply captivates my senses. Ask me to describe this beauty and words most certainly will fail me, for your beauty forever changes." He smiled as if his thoughts delighted him. "Your pale skin is smooth, clear and soft to the touch and your dark eyes can rob a man's soul of his senses and at other times display the strength of twenty men." A groaning sigh rumbled from him as his eyes settled on her mouth. "And those lips of yours beg for kisses time and again until a man goes crazy with the thought of satisfying them." He laughed. "And then your foolishness rears its stubborn head and you become a nymph who needs taming, an all-too-tempting prospect. So I say again, you are beautiful."

Her wish remained the same. She wanted to believe him. His words had touched her heart deeply so she asked, "When did you first think me beautiful?"

He stared at her over the rim of his wine goblet and sipped before answering. "As you remarked, everyone views beauty differently and keeping that in mind I must admit that I find courage beautiful. Harold possessed a beauty of courage I found remarkable for a lad so young and frail. So, as strange as it may sound, I saw beauty in you when we first met."

"You cared for Harold?" she asked, wishing he could feel the same toward her. It may not be love but it was a strong and honest feeling.

"I thought of him as a good friend," he said. "I still do."

She seemed confused when she asked, "You think me a friend?"

"You are Harold and Harold and I became friends as we traveled together. That friendship did not die when I discovered Harold was Hope." He held his hand up to prevent her from interrupting. "Upon discovering your deception I grew angry and part of that anger was because I thought I had lost a friend. It was not until I realized that your deception was not meant to hurt me or those you came to know, but meant to help you. I also understood that if Harold was my friend then Hope could certainly be my friend and the thought intrigued me."

"Then instead of your wife, I can be your friend," she said as if her words made perfect sense, though her heart wished differently. Her heart ached to love as only a wife and best friend could.

He stood and walked slowly over to her, bending down so that his face was level with hers. "Why not be both?"

"Impossible," she said on a hushed whisper, her heart beating too wildly for her to catch a solid breath.

He moved his lips near hers. "Anything is possible, Hope. You only need to wish it so."

Was it possible that he would kiss her? She wished it so.

He smiled as though reading her thoughts and moved his mouth to hers. His kiss was a gentle exploration of her lips that sent her senses hurtling completely out of control.

His hand moved to caress her neck while his lips ran in tender strokes over hers and she grew frantic for more, her own lips attempting to capture his fleeting ones.

He did not deny her her urgency and they were soon locked in a kiss that demanded much more than either ever imagined.

It was a kiss born of innocence, its intent to demonstrate possibilities and wishes. Instead it turned to magic—the magic of love.

Colin tore away from her in disbelief, standing in a flash and putting distance between them, if a few short feet could be called distance. He stood behind his chair, his hands firmly planted on the chair back for support. His legs trembled, his lips throbbed and his body grew hard with a relentless desire. And while he had always responded without a problem to ardent kisses, this kiss was different. It completely stole his senses and left him mindless.

Hope sat up, attempting to regain her own senses. She had not considered the consequences of her wish and there certainly could have been consequences if Colin had not ended their encounter.

She brought her fingers to her aching lips and briefly thought of how Colin had kissed her. There was no charm, only a need, a deep relentless need. She felt it in him. It was like an ache he wished to ease, needed to ease, wanted badly to ease but somehow could not find a way. And if she was not careful she would allow him his way.

Her fingers drifted away from her mouth to rest in her lap. The room grew heavy with silence. There was no place for either of them to go and no words either wished to speak. The silence grew heavy along with the passion that filled the air.

Colin attempted to control his raging desires and the thought startled him. He had always kept a firm control of his emotions. It was a way he pleased the women, keeping a tight rein on his desires and catering to their pleasure, only fulfilling his own when he knew they had been satisfied.

How then did this simple kiss gain control of his passion? He had almost lost control. His thought was to grab hold of Hope, strip her bare and make love to her with an urgency that bordered on primitive. Whatever was the matter with him?

Even now he was hot and hard with need for her. He was not thinking of gentle kisses and tender touches; his thoughts were more primitive in nature. He shook his head, stunned by his own wicked thoughts—which only served to torment him further.

She was to be his wife and it would cause no great harm if he made love to her before they exchanged vows. So why not just be done with it?

He could not answer his own question. He only knew that at the moment he was not himself and would not subject her to a primitive mating. Her first time with him would be loving and memorable.

He reached for the goblet of wine on the table and downed it, intending to drink himself into oblivion.

Hope decided to retreat silently to the bed and seek solace beneath the covers. She knew that their confined living quarters would only grow more confining after that kiss. Her lips still ached for him and her body desired him. She had never known that her breasts could ache with the want of a man's touch or that she could grow so moist with desire.

She wanted Colin. She almost cried with the want of him and she could do nothing to ease the unrelenting ache that throbbed mercilessly throughout her. And she feared, greatly feared, that she would not be able to deny him if he chose to come to bed and touch her.

The thought sent a shiver of desire racing through her and she almost wished that he would come to bed and ease the passionate torment she suffered. A single tear slipped from her eye and she allowed it to fall. Though small, it released a tiny bit of the tension.

After what seemed like an eternity of silent frustration her damp eyes grew sleepy and drifted closed, and it was in that moment just before sleep claimed her that she realized Colin himself had lost control. His charm had been replaced with a soaring passion foreign to him and that was why he had so hastily ended their kiss.

Colin found no peace in sleep that night. At first he

attempted to slumber in the stiff wooden chair at the table. When that proved too difficult and extremely uncomfortable, he sought the bed.

He remained fully clothed and slept on top of the covers. Hope, however, refused to remain on her side of the bed and rolled up against him, snuggling into his warmth and causing him great discomfort.

There was an added burden that finally drove him from the bed. Every now and then Hope would moan as if she were trapped in the throes of passion, a passion she seemed unable to satisfy. The moans would dissipate into a soft whimper and gradually fade, only to begin again just when Colin thought they were gone for good.

His body kept in tempo with her sensuous sounds and he found himself in a near constant state of arousal, not a comfortable feeling. He left the bed for the chair once again.

The situation needed immediate attention. He would have to deal with it sooner or later and he had a distinct feeling it would be sooner. If he were sensible he would simply satisfy his need and hers and be done with it. But his loss of control disturbed him and he had to address that issue before he paid heed to any other.

Tomorrow he would request to speak with Rath and see if their confinement could be supplemented with a daily walk or two. Perhaps he could convince Rath that the ladies would benefit from an occasional visit.

He would suggest that he and Eric be able to visit, though he doubted Rath would permit such a meeting, fearing that the time spent would be used on planning an escape. Eric, however, would never chance such a feat with Faith in her present condition.

He smiled, knowing Faith herself was probably attempting to convince her husband of an escape while he warned her against it.

Feeling much at ease with his newly devised plan, Colin decided to give the bed another chance. He was bone tired and would probably fall asleep instantly. He eased himself onto the bed and kept a safe distance from Hope.

With a soft sigh of relief he closed his eyes and was drifting off when suddenly he felt her snuggle up against him. He waited for the soft moans to begin and when none came he released the breath he held.

This he could manage. After all, he was exhausted and sleep was ready to grab hold of him. He would have no problem—none at all. He would sleep contentedly.

Hope snuggled closer, her small breasts pressed tightly into his back.

This time the moan came from him, and he knew he had a long night ahead of him.

Twenty-eight

Hope raised her face to the bright, sunny sky and breathed deeply. It was a beautiful day and she intended to enjoy every moment of her limited freedom. She had wanted to hug Colin for his persistence and success in getting Rath to agree to allow them daily outdoor sessions. They were instructed to remain within an appointed perimeter and if they failed to obey they would once again be sequestered in the cottage. Hope had no intention of losing the small amount of freedom given her, and besides, she hoped that daily outdoor activity would help her cope better when she was once again confined with Colin.

Her joy grew to excitement when Faith stepped out of a nearby cottage. She called out to Colin who was occupied with a group of young men training to defend themselves. He could not help but offer his expert advice and they appeared only too willing to accept it.

He acknowledged her shout with a wave and a smile to Faith, then turned his attention back to the group of eager students.

Hope and Faith hugged each other like long lost sisters finally reunited. Several women smiled at them as if in understanding and within minutes a blanket was spread under a nearby tree for the pair to use.

Hope helped Faith to sit and then joined her on the blanket, bubbling with the prospect of speaking with someone besides Colin.

Faith smiled. "Your confinement has proved difficult?"

Hope sighed, though her smile remained. "Very difficult."

"I find my time with Eric enjoyable."

Hope envied the look of pure contentment that Faith wore. She did not mind at all being isolated with her husband and Hope had no doubt that the devil himself enjoyed their seclusion.

Hope was curious as to the devil's whereabouts. "Is Lord Eric not permitted a bit of freedom?"

"He has tasted more freedom than I have."

Hope was surprised. "He has not been confined all this time?"

"He comes and goes almost at his will."

"How so?"

"He made it known upon our arrival that he wished to speak with Rath and the man was wise enough to pay him the respect he deserves. They talk daily, Eric wishing to learn more about this village and obviously why the people feel it necessary to hide away."

"Has he learned much?"

"Aye, though Eric was not surprised by what Rath told him. Eric has journeyed across most of Ireland and has seen what fighting and hatred can do to people."

Hope agreed with a nod. "My journey was not vast but what I did see taught me much. And I know from my own experience that hunger can cause an honest man to become a thief."

"That is right, you stole food from Colin. You must have been starving."

"I never understood the real meaning of hunger until I experienced it. And it was only myself and Lady to worry about. If I had a hungry child to feed—" She shook her head.

"Rath told Eric that most of the people here were once hungry and homeless. They banded together for the sake of survival and now they think of themselves as family."

"What of Rath? He does not seem a likely thief and when I met up with him he seemed more concerned about protecting than harming me."

"I agree. He is not your usual thief and his manner suggests good breeding, but he refuses to speak of himself."

"He keeps his camp well supplied. Food has been plentiful for us."

Faith nodded. "Rath is generous in his care of us."

Hope lowered her voice. "Lord Eric has not spoken of escape?"

"He knows we are in no danger. Rath would not hurt us. He but wishes the coins to keep his camp supplied and Eric cannot fault him for that. Eric will also not take a chance with me in my present condition." She ran a gentle hand over her rounded stomach. "The babe has been active. I think he is impatient like his father."

"You think him a boy?"

"I know him to be a boy. I feel it, as strange as that may sound."

"I believe you. I always thought that I would know whether the child I carried was male or female. A mother's instinct, I suppose."

"You wish to have children?" Faith asked, her hand continuing to calm the babe within.

Hope beamed with joy. "I love children. I wish to have a slew of them."

"Colin will make a good father."

The joy faded from her face.

Faith placed a comforting hand to Hope's arm. "You still refuse to wed him?"

"I do not think it a wise choice."

"Have you not come to know him better with the few days' confinement?"

She paused in her response. The confinement had managed to make her aware of her desirous emotions— much too aware. She had learned things about her body she had not known and things about passion she had only imagined. And that was the difficulty; she had awakened to the full potential of love.

"Aye," she said on a whisper. "And that is why I cannot wed him."

Faith patted her arm. "I think I understand your misgivings, though I think you do not see clearly enough. There is more to Colin that you stubbornly refuse to accept."

Hope grew angry. "He cares for me when I wish love. What more is there for me to see?"

"A man as stubborn as you," Faith said with a squeeze to her arm and a generous smile.

Hope laughed, though the sound had a ring of sadness to it. "We are both blind, then."

"Only by your own choice."

Hope stared at her strangely. "I do not always understand what you try to tell me."

"It is simple. It is right there in front of you, you only need to look to see it," Faith said with a gentle rub to her back.

"You are uncomfortable?" Hope asked while wondering how something of importance could stare her in the face and she would not be aware of it.

"A dull persistent ache that torments me."

Hope grew concerned. "You think the babe may come early."

Faith placed a finger to her own lips. "Do not let anyone hear you. If Eric should think so he would be beside himself."

"What think you?" Hope asked, her concern growing.

Faith lowered her voice. "I think there is a possibility that the babe may be far too impatient to wait."

"You should be home at Shanekill where there are many who would see to your care." The guilt of her actions overwhelmed her for she felt that she had placed Faith in a harmful position.

"I am fine, do not worry. And you are here if I should need help."

Hope almost panicked. "I know nothing of birthing a babe."

"Have you seen animals give birth?"

Hope remembered the many times she had watched with joy at the horses giving birth. Her response, however, was cautious. "That is different."

"It is similar and women have natural instincts that guide them through the process." Faith sighed and rubbed again at her back. "It matters not. The coins will be here soon and we will be home at Shanekill before we know it."

That was a prospect Hope prayed for.

"Have you considered your wedding?"

"Nay, I have given it no thought, since there will be no wedding."

Faith seemed to disagree. "It would be wise to give the matter some consideration. After all, you will be returning to Shanekill and once there I would imagine that your uncle Shamus will insist on an immediate wedding."

Hope remained silent.

"Think on it, Hope," Faith said seriously. "If you are to have a wedding then have one of your choosing. Eric and I will be only too glad to hold a celebration that will long be remembered."

A smile that Hope could not hide surfaced. "I always thought my wedding would be a joyous celebration."

"Then make it so," Faith urged.

"I will think on it," Hope promised as several women approached them with a basket of food, and the remainder of their time was spent in friendly conversation.

Colin kept a guarded eye on Hope and Faith. He was aware that Eric and Rath talked and he did not question Eric's suggestion that he assist in the training of Rath's men. It was a strange imprisonment of sorts, with a good amount of respect being shown to the prisoners. It gave

Colin time to pause and consider. There was more to Rath than one would surmise.

He noticed that Hope and Faith remained deep in conversation and that it lightened when the women of the village joined them. He wondered over their words. What did Hope feel safe to share with Faith? What secrets did she confide?

Did they talk of intimacy?

Colin walked away from the group of practicing men to get a drink of water from a pail that sat near the practice area. He needed a bit of distance, his mind churning with emotions he had thought a hardy practice session would eliminate.

The session had eased some of his tension, but his confused emotions continued to haunt him. He could not make sense of his reactions to Hope. He had always prided himself in his ability to handle a woman, and yet with Hope . . .

He shook his head and took another sip from the ladle. There seemed to be no way to handle Hope. She lived and played by her own rules—ones that were unfamiliar to Colin.

Hope was unlike any woman he had ever known. He recalled what the mother abbess had told him about Hope cherishing and protecting the man she loved. He fully comprehended her words and envied them.

To know that a woman could love that strongly was an indication of her character, her integrity and her honesty—not only with others but with herself. Hope was honest in her feelings and did not deny them, and she remained firm in her convictions when a choice was necessary. This was not an easy task and yet she faced the prospect with the honor of a true warrior going into battle.

He admired her strength of character and her tenaciousness though it often got her into trouble.

He smiled, knowing most certainly that she would not be a dull wife but one who forever challenged and cherished and, of course, keep him wondering as to what tomorrow would bring.

The one constant in it all was her love. It never questioned and never wavered in its belief. It remained firm, pure and forever.

A forever love.

He shook his head, certain he had lost his mind. This marriage was born of necessity. They had no choice. Or did they?

He shook his head more adamantly. They certainly did not. She would marry him and that was that. He would hear nothing to the contrary. She would be his wife whether she wished to or not.

"There is much on your mind."

Colin dropped the ladle, the water flying out to spray over him before he turned and faced Eric. "Too much."

Eric laughed and gave him a hardy slap on the back. "Is it love?"

Colin looked startled, his question asking more than he cared to answer. "It is a spoiled pint-sized woman who thinks she will do as she wishes."

"Love," Eric said with another laugh.

"Not love," Colin objected most adamantly. "Madness."

"One and the same."

Colin groaned. "Do not tell me this."

"At least I am able to warn you, as a good friend did for me, only I foolishly ignored him." He slapped him on the back once again. "The best advice I can give you is not to fight; merely surrender."

"I am a warrior," Colin said with an indignation that did not surprise Eric. He completely understood his reluctance.

"Who knows when surrender is wise, for within that surrender is the power he fights for."

Colin seemed skeptical. "Has marriage given you this wisdom?"

Eric thought a moment and felt most comfortable with his answer. "*Love* has given me wisdom."

"Then I should be a very wise man."

"You once told me that I refused to see the truth in front of me. Perhaps those words are good advice for you now."

"I see a stubborn woman in front of me who will fill my life with—"

Eric interrupted. "Love?"

Colin looked ready to disagree. Instead he simply shook his head. "I barely know her."

"You know her better than you think. You spent time with her when you thought her a lad and came to care for her as a friend first. And we both know the importance of friendship. It is the best place to begin a relationship. Friends trust and I think if you both would cease being stubborn you would see and value the friendship you both share."

Colin gave his dark hair a rough rake with his fingers. "She remains firm in her refusal to wed me."

"She has no choice," Eric said as if his words were a decree.

"Yet you gave me one."

"Of course, you must know this is what you want."

"What of Hope and what she wants?" Colin asked in her defense.

Eric had no problem providing a confident answer. "Hope's stubbornness stands in the way of her love for you. Marriage is what she truly wishes, but it is a marriage based on an equal love."

"I barely know her," Colin said, the words ringing familiar.

Eric placed a hand on Colin's shoulder. "Is it really Hope you barely know or is it yourself you are unfamiliar with?"

"You play with words."

"You often do the same yourself. Now it is your turn to understand the very advice you gave me."

"Is it an escape that is being planned?" Rath asked, walking up behind the pair.

Eric and Colin turned.

Rath stood with arms across his chest and a look that displayed not a bit of worry. The man was arrogant in his confidence and manner and won Colin and Eric's respect.

"With your generosity, what would be the purpose?" Eric asked, his own impressive stance demanding attention.

"You are much different than I expected the devil to be," Rath said, his smile broad.

"And you, my friend, are not a thief," Eric said boldly.

"There are many who would differ with your opinion and for now it is best you think me so," Rath said, his smile turning serious.

"Lord Eric!"

The excited cry caught the three men's attention, and when they turned and Eric caught sight of his wife passed out on the blanket, he ran like the wind to her side.

Colin and Rath followed.

Hope pressed a damp cloth to her face in an attempt to revive her and another woman had placed a folded blanket beneath her head. All cleared a path for the devil except Hope, who remained by Faith's side.

"What happened?" Eric demanded, going down on his knees beside his wife.

Hope attempted to explain. "She was talking and suddenly felt ill, telling me she thought it best if she laid down. The next thing I knew she was falling backwards and I put my hands out to stop her head from hitting the ground."

Faith began to moan softly.

Eric took his wife's limp hand and feeling the strength of him she immediately grasped hold of it. "I am here, Faith."

A soft sigh told him she understood.

"She is coming out of the faint and color is once again filling her cheeks," Hope said with relief.

Colin knelt beside Hope, and Rath kept a few feet away, making inquiries of the women who witnessed the incident.

A stronger sigh drifted from her lips and her eyes began to flutter open. "Eric," she said, sounding breathless.

"I am here," he assured her with a tender hand to her cheek. "Rest. Do not try to talk yet."

"I am fine," she said, her breath sounding more steady and her eyes opening wide. "I only fainted."

"Only?" Eric asked with surprise.

"It happens time and again when a woman carries a babe," Faith said as if it mattered not. "Do not worry."

Eric looked to Hope. "Is this true?"

Hope answered honestly. "I know little when it comes to carrying a babe though I do know of a servant in my uncle's home who fainted often when she was with child."

"And all went well with her?"

"She delivered a fine healthy boy," Hope told him with a confident smile.

"You doubt my words, husband?" Faith said on a laugh.

Rath stepped forward. "Agnes here admits that she suffers from fainting spells when with child."

Faith laughed again. "They all try to soothe the devil."

"The devil will be soothed when his wife is safely tucked in bed for the remainder of the day," Eric informed her, his hands slipping beneath her to gently scoop her up into his arms.

Faith looked ready to protest but one look in her husband's eyes warned her it would do no good, that he would have his way. She wisely remained silent and rested her head on his shoulder.

Rath spoke up. "If there is anything Lady Faith needs."

"Thank you," Eric said and turned, then walked to their cottage.

Colin stood and held his hand out to Hope.

She was hesitant to take it, hesitant to retire to the small cottage with him. At the moment she felt vulnerable. She felt the need to melt into the strength and comfort of his arms. And if she allowed her guard to drop, what would be the consequences?

"Come," Colin coaxed softly. "You could use some rest yourself."

His tender words tempted and she attempted to convince herself she could handle time alone with him. There was no problem. She was strong. She would not surrender.

She gave him her hand and his long lean fingers wrapped firmly around hers, and she knew as the warmth of him drifted lazily up her arm that she had made a mistake.

Twenty-nine

Colin took her into his arms as soon as the cottage door closed behind them.

She rested her face on his chest, heard the reassuring beat of his heart and began to cry. They were soft, silent tears, but necessary ones. It was time to release her emotions and face the fact that her heart was breaking.

"It is all right," he said quietly, holding her tightly. "Everything is all right, Hope."

But it was not all right. Nothing was right. She loved him with an intensity that frightened her. She did not think it was possible to feel such a deeply rooted emotion for someone. To care so very much for them that you would be willing to walk away if it meant their happiness. How could she confine him to a marriage to a woman he did not love? It was not fair to him and not fair to her.

She attempted to pull away but he would not have it. "Nothing is right," she mumbled against his chest.

He held her tightly, refusing to let her go. "Nay, Hope, all is right."

"You do not understand."

"I understand more than you think."

She struggled in his arms and he reluctantly gave her her freedom. "If you truly understood you would not force this marriage." She pressed at her throbbing temples. "And I grow tired of going round and round and round over this issue. There is no more to be said or discussed. I wish to hear not another word, I but wish this confinement over and done so that I may—"

She stopped suddenly, slowly shaking her head.

His voice turned stern. "Do you have plans you have failed to tell me about?"

She raised defiant eyes to him, though he could see pain in them.

"I have naught to say." Her hand went once again to her temple.

"Your head aches you." He softened his tone. "You need to rest."

Her eyes lost their blaze and her head drooped as if the effort was too much to hold it up. "What good will rest do me? I will only wake to face it all again."

He walked over to her and moved her hand away from her head to replace it with his own. He pressed a firm thumb to her temple and begin to stroke in slow circular motions, fanning out to cover a wider area.

She moaned softly and once again dropped her head to his chest.

"Rest clears the mind," he whispered near her ear. "Perhaps you will wake with a clearer vision of things to be."

"I know what must be."

"You think what will be."

"I will not argue," Hope murmured.

"Nor will I," he said and gently scooped her up into his arms and carried her to the bed. He followed her down, stretching out beside her and keeping his arms tucked protectively around her.

"I can take care of myself," Hope insisted, yawning.

"So you have attempted to prove on more than one occasion."

"I have survived, have I not?"

He hugged her tightly. "Aye, and glad I am for it."

"Then I have no need of your protection."

"I have need to protect you."

"Only because you think I am to be your wife."

He began to stroke her back and at first she tensed but as he continued she began to relax. "Not so. I felt the need to protect you from the first time we met."

"You felt the need to protect Harold."

"One and the same."

Hope laughed softly against his chest. "With your vast experience, I assumed you would know the difference."

His hand gradually and intentionally made its way down over her backside to give it a playful squeeze. "I definitely know the difference."

Why did his touch feel so good? Why could she not grow annoyed at his touch? Why instead did she hunger for it? *Because you love him, you fool,* she reminded herself.

His hand moved up to rest at her waist. "You do not mind my touch, do you?"

She almost laughed. He had to have read her thoughts, but then, does not a good lover know what a woman wishes, and did not he himself tell her that he knew what women wanted and gave it to them?

"What if I told you that I did?"

He rested his mouth near her ear so that he could whisper. "I would say you are being untruthful to yourself."

"Nay, I am being truthful with myself for I would not lie and say that I mind your touch, for I very much enjoy it. I mind you touching me for I feel it inappropriate since no marriage vows will ever be exchanged."

His fingers caught her chin and he turned her face away from his chest and up so that her eyes would meet his. "Your honor looks to have been compromised more than once—"

She attempted to argue the truth, but he would have none of it. He silenced her with a finger to her lips.

"It matters not whether your honor was damaged. It only matters how it appears to others."

"That is not fair."

"Fair or not, it is the way of things."

Hope continued to disagree. "I need not marry. I will take myself to the convent."

He stopped himself from laughing. "I will come get you."

She looked indignantly at him. "You cannot."

A laugh spilled out. "Aye, Hope, I can and I will."

She opened her mouth to continue her protest and he laughed, shook his head, and whispered, "So stubborn." He then closed his mouth over hers.

She was too shocked to react immediately and that moment of hesitation cost her dearly. He took command of her senses and like a fool she did not deny him. She did not want to. Not when his kiss felt as hungry for her as she did for him.

It was not his usual gentle, loving kiss, but one filled with a passion he himself found hard to ignore or deny. It was a kiss born of urgency and demand and filled with an unrelenting need.

She responded to that need, her arms wrapping around him and her own mouth pursuing him with a fervor she could not deny.

His body moved against hers, his hand running down her back to cup her backside and draw her closer to him. His tempo intoxicated, the rhythm all too familiar, even to one so inexperienced.

She rode the waves of pleasure that rushed over her body and yearned for more. His hands roamed intimately over her and his lips left hers to nuzzle at her neck and send ripples of shivers running down the length of her.

She was alive with passion and it grabbed her with an intensity that suddenly frightened. Her eyes flew open, her body tensed and she realized for a terrifying moment that she wanted, ached to surrender to this man she loved.

Sanity warned her of the consequences. If she gave herself to him now she would have no other choice but to exchange vows with him. Her destiny would be sealed forever.

Forever mine.

He wished for a woman whom he could love and call forever his. She was not that woman. The thought tore at her heart and sent her into action. She pulled away from him and ran for the door.

"There is nowhere to run this time, Hope."

Her hand lay on the door latch and she rested her forehead against the aged wood. He was right. There was no place for her to run or hide. The idea that she was trapped with no chance of escape, no way of dictating her own freedom, weighed heavily upon her and she pressed her palms to the door and choked back her tears.

She sobbed. Her frustration needed release and no amount of fighting would prevent her tears.

His arm slipped suddenly around her waist and he leaned in against her, though allowing her to remain as she stood. He simply joined with her.

"Stop fighting what you feel," he whispered, his voice heavy with desire.

"I cannot," she admitted on a hushed breath, almost afraid to confess the truth.

"It is done," he said firmly and gave her waist a gentle squeeze. "You are mine."

Forever mine.

She shook off the words that seemed forever to haunt her.

"Deny that you want me and I will leave you alone," he said, offering her a way out. But a whisper warned her, "Be truthful."

Tears ran down her cheeks and she was angry with herself for allowing her emotions to rule when she needed to deal reasonably with the matter, but then love was far from reasonable.

What good would denying the truth do her or him? What good was her stubbornness doing her? It but delayed the inevitable. She waged a senseless battle, one that would never taste victory. But would not victory leave a bitter taste in her mouth? She loved him and he was willing to wed her.

What foolishness did she mean in denying the very thing she wanted? Perhaps she could love him enough for them both. Perhaps love was a foolish fancy that she should forget. Perhaps she should surrender her emotions and see where they took her.

Perhaps she should simply love and be done with it.

She turned to face him, tears glistening in her damp eyes, and before she brought her mouth to his she whispered, "I want you."

Her kiss caught Colin off guard. He had not expected her to take charge of the situation. And he did not expect the torrent of emotions that poured out of her. She felt to him as if her body was on fire with desire and that it raged out of control. The sinful thought fired his own passion, sending it soaring. Suddenly all sanity escaped him and he wanted nothing but to strip her naked and take her with a primitive intensity.

He struggled with the burning urge and attempted to calm her kiss that had turned to a hungry demand. "Easy, easy," he attempted to soothe, his hands stroking her back.

She did not want reason or softness. That he gave to every woman he was with. She wanted the unleashed passion he guarded so closely. She wanted him to lose control and make love to her like he did to no other woman.

With her own desire raging through her and the love she harbored so deeply in her heart for him, it was easy to be bold. She slipped her hand down between his legs and cupped him, laughing softly against his mouth as she kissed him and said, "I cannot wait to feel the strength of you inside me."

Her hand closed more tightly around him and he thought he would explode right then and there. But he forced control upon himself, forced reason to prevail, forced himself to take a deep breath.

She plunged her tongue into his mouth and he gasped in shock, his body turning taut. She laughed again as she toyed with him, her tongue darting playfully and daring him to come join her. "I love the taste of you."

His breath caught again and he did not think it possible to grow any harder than he already was. He was wrong. He bulged with an ache that was painful and he knew that if he did not gain control soon he would lose his and take her as he had never taken a woman before.

Hope felt him fight himself and the thought soared her own confidence and desire. She wanted him not to think, only react. She wanted no planned touches or tender kisses that would lead to a loving performance. She wanted his emotions free and uninhibited so that he could love her with equal intensity.

Her mouth moved to his neck and her sensuous bites caused shivers to rush over him. Her hand continued to torment him and he tried to free himself and take charge. He only managed to work his way back up against the door, trapping himself.

"Hope," he said on a groan, his hands resting on her shoulders to attempt to ease her off him.

She acted as if she did not hear him and continued her seduction.

And he realized she was seducing him. This innocent, pint-sized woman had taken control and within minutes made him desire her like he had never desired anyone in his life.

He should be irritated by her brashness, but that thought took flight as quickly as it had entered his mind. His irritation was not with her but with himself for he did not wish to fight her. And he damned well did not wish to fight the raging feelings she evoked in him. And rage they did.

"Hope," he tried one more time and again she ignored him.

Her small hand inflicted a torrent of pleasure and her innocent and honest words seduced him even more.

"I never knew a man could feel so good."

Her caresses and words left him speechless, not a common affliction for him to suffer.

She nibbled at his throat and up along his ear to whisper, "I want us both naked."

With that she went to work on his tunic and had it off him in seconds, hastily discarding it aside. Her hands instantly went for his hard chest, her playful fingers causing tingles to rush over him. Her fingertips explored every inch of flesh as if she wished to know all of him.

He groaned when she squeezed his nipples and laughed softly while bringing her mouth down upon one hard nub. He braced himself against the wooden door, his breath catching and his hands fisting at his sides. He did not trust himself. He was close to losing all control and he feared the consequences if he did.

Her tongue enjoyed him, relishing the taste of him. And like a newborn who could not suckle enough, Hope feasted.

"Damn," he mumbled beneath a moan that rumbled low in his throat. He never knew such blatant desire. It was like a red hot liquid that ran through him, ready to explode and devour. It seeped through his flesh and rushed over him in a misty perspiration.

Colin realized that Hope had moved past seduction into a state of uncontrolled passion. She gave no thought to her actions; her emotions ruled and she let them take her where they wished to go.

Her mouth drifted down over his midriff, tasting every damp morsel of him, and she stopped to nibble at the more enticing places.

He thought to stop her; at least he gave it brief consideration, very brief. He was too lost in a swell of passion to think rationally. All sanity eluded him; he thought he had sunk into the very depths of seductive madness, and he did not care.

The thought startled him, but then Hope did something that further shocked him and sent him to the edge.

Her mouth drifted down his belly to rest over the bulge in his stockings. She licked at the soft wool with a gentleness that all but begged for more.

His ache turned painful and he shut his eyes against the intense and maddening pleasure. He should do something. He should take control, but all he wanted to do was surrender.

She lingered over the new and wonderful sensations that ran through her body as she lost herself in the sweetness of her own desires.

She slowly ran her hands up and down his legs, her fingertips lingering on the inside of his thighs while her tongue continued to seek and give pleasure.

He braced his head back against the door, squeezed his eyes tight and moaned loudly when she caught the tip of him with her teeth.

The tender bite brought him near to exploding and the only thought he had was that he wished her to do it again. And she did.

His moan echoed in the silence.

She savored the erotic sensations that made her own body throb and ache for fulfillment, and the heat that had tortured her flesh suddenly became unbearable. She moved away from him briefly, pulled off her tunic and undergarment and with a fast and slightly rough intimate nibble at him, she began to lazily crawl up the length of him.

His mind would not reason properly. He could barely make it function and when her small breasts rubbed against his belly he knew without a doubt that sanity had completely deserted him.

She worked her way up his chest, caressing his sensitive flesh with her small hardened nipples. That she brought them both pleasure was obvious from the moans that escaped her lips and the groans that rumbled from his.

Her fingers reached up to run through his hair, grabbing a tight hold and forcing his mouth down to meet her hungry one. They took hold of each other, their lips locking in a demanding kiss. His arms came around her, forcing her up firmly against him. And she met his body with an urgency she did not fight, pressing her hips into him and caressing his desire with her own intimate heat.

They were locked in intimate combat, too senseless to pay heed to reason, too lost to their shared passion to care. They shared one basic, primitive instinct.

They had to mate.

It was a necessity.

Nothing else mattered.

Their touch turned frantic, their kisses rough, and their passion surged beyond control. They fed off each other, fueling their already tumultuous desires.

She moved against him with a need to which he instantly understood and responded. Their bodies took on a rhythm of their own and she moaned with a building passion that consumed her.

"I want you," she cried against his mouth as she roughly stole a frantic kiss from him.

He could smell her desire. The sensuous odor drifted off her to attack his senses and when mingled with his own raging scent, it intoxicated. He warned himself to be careful, told himself to think, reason, grab hold of his sanity before he lost all control. But sanity was the furthest thing from his mind.

Nothing mattered.

And that was a dangerous place to be, for then he gave no thought to his actions; he merely followed his emotions. And presently his emotions raged out of control.

"I want you," she cried again and moved against him with such fervor that he thought he would explode.

"That is it," he said, issuing an order.

He pulled back away from her, his scalp feeling the sting of her reluctance to let go. He grabbed her beneath the arms, raised her up and walked toward the bed.

He threw her down on the thick mattress. "Now it is my turn."

Thirty

Colin stripped off the last of his garments and reached down to strip Hope bare as well. He then settled his naked body over her, his hands braced on either side of her head. He brought his lips down to faintly brush over hers and when she attempted to reach up and steal a kiss he pulled away.

"Nay, my turn, I told you."

He sounded as if he threatened, threatened with passion, and she shuddered.

He smiled, wicked that it was, and bit at her lower lip before whispering words that had her shuddering with a moan. He took her mouth then, claimed it for his own and made certain that she knew he marked his territory.

He followed down along her neck, causing her another shudder as her flesh raced with a sensitive tingle. Playful bites left gentle marks as he drifted down to her breasts and scooped a tender nipple into his mouth.

Her breath was stolen from her as she grabbed at the linens on the bed and allowed herself to enjoy the intense pleasure his tasting brought her. The flick of his tongue over the sensitive tips caused her body to arch and her moans to grow in volume.

He was true to his word when he had told her it was his turn. He followed suit and did to her what she had done to him. He worked his way down her body, nibbling and feasting on all the exquisite curves and mounds he found temptingly appealing.

She squirmed beneath him, the sensuous torture he inflicted driving her completely mindless. And when his mouth finally came to rest between her legs she cried out with the pleasure he gave her.

She could not think or reason. He drove her past all sanity with a tongue that worked absolute magic. She squirmed, she moaned, she cried out to him, and when her release came, she screamed his name.

Breathing was difficult, thought was impossible and when he moved over her, working his way up her body with a determination that drove her wild, she thought for certain she would die from the pleasure.

He thought to make her mindless again but she wished for him to join her in the madness and reached down to touch him.

"You play dangerously," he warned on a whispered breath.

"Then come taste danger," she challenged and caressed him with hands that promised fulfillment.

He moaned and arched his back, pressing against her and trying with an ounce of sanity to control himself.

She wanted none of his control. She wanted only his need. She took the length of him in her hands and squeezed. "Do I get to taste you?"

Her remark sent him over the edge, and he moaned low in his chest fighting against the primitive urge to take her fast and hard.

She could tell from the sweat on his brow and the taut tension in his body that he barely maintained control. And with a smile she pushed him over the edge with a whispered, "I want you in my mouth."

"Damn you," he muttered and with an urgency that was foreign to him he entered her with a swiftness that had her crying out.

He immediately stilled, throbbing with an aching need inside her. "I am sorry," he said on a shaky breath.

"I am not," she said and wrapped her legs around him. "Please, bring me to pleasure." She playfully nibbled at his chin. "But make certain you come with me."

He laughed, dropping his forehead to rest on hers and began to move within her. "I will join you only after I have given you pleasure several times."

"Promise?" Her question teased.

"Promise," he said, no charm in his smile, only wickedness.

He set the rhythm, she joined in and he kept his promise—her cries filled the cottage again and again until she fell limp and exhausted beneath him. He came then, fast, hard and furious and roared out a groan of satisfaction that brought a smug grin to her perspiring face.

When their breathing calmed and he settled beside her, he reached a hand out to her and ran gentle fingers down over her breast and stomach and then up again. "You never cease to surprise me."

She turned her gaze from his and sighed. "I was not proper in bed."

He laughed and gently squeezed her nipple. "And lucky I am that you are not."

She looked up at him in question. "Really, you do not mind my need for you?"

Her innocence showed but he would not let her know that. He kissed her softly. "I cherish your need for me."

"Truly?" Her hand went to stroke his face.

He sighed at the gentleness of her touch. "Truly."

She ran her thumb over his swollen lips—lips that she had swelled with her nibbles and bites.

He watched as her thoughts drifted and took her far away, and he would not have her leaving him. "Stay with me."

She looked with surprise at him. "I go nowhere."

"Aye, you do in your mind."

"I but think."

"Not now," he urged. "Now is not the time."

"What is this time for?"

"For us," he whispered and brushed her lips with his. "Only us?"

"Us and us alone," he assured her. "No thought of yesterdays or tomorrows; only here and now."

"And what will we do with it?" she asked, uncertain.

"We will enjoy *us*," he said, kissing her swiftly again and again. "We will not think, we will only feel."

She sighed and relaxed to his touch, enjoying the gentle intimacy.

"You are innocent, yet so knowledgeable. How is that so?"

She ran a finger over his chest. "Curiosity."

He seemed to understand. "Which means when you decided to learn about mating, you did."

"I was not satisfied with a mere explanation. I wished to see how things worked for myself."

He grinned. "This should be an interesting story."

She laughed and poked at his chest. "I was lucky."

"How so?" He appeared eager to listen.

She was eager to share the occasion with him, feeling him a kindred spirit. "I found out when my uncle would be mating the horses and decided that an early visit to the area would be worthwhile. I hid and to my amazement two of the servants decided to mate before the horses did."

Colin laughed. "And you watched?"

"I peeked," she said with a bit of guilt and a smile. "And I learned."

"What did you learn?" His hand rested on her stomach.

She covered his hand with hers. "I learned that sex could be fun and enjoyable."

"And?" he asked, sensing there was more she intentionally did not mention.

She decided that with the intimacy that had just passed between them there was no longer any point in keeping secrets. "I learned that love mattered."

"How so?" His intent eyes told her that his interest ran deep.

"With love there comes a trust that allows two people

to move past their doubts and insecurities. They can share without fear or disappointment. They can depend on each other and with that knowledge comes a deeper commitment and binding love."

"All this from watching a couple mate in the barn?"

She shook her head, her smile fading. "Nay, I learned from watching people and listening to their joys and sorrows. I learned that nothing is perfect, but in imperfection beauty can be found."

Her depth of intelligence amazed and intrigued him. He ran his finger over her lips. "I admire your tenacity."

She laughed. "Some would suggest it was a curse."

"They are fools," he said seriously.

"You truly believe so?"

"Your tenacity has brought you endless knowledge and the quest for more. You do not fear to search for answers, you eagerly seek them, and they take you on exciting adventures."

She laughed again. "Many would disagree with you. I have been called spoiled and selfish."

He kissed her. "Nay, you possess too caring a heart to be spoiled or selfish." He teasingly poked at her. "I like your curiosity."

"Truly?" She looked at him with hope, wanting him to speak the truth.

And he did. "Truly, your curiosity makes you unique. A one of a kind. A rare gem."

"You do not think me a troublesome burden?" She almost seemed afraid to ask but again her curiosity got the better of her and she needed an answer.

He tapped her nose lightly. "How can a pint-sized female be a burden?"

She gave a brief wave to the small room. "Look where I have gotten us."

He leaned down and nuzzled her neck. "Aye, look where you have gotten us."

"I will not change," she said on a sigh, his eager nibbling causing her flesh to tingle with anticipation.

He spoke into her neck as he continued to feast on it. "I have not asked you to, though—" He paused and looked at her with a teasing smile. "We will work on your stubbornness."

She shoved playfully at his chest and he fell back as if her strength was no match for him. "I am not stubborn," she insisted as she settled herself comfortably on top of him, her hands braced firmly on his chest.

He grabbed her around the waist and positioned her over him.

"I wish to ride you," she said boldly.

He shook his head. "You are not too sore?"

"Should I be?" she asked innocently.

He reached down between her legs with a gentle hand to touch her and she moaned when his fingers found her.

"That feels so good."

He shook his head again. "You are a rare woman, Hope, and I am glad to have found you."

She laughed and attacked his lips with teasing bites. "You could not find me, Colin. It is I who found you."

"Aye," he agreed, his fingers gently exploring her. "But it is I who caught you."

She moaned when he slipped a finger inside her and responded immediately to his gentle persuasion.

They were soon lost again in the throes of passion and the small room once again filled with cries of pleasure.

Late that night Hope woke from the sleep she had drifted into after they had made love for the third time. Colin slept peacefully beside her. She turned on her side to look at him, tucking her hands beneath her cheek to prevent herself from touching him.

It seemed that all she wished to do was touch him. She loved the feel of him, hard and powerful in so many places. She giggled quietly to herself. She liked very much his hard places—they made her feel alive with pleasure.

He was a considerate lover, though she liked when he

lost control and had no choice but to surrender. The feeling gave her power and aroused her all the more. Actually she felt almost a constant arousal around him but then this was all new to her. And yet . . .

She sighed softly. She would forever want him because she would forever love him. Was not that the reason for her surrender? Did she not realize the foolishness of her actions and know that there was nothing left for her to do but to surrender her heart?

Would he ever come to love her?

She knew that was a question that would forever haunt her. And she thought, or perhaps it was more of a wish, that when they made love that she saw a spark of love in his eyes when he looked at her.

She could dream, or wish, or pray that someday it would be so.

For now she would accept her fate and do what was expected of her. At least it would not be a chore to be married to Colin. And it would certainly not be a chore to share a bed with him.

A sudden thought nagged at her, a thought she did not like. She wondered whether he would be a faithful husband to a wife he did not love. Would he continue to charm other women? The idea disturbed her and the more she thought on it the more upset she grew.

She understood that many men did not remain faithful to their wives, but she wanted no such husband. And she wanted to know now what to expect of him.

Without thought to the consequences, she gently poked at him.

He stirred only slightly.

She gave him another poke.

He mumbled incoherently.

This was not working and her frustrated sigh turned to a sudden smile when she reached out and ran a loving hand over his napping manhood. With a few caressing strokes she brought him to full attention.

She also brought herself to an unexpected arousal. She

thought to torment him but it seemed that she tormented herself.

Her passion grew with his and when he felt thick and heavy in her hands, she was suddenly grabbed around the waist, flung backward on the bedding and with a need that mirrored her own Colin entered her swiftly.

She cried out—not from the twinge of soreness that struck her briefly but from the immense pleasure the full, hard length of him brought to her. She could feel the intense swell of him and she moved to take him deeper inside her, moving in a rhythm that he matched.

She moaned and tightly grabbed hold of his shoulders.

He kissed along her neck and whispered in her ear. "I do not hurt you?"

"Never," she whispered back.

"Then hold on," he ordered firmly, "for I want you with a need I never thought possible."

His confession fanned her arousal and she herself swelled with passion for him.

He took her like a man long denied, though she took from him with the same intensity. It was a fast and furious mating that had them both crying out in their combined and sudden climax.

They clung to each other, refusing to let go, refusing to allow the ripples of pleasure to die away.

When the last shudder was released and the last breath finally gasped, he moved off her though he wrapped her in his arms and held her tightly to him.

She had barely caught her breath when she asked, "Will you have other women after we wed?"

Her question stunned him speechless.

"Does your refusal to answer alert me to your intentions?" she asked on a shaky breath.

He was finally able to speak and it was with a note of annoyance. "You ask me this after what we have just shared?"

"I wish to know," she said candidly, though a shred

of doubt entered her tone. Did she wish to know the truth? Or was it better she did not know?

He rolled her onto her back and took an authoritative position over her, his hands locking with hers and stretching them up and out above her head. "Listen closely," he said, his face a mere inch from hers.

Her body tensed, fearing his reply though her wide, bold eyes belied her true emotions.

"As far as I am concerned our vows were sealed the moment I took your virginity. To me you are my wife. We will make it official in the eyes of the church but the ceremony matters not to me. I will cherish, care and protect you for all my life. I need no clergy to speak these words to me and though I have yet to exchange vows with you, my heart and soul have already done so. I will not break them nor will I dishonor them." He smiled and brushed a kiss across her lips. "And you, dear wife, please me in bed, so why should I look to another woman?"

She opened her mouth and he kissed her, his tongue darting, playing and teasing hers.

"I look for no answer," he said, ending the playful kiss. "I but wish to know why you feel the need to ask such a ridiculous question of me?"

"Your reputation," she said without hesitation.

He rested his forehead to hers, stole a brief kiss and rolled off her, taking her with him to nestle in his arms. He seemed to pause and consider her words and then with a tight hug, he said, "I will be a faithful husband to you, Hope."

He did not expect her response. "Why?"

He sensed her frustration and doubt and he wished to ease her worries. "Because I take my vows seriously."

Had she expected him to declare his love for her? *Foolish.*

Would that word forever haunt her? Would she forever want a love from him that he could not give? And why did the thought upset her so? Why could she not accept and admit that she must wed him no matter what he felt or did not feel?

Why was love so important to her?

"I will be good to you, Hope," he said, his remark spoken with a confidence that was meant to ease her concerns.

"I have no doubt of that, Colin," Hope said.

"Then what disturbs you? Tell me so that I may ease your worries."

"What if you cannot?"

He sounded confident. "I can and I will."

She thought of the deep, soul-reaching love she felt for him and the thought that if he could love her with a mere fraction of what she felt for him . . .

She shook her head. *Foolish dreams*. But then was not one allowed to dream foolishly?

"You are mine," he whispered with a strength that challenged her to deny him.

She could not deny the truth. She was his, her heart belonged to him and as much as she fought her emotions, she also surrendered to them.

She loved him, plain and simple, and she told him so. "I love you, Colin. With all my heart I love you."

He hugged her tightly to him and felt her love, and at that precise moment he realized that it was not only her love for him but his love for her.

The realization startled him and words failed him. Actions, however, did not and he did what he did best. He turned and with a gentleness that disarmed her he began to make love to her.

She surrendered easily and most willingly and she understood that she could not deny her love for him, nor did she want to. However it was to be she would accept, and right at this moment she wanted him with all her heart. That was how she surrendered to him—with all her heart.

Thirty-one

Hope was grateful for the change of clothing and the chance to bathe in the nearby stream. The daily pitcher of water had helped her keep herself as fresh as possible but a good bathing was what she needed.

She and Faith eagerly joined the village women as they gathered to talk, bathe and wash garments. A woman close to Hope's size provided a fresh linen shift and another offered a tunic that she was able to make fit with the help of her cloth belt.

Faith was also provided with fresh garments while hers were washed and though she had insisted on seeing to the task herself, the other women would not hear of it. They were most insistent that she rest and grateful to her for having seen to a few ailing villagers.

Hope sat beside Faith on a brown wool blanket, each of them busy combing their wet hair.

Faith sighed and gave up almost as soon as she had started. "I seem to grow tired much too often lately."

Hope finished her own hair with a few rough strokes, the short cut making it easy to handle when wet or dry. She took Faith's comb from her hands, kneeled behind her and with a gentle touch, began to comb the mass of flaming red ringlets.

"Are you concerned about the babe?"

"I feel well and I have experienced no discomfort."

Hope waited for her to continue, for something obviously concerned her.

"I wonder if my child grows impatient inside me."

"You think the babe wishes to make an early appearance?"

"I have no signs of early delivery," Faith said, but doubt could be heard in her voice.

Hope worked the bone comb through the thick ringlets. "You sound as if you may feel otherwise."

"A feeling is all I have."

"Is not that all a woman needs? A simple feeling tells a woman much."

"Aye, that it does," Faith agreed. "If a woman would listen and follow what she knows to be so."

"But we can be a stubborn lot," Hope said with a laugh.

"True enough. Even when a feeling nags at us we sometimes ignore it and suffer the consequences."

"Then we must not ignore your feeling about the babe," Hope insisted. "We must return you to Shanekill as soon as possible." Hope continued to run the comb through the mass of wet curls, the tangles nearly gone.

"It should not be long now. Borg should arrive any day, and besides, there are many experienced women here who could help birth a babe. And, of course, I have you. I would be in safe hands."

Hope was honored that she trusted her and though her experience with actual births was limited she was confident she could provide the necessary care. "I would do all I could to help deliver your babe safely."

"The babe sees to most of it," Faith said with a yawn.

"Have you spoken of your concerns with Lord Eric?"

Faith laughed. "Good heavens, never. He worries enough now as it is. If he thought there was a possibility of me delivering early he would not be fit to live with. Nay," she confirmed with a shake of her head. "I will not speak of this to him."

"Not speak of what to me?"

The two women did not bother to turn around, though

the sudden sound of the devil's voice behind them had caused their bodies to jump in surprise.

Eric walked around to confront them and Hope was not surprised to see Colin with him.

"Do I get an answer, wife?" he asked, the confidence in his voice obvious.

"Nay," Faith said on a sigh and took the comb from Hope so she could comb at the curly strands that lay over her chest.

Hope watched the way the devil grew annoyed and Colin smirked. He seemed to delight in the confrontation that was about to take place, but then he had often commented how right the pair was for each other.

Hope moved from behind Faith to sit at her side and in a way demonstrate her support.

Faith acknowledged her support with a pat to her hand.

The devil had remained silent long enough and while he attempted to control his annoyance he was obviously having difficulty doing so. "Nay? I ask you a question and you refuse to answer me?"

Faith spoke calmly. "You asked me if you would get an answer and I spoke the truth."

Colin covered his smile with his hand.

Eric turned to him. "You have something to say?"

"Nay, my lord," he wisely responded.

"Do not pick at Colin, he has done nothing," Faith said, remaining calm.

"You forever defend him," Eric snapped.

"He is my friend and would do the same for me."

"Aye, I would," Colin agreed.

"Very well," Eric said, looking from one to the other. "Then I shall ask an impartial person." He turned his attention on Hope. "What does my wife not tell me?"

"That is not fair, Eric; you ask her to break a confidence," Faith demanded, annoyance now evident in her voice.

"This was spoken to you in confidence?" Eric asked of Hope.

Hope looked to Faith and then at the devil. "I took it as such."

Eric crouched down in front of Hope. "I love my wife very much, Hope. I would give my life for her. I worry needlessly more often than not but it is my way. I ask you as a friend to her and me. Please tell me if I should worry now."

Hope understood love, having fallen so deeply in love with Colin; therefore she understood how Eric felt. It was a vulnerable feeling and one foreign to a warrior, and yet he admitted his emotions. He was not ashamed of them and that won her heart.

She looked to Faith. "You are lucky he loves you so very much."

Faith understood her dilemma and quickly took charge. "He was stubborn about loving me at first."

"I was not," Eric objected vehemently.

"Was he not, Colin?" Faith asked.

"I must agree with Lady Faith," Colin said. "You were a stubborn one."

Eric stood. "And you are not?"

"I have my moments," Colin admitted.

"We are not talking about moments of stubbornness. We are talking about stubbornness when it comes to love, and if anyone is stubborn about love it is you," Eric said adamantly.

"True enough," Faith said.

Colin looked wounded that Faith should agree with her husband.

Hope remained silent and deeply interested in the exchange of opinions.

Colin disputed their claim. "I am not stubborn about love—"

Eric laughed, interrupting him. "You charm your way around the elusive emotion."

"Are you suggesting that I avoid love?"

"Aye," Eric and Faith said in unison.

Hope simply smiled.

Colin shook his head and insisted, "Love did not see fit to find me."

"You never looked with open eyes," Eric challenged.

Colin was about to respond when Hope spoke up, capturing everyone's attention. "Perhaps you fear to love."

Colin looked ready to object when suddenly he held his tongue and remained silent.

Eric reached down to help his wife up. "Come, we need to talk."

Faith agreed, grateful for her husband's strength as he easily lifted her up to stand. "Aye, that we do. I will be honest with you, my lord."

"You always are," he said with a nibble to her neck and a supporting and loving arm around her waist. They walked off together, content in each other's arms.

Colin watched them for a moment before joining Hope on the blanket. He looked directly at her. Last night the realization of his feelings for her startled him and he was still coming to understand and accept them. He had wished to find love, thought he looked for it, but never had he thought he avoided it. Had he feared to love all these years? And why was it different now with this pint-sized woman?

She felt uncomfortable, as if her words had somehow personally intruded on him, and she attempted to take them back. "I sometimes speak without thinking."

He shook his head. "Nay, your words were spoken in haste but they were spoken with good intention." He gave her a teasing poke. "Though your mouth does not mind itself at times."

"It minds itself all right," she said with a heavy sigh. "That is why I find myself in trouble more often than not, for I speak what I feel."

"You feel that I fear to love?" He wanted to know more of what she thought.

"It is possible. We often run from our deepest fears."

"Have you?"

She laughed. "You were sent to find me, were you not?"

He smiled, though it faded as he asked, "What did you fear that made you run?"

She paused in her answer.

He poked at her. "And do not tell me that you feared you would never experience a grand adventure."

Her smile was childlike. "I like adventures."

He ran a gentle finger down her cheek and across her lips. "What was your fear?"

She was honest. "I feared I would never know true love. Never know what it was like to love someone so very much that it actually hurt when you were parted from them. To crave a man's touch or hunger for his kiss and know that he was the only one who could ever please or satisfy you." She paused and with reluctance added, "And to know that he felt the same in return."

"So you ran away to find love?"

She covered his hand where it rested on her cheek with hers. "I ran to find love. You ran from love."

All these years, all the women. Had he truly run away from love? Had he truly feared finding love?

She offered him more answers, their joined hands drifting to rest in her lap. "My mother and father loved deeply and I will always remember that special love they shared. It was rare and it was beautiful. And I wanted to know a love such as theirs. And while I knew it would not be easy to find, I knew I must at least attempt a search or I would always wonder."

"Your courage took you on your search."

She shook her head and smiled. "Nay, it was my fear that urged me to go."

He never spoke of his family to anyone but he felt the need to share his past with her. "My mother and father cared naught for each other. Theirs was an arranged marriage, loveless and emotionless. What love I did find was with an older woman who understood what

I needed. She taught me that true love is unselfish and what your parents had discovered . . . true love is rare. Having tasted from her a mere sample of what true love could be and never having known it from my parents, I suppose my inclination was to run so I would not suffer the hurt and disappointment of never finding love."

He shook his head and gripped her hand tightly. "Love is difficult."

"Only if we choose to make it so."

"You chose to make it difficult," he said.

"How so?"

He explained. "You love me and yet you—" He paused, a question popping into his head that made him wonder. "When did you realize you loved me?"

"When we were traveling."

"But—" He shook his head. "I do not understand. I never kissed you or touched you and yet you fell in love with me?"

"Aye, I fell in love with *you*."

"You barely knew me."

"Nay, I got to know you well. And glad of it I was. You became my best friend, someone who cared for me, someone I could trust, someone I could depend on if need be." She smiled. "You showed me who you were in many ways. Ways I would never have gotten to know if we had met as a man and a woman."

Colin cringed, recalling the many discussions around the campfire. "You heard much you should not have."

She laughed with delight and squeezed his hand. "Nay, I loved listening to the men and learning about them. I had no knowledge of how men actually thought or felt. Most seemed selfish and self-indulgent. Talking with the men made me realize that most of their bluster is an act to hide their true emotions. They fear their own feelings, thinking of them as weaknesses instead of strengths."

He looked at her with amazement. "You are remarkable."

She blushed at the compliment. "You think so?"

"I have known only one other woman who could talk with such intelligence and never did I imagine I would meet another."

Her smile teased. "But you wished for me, did you not?"

He brought her hand to his lips and kissed it. "Aye, I wished for you on every bright star and every whispered breath." He gently kissed the back of her hand again.

She felt the sensual tingle grab hold. It tickled, tormented and tempted at all her intimate places. And she could have surrendered right there and then to him, but she had to ask the one question that continued to nag at her. "Could you love me?"

Her boldness should not startle him, and yet it did.

Her fingers rushed to still his lips. "I need you to love me as much as I love you. I want no less of a love. It must be a forever love. If you cannot give me this then please never speak of love to me. Cherish and care for me as I know you will, but please do not hurt me with meaningless words."

He admired her courage and respected her request and at that moment he could have spoken of love to her. But would it be a forever love? Did he feel that strongly or was it the moment and their surroundings that made him feel so emotionally attached to her? He wanted to be certain. He did not wish to disappoint her or himself. It would not be fair to either of them.

His hesitation spoke loudly in the silence and her hand dropped away from his mouth. She eased the tension with a change of conversation. "I should tell you that Faith feels the babe may arrive early."

It worked. Colin grew alarmed. "This is what she did not wish to tell Eric?"

Hope nodded, relieved that she had succeeded in diverting his attention so quickly.

"He will worry when he learns of this and make demands of Rath."

"Faith is in good hands here. The village women have delivered many a babe and they are good, caring women."

"True enough," Colin agreed, worry remaining heavy on his face. "The small group is a close lot and protective of each other. And they have treated us well. They are far from the common thieves that prey and rob with malice."

"I have thought the same myself." Her heart continued to feel heavy over his silence to her question, but she would not allow him to see her hurt. She did as a man would and hid her true feelings.

"Rath speaks little of himself and of this group. He did mention that the law was meant to benefit only a chosen few and the rest of society was forced to follow their harsh dictates. He felt otherwise. And I think his firm convictions are the reason he is presently in this situation, for he certainly is not a common thief."

Her hand continued to rest in his and he made no move to release her so she lingered in the warmth of his touch. "I agree. The villagers speak highly of him and it would seem that they follow him with trust and devotion."

"The men fight at his side without doubt to their cause." He shook his head with a smile. "But then I did the same with Eric."

"You trust him."

"Aye, from the first moment we met, I knew he was a man of his word and a man who would march into battle leading his men. He would expect of his men what he expected of himself. He is a man of honor and I am proud to call him friend."

"And these people feel the same of Rath as you feel for the devil, do they not?"

Colin squeezed her hand. "I felt it when we first arrived. It was strange to see the same respect and admiration given to the devil also given to this thief by this small lot. Yet their trust is palpable."

"You sound as if you respect him as well."

He shook his head. "Crazy as it seems, Eric and I were speaking of our admiration for the thief. The more we come to know him, the more of our respect he earns, and he does treat Eric with due respect. I almost feel that he would not stop us if we chose to leave, though the promised coins are important to him. They will supply these people with needed supplies."

Hope looked around the camp at the women and men who talked and laughed and the children who ran about playing. They were a content group thanks to the man who led them.

"During my journey I met up with many who were hungry and homeless. Theirs was a sorry lot and it hurt me to discover that many suffer while many others indulge."

"It is the way of life. The strong always rule and the strong always survive. You survived, though you were near to starving when I found you."

She poked at him. "It was I who found you. I watched you set up camp and I waited."

"You spied on me?" he asked with surprise.

"For a time," she said proudly.

"I cannot believe I did not discover you lurking about earlier in the evening. My men combed the area before we settled for the night and then stood guard."

"Lady and I easily avoided them. They are not hard to miss while I, this skinny lad, could hide without difficulty."

"For a lad you were skinny. For a woman I find you perfect."

She did not believe her ears. "You think me perfect?"

He leaned down and stole a brief kiss before he answered, "Your body is pure perfection."

The sensual tingle started all over again and this time she did not wish to ignore it. She wished to surrender to it. She sighed lightly and grabbed hold more tightly of his hand.

He understood her need for he felt it himself.

He ran a faint kiss across her lips and whispered near her ear. "I want you."

She shuddered from the tingle that rushed through her body and nestled between her legs to leave her moist with the want of him. And she told him so. "And I you."

He stood, his hand tugging at hers to pull her up along with him.

He slipped his arm around her and tugged her close to his side as they walked to the small cottage. "My need is great."

"Then we should take our time and make certain your need is satisfied."

As they neared the cottage he scooped her up in his arms and she laughed, throwing her arms around his neck. He shoved the door open with his shoulder and kicked it closed after they had entered. He went straight for the bed and they went down on it together.

He pressed his forehead to hers and admitted, "I have no patience; my want overwhelms me."

She reached down, running her hand over the bulge beneath his tunic. "Then let us assuage your ache quickly."

"Once will not be enough," he warned her as he began to kiss her with a demanding urgency.

"Once is never enough," she whispered and bit playfully at his lower lip as her hand moved beneath his tunic and cupped him with a roughness that had him moaning aloud.

A hard knock at the door tore them apart just as Eric entered the cottage. "Colin, we need to talk," he said and walked out, leaving the door open for Colin to follow.

He stood and adjusted his garments. "We will finish this when I return."

She walked on her knees to the edge of the bed where

he stood and ran one hand over the bulge that remained hard under his tunic. Her other hand drifted up around his neck while her lips went for his mouth.

She kissed him with a fervor that left him breathless. "I will be waiting *impatiently*."

He shook his head, groaned, grumbled and reluctantly left the room.

Thirty-two

Colin assumed Eric was worried about Faith, but it was not only Faith's condition that disturbed him.

"At first when she informed me that the babe may arrive early I grew concerned with our present situation. Faith alleviated my fears by making me realize she would have much experienced help here. I would, of course, prefer her to be at Shanekill where I know for certain she would be safe."

"Then there is naught for us to worry about," Colin said with relief.

It was a short-lived relief, however, for Eric said, "Nay, there is much for us to worry about." Eric sat on a nearby fallen tree, Colin joining him. "Rath has just informed me that a lord from a neighboring land has a troop of his men out searching for him and that they draw dangerously close. He does not think it is safe to remain here much longer. A day or two at the most, he suggests."

Colin stood and paced before him. "Perhaps it would be best for us to leave immediately and return to the safety of your land. Rath and his people would find safe shelter there."

Eric grinned. "You do me proud by thinking as I do. That is why I trust you to lead many of the missions requested of me."

"You have taught me well, my lord."

"We are friends, Colin, friends long before I bought this fancy title."

"It is a title you earned and a title I respect. You are my lord and I will serve you well."

Eric stood and held his hand out to him. Colin took it. "Thank you, and it is glad I am to call you friend."

Colin nodded, feeling a strong bond with the devil and knowing he would give his life for him and his wife. "Shall we make plans to leave immediately?"

"Rath suggests that a day or two should not harm us. And I worry over Faith."

"I think we would be wise to move as quickly as possible," Colin said. "There is no point in taking a chance, especially with Faith's condition. The closer we are to Shanekill land the better it will be for her."

"I thought of this, but she grows tired much too often and I do not know if this journey will be too much for her."

"There is a cart here. We can make it comfortable for her and she can sleep when necessary. Hope will look after her."

"You grow fond of her," Eric said, as if he declared it so.

Colin felt at ease talking with Eric. "More than I expected. She is different from most women I have known. She intrigues me."

"That is a good start. For one so small in size she defends herself and others when necessary. I admire her courage and I am pleased that she is here now."

Colin laughed. "*We* are here now because of her."

"Faith is here because of her obstinacy and because she has a husband who cannot seem to deny her her way."

"Hope need not have run away again," Colin said, feeling a sense of guilt for their dilemma.

"I would have been surprised had she stayed and remained compliant."

Colin looked confused. "You expected her to run?"

"She possesses too much courage to surrender without a fight. Remember that during your marriage. She will not retreat easily and she will defend herself endlessly. Her willful nature will not allow her to respond otherwise. Have you not learned this by now?"

"It is easier to see when you stand outside the situation," Colin said. "But when you are in the thick of things nothing is clear."

Eric nodded. "How true are your words. I could see nothing clearly when Faith and I first came together."

Colin grinned. "Aye, I remember."

"And enjoyed."

"That, too."

Eric returned his grin. "Now it is my turn to enjoy."

"Will you have no mercy, my lord?"

"Not a lick," Eric assured him.

"At least have mercy on me now and allow me to return to Hope and finish what I had begun."

Eric laughed and slapped Colin on the back. "I disturbed you at an inopportune time?"

"Most inopportune time."

"My regrets," Eric offered. "Go enjoy."

"Thank you, my lord," Colin said, and with a respectful nod walked away.

The devil called out to him and he turned. "First thing tomorrow we make plans and by the next sunrise we are gone."

"A wise choice, my lord. I will see to it." A nod and they both went their separate ways, returning to their women.

Hope was naked beneath the soft wool blanket and sound asleep. Dusk was near to drifting into the night and the room's only glow was the soft light from the moderate flames in the hearth.

Colin at first thought not to disturb her. His immediate second thought was that her nakedness was a sure sign that her intention was the same as his. And she would not at all mind if he woke her.

He stripped out of his garments with haste and slipped carefully beneath the covers. She was turned on her side, her back to him, and he nestled himself gently up against her, his hand drifting slowly down her waist, over her hip, splaying along her belly until his fingers tickled at the triangular mound of dark hair.

She responded to his familiar touch though asleep, a soft, sensual sigh spilling from her lips.

That sigh encouraged him and he went to work at her neck, raining endless, provocative kisses along the sensitive skin. His hand worked its own magic, tempting her with a flicker of a touch here and there until he had her moving to the rhythm his hand finally set.

Her eyes drifted open and her voice was heavy with sleep and desire. "Why did you not wake me?"

"I have," he said on a laugh and bit playfully at her neck.

She shivered and when she did, his fingers entered her with a force and rhythm that had her climaxing in seconds, her cries of pleasure filling the room.

"Not fair," she said when she regained her breathing.

"I do not play fair with you," he whispered in her ear.

The thought that he made love differently to her excited her. "Why?"

He was honest. "I lose control and think naught but of my need for you." His fingers began to move inside her again, and again she responded.

"You need me now?" she asked, her sighs beginning to rise with the tempo he set.

He moved his swelled manhood against her. "Do you doubt my need?" She rubbed against him, a laugh mingling with her moans. "Nay, I am glad for your need."

His hand drifted away from her and he turned her on her back, slipping over and into her in one skillful stroke.

She welcomed him with a deep sigh and he moved in and out of her with strong purposeful strokes. His mouth came down on her aching nipples and he soothed them with his lips and tongue, paying each much needed attention.

"I never imagined . . ." Her words drifted off on a pleasurable moan.

He finished them for her. "That it could feel so good."

She nodded and ran her hands over his broad shoulders. "Aye," she said on a sigh that grew as he hastened the tempo. She wrapped her legs around him and took him deeper inside her, feeling the strength of him and relishing in the exquisite sensation.

His lips left her tingling breasts and moved to capture her lips swollen with the want of him. She eagerly responded to his kiss and her movements grew more demanding, more needy. Her moans turned to a frantic ache and he made certain to satisfy her every need, giving her what she craved with an intense craving of his own.

They came together in a fast and furious climax that neither expected. They clung to each other like lovers drowning in the aftermath of a rich sexual encounter and not yet realizing its ramifications. They drifted listlessly, letting the ripples of pleasure ride through them and forgetting everything but the passion they had just shared.

They came apart out of need for air and lay sprawled on their backs, their arms stretched above their heads and holding hands to keep them connected.

Their breathing slowed and their senses returned and with it they turned on their sides facing each other. He kissed her gently. She kissed him back. He touched her here and there and she did the same. They could not keep their hands off each other.

It was a gentle intimacy they shared, a bonding of lovers.

"I like the feel of you," he said. She smiled softly. "And I you. I do not think I will ever grow tired of touching you."

"That is good," he said with a kiss. "For I will be the only man you ever touch."

She looked at him strangely. "Why would I ever wish to touch another man? I want only you. I love you." The words came easily to her, for they were truthful and spoken from the heart. And she could be no less than honest with him. No matter how he felt.

His fingers teased at her nipples, his mouth fed on hers and he demonstrated his feelings as only he could at the moment, through touch.

She enjoyed his inquisitive fingers and relaxed with every stroke.

They talked, they kissed, they touched and they loved into the night until finally exhaustion claimed them and they fell asleep in each other's arms.

Dawn brought a new day and Hope woke with a promise of a new beginning. She grew excited at the challenge and was eager to begin the day. It was delayed with a brief but satisfying bout of lovemaking and then she was up, hungry for food and for the new day.

Eggs, bread and cheese were served to them for breakfast and Colin decided while they ate that it was best to be honest with her about their circumstances. He told her of his conversation with Eric.

She finished eating a chunk of cheese. "Do you feel we are in danger?"

"Not immediate danger, but close enough. Lord Eric wants us gone from here by sunrise tomorrow. A wise choice."

"Then there is much to do, especially making certain that Lady Faith's comfort is seen to for the journey."

"You are a lady yourself, born of a respected lineage, and yet you demand no pampering or special treatment."

She reached for a small piece of cheese. "I am proud of the courageous bloodline that I am a descendent of but my heritage also possesses a strong sense of independence. I need no special treatment nor do I want it. I enjoy doing for myself and have done so since I was a young girl."

"I would guess that your uncle is disappointed that

you were caught in a compromising situation that forced him to agree to a marriage he would never have sanctioned."

"Are you saying that my uncle is disappointed that his niece did not have a better choice of a marriage partner?"

He shrugged. "You did not have a choice. I am sure he would have preferred someone with a richer lineage than mine."

She laughed, pressing her fingers to her mouth to contain her laughter.

He grew annoyed. "You think it funny?"

"Aye," she admitted, and bit at her lip to keep from laughing out loud.

"Why?" His curt query sounded stern.

She tempered her laughter and took a deep breath so that she could explain. "My uncle wished me to be happy. He had all intentions of presenting me with a list of potential husbands and allowing me to make my own choice."

"You were to choose your husband?"

She nodded. "Uncle Shamus would never have forced me to marry a complete stranger. He wanted me happy; therefore, when he found us in bed together he was actually more relieved than angry."

"Relieved?" he asked, confused.

She nodded again. "Aye, he assumed since I slept with you that you would be the husband of my choice and he no longer needed to worry about finding me someone. I had seen to finding my own husband."

Colin shook his head. "I do not understand."

"But I have explained it."

"Nay," he said, shaking his head again. "I do not understand why you ran away if your uncle intended for you to choose your own husband. Could you not have found one to love?"

She looked directly at him, raising her chin a notch. "I was looking for a special man. I searched for someone who would not only love me but understand my willful ways, my need to explore, my need for a sense of freedom."

"Some would think that was much to ask of a husband."

"That is why I searched for a special man, for only a kindred spirit would understand my needs and be able to meet them."

Colin leaned across the small table and tapped her playfully on the nose. "As I told you, Hope, I will be a good husband." He stood and held his hand out to her. "Come, there is much work to do before our departure tomorrow."

She took his hand, wondering over his remark.

The day was beautiful, the sun bright and the air warm. Everyone in the village was busy running about gathering, packing and preparing for tomorrow.

Hope immediately went to work helping a few of the women prepare a small cart for Faith. Colin joined Eric and Rath who were deep in discussion.

Faith sat on a blanket complaining that she should be helping along with everyone else.

"Be sensible," one of the women said. "You need to see to the safety of your babe. Rest and do not worry. All will be seen to."

Faith rested a hand to her stomach as if realizing the wisdom of the woman's words, and remained silent as preparations continued.

Early in the afternoon Hope joined Faith on the blanket for a light meal while the men continued to talk. It was not surprising to see that weapons had been dispersed amongst the villagers. Even a few of the women carried knives.

But the impending danger came to full realization when Colin and Eric's swords were returned to them.

"I will be glad when we are home," Faith said, her eyes on her husband in the near distance but her remark directed to Hope.

"Do not worry," Hope said, laying a comforting hand on hers. "We are well protected."

"I know. Eric and Colin are fierce warriors and will guard us well, but I am a cumbersome lot in my present condition and fear I will slow us down on the journey."

"Are you not feeling well?" Hope asked with concern.

Faith shook her head. "It is nothing I can say for sure and since I cannot I do not speak of it to Eric, but . . ."

"You think the babe will arrive early."

"It is only a feeling."

"One that needs to be paid attention to," Hope insisted. "And I will be by your side the whole return trip. I will see to your every need."

"Nonsense, you need not—"

Hope interrupted. "I want to do this for you, and besides, I am too stubborn to take nay for an answer. I will do as I please."

Faith took hold of her hand. "I am glad you are here with me."

Hope thought a change of topic wise. "And glad I am that you will be with me on my wedding day."

Faith smiled and hugged Hope. "You have decided to wed Colin."

"Aye, I have," she admitted and felt good that she had made the choice that had so haunted her.

"It is a wise choice you have made," Faith assured her. "And when we return to the keep we will begin immediate plans for your wedding. Bridget can stitch a dress for you. Mary will cook a grand feast. There will be music and merriment." Tears gathered in her eyes. "I love weddings, especially when two people are in love."

Hope looked at her strangely. "Colin does not love me. He weds me out of duty."

Faith stared at her oddly. "Colin would only wed for love. He does not marry you out of duty."

"You believe this?" Hope asked incredulously.

Faith shook her head. "I know this. He is as willful

as you are, and would do nothing if it was not his choice."

"Aye, he chooses to wed me out of duty."

"Nay," Faith insisted. "Duty has nothing to do with why he weds you. And Eric himself told him he would not force him to wed you if it was not what he wished."

"He did?" Hope asked in disbelief.

Faith nodded. "He did and Colin did not hesitate in his decision. He may not have realized his love for you immediately but he felt something strong enough that made him wish to wed you."

"He was confused, thinking me the lad, and probably felt sorry for me and my foolishness."

Faith smiled. "Nay, he admired your foolishness, for he is often foolish himself."

Kindred spirit. Was he more like her than she thought? Could he truly understand her? Could he truly love her?

"Give him time," Faith said, yawning.

Time. They had much of that to share together and perhaps time would prove to be their friend.

"You should nap," Hope said and stood, reaching her hand down to her.

"You are right. I wish to be strong for the journey tomorrow." Faith took her hand and Hope easily helped her up. "You are strong for one so small."

"Aye," Hope said with a wink. "It fools many."

"And makes fools of many," Faith said, laughing.

Faith saw that Eric approached with Colin and waited for him with a smile.

The blast came out of nowhere and the soldiers descended on them in a fury.

Chaos reigned in seconds, smoke filled the air along with screams, swords clashed, arrows flew and Hope grabbed Faith, pushing her toward the surrounding forest.

Thirty-three

Hope kept her small body protectively in front of Faith as she pushed her toward the safety of the woods. They dodged several sword-wielding men and frantic women who were attempting to get the children to the cover of safety.

Anguished screams pierced the warm air and Hope tried not to think of Colin. He was a skilled warrior and he would survive. Her concern now had to be for Faith. She was in no condition to be on her own and Hope knew she had to protect her.

Hope grabbed for a knife from a felled villager and with steady though unsure steps she kept working her way toward the woods. She caught sight of Colin and Eric fighting side by side and saw that they were attempting to make their way toward her. She understood the anguish Eric must be feeling, unable to be at his wife's side to protect her, and she had no doubt that Colin fought with the same intentions, though he would know that her own willfulness would serve her well.

They were not far from the thick covering of the surrounding woods. Once in there she realized she could make certain Faith was safely tucked away and return to help those in need.

The soldiers seemed to multiply in strength and the fighting roared out of control. Villagers fell one after another and it was obvious that retreat was the only solution for the small band of innocents.

Eric and Colin appeared to be in the thick of things. Hope heard Eric scream his name and watched as soldiers gave him and Colin a wide birth since they stood back to back.

Rath, however, was not so lucky. He fought bravely, but it was obvious the soldiers were determined to capture him.

Hope managed with a kick and a tussle and a warning of a swinging knife to get Faith to the safety of the woods.

Faith dropped with a heavy sigh to her knees once under the covers of the dense bushes. "Eric, is he all right?"

Hope attempted to ease her worries. "Last time I saw, he was fine."

"And Colin?"

"They both do well."

"Rath?" she asked with wide eyes.

Hope's silence answered for her.

Tears filled Faith's eyes. "Go do what you can. I am fine."

"Are you sure?" Hope asked, not wanting to leave her.

"I can hear the children's screams. Go help them, Hope. I am safe here."

"I will return soon," she assured her and hurried off.

It took time to get the scattered and frightened children together and finally to safety. Faith took charge from there, quieting the children with her soothing voice.

Hope made another trip out into the melee to make certain she had gotten every child. Her eyes caught briefly with Eric's and with a simple nod of her head she informed him that Faith was safe. His look of pure relief brought tears to her eyes and when they caught with Colin's he seemed to understand, and what she saw in his eyes stunned her even more. He was proud, so very proud of her.

She guided the last lone child to safety and returned again to see if she could help. The smoke from the burning cottages hung thick in the air and it was difficult to see clearly. The clash of swords had lessened and it seemed the fighting had abated. No cries were heard. Instead silence hung heavy and a sense of defeat was felt.

Hope went to take another cautious step when she heard the devil speak.

"Hold your sword or I will kill you where you stand."

The smoke began to clear and she stood where she was, watching, waiting, holding her breath and wondering to whom the devil spoke.

He held his sword to a man's throat and it was obvious the man was in command for his men froze around him.

"I am Lord Eric of Shanekill."

Gasps and whispers circled the area and many took a step back as if in fright.

Colin stood protectively at the devil's back and when he caught sight of Hope he could not hide his relief.

"I offer these people my protection," Eric said with a forcefulness that had the soldiers trembling.

Hope noticed the few wounded and remaining villagers breathed a sigh of relief and helped each other to crowd closer together.

The man with the sword at his neck attempted to keep his command. "You have no right to speak for these people."

Eric pressed the sword to his throat and caused him to choke and take a cautious step back.

"I have every right to extend my protection to whomever I choose, and you will do well to realize the wisdom of a silent tongue."

He foolishly did not listen. "My orders—"

"I care naught for your orders," Eric bellowed. "You will take your men and return to your lord and tell them that the people of this village belong to the devil and will be given safe passage away from it. If he chooses to confront me, then he will face my wrath. An unwise choice."

The other soldiers were already backing away, ready to take flight, and when the commander saw retreat in their frightened eyes he himself acquiesced with a nod.

"I will deliver your message."

"A wise choice," Eric said and lowered his sword.

The man fled in haste, his soldiers fast at his heels.

"My wife . . . ?" Eric inquired, turning to Hope.

"Safe in the woods," Hope answered and went to Colin who extended his arm out to her.

He wrapped her quickly in a tight embrace and they followed the devil to the woods so he could collect his wife.

Unfortunately the woods were empty and silent. Not a sound could be heard. The birds had taken flight, the animals had scurried off and Faith was gone.

Eric turned to Hope. "Where is she? I saw you guide her here."

"I did," she said frantically, her wide eyes searching the surrounding area in disbelief. "I left her right here with the children and a few of the women. They were safe."

"Rath?" Colin asked as if his name gave answer to the question.

Eric looked ready to explode, but spoke with a frightening calmness. "Did he escape?"

Hope answered. "He does not appear to be among those left behind."

Eric began to breath heavily and pace the wooded area. "He took her. He took my wife."

Hope attempted to reason. "Perhaps he thought he was protecting her."

Eric would have none of it. "He knew she would be safer with me. Once the soldiers found out my identity they would not fight me. He understood this and he took her anyway."

"Do you wish to follow?"

"I know not this area, and he does. I would be foolish

to follow him blindly. Borg will be at the river in a day or two with the coins, horses and men. And Rook, he will find Faith. We go after him then. For now see to the wounded and those needing help."

"Aye, my lord," Colin said, and he and Hope walked off.

"Hope," the devil called out.

Colin and she stopped.

"Thank you for seeing to my wife's safety."

"I should have remained with her."

"Nay, you did what was necessary. You saved the children and Faith would have had it no other way."

Hope was at a loss to respond and simply turned with Colin and walked away.

They were only a few feet from the woods when a fierce cry of anger ripped through the air and sent shivers racing over everyone.

The devil had made his wrath known and there was no escaping it.

Hope cast a silent prayer for Rath, for when the devil found him there would be hell to pay.

Hope did what she could for the wounded. Gratefully there were no serious injuries—only minor abrasions. Colin hunted the woods for food and returned with enough game for all.

It was a quiet night with many too lost in their thoughts to speak. They missed loved ones and their faithful leader though none would mention his name in front of the devil.

Hope did not feel Rath meant Faith harm and she wondered why he took her along. He had known she was not feeling well and it would have been safer for her to remain behind with her husband. So why did he take her with them?

She sat away from the fire on a bedding of blankets she had prepared for herself for the night. She missed Lady and wished that she was there with her. She wished that she had not run away. Then Faith would now be safe at Shanekill. She wished that she had not run away at all for then she would never have upset so many lives, including her own.

The tears fell one by one, landing on her linen tunic, and she wished that she was wearing the lad's garments for then perhaps she would find some of his courage and not feel so guilty for all the harm she had caused.

She heard Colin approach and wiped at her tears, not wanting to appear vulnerable or weak.

He crouched down in front of her. "Have you ea—" He reached out and caught a descending teardrop. He asked her not a single question; he simply moved in beside her and took her into his arms.

She cried then in earnest, holding tightly to him, her head resting on his shoulder. Her fear, frustration and worry flowed out in an ebb of continuous tears and he continued to hold fast to her, protecting her from her own weakness and vulnerability.

"I am sorry," she finally said when she was able to control her emotions.

"You have nothing to be sorry for. Battles leave scars that must be faced."

"This is not my first battle," she reminded him with pride.

His pride in her caused him to smile. "Nay, it is not, though after your first battle you were ill. Not so with this one."

Hope remained silent, for she remembered that battle well and had wished she could cry. She had also wished she could have remained in his arms.

Colin must have remembered also, for he slipped a finger beneath her chin and with a gentle lift he forced her eyes to meet his. "I recall after that battle how you clung to me. You must have been frightened and close to tears, but you shed none."

She was honest with him. "I wanted so badly to remain in the safety of your arms, but I could not. A young lad would not seek the shelter of a man's arms."

"A woman would," Colin said and began to realize just how difficult it must have been for her to be disguised as a lad. He wrapped her tightly in his arms. "You are safe in my arms now and may remain so as long you wish, though I must tell you how proud I was of your courage today. I feared for your well-being when we were attacked. I could not stand the thought of losing you."

She allowed her tears to run dry. "You worried over me?"

"Of course I did. Life would be meaningless without you."

She looked up at him in surprise. "It would? I thought I was a nuisance to you."

He captured her chin in his hand and leaned down to place a firm kiss on her lips. "Nay, a nuisance you are not. You have come to mean much to me."

She pursued his remark. "What do I mean to you, Colin? I wonder, for you have agreed to wed me, committing us to a lifetime together."

He had thought much while hunting game for the camp. He had thought of how frightened he was that he would lose her during the attack. It left a hollow pit in his stomach that he continued to feel from time to time. He thought of how much he enjoyed talking with her and how stubborn she could be in her ideas and ideals, yet she was determined to defend her opinions. He thought of how free and unrestricted she was when they made love and he thought of how he felt when he was not near her.

Empty. So very empty. And he ached until he once again was reunited with her.

Love.

He had to admit it. He loved her. And it was a powerful love, one he had hoped to find but had never thought he would. It was a forever love and perhaps that was why he was reluctant to admit it to himself. But now that he had, he felt good about it. He felt strong and sure and safe in the knowledge that a forever love was theirs to share forever.

"*Forever mine*," he whispered to her and kissed her gently.

She was not certain she had heard him correctly, though her heart raced at what she thought she had heard. "What did you say?"

"*Forever mine*," he repeated with a stronger whisper. "You are forever mine."

She was stunned, for she recalled how he had wanted someone to say those words to, someone whom he loved, but he had not mentioned love to her. Were they words of love? She wanted to know, but was uncertain if she should ask. Or perhaps she was fearful of the response.

He smiled as if he understood her inner turmoil and with a gentle laugh and several teasing kisses to her lips he said, "You have found what you searched for, Hope. I cannot go another minute without telling you how very much I love you. You stole my heart when I was not looking and now I willingly give it to you."

Her tears began again and he wiped at them with his thumb.

"I warn you now that my love for you is forever. It will not fade with the years; it will grow stronger and richer in emotions. My love will follow you throughout your days and comfort you in your times of need. I will be by your side even when I am not near you. I love you more than I ever thought possible. You will always be forever mine."

Hope burst into tears and flung her arms around his neck, hugging him tightly to her. She could not believe his words. She heard them, she understood them, but she thought for a moment that she was dreaming.

She cried harder.

He laughed softly. "I tell you I love you and you cry."

She sobbed, unable to speak.

He laughed again, feeling delighted, knowing her tears were in response to her overwhelming joy.

"I—I—I—"

He kissed her with laughing lips. "I love you."

"Truly?" she asked between sobs.

"Truly," he said and took her face in his hands. "I truly, truly love you." His kiss was gentle and loving, and welcomed.

"I love you," she said against his lips.

"I know," he said, reluctantly holding back another kiss so he could respond. "And glad I am that you loved me enough to admit your feelings to me. Your love made me focus on my own emotions and made me face feelings I had not thought possible."

Their kisses grew hungry, as did their bodies.

Colin looked around the camp. Eric sat by the fire lost in his thoughts, though Colin knew he was alert to his surroundings. Many were asleep; two or three villagers spoke quietly together.

He ran a tender hand along her neck and whispered, "Would the dark woods frighten you?"

She smiled, for she recalled the many nights she and Lady had spent in the woods together. "Nay, I find it peaceful."

"I should have known," he murmured. "You are not like other women. You are unique."

He kissed at her neck and she shivered.

"Why do I always want you?" she asked more of herself than of him.

He answered for her. "Love."

"It makes no sense."

"It is not meant to." He stood, pulling her up with him, and then reached down to grab a blanket. "Come with me so that I may show you how love can be."

With a nod to Eric, Colin directed Hope into the woods and the shadows of the night.

They found a secluded spot—a small clearing not far from the stream that ran behind the village. Colin spread the blanket on the ground. An abundance of bushes and trees provided privacy and a half moon cast the only light in the darkness.

They took their time undressing each other, wanting this time, this moment of love to be everlasting. He touched her gently, she touched back and a chilled breeze suddenly whispered over them.

Hope shivered and Colin took her in his arms. "Come, I will warm you."

He lowered her to the blanket, covering her with his warm body and raining kisses on her face, neck and finally settling on her hard nipples.

Her moans began softly and he warned her she must remain quiet for the woods could harbor unwanted guests.

She bit at her lips to prevent her cries of pleasure from escaping and dug her fingers into the strength of his muscled arms.

Hope had never imagined she could feel more than she had before with Colin but she did. Knowing he loved her, truly loved her, stripped away all her doubts and fears and her surrender was complete, as was his.

Love brought them together in a whirlwind of passionate emotions and continued to do so well into the night.

Much later, exhausted from their continued lovemaking, Colin and Hope returned to camp. All were asleep except Eric. He remained as he had been, staring into the campfire.

"Go to him," Hope urged.

Colin looked reluctant.

"He needs you."

Colin nodded and kissed her lips. "I love you."

She smiled. "I know, you showed me just how much."

"Aye, I did," he admitted with a sense of arrogance. "And I will show you every day of our lives together."

"Promise?" she whispered and leaned up to peck at his cheek.

"Promise," he assured her and with a quick kiss he left her to go join Eric.

Hope retreated to the bed of blankets and stretched out, covering herself. She was exhausted, happy and sad. She felt guilty feeling happy while knowing Eric suffered with concern for his wife. She herself worried for Faith though she honestly felt her to be safe. She did not think Rath would allow any harm to come to her and if the babe should come early there would be a few women there to assist her. At least she hoped there would be.

The long day swiftly caught up with her and she quickly drifted into a much needed slumber.

It was a wet tongue that greeted her early the next morning and a booming voice that echoed.

"Rook, find Faith!"

Thirty-four

Hope jumped up.

Eric's men had arrived.

Rook immediately obeyed the command. He barked once at Eric and once at Lady and then took off into the woods.

"We follow?" Borg asked anxiously and Hope realized that he must have been informed of the situation for he wore a mixture of anger and worry.

"Nay," Eric said confidently. "Rook will return and take us where we need to go. I do not want to take a chance of alerting anyone to our arrival. I know not what waits for us."

"I do not think Rath means any harm to Faith," Colin said, attempting to ease the tension filled air.

"He took my wife," Eric reminded angrily.

"We do not know why," Colin said. "Perhaps he thought to protect her."

"No one takes Faith from me for any reason," Eric said through gritted teeth.

"Could Faith have gone of her own volition?" Borg asked.

Hope approached the men with Lady at her side and answered his question. "Faith would never have left her husband."

Eric nodded his appreciation. "You understand my wife well."

"I understand her strong love for you and that love

would never have permitted her to leave your side in battle or any other time. She worried over you during the attack, asking me if you were all right each time I returned."

Eric tensed, his hand gripping the hilt of his sword until it turned pure white. "I will hold my wife in my arms by nightfall or there will be hell to pay."

"Aye, my lord," Colin and Borg echoed in unison.

"Lady Hope, I wish to speak with you," Eric said sternly. "Borg, Colin, see to it that the men are prepared to leave and that the people here are given sufficient food and shelter until our return."

Colin moved to stand beside Hope.

She placed a hand to his chest. "I will be fine."

Eric understood his concern. "You may remain if you wish."

Colin looked to Eric and smiled. "It is you I should be standing beside, my lord. Hope is a stubborn one to deal with."

For the first time since the attack, Eric smiled. "Then I will have no trouble handling her for she is exactly like my wife."

Hope smiled along with them. "From what I hear Faith handles the devil quite nicely."

Colin and Borg roared with delight as they walked away and Eric simply shook his head.

"Come join me," he said to Hope, his mighty hand extended.

She accepted his invitation and sat by the fire, Lady resting at her side.

"Tell me of you and Colin. Have you settled things between you?"

She had not expected this question from him and her surprise showed on her face.

Eric understood. "Colin is a good friend and I will see him happy and I will not see you forced to wed. Now tell me, have you both finally realized you love each other?"

She nodded. "You knew we loved each other?"

"Only a fool could not see it. Colin worried incessantly about the lad. He cared for you from the start, in a different manner, of course, but he cared. Once he discovered you were a woman, he was angry and also intrigued. He had first thought you robbed him of a friend and then realized you were still that friend and could be so much more. You confused him and thrilled him and completely frustrated him. And it was a delight to watch."

"I sense he received the same pleasure from your relationship with Lady Faith."

"She led me on a merry chase, though it was of my own foolish choosing. Colin attempted to warn me of my rash actions but a fool in love listens to no one, which Colin has recently learned."

"Aye, he has and so have I."

"Then you both agree to wed?"

She answered with a smile and without hesitation. "Aye, that we do."

"Good. Now that we have settled that, tell me of my wife."

"What do you wish to know?"

The conversation took a serious tone. "Do you think the babe will arrive early?"

Faith hesitated.

Eric would not have it. "Be honest with me."

"Faith worried over the babe arriving early and I trust a woman's instincts. I also worry that she was subject to the unexpected excitement of the attack. That cannot do well for her."

"Then you think there is a good chance the babe will arrive early?"

"Births are unpredictable, but I would tend to believe your babe is impatient."

Eric rubbed at his jaw. "I wish to be with her when her time comes. I do not wish her to suffer alone."

Hope placed a comforting hand on his arm. "I am sure

she thinks of you and knows in her heart that you come
to rescue her."

"Do you think she needs rescuing?"

"I do not believe Rath intends her harm."

"He seems like a good man, but he took her away
from me. That I cannot forgive."

"As long as she is well, does it matter?"

Eric needed no time for thought. "Aye, it matters. She
is the devil's wife and no one touches what is mine."

Hope could understand why many feared the devil's
wrath. His size alone would make one quake and his
blue eyes looked as if they could reach down to one's
soul. Yet Hope sensed compassion, understanding and
love in the depths of the devil and that made him all the
more human.

"I should prepare for the journey," she said, anxious
to change from female attire to the lad's durable garments.

"Colin will be concerned with your safety. He may
not allow you to go."

"Allow" was the wrong choice of word. Hope simply
smiled at the devil and stood. "I will soon be ready to
join the men."

"I will leave it for you and Colin to settle."

"A wise choice, my lord." She walked away, Lady
following close by.

"Lady Hope," he called to her and she turned.

"I would be pleased if you joined us."

She smiled. "I appreciate the invitation, my lord."

He nodded. "I thought you would."

"I do not care if the devil invited you; you are not going," Colin said for the third time, and shook his head
at her. "I intend to burn those garments when we return
to Shanekill."

Hope looked down at the worn but comfortable lad's
garments she wore. "Burn them if it pleases you but I
will find others to wear if need be."

"More adventures?" he asked, his glance busy on the

men who were making ready to depart the campsite.

"Only if you join me."

He looked with surprise at her. "Perhaps I will have a set of male garments made for you."

"I would cherish them," she said with delight.

He leaned down and kissed her. "I cannot prevent you from coming with us, can I?"

"Lady Faith may need me."

She need say no more. He nodded his permission, though she had all intentions of going regardless.

"You will pay me heed and do as I direct."

"Must I?" she asked, her tone serious.

He stared at her until a smile peeked at the corners of her mouth. "You will be a handful, I can see."

She stepped up to press against him. "A handful that will not disappoint you."

"Nay, never disappoint me." He hugged her to him. "You will stay close to my side and follow my direction."

Hope gave his order thought.

"You will heed me on this, Hope, or you will remain behind."

"The devil invited me."

"And the devil will uninvite you if I request it."

"That is not fair," she said with an angry stamp of her foot.

"Not all things in life are fair. You will do as I say."

She agreed with reluctance, knowing she had no choice. "Aye, I will."

The small troop of men and one lone woman who resembled a young lad moved out of the camp. They traveled slowly, following the path of a lone dog, Lady heavy on Rook's scent and helping to guide them, to everyone's amazement.

Hope rode beside Borg. Colin and Eric were at the lead, deep in conversation.

"I thought the exchange of coins was to be at a designated spot by the river?" Hope asked.

"Rook decided to travel ahead and he returned with Colin in tow," Borg informed her. "Or else we would have continued to wait by the river."

She realized that Colin had gotten little sleep last night while she slumbered peacefully. But then he would wish to guard and protect her well.

"You arrived earlier than planned."

Borg nodded. "Aye, I thought it wiser to be in the area before the designated time. One never knows what may happen or when one may be needed."

"Eric knew this," she said with sudden realization.

"He knew what to expect from his warriors. He had no doubt we would be near."

"That would explain why he did not rush to leave camp. He knew the longer he lingered the closer you would draw near."

"Aye, but not near enough. If I but knew of the danger to all of you I would never have remained by the river."

"Colin, Eric and you are close."

"We fought many battles together," Borg said with pride.

"And battles draw men together."

"You understand this?" he asked, surprised.

"I learned from experience the truth about battles."

"Aye, you have faced two now—a remarkable feat for a woman."

"I am no ordinary woman," Hope said with pride.

"Nay, you are not; but then Colin could never wed an ordinary woman. He needs someone who will challenge him."

"I do that," she smiled.

"Aye, that and more."

She laughed. "That I do."

"A challenge you will be and a good one," Borg said, joining in her laughter.

Hope had thought of finding love but she had never dreamed that with that love would come a family who cared so very much for each other. These people had become an important part of her life. She worried about Faith as she would a dear sister. Never having had siblings, she cherished her newfound friends even more.

The day wore on, a cloud covering turning the blue skies gray.

The trail was difficult to follow as the clear path turned dense with bushes and trees. The horses were finally abandoned, two men left behind to guard them.

Lady took the lead, sniffing frantically along the ground as she continued to follow Rook's scent. Colin and Eric kept close behind Lady, and Hope trailed them with Borg beside her. She noticed that Colin kept a watch over her out of the corner of his eye and she was well aware that the three men had her safely pinned around them. They had no intention of any harming befalling her, and that knowledge warmed her heart.

Hope was grateful that her legs were accustomed to such vigorous walking. Several hours had passed and they had not stopped once. To Hope's surprise, Lady remained vigilant in her tracking. She wondered whether Lady missed Rook and was as intent in finding him as Eric was in finding Faith.

Her mouth grew parched and a muscle caught in her calf but she ignored it. She would not slow the men down. She had insisted on joining them and she had no intention of delaying their mission.

She forged on, keeping up with the brisk pace.

Suddenly Lady stopped, bringing those around her to an abrupt halt. She waited, her head up and her nose sniffing the air.

Silence reigned, each man ready and waiting.

Lady's head snapped to the right and within seconds Rook darted out from the bushes, ran up to her, gave her a quick lick and went straight to Eric, sitting down in front of him.

Eric spoke just above a whisper. "He has found her."

The men stood ready for their orders.

Eric turned to Colin. "You and I will go see what we

face." He looked to Borg and the waiting men. "Remain ready."

Rook took the lead with Colin and Eric close by. Lady decided she would not be left behind and joined Rook.

Hope decided to do the same and hurried up behind Colin.

"Go back," he ordered on a whisper.

"Nay, I stay with you and Lady."

Colin delivered a more firm demand. "Go back."

She simply ignored him.

He mumbled beneath his breath, halted in his tracks and grabbed her arm. "Return now."

She understood his concern, saw it in his eyes, but her own concern shined just as strongly in her eyes. "I cannot leave your side. Please, Colin, do not make me."

The devil solved the problem. "No time to argue, let her be."

"Stay close," Colin commanded, and she nodded.

The trio continued on.

It took longer than Hope had thought to reach the campsite. They remained hidden in the bushes a safe distance away. Faith was not spotted but several men guarded the perimeter of the camp with drawn weapons and it could be certain that men also patrolled the surrounding woods.

With a hand signal Eric directed them to retreat.

Once a safe distance away he turned to Colin. "They look ready for the soldiers' men, and I fear that since we remained behind they may think us part of them or else I would simply walk into camp and demand my wife." He shook his head. "I cannot take a chance with her safety so we will place our men strategically around the camp and overpower them with little difficulty."

Colin nodded and the three of them along with Lady and Rook made their way back with haste to the waiting men.

Eric explained the plan, cautioning the men to use limited force and to take no lives. He detailed the ragtag group and their fear that it might be the soldiers attacking once again. The men instantly understood.

Borg was directed to lead the men in circling the camp. Colin was to remain at Eric's side and Hope was to remain concealed in the safety of the woods.

That was not to her liking and she made her objection known. "I could enter the camp without a problem and locate Faith."

"Nay," Colin and Eric said in unison.

She was more insistent. "I wish to help."

"Then do not make us worry needlessly over your safety when we have Faith to concern us," Colin said adamantly.

Her chin went up. "I can take care of myself."

Colin walked up to her and tapped at her defiant chin. "Not any longer. I take care of you now and you will obey me on this one, Hope."

She opened her mouth and Colin pressed a firm finger to her lips. "Not a word."

One more attempt and it was no longer his finger that silenced her lips but a solid kiss.

His tactic worked. She remained silent when he drew away, though it was his whispered words that had her holding her tongue. "I love you too much to lose you."

Eric warned his men once again to be cautious with their weapons. He did not feel that Rath's group was a threat, but he would take no chances. A good warrior never did.

Silence followed them as they made their way to rescue Faith.

Eric's skilled warriors had no trouble circling the camp without anyone's knowledge and lying in wait ready for a signal from the devil.

Hope watched with Lady from the bushes as Colin, Eric and Rook approached the campsite. Their steps were sure and steady, their hands grasped the hilts of their swords and their eyes bore the look of seasoned warriors ready for battle.

She shivered, feeling sorry for those who glanced into their chilling eyes for they would surely freeze with fear.

Another step and the two would be ready to signal the men.

That is when it happened.

An anguished scream ripped through the warm air and sent a shiver racing through Hope. There was no doubt who had unleashed the tortured scream.

It was Faith.

Thirty-five

The devil roared his rage.

Rook growled.

The two charged the camp.

Colin was fast on the devil's heels and Hope fast on his along with Lady.

Eric broke from the woods into camp and stared in disbelief at the sight that caught his eyes near the fire. His wife lay prone and writhing on the ground, her knees bent and her legs spread wide, and between hovered Rath.

Eric roared his rage so loudly that everyone scurried out of his path as he descended in fury on Rath.

Rook ran alongside him, teeth bared and ready for attack.

Hope was small and agile, and when she realized the situation she raced past Colin and shouted, "The babe!"

He realized what she attempted to tell him and hurried his steps toward Eric.

The devil was too enraged to listen to reason and Hope feared the consequences of his rash actions. Though her steps were quick they were not quick enough.

The devil's mighty hands reached out to grab Rath from behind and Rook was ready to join in the attack.

Faith screamed her husband's name when she saw his intention and then yelled to Rook. "Eric, nay! Rook, stay!"

Rath made no move—he remained as he was, busy delivering the devil's child.

Eric halted and after a quick assessment of the situation, he dropped down on his knees beside Faith and grabbed her hand.

Rook kept a respectful distance but remained close by, ready to protect his master.

Faith released another anguished scream that tore at Eric's heart and she gripped his hand tightly.

Hope joined Rath, and Colin went down by Faith opposite the devil.

"What is wrong?" Eric demanded and caught a quick glimpse of Borg, who looked to have everything in the camp under control.

"The babe . . . is not turned . . . the right way," Faith said on a labored breath.

"He must be turned," Rath said and looked around. "You frightened the women away who were helping me."

Hope spoke up. "I will help you."

"What can I do?" Eric asked, feeling helpless.

Rath answered honestly. "Hold her hand and pray."

Eric turned pure white and Faith attempted to ease his concern. "It is all right."

"It is not," Rath argued. "The babe will not turn."

"Make him turn," Eric ordered.

"This is one time your orders will do little good," Rath said sympathetically. "The babe is a stubborn one."

Faith could not hold back another scream and Eric cringed when he watched the pain his wife suffered. "Do something," he demanded.

"Move," Hope ordered of Rath. "It takes a stubborn one to handle a stubborn one."

Colin smiled down at Faith. "All will be well now, for Hope is a most willful one."

"Aye, that I am and that is why this babe will obey me."

"Good," Eric said with confidence. "Hope will deliver

the babe safely." His blue eyes begged her to make it so.

She folded her sleeves up past her elbows and one of the younger women who had been attending Faith bravely returned with a bucket of heated water and fresh cloths, placing them beside Hope. She kneeled beside her and pushed her own sleeves up, ready to help.

Hope wet her hands and with a gentle touch she went to work on the stubborn babe.

Time passed slowly and Faith tried bravely not to scream but it was near to impossible. Eric held tightly to her hand and Colin mopped at her perspiring brow with a damp cloth.

Hope continued to coax the babe.

"I grow tired, Hope," Faith said, letting her know her strength was ebbing.

"Hurry," Eric snapped at Hope.

Colin cast Hope a supportive glance and she smiled her appreciation in return, though it was weak.

"A little more and I think he will be ready," she said with a confidence that had them all smiling.

Faith released another scream, looking with tear-filled eyes to her husband.

He pressed his cheek next to hers. "I love you more than you will ever know."

His words soothed her. "Nay, I do know, and it gives me strength."

"Get ready, Faith," Hope said with excitement.

Everyone looked to Hope.

"He is ready."

Faith sighed and screamed with relief as she pushed her babe into the world.

The babe wailed loudly as soon as he slipped out of Faith into Hope's hands.

"You have a son," Hope shouted with joy and the whole camp cheered.

Hope placed the babe on Faith's stomach while she tended to the cord.

Faith reached down to touch his head and Eric simply stared in awe at him.

"He is a big one. A warrior's son," Colin said with pride. "No wonder he gave you so much trouble."

Faith laughed softly. "He is like his father, wanting his own way even before he makes his entrance into this world."

Eric reached out and touched his tiny clinched hand. "Our son," he smiled and looked to Faith. "Thank you."

"You are wel—" She yawned.

Eric looked to Hope. "She is tired."

"Nay," Hope said. "She is exhausted and needs rest and a more sheltered spot where I may tend her and in case it should rain." She glanced up at the clouds that hovered overhead.

Colin stood. "I will see to it."

Hope did what she could for Faith at the moment and was grateful when Colin returned shortly, happy to inform her that Borg had thought ahead and had had the men construct a sheltered spot for Lady Faith.

Hope wrapped the babe in the fresh cloths and carried him while Eric saw to moving his wife. When Faith was settled she chased the men away, promising a worried Eric that he could return as soon as she had seen to cleaning up and settling his wife and son.

Reluctantly he left Faith's side, insisting he would return soon whether she was ready for him or not.

"Like father like son," Faith said as he walked away.

Colin left with Eric, sending Hope a quick nod to let her know they would speak later. She looked forward to that time. Time for them to talk, time for them to be together. Time to rest in his arms.

Hope and a few other women set to work tending to Faith.

Eric and Colin joined Borg and Rath at the campfire.

Eric's men were seeing to the safety of the camp while two of his men joined Rath's men to hunt for food.

"Explain," Eric said, sitting beside Rath and accepting the jug of mead passed to him.

"First let me congratulate you on the birth of your son," Rath said with an extended hand.

Eric took his hand without hesitation. "Thank you, but my wife would have been in the safety of my protection had you not taken her from me. And you did take her from me."

Rath offered an explanation since he knew the devil expected one. "I had no choice. One of my people was seriously hurt and needed her skill as a healer."

"You placed her life in danger," Eric accused.

"I never would have allowed harm to come to her."

Eric raised his voice. "You placed her in harm's way when you took her from me."

Rath remained silent for a moment and then looked the devil directly in his eyes. "I meant no disrespect, but I did what was necessary for the safety of my people. And I would do it again."

Colin and Borg waited for Eric to erupt and were surprised when he did not.

He spoke calmly. "I understand your reasoning and I respect your choice. You must understand my reaction."

With that he drew a fist and threw it directly in Rath's face. The man went over from the force of the punch and groaned, his hand going to rub at his injured jaw.

Eric offered him his hand. "All is settled now."

"Aye," Rath acknowledged, accepting his help to sit up. "All is settled."

"Then I offer you my protection."

Rath thought a moment. "I will consider it."

"Good," Eric said and stood. "Now I go to my wife. Borg, you are in charge of the men. Colin, go see to Hope. She has done much for my wife and I am grateful, but she herself must be weary from this long day."

"She will not leave Faith's side until she has seen to her care."

"Then let us go together and see that both our women get what they need."

"Which is?" Rath asked with a smile.

Eric grinned and threw an arm around Colin. "Us."

Faith was nearly asleep when Eric stretched out beside her and beside their sleeping son. He was wrapped in several warm cloths and a wool blanket.

"He is handsome like his father," Faith said with a proud smile.

"He is wrinkled," Eric said and kissed the sleeping babe's forehead. "You think me wrinkled?"

Faith laughed and welcomed his lips as they claimed hers.

"Rath tells me you went with him to help the injured." He snuggled next to her, wrapping his strong arm around her and his son.

"I knew you would follow or else I would never have left you and there were those who required healing. I could not save one; his wounds were beyond my skills."

"I am sorry," Eric said, knowing his wife held a strong compassion to help the wounded and when she could not she suffered their loss.

"I saved others," she said with a yawn. "And I knew you would come for me. I had no doubt." Another yawn escaped from her.

"She needs rest," Hope said, tucking the blanket around Faith's legs.

"She will get her rest," Eric said as if it were a command. "And so will you. Go with Colin. I will see to my wife now."

Hope looked to Faith. "Aye, you need rest as well and you have done much for me. I do not know how to thank you."

Hope smiled. "You can be there for me when my time comes."

Colin slipped his arm around her. "Her time will come many times, for we both love children."

"Aye, this is so," Hope said, snuggling against him.

"Then go and begin your family," Eric said with a dismissive wave of his hand.

"Do you hear that, Hope?" Colin asked with a grin. "The devil orders us to start a family."

Hope laughed. "He is too late—we have already begun to do so."

They ran off laughing together like two young children, leaving the devil and his lady time alone with their newborn son.

Colin directed Hope away from the camp.

"Where do you take me?" she asked while eagerly following.

"To a place meant only for you and me," he said and stopped briefly to kiss her.

The rain started just as they slipped beneath the branch structure, soft splatters of raindrops falling down around them. They fell into each other's arms, embracing as if they had not been together in a very long time.

"I cannot believe where my adventure has brought me," she said in the comfort of his loving arms.

He hugged her close to him, feeling the gentle strength of her. "I am glad you are adventurous or I would never have found you."

She laughed softly. "I must always remind you that it is I who found you."

"Nay," he said, shaking his head before kissing her temple. "I have searched for you for a very long time and I finally found you. I finally found love. A love that is forever."

She turned in his arms and captured his lips in a hungry kiss that she never wanted to end. Their hands grew frantic, their passion soared and Hope whispered the words to him that meant so very much to her.

"You are *forever mine*."